"He's going to be a great responsibility and he's *not* going to change..."

The story of a dyslexic 18-year-old, who just happend to be gay, and how with love he *did* change, not only his own life but the lives of those around him.

KILLARNEY

by

BRIAN STUART PENTLAND

Order this book online at www.trafford.com
or email orders@trafford.com

Most Trafford titles are also available at major online book retailers.

Printed in the United States of America.

ISBN: 978-1-4269-5785-7 (sc)
ISBN: 978-1-4269-5786-4 (e)

Trafford rev. 02/07/2011

 www.trafford.com

North America & international
toll-free: 1 888 232 4444 (USA & Canada)
phone: 250 383 6864 ✦ fax: 812 355 4082

CHAPTER ONE

A Harsh Beginning

CHAPTER 1

A Harsh Beginning

"Please Peter, just let it go. We haven't seen Paul for months, and this is our first opportunity! The children are away, so let's enjoy ourselves!"

"Very well, very well!" replied Peter, who liked his brother-in-law very much. "I must say I have missed Paul, but I'm not going to put up with any of this idealized past love affaire." The past love affaire that Peter spoke of was Paul's affaire with Malcolm, which had survived for six years: the longest affaire and, as his sister Janet had said, probably the only one of any length.

Janet and Peter had been married almost fourteen years now and had, as Paul would say, three extremely noisy children; not liking children at all, Paul rarely visited the house, but tonight was an exception: all the children were away.

3

Peter worked as a psychiatrist in a Government institution for disabled and handicapped children. Parents took their children to this institute on Parson Street as day students, but the moment a permanent vacancy occurred, there was a rush to fill the position. A great many of these children lived there permanently; some had done so for most of their lives. Paul had often said to Peter that he would end up being a saint. The work was difficult and rarely did he ever see a great change in this field of work, as progress was in every sense difficult for the children there permanently to achieve in this restricted environment. But this evening he had returned home knowing his brother-in-law would be present: he brought with him a case file, something he rarely did.

Paul arrived exactly as bidden at seven-thirty. The large weatherboard house in Camberwell, with its obligatory high picket fence, had, as a result of many years of renovations and extensions, become a very pleasant and comfortable home for Janet, Peter and the three children. Paul parked in front of the house and did not drive in, even though the gates were open. He rang the bell and his sister greeted him with a kiss. "Well! Long time, no see!" she smiled. "Come in." She took the two bottles of wine from his hands and they proceeded down the corridor to the living room. "Oh!" said Paul, "don't tell me we are using the dining room tonight", and laughed. "Yes, sweetie: just for you! Peter! Paul's here!" Peter came around the corner and smiled. "Come and have a drink", he said, "you can relax in a child-free home tonight. Well, how's work?" "Much the same", said Paul, "It doesn't change much. Mr. Robinson is great and allows me quite a lot of leeway." "He's very fond of you, you know", said Peter. "I saw him at a dinner party a week ago, but I thought he looked much older than I remembered."

Paul accepted the glass of red wine from Peter and they sat down. "And your work?" "Well, it's very frustrating at present" said Peter. "I'm trying to battle bureaucracy and I'm not sure I'm going to win. You wouldn't like to do me a favour and look after someone for eleven days starting next week, would you? I could organise for you and Michael to go and stay at the farm."

"What, me!" Paul said with a startled look on his face. "Definitely not! You know I can't stand children." "But he's not a child, he's almost eighteen years old. In fact, he'll be eighteen in three days' time, and that's the problem."

"Why is it a problem?" said Paul, putting his glass down and noticing at the same time that he had almost emptied it. Peter noticed the same. "Help yourself to some more", he said, which Paul duly did. "You're owed three weeks holiday from last year, you told me, so you could take them and help me." "I can't! I don't like children, and besides it's so close to Christmas and I have so much to do," said Paul.

"So did we eighteen months ago, but Janet and I didn't ignore a certain responsibility."

"That was a completely different situation. Malcolm was dying."

"I'm aware of that, Paul, but just remember that when you wanted us we were there, and with three children that was not always easy."

"I shall always be grateful to you both", said Paul and turned his head as Janet came through the door.

"Darling," she said to Peter. "Can you help me in the kitchen for a moment?"

"Sure, on my way. Look at this for a minute and see if it makes sense to you," Peter said and handed Paul the manila folder he had brought from work. "Especially the second last page."

Paul took the file that Peter thrust into his hand. "Oh! Help yourself to a drink!" Paul opened the file to find that the name at the top read MICHAEL, with no surname, and the sheets inside the folder as he turned the cover over threatened to spill onto the floor: he quickly gathered them together. Of the technical terms he understood little, except 'extreme dyslectic', etc., 'withdrawn'. "Oh, what's this got to do with me", he thought, "a dyslectic eighteen-year-old is not my concern". The file was quite large and seemed to Paul very repetitive, with different reports being made on Michael year after year, but seemingly saying the same thing. He idly flicked through the sheets. He was not reading them at all, but just turning the sheets over one after the other. Just as he was about to close the manila folder, he remembered his brother-in-law's comment: the second last page. This he turned to, prior to putting the file back on the writing desk. He read "it is the opinion of (obviously a summary of three or four psychoanalysts) that Michael is a homosexual youth of eighteen years with some sexual experience in this field, be it his choice of companion or not".

Peter returned. "What the hell does that mean?" Paul asked as he handed the file to Peter, still open at the second last page, "and, why doesn't he have a surname?" "It means, Paul, that he was abandoned when he was about two years old, we think, and the only information we have is the name 'Michael', written on the box that held him. As for the information on the second last page, it means exactly what it says." "But what does 'his choice of companion or not', what does that mean?" "Think about it for a moment", said Peter. Paul began to feel very uncomfortable. "You mean he was forced into sex?" "I'm afraid so. In an environment like the Institute these things occur unfortunately. I need you to take Michael up to the country for eleven days before Christmas. There's tons of time."

"Why me?" said Paul. "First, you owe me a big favour for when Malcolm was dying and we were there. You know damn well he was not my choice of a fine friend!" Peter had disliked Malcolm intensely, as he had said to Janet that Malcolm was the vilest bitchiest queen he had ever known, a social-climbing upstart who used everyone as often as it suited him, and he was particularly unattractive. Peter could never understand what his very handsome brother-in-law ever saw in this nasty piece of work. Malcolm was short and fat, and quite a contrast to Paul, who was tall and elegant. Malcolm, according to Janet, always looked as if he needed a shower. He was always with that red-blond thin hair that was forever greasy and lying all over his forehead. Peter had said to Janet that the relationship was bad for Paul, and indeed this was the case. Malcolm had picked Paul up and manipulated him with great ease. Their sexual relationship had finished short of their first year, but Paul remained with Malcolm. Paul had a beautiful terrace-house in Darling Square, East Melbourne, large and beautifully decorated inside, which Malcolm felt was his domain. Many of Paul's friends stopped calling in and stopped telephoning. Malcolm was just too negative. His sexual relationship had finished with Paul, and he returned to his nighttime excursions for casual sex, which he liked much more. This led to a predictable situation. Malcolm had known for some time that he was not well, but sought no help nor told anyone, not even Paul. He had been quite stocky, but as his weight fell away and his clothes began to hang on him, Paul began asking questions. "I'm on a strict diet", he told Paul, "and it makes me very tired." Eventually, a collapse at his work in a large real estate business one busy Saturday morning, a rush to hospital and a complete check-up showed that Malcolm had an advanced case of AIDS. It took only seven months for the inevitable to occur.

Paul took the stand that Malcolm could have done no wrong, that he missed him terribly and that his life was virtually finished. It was this attitude that made his brother-in-law very, very angry, considering that he had, with Janet, spent seven long months helping where necessary and putting up with the visits to Darling Square and later to the hospital, where Malcolm, knowing his time was marked, vented his spleen on all.

"Come on boys. Dinner is served", said Janet, poking her head around the corner of the door. "Tonight, the dining room!" This was an occasion, since the room was rarely used, because when the children were home, everyone ate in the extended kitchen-family room.

The three chatted generally about the onslaught of Christmas. "Do you want to come up to the farm for Christmas, Paul? You're most welcome!" said Janet. A definite "No!" was the response: Paul had once foolishly spent Christmas at the farm, when Malcolm had gone somewhere else, disliking Peter intensely, although he tolerated Janet and, strangely, got along with the children in a sort of way.

It had been a shocking four days for Paul. The farm belonged to Peter's aunt, and when she died she left it to him, with two hundred acres set in rolling hills, an hour out of Melbourne. There were two houses on the property: the larger, where the aunt had lived, and the other nearer the main entrance, where the caretaker family lived, the Cunninghams. Mr. Cunningham was a quiet hen-pecked man, who went about his work in a pleasant and orderly way. It was Mrs. Cunningham that Paul hated: she was a very stocky woman of about fifty-four, and was as invasive and as bossy as can be. She was the head of the local Brownie Pack and as Brown Owl she controlled all. Behind her back, Paul always called her Brown Vulture, considering the name much more appropriate. So the last Christmas spent at the farm with Janet, Peter, three screaming children and Brown Vulture always hovering about giving advice and directions to all, was something Paul had promised he would never do again. The dinner passed very pleasantly and Peter was glad to see Paul relaxing a bit, as he had been quite stressed and sharp with everyone after Malcolm's death.

"Well!" said Peter, as a delicious dessert of Black Forest cake was being served, "Have you thought about my request to look after Michael for a few days?" "Why does he need looking after anyway?" said Paul. "What's the problem?"

"The problem is this", came the reply, "he is now too old to stay at the Institute and they want to transfer him to an adult centre. Do you see the danger? Remember, he is only eighteen and as a homosexual youth in an adult environment there is bound to be real trouble for him. I am searching for a custodian for him, if I can find one. Then, as an adult of eighteen, he can be given over into their custody. I need someone to look after him while I am trying to work all this out", he said with a pleading look and to dead silence from both Paul and his sister. Peter played his last trump card. "Paul", he said, "Where is your Catholic charity?" Paul glared at Peter, considering this comment from a Protestant totally unnecessary, refilled his glass and slowly looked at him. "Can't you find anyone else to look after him?" he pleaded. "If I could", said Peter, "believe me, I would. This is a very urgent case."

"I mustn't drink any more, or I shall be pulled over by the police", said Paul. "I must go". He stood up and walked toward the dining room door. Janet and Peter were also on their feet. Paul turned to them both and said, "Very well! I accept this *charitable* work on one condition". "What's the condition?" asked Janet. "At the farm, absolutely no Brown Vulture flapping around the main house! Is it a deal?" he asked. "A deal!" said Peter and gave him a hug. It was the first male contact Paul had had for some time and he felt very good about it.

He turned on the ignition and pulled the car out into Highfield Road. "What have I done?" he thought. "How much have I had to drink? This boy may be violent; he may be totally aggressive; he may not be able to speak." At that moment, some passing car sounded his horn and Paul realised he was not exactly on the right side of the road. "Pay attention, pay attention!" he thought. "Oh, what have I done! What have I done! Oh, I could become very ill and have to rest completely for a month on the Barrier Reef, or in South America, or, or …"

Coming close to East Melbourne and Darling Square, Paul realised that he needed milk. He had used the last for breakfast that morning. "Oh, why me, why me? It's so unfair, and it's also Christmas." He found his local shop on Wellington Parade had no parking places, so he was obliged to go round the corner and walk back. "Just my luck", he thought. When he passed a lane between a large eight-storey building and a two-storey doctors' clinic, he heard shouts from a man. "Go away! Go away!" When he looked up the lane, he saw in the dim light two youths attacking an elderly man. "This is all I need" though Paul. He yelled for all he was worth, "Get lost, you two!" and, armed with a garbage lid from an overturned bin, he went to the aid of the old man. The old man was on the ground. Paul took a swipe with the lid at one of the youths and missed him completely. The second time he did not and the youth let out a scream and a string of expletives and ran past him with blood running down the left side of his face. The other youth realised all was not to their advantage and hurriedly made a retreat with his battered friend.

Paul went forward to find a very well-dressed man of about sixty-five lying on his side on the ground, and said, "Are you all right? Can you stand up? I'll call the police." "Don't bother", came the reply. "Help me up!" The man limped to the main road whence Paul had come. Paul noticed he had a cut above his right eye, and took out his handkerchief and offered it to the man. "You silly old coot! Fancy taking two young guys down a lane and not expecting the worst!" "I did NOT take these two delinquents down the lane. I was dragged down. They probably thought I had money. My car's broken down: second time in a week, and I was going to Hoddle Street to catch a taxi home." Paul wasn't sure he believed him, but said, "Listen, I'll take you home in my car, which is just back there. Or shall we stop at the hospital and get them to have a look." "No, no. Just take me home, please." Paul opened the passenger door and said, "Don't spill any blood on the car, you old coot! Two boys and a dark lane! Really!" "It's not what you think", the man said indignantly. "Which way is home?" "Toorak, St. George's Road." In a short time, due to no traffic at this time of night, Paul pulled up in front of a very imposing set of gates, and the man alighted. "What's your name and address", he asked Paul. "It's OK", said Paul, "Catholic charity", and wondered why on earth he had used his brother-in-law's annoying comment from earlier this evening. The man closed the car door and opened the side gate with a key, which must obviously, thought Paul, not have been stolen. The man disappeared inside. Paul then turned the car about and headed back for a carton of milk, only to see on arriving at the store that all the lights suddenly turned out. "I don't believe it!" he said aloud. "No milk, a retarded eighteen-year-old, and an old coot picking up two youths! It isn't possible!" And with that he headed home with the knowledge that breakfast was to be had with black tea.

Peter telephoned early next morning to make the arrangements and spoke to a very unsure Paul. "Listen carefully. I want you, Paul, on the 15th of December. Do you have a pen?" "Just a minute," said Paul, and Peter heard footsteps leave and return. "Yes, I have a pen and paper now." "Good. Write this address down: 64 Corbel Avenue, the Tennant Centre for Adults. It's in Coburg, not far from the freeway. You have an appointment to see Dr. Beverley Roberts at 10 o'clock." "Heh! Just a minute! I thought I had to pick up this boy at your Institute. Has he been transferred already?" "No", said Peter, "he hasn't. Please just do what I tell you. When you have finished seeing Dr. Roberts, then come over to me and collect Michael. Do you have any spare clothes?" "What?" said Paul. "Michael has very little, so pack what you can spare." "But how big is he? Is he tall? Thin? Fat?" "He's about your height and very, very thin." "Peter, I don't have anything much." "What about all the clothes that Malcolm purchased when he lost all that weight?" "I'll have a look. Anything else?" "Yes. The farm will be fully stocked. Mrs. Cunningham will have it cleaned and there will be sufficient food for the period. If you need anything else, just tell your favourite Brown Vulture and she will go into town and get it for you. She has been told not to come to the house while you and Michael are there." "Thanks!" said Paul. "I'll see you the day after tomorrow. 'Bye!" Paul hung up and still in a dressing gown went upstairs from the kitchen where he was having his breakfast with his black tea to a smallish dressing room: wardrobes on all sides, with mirrored doors, and an antique mahogany table in the centre. He opened the wardrobe doors on the left. It was the first time he had opened them for a long time. Hanging inside were all Malcolm's clothes. He stared at the clothes as if they were going to give him a signal, but no signal came. Eventually he roused himself and pulled out two pairs of trousers. "These are just too short", he said to himself. He disliked all the shirts, but two jumpers were quite satisfactory. He withdrew them and placed them on the table and then turned to his own wardrobe. He opened the mirrored door. On the top shelf lay four pairs of trousers, now too tight, that he had kept since taking up bodybuilding. A great deal of his clothes were now too tight, but this Michael may not like these hand-me-downs, he thought. "What on earth do eighteen-year-olds wear?" He put the clothes he had selected into a bag which he pulled down from the top of the wardrobe. "Well, if these aren't any good, I'll buy him some jeans and some tee-shirts. The weather is hot, so I don't think he'll need much." He was about to close Malcolm's side of the wardrobe when suddenly he thought, "Why am I keeping all this stuff? Malcolm's gone". But rather than doing anything immediately, he slowly closed the wardrobe door.

He made his way downstairs and left the bag on the hall table. He then returned upstairs and took a shower, realising that the cleaning woman – a certain Mrs. Lamb – would be here in a few moments.

Paul had made arrangements for the time off and Mr. Robinson had been most accommodating when Paul explained why he needed the time off now. The following day, Paul spent the morning at the gym, and was very pleased at the result he could see in the mirror. His chest and biceps had developed very well. "Not bad at all", he thought, as he surveyed his image. He was a handsome man, with a furry chest, tight thick brown hair and pale brown eyes. He was slightly taller than average, and with all this bodybuilding he had developed quite a fine physique.

The afternoon was spent organising Mrs Lamb to look after the house for eleven days, checking burglar alarms and so forth, and to do some shopping so that when he returned he would find food and drink ready for him.

Next morning, Paul woke early, showered and shaved and had breakfast and was ready well before time to go to Coburg. He watched the news on the television, but realised he was very nervous and uncertain about this venture. He then took the bag from the table in the hall, as well as his own, and headed out to the car at the rear of the house. He placed the bags in the boot and then pressed the button and the automatic garage doors opened. Paul got into his black BMW and drove to Coburg.

When he arrived, having had to check the street directory three or four times, he saw a most disturbing sight: ten-foot-high wire fencing surrounding the place, and the tone of the entire structure seemed to be grey. He parked the car not far from the entrance and walked back. The front of the building was single-storied, and as he came to the entrance path, he became very aware of the high wire fence that accompanied him down both sides of the path and joined on to the building. He pressed the bell on the bright red door, and in a moment, a short, fat man let him in. "What do you want?" he said in a toneless voice. "I have an appointment with Dr. Roberts." "Just wait here", the man said and disappeared down a depressingly long grey corridor, with a cream asbestos ceiling and long unshaded fluorescent tube lighting. Not a picture on the wall, nothing except a series of olive-coloured doors opening on to the corridor. "It's the smell; it's terrible: that cheap antiseptic smell: ammonia, that's what it is. It's hideous", thought Paul. Eventually, a tall thin man came out of one of the doors and said, "Mr Paul Moran?" "Yes", replied Paul. "Dr. Roberts can't see you, so I will take you around." He introduced himself as James Stilton, and said he had worked there for over twelve years. James Stilton had a face that seemed to be carved from soapstone. His eyes were a watery green-yellow, like a cat, Paul thought, and completely expressionless. His pale parchment-like skin made the whole effect very sad indeed. He wore a green top and loose green trousers. Paul later noticed that all the staff seemed to be wearing this sort of uniform. Stilton said, "I'll show you the dining room first". Paul looked surprised. "Why exactly am I here?" he asked. James Stilton looked at him in a puzzled way. "Aren't you here to look over the Institute?" he said. "We have had a note from Dr. Peter

Simmons saying you are to be shown over the complex at eleven o'clock today." "Oh, yes!" replied Paul. "Of course!" and wondered what this had to do with a boy at an institute on the other side of town.

"Because we have about two hundred handicapped people here, we start lunch early, but some eat in a special room." There were approximately thirty people in the dining room. A dreadful din, accompanied by individual shouts, a yell here and there and a fearful empty expression on most of the faces. The dining room was ghastly, painted pink with the same ceilings as the corridors, and the ever-present fluorescent tubes. The ceiling was not horizontal, but sloped from a high section with a clerestory to the lower side with windows, looking on to an asphalted courtyard. The windows were hung with narrow skimpy cretonne curtains of a nondescript design in pink and beige on a cream background. The furniture was chrome and formica and the chair design matched the tables, with upholstery in beige vinyl. There were no pictures on the walls, only a large noticeboard at the entrance: this was the entire decoration.

The sight of these people and staff was extremely depressing. Some were eating with their hands and every so often one would take a piece of bread or something from a neighbour and a yelling match would begin, the others just sitting looking into the middle distance, not caring it seemed and not interested in anything, being fed by the staff, just like little children. They were mostly dressed in tracksuits of every imaginable hue. Sometimes the tops didn't match the bottoms. Paul felt terribly afraid, not because he thought one of them might hurt him but because of the concept that nothing would ever change for them: three meals a day in the same depressing dining room, or did *they* see it as depressing, he wondered. Perhaps they thought it was fine. The noise echoed back and forth, and it was Paul who said, "Shall we have a look about?" "Sure!" was the toneless reply. The complex at 64 Corbel Avenue was laid out in a series of courtyards, the buildings forming the four walls and no view out. "Good Heavens" thought Paul, "not only no view, but no prospect of ever going out". The thing Paul noticed was the doors, all painted different bright colours, like at a kindergarten. But these were adults. When he asked Mr. Stilton why this was so, the reply was quite sharp. "They can't read, most of them, so what's the point of putting up signs? But they can – some of them – recognise different colours, so with time, they get used to the complex."

There was a noise that was eerie, a yell or a droning of voices together, and indoors that ever-present smell of ammonia antiseptic. "I will only show you one of the dormitories", he said, and they started across a courtyard that had a veranda on one side, obviously for bad weather, and into a vestibule that lay behind a glossy bright-blue door. There were twelve single beds, a dull green paint had managed to spread all over the walls, and the ubiquitous fluorescent tubes lay waiting for the night on the ceiling. The bedspreads were all different, which gave an even more confused look to the room, at the end of which were lockers for clothes, or that's what they seemed to Paul. And again, that hideous ammonia smell. "I'm not going to take you to the section where some of the patients are confined. I think you've seen enough, haven't you?" "Yes," Paul replied, "I've seen enough." With that, the lack-lustre Mr. James Stilton accompanied Paul to the entrance where he had started one hour before. "Thank-you so much", he said. "It's nothing," said Mr. Stilton, and turned and walked down the long corridor with all the olive-green doors. He found the one he was looking for, and disappeared inside.

Paul opened the red front door and walked out. He suddenly became aware that he was shaking a little and felt quite nauseous. The smell of sunshine and fresh air was amazing, a sensation he hadn't noted for years. He made for his car as quickly as possible, unlocked it and got in. He just sat there, not moving, staring blankly through the windscreen. After five minutes, he started the car and headed off to his brother-in-law's institute, feeling completely drained of all emotion. "I can't go through with this. It just isn't possible! I can't do it!" He realised he was speaking to himself. "I'll end up in there myself soon."

He found a parking place and pulled his car up, half a block from Peter's institute. He got out, locked the car door and made for the building. He realised that what he had seen that morning had affected him considerably and knew he wanted to get out of this arrangement with Peter. Again, a high wire fence both sides of the path guided Paul to the front door. He entered and spoke to the receptionist. This building was similar to the previous one, except it seemed someone had gone berserk with bright colour everywhere, brightly-coloured posters, huge cartoon characters all over. "Hi!" said Peter, the receptionist having sent a message to his office. "How was your tour this morning?" "Hideous! What do you think?" said Paul, looking very pale. "I think you need a cup of coffee. Come with me to my office." "Peter!" "Yes," replied his brother-in-law. "Why do these institutes stink of ammonia?" Paul had noticed that this place had the same smell. "I don't know. I've never thought of it."

They entered Peter's office and Paul sat down. Peter disappeared and returned with two cups of coffee. "I can't do it! I'm not trained. I can't handle it," said Paul. "Do you know why I sent you to 64 Corbel Avenue?" "No idea, unless you wanted to shock me." "I sent you there to see exactly where Michael is to be sent, if I can't organise a way out for him. It's essential for you to realise how serious this is." "Does he know about this transfer?" Paul asked. "No, not exactly, but he knows something is about to happen, and that's all." "Peter, isn't it possible for someone else to do this? I really do feel inadequate." "Imagine how *he* will feel if he's transferred to Corbel Avenue", said Peter sharply. "Finish your coffee and I'll introduce you to him. Stop making problems! In the name of God, think positive! Michael deserves this at least!"

Paul dutifully followed Peter down a colourful kaleidoscopic corridor to the dining room. As it was now one o'clock, the noise was absolute, with children moving about, yelling, and the clatter of plates and cutlery, some children eating with their hands, and the staff returning children to their places and attempting to feed them.

The pushing, shoving and hitting was to Paul a concept of complete chaos in this brightly decorated room where everything was a different colour, the chairs, tables, all different. Posters and large cartoon characters were plastered all over the walls. If the previous institute had been depressing, this was impossible. A siren shrieked and the children began to empty out of the dining room. Paul was now really feeling nauseous, and very weak. All he wanted to do was to get out, have a drink and go home. The room was now almost empty of children and the staff were making just as much noise by scraping chairs across the brightly patterned floor and clattering all the empty plates and multi-coloured plastic beakers onto the trolleys to be returned to the kitchen. At the far end of this large room was a lone figure, sitting with his face down and his hands on the back of his head, as if he were protecting himself from someone invisible.

"Oh God, I can't do this", thought Paul. "Paul, a word of advice. At the end of the room is Michael. Don't, whatever you do, walk behind him, or touch him from behind, or he will do what he's doing now. He puts his hands over his head and just freezes and it can take quite a while to relax him." "But why is he like this?" Paul asked in a worried manner. "Because he has been hit by other children from behind and hasn't learned to hit back to defend himself."

As they walked the length of the dining room, Peter instructed Paul to take the initiative and introduce himself and speak to the boy. Paul looked completely blank. "Go on!" said Peter and walked away to the other side of the room and watched this first encounter. Paul moved closer to Michael and sat down beside him. "Michael, my name is Paul, and I'm going to take you on a holiday." It was the tone of Paul's voice that made Michael remove his hands and look up. Paul almost died. The boy's face was cut and there was blood, dried blood, all down one side and on his chin and neck. He had obviously had a disaster with a razor while shaving. The blood had also dripped onto his white tee-shirt, around the neckband. He was wearing a tracksuit, a red top and blue trousers, both looking as though they had been washed many times, and he had beige sandshoes.

But it was the eyes, Paul had never seen anything like them. Cobalt blue, enormous, fringed with long black lashes; he had thick black eyebrows and a strong nose. He had high cheekbones and very sensual, full lips, and a slightly cleft chin. His ears seemed to stick out, but that was the result of his head having been shaved. His skin was slightly olive-toned and the combination with the blue eyes was hypnotic. But the blood was very disturbing: he looked as if he had been in an accident. Even with the terrible shave, it was easy to see his dark beardline, and his forearms showed fine black hair. He looked at Paul without showing any emotion at all, no curiosity, just an empty gaze.

"Michael, shall we go now?" said Paul, who was beginning to feel a very strange sensation and was very aware of his brother-in-law watching him. Michael stood up. He was approximately the same height as Paul, perhaps a centimetre less, but without his hair, he probably looked shorter, and Paul could see that he was extraordinarily thin. Michael followed him, and Paul said to Peter, "I'll call you tomorrow". With that, Paul left this colourful wonderland and walked beside Michael down the corridor into the entrance hall and out of the glass front door. Michael had a tiny supermarket bag in one hand. When they got to the car, Paul opened the passenger door for him and then got in. "Put your safety-belt on Michael," said Paul, as he clipped his into the locking device. This obviously confused Michael, so Paul did it for him. It was then he remembered Peter's advice not to treat him as a child, but as a friend, as an adult. Paul pulled the car out and headed in the direction of the freeway, and then toward the farm at Greendale. Paul tried all forms of conversation, but to no avail. Michael stared straight ahead, as if he heard the conversation, but was just not interested, and did not reply to any of Paul's questions.

"This is going to be just great," Paul thought, "Really great! No conversation for eleven days! Wonderful!" After an hour and a quarter, they left the freeway and drove onto a country road. The car slowed down, since the road was not in the best of conditions. Suddenly, to Paul's surprise, Michael spoke. "I feel very bad", he said. Paul instantly thought of car-sickness. He pulled the car over and got out, but had barely extracted Michael from his seatbelt and helped him to his feet when he began to vomit. "Oh what do I do now!" thought Paul. He held Michael in his arms, and the vomiting continued, all over his trousers and Paul's shoes. Michael began to cry. The tears flooded down his cheeks and onto his tee-shirt and the red tracksuit jacket. "I didn't do bad", he said, still crying. Paul tried to console him. "It's OK, there's no problem, you didn't do bad". He reached into the car and fetched a box of tissues and began to clean him up. Michael suddenly stopped crying and stared at him. Paul felt extremely odd. The look on Michael's face was the first time he'd shown any emotion, apart from the tears. "We only have a little way to go now, so shall we be off?" said Paul. Michael said nothing, but returned to his seat. The smell of vomit did nothing to make Paul feel that these eleven days were going to be easy.

Finally, the gates of the farm appeared and, since they were open, Paul drove right in. As the road to the big house passed by the caretaker's cottage, Mrs Cunningham, who Paul was sure had waited all day to pounce on him as he came up the drive, appeared in front of the car, forcing him to stop. "I wonder how many years I would get for running her over", he thought. "Good afternoon Mrs Cunningham", said Paul. "I trust everything at the house is in order?" "Of course! Of course!" she retorted. "And just who is this young man?" "He has been ill, and so he's going straight to bed. I will call you if I need anything, otherwise please don't disturb us. Goodbye."

She moved to the side of the drive to let the car go by, and glared at Michael as they passed. "The cheek of him. Mr Moneybags himself!" she said under her breath, and returned to her manicured garden to see if a snail had dared to enter.

Paul helped Michael out of the car and grabbed the things from the boot. "You can have a shower and everything will be fine", said Paul. He was beginning to have a sensation about Michael, but couldn't work out exactly what it was. They went through the living room and to the bedrooms. Paul looked through the clothes he had brought and the forlorn little supermarket bag Michael had with him. He located a pair of his trousers and a pale blue shirt of Malcolm's. It was then he realised he had forgotten underwear. "You can use mine", said Paul aloud, then realising that Michael could have no idea of what he was talking about. Paul said to Michael, "Take off your clothes, and I'll soak them while you have a shower". Paul placed the fresh clothes on the chair in the very 'fifties bathroom, complete with the pink and white chequerboard effect tiles. "Hideous", thought Paul, "I always hated this house".

Michael seemed confused as to what to do, so Paul helped him undress and turned on the shower. Despite the blood, cut face and shaven head, totally naked, he was unbelievable. Paul gasped. Michael's legs were covered with fine dark hair, and his pubic hair formed a pyramid up to his navel. He also had a little hair on his chest. He was, as Paul noticed at once, extremely well-endowed. With his beautiful pale olive skin, although very, very thin, he was most handsome.

Michael showered and was not at all embarrassed at being naked in Paul's presence. Paul helped him to dress, having unpacked his own bag to find some underwear for him. With the trousers, although loose at the waist, but the right length, and the blue shirt, Michael looked a different person. Paul took Michael's clothes and soaked them in the laundry sink. He returned and, as it was nearly six o'clock, asked Michael whether he was hungry. Michael was non-committal. Paul went to the refrigerator to see what Brown Vulture had organised, and organised it was! Plastic containers with different days marked on them and he noticed on the refrigerator door a note that read "Please wash and sterilise the plastic containers and stack neatly in the basket supplied in the pantry". "Stupid bitch!" Paul murmured under his breath. But, from Brown Vulture's plastic containers, Paul managed to organise a meal, which he and Michael ate together in silence.

Then Paul made the mistake of walking behind Michael and putting his hand on his shoulder. Michael froze completely and placed his hands in such a way as to protect his head from being hit. Paul turned Michael's chair toward him and knelt in front of him. Instead of continuing in his defensive position, Michael opened his eyes and gazed at Paul on his knees before him.

"Michael", said Paul, "Listen! If you ever feel frightened or you feel bad" – remembering his only comment of the day so far – "take my hand and hold it like this", and he took Michael's hand and held it in his. This was the first real contact they had had, and Michael tightened his grip on Paul's hand and looked into his eyes as though to say, "I understand". The rest of the evening passed quietly, with Paul feeling very tired. He was watching television and realised that Michael was looking the other way, as if he weren't interested in it, or just couldn't be bothered. Paul left Michael for a moment to go to the bathroom. He opened the drawers of the pink vanity unit and there it was, an electric razor! "Hurray!" he thought, "no more blood or cuts!"

It was time for bed. Paul remembered that Peter had said, "Sleep in the room closest to him, in case he needs anything. He may just have trouble, since he usually sleeps in a dormitory with other, and may feel abandoned all alone." Michael's pyjamas were, as expected, terrible. As Paul had not thought of bringing another pair with him and could not find a spare pair in the chest-of-drawers or wardrobe, he helped Michael into his own pyjamas. Since Paul himself usually slept naked, it was no problem. Michael was duly popped into his bed and Paul explained that if he needed him, he was just across the hall, just ten or twelve steps away. Michael seemed content and Paul switched the light off, said goodnight and went to his own room, where he prepared for bed. He took the side of the double bed furthest from the door. As he was about to turn off the lamp beside the bed, his finger almost on the switch, he felt a shock – not an electric shock, but a strong sensation. He span around to see Michael standing very close to the other side of the bed. "Whatever's happening? What's wrong with this boy?" he thought. He started to get out of bed to take Michael back to his own room, and realised he was naked. At this point, the two of them just stared at one another, but this time it was Michael who made the first move. He took off the pyjamas Paul had found for him and slid very smoothly into bed with Paul. "Peter is never going to believe this, I just know it", thought Paul. Michael moved very close and rested his head on Paul's hairy chest, stretching one arm across his stomach. Paul was terrified of breathing normally in case he disturbed Michael. After ten minutes, which to Paul seemed like an hour, Michael slid his hand much lower down and touched Paul very gently. Paul gasped. Michael looked up and said, "Paul, I love you!" With that, he rolled against Paul, his head now on the pillow, and began breathing more slowly and deeply. Soon, he was fast asleep.

Paul turned off the light. Being close to Michael brought an exhilarating sensation that swept through his whole body. So this was Michael… In the moments before sleep, Paul began to think of the negative aspects of this situation. He was almost exactly twenty years older than Michael. What would people say? "Cradle-snatcher!" And Peter, what would he think, on a professional level? He felt Michael move against his side and he drifted into a more positive and happy mood and thence into sleep.

In the morning, it was Michael who woke first, and moving his head on Paul's chest awoke Paul suddenly. This was the first time in six years that Paul had woken with a male companion beside him. It felt strange but good, successful in an odd way. He put one arm around Michael and lay very still. Michael spoke first, "Paul, we can have sex". Paul did not know exactly what he should do or say in such a situation. It was Michael who took the initiative, one hand moving down Paul's chest and caressing his already alert sexual organ. Then there was no stopping either of them. Paul had never been a brilliant lover, but, with Michael, suddenly everything worked. At the beginning of his relationship with Malcolm, sex had been a clumsy and never spontaneous event, yet here was an eighteen-year-old, supposedly with many problems, bringing him naturally to sexual heights he had never experience before. It was lovemaking on a completely equal basis. Paul enjoyed Michael's body: thin though he was, he was very exciting. Paul had always been wary of letting any man penetrate him, he found it awkward and rarely pleasurable, but with Michael, for the first time, it was exhilarating and extremely good.

Paul lay with Michael in his arms, thinking that he had almost rejected this marvellous opportunity. Michael had said, "Paul, I love you". But how could he? A boy from an institution that had compiled a report saying that he was incapable of making or sustaining a relationship. Yet, Paul thought, here he is with me! The enormous cobalt-blue eyes looked up at Paul and, for the first time, Michael's sensual lips shaped themselves into what could be seen as a smile.

Paul noticed that when Michael spoke, which was rare, he always prefaced the sentence with Paul's name, as if making sure Paul was completely aware that the message was exclusively for him.

"Come on", said Paul, "let's have some breakfast!" It was a beautiful hot morning. They walked naked together to the bathroom, where for the first time in many years, Paul showered with another man. After dressing, as Paul got out the electric razor for Michael, not wanting another blood-letting exercise, he suddenly realised that he had, in his bag, a digital camera. He went to fetch it, his instinct telling him that this could well be an aid for the future, and photographed Michael's face from several angles, with the still visible scars and shaven head. He them took a photo of him without his shirt on, showing how thin his torso was. In was then Michael's turn to use the electric razor! "I must get him a good one", Paul thought, since this old one was Peter's. The shave was moderately successful. Michael had missed a couple of places on his neck. Paul took the razor from him and did the parts he had missed, although his concentration was not as focused as it should have been, due to the fact that Michael had put his hands on Paul's hips.

Breakfast was served, with Michael eating what Paul put in front of him, but passing no comment at all. After breakfast, in the warm sunshine, they went for a walk to the creek at the bottom of the property. Part of it had been dug out to provide a rustic swimming hole for Peter and Janet's three children. When Paul asked Michael whether he could swim, he looked blank as if the question meant nothing to him, and just kept walking toward the trees a little further on.

When they returned to the house, Paul rang Peter, while Michael sat at a strange angle on the sofa and looked around the living room. "Well, how is everything", said Peter anxiously. "Very good", replied Paul. "We don't seem to have any problems at all. He's really a nice young man. Listen, what happened to his face, all the blood? Why don't you provide them with electric razors? He's very badly cut up." "We did that once", said Peter, "but unfortunately one of the boys dropped it in the water, while it was connected to the electricity supply and, in attempting to retrieve it, he electrocuted himself. From that moment on, no electric razors." "Well, he's using your old one here, and when I get back to town, I'll get him a really good one."

"Am I to take it that you'll be looking after him after you return to Melbourne?" said Peter. There was a pause in the conversation, and a very quiet "yes" was the reply. "Great!" said Peter. "I knew you two would hit it off!"

So the eleven days passed gently by, with both of them discovering that they were, in fact, changing… Waking up every morning with this youth beside him was wonderful, and Paul realised, on about the ninth day, that he was feeling something that he had never felt for any human being in his entire life. Every evening before they went to sleep, Michael always said "Paul, Goodnight! I love you!" and Paul, to his surprise, found that he was repeating the phrase and meant every word of it. In these days, Michael had changed physically: he was just as thin, but after ten days the scars had vanished and his head was covered with thick black bristle. Having been in the sun – they were sunbathing every day for a few hours, well away from the ever-inquisitive eyes of Mrs Cunningham, Michael's skin quickly became a much deeper olive. But he remained relatively silent: it was only after the ninth day that he started making short responses to Paul's remarks. On the tenth day,

Paul was absolutely convinced that he had fallen in love with Michael and was just as convinced that he was not going to return him to the Institute: he had no idea of the ramifications of it all, but he was not going to let him end up at 64 Corbel Avenue, Coburg.

He rang Peter just before lunch, as they came in from taking the sun. Peter replied in a business-like voice, "Yes, may I help you?" "Peter, it's Paul. I have a request to make." At this moment, Michael moved across the room and stood beside Paul and took his hand, as if he knew instinctively that this telephone call was going to change his life,. "Anything you want", said Peter. "I'm so grateful to you for helping me out with Michael." "I should like to take legal custody of Michael." There was silence at the other end of the line. "Did you hear me?" asked Paul. "Yes, I did. Are you sure you know what you're getting into? He's going to be a great responsibility and he's not going to change very much." But Paul had seen a change in Michael in just ten days, so this latter comment he dismissed at once. "Will you help me?" asked Paul quietly. "I'll begin the legal work immediately. When you come back tomorrow, keep Michael with you and I'll see if I can organise a judge to make the necessary arrangements. You realise you'll have to go for an interview, but I'm sure Judge Stephen Spender will be most sympathetic to the case." There was a pause, then, as Paul expected, Peter began, "Let's be honest, Paul. What exactly *is* your set-up with Michael. I mean…" "It's fine", interrupted Paul. "Yes, we have become lovers if that's what you want to know". "Well, you didn't lose much time", said Peter. "If I tell you I was not the instigator of this relationship, would you believe me?" "Certainly I believe you. I didn't study psychology for five years for nothing. But you must admit, it's rather a surprise, but not a bad one. OK, my dearest brother-in-law, let's see what Judge Spender has to say." Paul said goodbye and hung up. At this precise point, Michael put both arms around him and kissed him. Paul grasped Michael by the waist and swung him round. "By the grace of God and a judge called Spender", he said, "you are going to stay with me forever". Michael nestled his head between Paul's neck and shoulder and repeated his declaration, "Paul, I love you. When do we live together?" Paul was certain Michael had no idea of what living together entailed, but replied, "We start right now", at which Michael smiled. "Paul, I like that!" he said.

The couple that returned to the city was much happier than the one that had arrived eleven days earlier. They had said goodbye to Mrs Cunningham and returned the keys. She was extremely curt, having expected to be called regularly to the house to sort out the daily problems, but this had not happened. She had been virtually ignored on her own territory. As she took the keys, she noticed a much healthier young man sitting beside Paul. "I'm sure Peter, Janet and the children will be here for Christmas, but they will be sure to call you before. Goodbye!" "*You* won't be here for Christmas, then", she said with a certain satisfaction. "No", said Paul, "I'll leave them all to you", and he drove through the gates and headed back to Melbourne.

On the drive back, Michael began little by little to make conversation with Paul. Paul was surprised and somewhat confused that Michael only recalled things he thought relevant at that moment, otherwise he stayed silent. Occasionally, he would repeat some phrase he had heard, using it completely out of context. The car purred down the freeway and through the city to East Melbourne and the terrace house on Darling Square. Paul wondered how he was going to explain Michael to Mrs Lamb. But she would have to cope. "Good heavens!" he thought. She had loathed Malcolm and stayed on, cleaning, doing the shopping and maintenance because of her affection for Paul, not for "that nasty piece of work" as she used to call Malcolm.

Paul was worried that Michael would have trouble settling in, but it seemed this was not to be. Whenever he felt confused, he simply took Paul's hand and they worked the problem out. No one was more surprised than Paul. He showed Michael his new home. He didn't show much interest, but was delighted when he found he was going to sleep in the double bed, which meant he was going to be with Paul.

The three french windows of the upstairs bedroom gave onto a balcony overlooking the little park that formed the centre of the square, with people passing through. They spent the afternoon and early evening together. Paul, noticing Michael's growing hair, ran his hand over the tight black bristle. "Beautiful!" he thought. "I wonder what he will look like when it's fully grown." Michael's cobalt-blue eyes signalled that he was ready to go to bed, and so to bed they went.

This was the first time in six years that a man had shared Paul's bed in this house, since after a year, Malcolm had taken over the bedroom off the landing and left Paul to his own devices. *This*, however, was not an old rerun, it was a completely new experience, and a wonderful one!

An hour later, after they had enjoyed each other, Michael said, "Paul, goodnight. I love you", and Paul repeated the phrase, and felt very good about using it.

Two days later, the telephone rang very early in the morning, while they were still in bed. Paul picked up the receiver and said happily, "Good morning!" "Paul, it's Peter. You have a meeting with Judge Spender the day before Christmas at ten o'clock. I'll give you the address, but I shall be there to give you a hand. I'll bring all the files on Michael, since they usually call for a psychiatrist's report before releasing a ward of the State into private custody." "But that's only two days away! What should Michael wear? Collar and tie?" "Paul, come on! It's very hot weather. I would suggest as Ralph Lauren as possible! I'll see you at quarter to ten at the court house."

Paul wasn't at all concerned about the meeting. After all, in eighteen years, no one had come forward to help or take custody of Michael. Besides, he would be saving the State a fortune, he reckoned.

Michael had met and totally charmed Mrs Lamb, who sang his praises to Paul from morning to evening. Nothing was too much trouble for her where Michael was concerned. Paul having explained the problem to her, never once did she walk directly behind Michael or touch him from behind. On one occasion they had even walked hand-in-hand to the local store to fetch a carton of milk. For Michael, all this was very new, but when he heard a group of schoolboys passing on the other side of the street, yelling and shouting, he grasped Mrs Lamb's hand tightly and was very glad to get safely back to the big terrace-house on Darling Square. "He's an angel, Mr. Moran, an angel! And so beautiful! Yes, he's an angel!" she exclaimed, leaving him with Paul who was working with his laptop. Michael leant down and kissed Paul on the neck. "Did you see any interesting people in the street?" Paul asked.

Walking along the street with Mrs Lamb was a novelty for Michael, since at the institution they were always transported by bus from door to door in large groups. It was all new to him, but it was the noise he didn't like, especially the groups of yelling school children, revelling in their freedom after a day of school discipline.

The next day, following Peter's advice, Paul took all Michael's measurements, left him with Mrs Lamb and returned later with two large bags of clothes. On the day, Paul dressed in grey trousers, white shirt and a black blazer. Michael wore a blue shirt, almost the same colour as his eyes, and beige trousers, with dark blue jumper, but since it was quite warm, he didn't need to put it on. Paul then remembered that he had taken those photos of Michael when he had not been looking so good, and placed them in his blazer pocket. "Just in case...!" he thought.

When they arrived at the court, Michael became very bewildered and frightened by the people rushing about in and out of doors and large groups standing and waiting. He reached out and grabbed Paul's hand. Paul squeezed it and smiled. In his entire life he had never held a man's hand in public, but was now proud to do so, feeling an inner satisfaction.

He saw Peter at the end of the corridor, talking to someone. Then Peter saw them and hurried towards them. "Good morning, Paul! Good morning, Michael!" Michael did not reply. Paul said to Peter, "What's the matter? You look very agitated!" "Paul, we have a real problem! Judge Spender is ill and the hearing has been taken over by Judge Bernard Mahoney." "So", said Paul, "what's the difference?" "Judge Mahoney is not exactly pro-gay. We're going to have trouble with the custody." Paul went quite white, his stomach cramped. He had never even thought of it. "And what if they won't give me custody?" said Paul. "I think you know what will happen to Michael." It wasn't fear, it was terror, a terror he had never known in his entire life. What would he do without Michael? He knew he couldn't live without him, and if there was a battle to be fought for someone he loved, he was ready, but extremely nervous. Michael was wholly oblivious to the situation and either didn't understand or chose not to. A clerk came along and said that Judge Mahoney would see them now. This was his last hearing before the Christmas break. The three of them followed the clerk into a relatively small room, with a table in the centre. The clerk motioned them to sit down. The air-conditioner seemed to Paul to be making a noise like an aeroplane. He was starting to perspire: this disaster had not been foreseen and he was totally at a loss as to how to deal with it. The door opened on the other side and in came Judge Mahoney. Paul rose quickly and said, "Good heavens! I know you! You're the old coot the delinquents knocked down three weeks ago! By the way, how's your head?" Peter thought Paul had gone absolutely mad, calling one of the most conservative judges an old coot, it was suicidal for Michael's case. "My head's fine now, thanks to you. What are you here for?" "A custody case", said Paul, a little more quietly. At this point, Peter intervened and began to explain the situation. Judge Mahoney's eyes went from Paul to Michael, without looking at Peter. "Fine! Fine!" he said to Peter. "Would you wait outside a moment? I want to speak to these two young men alone." Peter left the room. The door squeaked before banging shut. "Well! So we meet again!" said Judge Mahoney. You never gave me the opportunity to thank you. I've read the custody case. Stephen (Stephen being Judge Spender) sent it to me. He's very ill at present. What do you want me to do about this situation?" He looked gravely at the open file in front of him. To Paul's surprise and horror, Michael just took over. He did not relate to many people, but in his own way, when he sensed love, security, something he felt was positive for him, he opened up, and with Judge Bernard Mahoney, he sensed this warmth. "Mr Coot, I want to live with Paul", he began. "I don't want to be in that place with all those people. They hit me and they took Toby away." Bernard Mahoney had never in his whole life encountered anyone like Michael. He asked Michael who Toby was. "Mr Coot! Toby was mine! He was a bear, a beautiful little bear, and they pulled him apart. I found one arm and I hid it in my bed, but the ladies that change the bed took it away." Judge Mahoney looked into Michael's huge cobalt-blue eyes and was somehow aware that something was happening. Michael's magnetism was working on him. Paul had never heard Michael speak like this and was genuinely surprised. He felt in his blazer pocket and handed the Judge the photographs of Michael. Bernard Mahoney's face showed no expression at all. He closed the file and stood up. "What's your Christian name?" he asked Paul. "On the application for custody it just says 'P. Moran'". "It's 'Paul'" was the quiet reply. "What are you doing for Christmas dinner?" asked the Judge. Paul felt he was totally losing track of everything. "Michael and I will be at home. My brother-in-law, sister and their children are off to the farm, but neither Michael nor I like noisy children." "Neither do I," said Bernard Mahoney.

"Listen carefully: I'll give you custody for one year, with provision for permanent custody if everything is all right. Despite what you think of me, I have visited the Institute where Michael would otherwise have to be sent, and am well aware of the problems he would encounter. However, custody is given with the proviso that you and Michael have Christmas dinner with Lorna and me. Where is it you live?" Paul pulled out a business card with his home address on the reverse. "Very well", said the Judge, "I take it with a name like yours that you're Catholic?" "Well, sort of…I haven't been to mass for a while." "I see. We will pick you up for the eleven o'clock mass at St Patrick's and then back to St. George's Road for lunch. It's my way of saying thank-you for the other night. At the same time, you will be able to sign all the other legal documents."

Paul stood up, shook hands with Judge Bernard Mahoney and thanked him, saying that they would be ready on Christmas Day. He felt a great sense of relief when, to his utmost horror, Michael went up to the Judge and kissed him, with the words, "Mr Coot, I like you very much!" Bernard again said goodbye and Paul and Michael left the room, leaving behind a man who, for the first time in sixty-five years, had been kissed by a beautiful young man with blue eyes. He stood motionless, his mind a complete blank, but he felt remarkably happy.

Paul walked out with a straight face to encounter a most worried and anxious Peter. "Well, what happened?" Followed immediately by "You didn't get custody!" Paul came up very close to Peter, with Michael beside him, and whispered, "He's mine! He's all mine! Yes! We got custody on condition that we go to Christmas mass and have lunch with the Mahoneys at their home". "I don't believe it! Judge Mahoney gave a custody case a 'yes' in ten minutes, and a gay one at that!"

"Times change", said Paul. "You're both very lucky! Congratulations! I must phone Janet and tell her at once. She'll be delighted. She's dying to meet Michael!"

Paul left the court with Michael and then realised that he had nothing to take to lunch tomorrow, so they took a taxi and went to a large department store in the city centre. The Christmas crowds were terrible with the last-minute shopping rush. When they entered the store, it was extremely crowded and, since Paul wished to go to the second floor, he told Michael he would leave him in a place where there were fewer people, rather than have him touched or pushed.

So Paul left Michael for ten minutes or so, and hurried up to the second floor to the bottle shop to purchase a couple of bottles of champagne. As far as money was concerned, Paul was always afraid that if Michael did get separated, he would be in real trouble, so he had put a list of telephone numbers in his shirt pocket and fifteen dollars in his trouser pocket to cover costs until he could be rescued. He left Michael beside a special stand erected for the sale of Christmas decorations, but at this late hour – the day before Christmas – few people wanted to purchase last-minute decorations. Michael noticed a ten-foot fringe of burgundy red with wording on it, so that when the fringe moved, the words shimmered. He thought he would get one for Mr. Coot and one for Paul for Christmas, but since he had no idea of how to do it, he was most perplexed, and just stared at the fringes.

"What do you want?" asked an abrupt voice. Michael froze. He didn't know what to do. "Well, move on if you're not going to buy anything!" said a very thin-faced man in his early forties. Michael moved to the side and began to cry. He couldn't understand why the man was angry with him: he hadn't done anything bad! At this very moment, a woman of uncertain age came past, wearing extremely heavy makeup and bleached hair that looked like straw. She had very high heels and tottered rather than walked, a black miniskirt, a white see-through blouse with a bright red bra nestling in behind, and a copious bag swinging from her shoulder. "Hey!" she said abruptly, "You giving my friend a bad time, are you?" and glared at the thin-faced vendor. "What do you want, beautiful?" she asked Michael, and he replied that he wanted to know what the fringe spoke. "'Spoke'?" She looked quite taken-aback. "Well, beautiful, it says 'Happy Christmas'." "I would like two, one for Paul and one for Mr. Coot." "Well!" said the woman, "You shall have them! Rat-face, we'll have two of these." "Really!" said the vendor, obviously having had a trying Christmas season, "that's all I need, a retard and a hooker!" "Watch your tongue, Rat-face! I am a regular customer here! Give the Rat the money, beautiful! They're eight dollars each, so that will be sixteen dollars." Michael handed the money to the woman and she in turn handed it to the irate vendor. "Ho! We seem to be a dollar short!" "Oh, come on!" she said, "it's all he has and it's Christmas!" " No dollar, no Christmas fringe!" replied the vendor with a nasty smirk. The woman turned round as an extremely tall basketball type passed behind her. "Oh darling!" she said, "You don't have a dollar, do you? I've left my purse at home!" "Is that all you're charging these days?" he said with a laugh, "Haha!" She glared at him, "This rat-faced assistant is giving my friend here a really hard time and he is one dollar short for buying his friend a Christmas gift. This louse really hasn't got any Christmas spirit and refuses to help him out." "OK, here's the dollar." But the tall basketball player had entered into the spirit, not of Christmas, but of the banter between the woman and the vendor. "Here's the missing dollar. Give my friend the goods or there'll be trouble! Wrap them separately." "We don't do that at this counter. If you take the goods and receipt, they'll do it just over there." He pointed to a counter where two young assistants were wrapping up customers' purchases. "Thank you Rat-face" said the woman sarcastically and tottered with Michael and the six-foot-three basketball player to the counter.

There were two queues: both were short, but they joined the shorter, which had only one elderly lady in front. In the other slightly longer queue, an overweight, smartly dressed matron complained loudly that they had taken her place. "Oh, shove off, fatty!" was the retort from the woman, bringing gales of laughter from the others in line. "Well!" screamed the matron, "How dare you! I didn't come here to be insulted". As quick as a flash, the woman with the straw-like hair replied, "Where do you usually go?" This had the basketball player in hysterics. "Cheap tart!" was the matron's comment.

Finally, the three of them reached the counter, and an overdressed little queen asked for the receipt. On seeing it, he said, "You haven't spent enough to have it gift-wrapped. That's only for goods over twenty dollars!" Michael looked up at the tall youth and took his hand. He was now completely confused. The basketball player yelled, "Wrap the two fringes separately, or else I'll take out my 10-inch cock and shove it up your arse!" There was dead silence in the queue, and quite a few people had gathered around to watch the scene. "Really!" said the snappy little queen. "Yes, really!" said the tall youth, and with that he unzipped his shorts and waved his extremely long member at the queen, whose eyes widened like never before: the matron feigned shock and the woman with the straw-like hair smiled knowingly. Michael seemed oblivious to the whole drama.

"What colour would sir like the wrapping paper?" asked the breathless assistant. "What shall it be, my friend?" asked the basketball player. Michael replied, "Red would be nice". "Two parcels in red with red bows – and large red bows!" said the basketball player, rubbing his groin. The assistant dropped the roll of ribbon, which ran right across the floor.

The matron had had quite enough of all this, and spat out at the woman with the straw-like hair, "You prostitutes are all the same, common as muck, standing on street corners with cheap dyed rabbit coats!"

"Really Fatty! With your figure you would need four dozen rabbit pelts to go round your waist!"

"I", came the reply, "happen to wear only mink!"

How Michael remembered, where he had got it from, remains a mystery, but it must have been the word 'mink' that sparked something in his memory, and his recall was excellent: "You have to be up early in the morning to catch a fox, but you have to stay out late at night to get a mink."

The effect on the rather large crowd that had by now gathered was electric; laughter was spontaneous. The tall youth who had helped Michael was laughing so much that tears rolled down his cheeks; even the boy wrapping the presents for Michael had lapsed into hysterical giggles. Not to miss a trick, the woman in the mini-skirt and very high heels shot another verbal arrow at the matron, "Honey, you could work all night and you wouldn't earn enough to buy a mink button". The crowd was now entering into the spirit of this debacle, with comments and very loud laughter. The matron was so angry that she slammed one of her gifts on the counter for wrapping, only to hear a nasty sound from inside the shallow box. She glared down and wrenched it open to discover that the Copenhagen Christmas plate for her sister was now in five separate pieces. Her face paled. "I suggest", said the snappy little queen, "that you return to where you purchased it with your receipt and see what they can do for you". With that, the matron snatched up all her parcels and, ramming them into a large loose bag, stormed off toward the lift. Her parting comment, at the top of her voice, was, "Common, you are, all common!" and she disappeared into the crowd.

The tall youth put his arms around Michael and said, "You're the best value I've ever known, and all for a dollar!" before disappearing in turn among the busy last-minute Christmas shoppers.

Having received his two luxuriously-wrapped parcels in separate store Christmas bags, Michael returned to the point where Paul had left him, but not before saying to his slightly-fallen angel, "Thank you very much. You are a nice person". But it didn't finish there, for our fallen angel had forgotten her contact lenses. She left the large group she had entertained, who would all dine out on the experience for months, and moved forward, saying, "Out of my way! Out of my way!" She tottered directly into a pillar, covered in mirror, and ended up in a horizontal position on the floor. She was surprised when two – or was it three – men dashed forward. Where she had her accident was only four yards away from the counter and when she had fallen, with her legs in the air, her reflection in the mirror had caused quite a stir, since underwear is not a prerequisite for ladies of the night. "May I take you for a coffee", asked a good-looking executive type. She looked surprised as he helped her to her feet. "Well", she said, "take me for a late lunch and you'll never regret it!" With that, Michael's guardian angel hobbled away toward the exit on her five-inch Ferragamos, accompanied by a rather breathless and not at all bad looking young man.

Michael waited and after what only seemed a moment Paul was there. "Where did you get the bags?" he asked, looking at the store's de luxe carriers. "It's a surprise", said Michael. For Michael and his future extended family, this statement was to become an important signal that he was waiting for something special.

But this wasn't the only drama in the store during this last-minute scurry for odds and ends for the festive season. After Michael and Paul left, Bernard phoned his wife to say they would be four for Christmas dinner and that it would be a surprise for her. Then he telephoned the switchboard of the same store where Michael had had his adventure with Christmas fringe. "I wish to speak to the manager", said Bernard in his driest voice. "Who's calling?" came the pat reply. "Judge Bernard Mahoney." "Just a moment, Judge, I'm connecting you." "Yes", came a very tired voice. "Is Christmas a worry this year Teddy?" "Oh, Bernard, you have no idea! Complaints from morning to night. How are you, anyway?" "I'm fine. I need you to do me a favour." "Oh, anything, Bernard. What is it?" "I need a Steiff teddy bear, with a brass or similar label round his neck saying 'Toby', delivered to St George's Road tonight." "Bernard, are you aware what you are asking me? It's the last day before Christmas. It's chaos here!" "Tonight, Teddy. Lorna's home, so she can receive the package. Leave the gift label blank and I'll fill it in", and he hung up.

'Teddy' was in fact Edward Smith, managing director of the whole enormous store, and this was the last thing he needed: Judge Mahoney demanding a teddy bear, suitably wrapped, as a present. He thought it rather odd. They were both members of the same prestigious club and he had known Bernard for years. "But Bernard *hates* children, I know he does. How strange!" He immediately telephoned the display department, "Tell Kevin to come to my office at once. It's an emergency!" Ten minutes later, Kevin Riley appeared at the manager's door. He was tall with receding reddish hair and carried a walking stick – the result of a bad fall in one of the front windows. His face seemed to say 'I know it all', with only a slight trace of superiority. He was always impeccably dressed, and was a master of understatement. "Well!" he said, "London burning?" "No!" came the sharp reply. "I need you to get a Steiff teddy bear. Gift-wrap it, but it must have a brass or silver tag or something around its neck that says 'Toby'." "Shall I pack the champagne bottles alongside him?" "Don't be smart! This must be delivered to St George's Road this afternoon, and it's already four-thirty." "What number St George's Road?" When told, Kevin Riley said, "What on earth would Bernard and Lorna want with a teddy bear?" "I don't know, and frankly,

I don't care, but get it there at once!" "It will cost you a bottle of champagne!" "Very well! But get going!"

With the aid of his silver-topped cane and great aplomb, Kevin Riley made his way to the lift and took it to the seventh floor. "Toys", it said boldly as he stepped out. He walked directly across the floor to a young woman and said, "Steiff teddy bears! How many left?" "Why Mr. Riley," – since he was an institution at the store – "we only have two, a large one and a tiny one". The larger one seemed fine except that it was in the hands of a prospective buyer. With his cane, Kevin walked right up behind the customer and with his free hand snatched the bear from her. "I am so sorry", he said to the woman, who was both startled and angry at having the bear snatched from her grasp. "You see", he said, "we are to be married the day after Christmas, so I couldn't possibly leave him with you. We've been lovers for years". The woman was totally confused. The bear being married to this imperious man with a walking stick! Nothing made sense! "Come along, Toby" Kevin said, and with the bear under one arm, his head held very high as usual, he stalked his way across Toyland – as it was called – back to the lift. On reaching ground level, he found himself again among the frenzy of last-minute shoppers.

He moved to the engravers' stand, which did anything from 'I love you' to 'Fido' and insisted they make the necessary engraving. "No way, man!" came the reply. "We're up to our arse in last-minute work". Kevin Riley looked at the manager of this tiny stand – just two men worked there – and said, "I suggest you should do this at once, or find another store to give you this sort of franchise". The manager, who worked with his son, looked a trifle threatened. "I'm not joking", said the poker-faced Mr Riley, "and now I'm waiting!" With a somewhat changed manner, the manager brought a choice of disks or shields on which 'Toby' could be engraved. Kevin selected a small, gold-coloured shield, already with decorative engraving around the edges, but, alas, the chain was too short. "Take another and join it on. Hurry up! The taxi is sure to be waiting."

'Toby' was duly engraved; the chain was fitted around the bear's neck and six links were added to make the whole thing look as though it had been designed just for the bear. Then off to the gift-wrapping department went Mr Riley, where he encountered the same young assistant who had had the adventure with our lady of the night and the tall young man with something to remember.

Kevin Riley was an institution with his stately appearance and mastery of the understatement: he was the store, and the store was him. At sixty-seven, he was past retirement age, but he and the store were both sure that one could not do without the other.

"Mr Riley", said the young assistant. "You won't believe it!" There was a queue of people, which Kevin Riley jumped. "Wrap him deluxe. I know", he said, "six foot three inches and a 10-inch cock. It's been the happiest Christmas the store's ever known!" The assistant was somewhat taken aback that he already knew. But, in actual fact, within twenty minutes, the lunchroom and every department had joyously passed on the news, amongst hoots of laughter.

The bear Toby, duly packed, made a slight detour past the liquor store, where a bottle of vintage Tattinger was put on the Manager's account. Then Kevin Riley took a taxi, with Toby the bear and a bottle of champagne to one of the most prestigious addresses in Melbourne.

Kevin phoned Lorna from the cab to say he was on his way over. When the cab arrived, the driver got out and pressed the bell. The gates opened and he got back in and drove up to the front of a most imposing Toorak mansion. Kevin got out with some difficulty owing to the cane, the bear and the champagne, but with the driver's help, he managed. He pressed the doorbell, as the taxi headed back up the drive.

"Kevin, darling! How are you? What a marvellous surprise!" said Lorna. "It's so long since we last saw one another." "True, true!" was the reply. "Let's go in and open this thing", he said, "pushing the champagne bottle into Lorna's hand.

They passed through a white marble-floored entrance into a very gracious living area on the right. "Do sit down, darling!" she said, "and tell me why you're here. What can I do for you?" "Oh no!" he said. "It's what I'm doing for Bernard". "I don't understand", said Lorna. "Well, Edward phoned me to say Bernard wanted a de luxe teddy bear with the name 'Toby' smartly engraved around its neck. And here I am!"

"But what on earth would Bernard want with a teddy bear?" asked Lorna. "Second or third childhood, I should think", said Kevin, in a slightly sarcastic manner. Lorna laughed, "Do open the bottle, Kevin! You're impossible!" She rang the bell and a maid appeared and returned with two glasses. They drank to their lost youth and screamed with laughter about friends they were happy to have lost. Kevin then told her the funny story about the store's gift-wrapping department. "Quite the thing, never has anything so exciting happened before! Imagine, in every department – and there are eighteen – this is the only thing they're talking about: six feet three inches and a ten-inch cock! Isn't Christmas wonderful!" They both burst into peals of laughter.

"Have you seen Anne?" he asked. "Not for a while, but you know Anne. She's a whirlwind of energy, always here and there!" "Exactly!" came the reply. "She's very popular with every queen in town, you know!" "Oh! I do!" Lorna said, "but how she keeps her strength up night after night, I'll never know!" "Well, that's easy!" Kevin replied. "She doesn't have a husband, just his money! Isn't she lucky?"

At this moment, the front door was heard to open and close, and Bernard appeared. "Hello, Kevin", he said. "What brings you here? We haven't seen you for ages." "Your bloody bear is what brings me here", Kevin replied. "Oh yes, the bear! Is everything complete?" "Yes, absolutely!" said Kevin, "everything's complete! Listen, would you call me a cab, Lorna? I must go. I've a million things to do before the store closes at ten tonight." Kevin sped back for the last four hours of Christmas trade at Melbourne's largest department store.

"Bernard, what's the story about the parcel with the bear?" Lorna asked. "It's a surprise for Christmas Day", he said. "Don't ruin the surprise!"

Christmas Day in Darling Square began, as every day, with the two young men enjoying each other amidst lots of laughter and love. Michael told Paul he had to stay in bed and went to collect his gift for him. He had never given a present to anyone before: he had never had the money to do so, or the opportunity or person to give it to. So for Michael this was an exciting moment. He gave Paul the package, sumptuously wrapped with two red satin bows. Paul opened it, and there was the fringe with Happy Christmas written on it. Paul was overwhelmed.

With his gift, Michael expressed exactly what Christmas was all about: being happy! Paul kissed him and told him it was the most beautiful present he had ever had, and he really meant it! It was real, a dear sentiment three yards long and ten inches deep. Paul strung it up in the bedroom in front of the windows. Then he gave his gift to Michael. "It's not as nice as yours!" he said, and felt stupid because he hadn't thought of a sentiment rather than a fashion object. Still, Michael seemed very pleased with his beautiful black jumper and put in on at once. Having just risen from bed, he was totally naked, his now bristly black hair not quite the mane it was soon to become, and the jumper his only covering. In Paul's eyes, he wasn't just beautiful, he was almost divine. They had three or four hours before being collected by the Mahoneys. They went down for breakfast: Paul's was low-fat; Michael's just the opposite. He was starting to lose his skeletal look and was thickening up a little. After breakfast, he came up behind Paul, put his arms round him and said, "Where is the man in the pictures?" Paul looked around and saw that Michael was looking at the photos of Paul and Malcolm together. "He's dead now", said Paul. "Then why is his picture here?" "I don't know", said Paul, simply because he had never thought of it and it had never occurred to him that Michael might think of it. "When people are dead, they go away, and so should their pictures." Michael stood up, went upstairs and lay down on the bed.

In a sudden burst of real strategic energy, Paul collected the photos in the living room from their silver frames. He went upstairs and removed them from the frames in the dressing room and went into the bedroom, where Michael was lying on the bed clad only in his new black jumper. In the bedroom too, Paul opened four silver frames and took out each photo without a word to Michael. Then he went back downstairs and put all the photos into the metal grate of the white marble fireplace. Fetching a box of matches from the kitchen, he lit the photos all together: after a slow start, there was a flash of flame and it was done. He went to the phone and dialled Mrs Lamb's number and wished her a very happy Christmas on behalf of Michael and himself, and hoped she had liked her gift. She returned his wishes warmly and said that his gift of a new dinner service was beyond her wildest expectations.

"When you come in on Wednesday", he said, "please empty Malcolm's wardrobe completely, and remove everything of his from this house. Do what you want with them, but get rid of absolutely everything!" "It will be a pleasure, Mr Moran", she said. And Paul knew she meant it, aware as he was that she had loathed Malcolm and that this was the final purge, throwing away every last thing.

Paul went back upstairs and said, "Get dressed! There's something we have to do". Twenty minutes later, they were both suitably dressed for the Mahoneys, but were forty-five minutes early. Paul took his digital camera in one hand and Michael in the other, and together they crossed the road to the middle of Darling Square. The first person Paul saw was a woman he knew vaguely, having met her once or twice at the East Melbourne Association: a charming woman, who was very surprised at being marshalled into action on a warm Christmas morning.

Cecil Beaton in Darling Square: she did her best, being very aware of aesthetics, and made sure that the background was unmistakeably East Melbourne. Although she knew only one of the two men, her instinct told her she was photographing two men who were very much in love with each other. After twenty minutes of formal and funny poses, they thanked her, wished her a Merry Christmas and a bright New Year. With Michael, Paul at once returned home to the room he used as an office and downloaded the photos. They selected the best ones and using "Photoshop", he printed sufficient photos to fill the now empty silver frames. Michael said absolutely nothing, but this burst of energy to change everything for his and Michael's future was for Paul a cleansing process. He should have done it before, but with all the necessary adjustments when Michael had moved in, he hadn't even thought of it. Now it was done, and he felt a kind of freedom as he moved from room to room, seeing only himself and Michael and feeling ashamed that Michael had had to tell him that they didn't need a dead man between them.

The car pulled up in front of the terrace in Darling Square. Bernard alighted and pressed the doorbell. The door opened and two handsome young men said "Happy Christmas" together. "Shall we go?" Bernard said. Paul had a bag with two bottles of champagne and Michael his de luxe department store carrier bag, which they put in the boot.

In the car, they found Lorna in the driver's seat, very elegant in a light cream silk frock and magnificent string of large-grade Broome pearls, all of the same colour, her Christmas present from Bernard. "How do you do?" she said formally. "Happy Christmas!" "Thank you", said Paul, "and the same to you!" Michael remained silent. Not having expected to see a woman with Bernard and being rather unsure of the situation, he seized Paul's hand.

Lorna drove off in the direction of St Patrick's. Lorna's first instinct was that Paul was marvellous, and she liked him at first sight: his thick hair and brown eyes, well-dressed, but not overdone. With Michael, she felt she was seeing him through a sheet of thick clear glass, and sensed he had raised a barrier as a kind of protection, but realised how right Bernard had been when he said the boy was beautiful and had magnetic blue eyes. She felt an ever-so-slight touch of that magnetism, but it wasn't just his eyes: it was the whole presence of Michael sitting with Paul on the back seat.

A place in the carpark had been kept for Judge Bernard Mahoney, and the Bishop had clearly been waiting for them inside the Cathedral. After greeting them, they were led to reserved seats two rows from the front. Paul noticed that for the first time in a large group of people Michael did not appear agitated or afraid. To Paul's knowledge, this was the first time Michael had ever been to church, and this one was particularly large and crowded, with everyone sitting very close to each other. This would be the pattern with Michael in future: he felt protected in church, despite the large numbers, and found that their simultaneous movements of standing, kneeling and sitting were calm and harmonious, leaving no room for fear. But in other situations, Michael just froze.

During mass, Michael sat between Paul and Bernard, and it was Bernard – not Paul – who took his arm, directing him when to stand, kneel or sit. Michael thought it very nice that he could do the same as everyone else, and enjoyed the feeling of success.

After mass, Bernard drove them back to St George's Road, where they were ready to settle down to the splendid Christmas dinner that Lorna had arranged. Before lunch began, Bernard said to Paul, "Let's sign the custody papers now", and he left the room and returned with a folder containing two sheets of paper. He produced a fountain pen from his pocket and handed it to Paul. "Sign here on this sheet, and here on this other one. Good! Now, Michael, you sign here." Paul wasn't sure what to do. He said to Bernard, "I'm not sure Michael can write". Bernard looked at Paul. It was Lorna who saved the day. "Give me the documents and put a cross where he has to sign." When this was done, she sat beside Michael and, on another sheet of paper, wrote his name: 'Michael'. Then, with some effort, she got him to copy it underneath, which he did with a very shaky hand. Lorna then passed him the documents, with her sheet just above where he was to sign, and he copied his signature on both documents, an unfortunate necessity now that he was eighteen years old.

Michael had shortened 'Mr Coot' to 'Cooty', and 'Cooty' it remained! No one else would have dared address Bernard by a nickname, but he accepted it from Michael and seemed to enjoy it. Michael related to Bernard and had even started to warm a little to Lorna. By this stage, everyone was on first name terms. Michael brought in his bag with his gift for Bernard, but seemed perplexed: whereas Paul had two bottles of champagne, which he thought meant one for Lorna and one for Bernard, he had only a single gift.

"What's up?" asked Paul. Michael raised his left hand to his face and frowned. "I have only one bag", he said. Lorna immediately dealt with the problem. "Oh Michael, the bag you have is for Bernard. I don't need a bag because Bernard gave me my present this morning." Michael seemed a little confused, but was happier at once. He gave the bag to Bernard. "Let's have a drink", said Lorna and in a moment a chilled bottle of champagne was opened and the maid took Paul's warmish bottles to the refrigerator. Paul said that Michael would prefer orange juice.

Bernard opened the bag, withdrew the package and carefully unwrapped it. Michael moved to sit beside him on the sofa. Bernard took out the Christmas fringe and declared it was the nicest gift he had ever received. Michael was very happy and kissed him, at which Bernard gave him a hug. Lorna was genuinely surprised, since Bernard never showed any emotion in public, and this was something she had never seen before.

"Well, young man! Let's see what we have for you." With that, Bernard got down on his knees and from under the tree pulled out a large box, wrapped in red paper with an enormous green satin ribbon wound all round the parcel, which he handed to Michael. He turned to Paul and winked, "You'll have to wait till next year!" "Very well!" said Paul, smiling. Michael just sat on the sofa with the large box on his lap. He looked at Bernard and said, "Cooty, it's very nice red paper!" Bernard replied, "Shall we open it?" "Yes, I think we should!" said Michael. With that, Bernard untied the bow and ribbon and helped Michael take off the red paper. Michael was very careful not to tear the paper. He clearly thought it worth saving, or perhaps it meant something very personal to him. The box's lid came off and inside, when all the tissue paper was removed, was the bear. Michael just stared, not touching it, but he looked at the gold tag on the chain and asked Bernard, "What does it talk?" Bernard smiled, "It says 'Toby'". Michael then took the bear from the box and held it, not as a child would do, squeezing it, but lifted it with great care and sat it down beside him. "Cooty, how did you make Toby come back?" "Oh!" said Bernard, "I'm very clever!" "Oh Cooty, you *are* very clever. Now I have Toby again. He's very beautiful, but he has a silver button on his ear." "That", commented Bernard, "is to show he's a quality bear. "Hmm", said Michael, and repeated, "a quality bear!"

After hearing the story about the original Toby from Bernard, Lorna was surprised that Michael was not more emotional, but he seemed most contained and accepted everything Bernard said in a very matter-of-fact way.

Later, when they returned to Darling Square, Toby was ensconced in the bedroom, where he remained like an eternal watchdog, keeping everything safe. In Michael's mind, this was Toby and Toby was Bernard's gift. The bear from the past was completely forgotten: for Michael, Toby was in the bedroom upstairs, waiting for him every night.

"Come and help me hang up the fringe, Michael!" said Bernard, but they weren't tall enough to loop the ends over the finials of the curtain rods. "We need the tall man!" said Michael. "What tall man?" Bernard asked and Michael recounted word for word his adventure in the store. They were all in fits of laughter and, because they were laughing, Michael laughed too. Paul moved over and put his arms around him, "You didn't tell me!" he said, wiping the tears from his eyes.

"I heard the story from Kevin yesterday", Lorna said. "The whole store was shrieking with laughter. I wonder who the fat woman was?"

If there was any ice to break, it was all broken after Michael's tale. Lunch proceeded very smoothly. Paul had taken Lorna aside and asked whether it would be possible to cut any meat for Michael into small, manageable pieces. Lorna saw to everything calmly and efficiently. She and Paul had a few mutual friends, so they chatted together splendidly, while Michael and Bernard spoke on whatever subject came into Michael's head.

After lunch, Bernard asked Paul "What are you doing after Christmas? Are you going away at all?" "No," came the reply. "Well", said Bernard, "why not come with Lorna and me to Killarney for a week. We would love your company."

Paul looked at Michael. "Would you like to go on holiday with Bernard and Lorna?" He looked back at Paul and asked, "Are you coming too?" "Of course I am! I wouldn't leave you alone!" "Oh!" said Michael, "I think a holiday with Cooty would be very nice". Paul wasn't sure that Michael understood exactly what a holiday would entail, but there it was: everyone agreed, so they would be off to Killarney!

CHAPTER TWO

Killarney & New Friends

CHAPTER 2

Killarney and New Friends

All the necessary arrangements were made and three days after Christmas, they set off for Killarney

Between Christmas day and their departure, however, Lorna received a phone call from Anne Rochester, whom she had not seen for six months or so, and agreed to have dinner with her at their club on Collins Street. At seven-thirty, a taxi pulled up in front of the club – much to the annoyance of the driver behind – Lorna alighted, received the change from her fare and went up the main stairs.

"Darling! I've just arrived!" said Anne. "You look marvellous! Oh!" she squeaked, "What stunning pearls from Father Christmas! Oh, I'm so jealous!" "Anne, you're too much! You have the finest jewelry collection in Melbourne!" "But, darling, the pearls are fabulous!" retorted Anne.

Anne Rochester was rather small and immaculately groomed: it was her hallmark, with her perfect figure, her hair always in place and always some magnificent piece of jewellery attached to her somewhere. Tonight she wore a classic midnight-blue chiffon frock with tightly-pleated skirt – not a pleat out of place – and a Cartier *art deco* broach on her shoulder.

Anne and Lorna had been to one of the best girls'schools together. Their families knew one another and they had been good friends all their lives. At school, Anne had been sports-mad, but her great passion was for horses. Anne had a house next to Killarney, called Bellevue, where she kept her horses. When she was away for some time, the horses were trailered over to a large riding school-come-livery stables where they were looked after by a certain Margery Robins.

Tonight Anne was in fine form, her blue-grey eyes darting about the lounge to see who was there. She attracted the waitress's attention and ordered champagne. "Now, tell me all!" said Anne. "I've been speaking to Kevin Riley – oh, he's such a dear! – and he told me about Bernard buying a bear called Toby. What's it all about? Do tell!" So Lorna told Anne about the boys and how marvellous they were, and what a great Christmas Day they had had, and that the day after tomorrow the four of them were off to Killarney. "I don't believe it! How long is it since you were last at Killarney?" "Probably", Lorna replied, "two years. Bernard rang Mary Ryan to get the house ready. We shall be there for a week, I think. I'm so looking forward to it!" "But Lorna, I shall be at Bellevue at the same time! Oh, how splendid!" said Anne. As they were about to continue, a certain Mrs Horton Wills blustered into the lounge and took over. "Well, girls", she said loudly, "you'll never believe the ghastly, humiliating experience I went through the day before Christmas. It's enough to make your blood run cold! In this city we have to put up with common people, who bully one and push one about!" In a loud voice, she began to recount her version of the story that Lorna and Anne had heard from Kevin Riley, and Lorna had the advantage of Michael's version as well. "Oh!" chuckled Lorna, covering her mouth. "The fat woman was Kathryn Horton Wills. Oh how splendid!"

Though considerably different from the other two versions, Mrs Kathryn Horton Wills had her friends gasping at the indignities that poor Kathryn had suffered. Lorna said to Anne, "Come along, let's go in to dinner" and, as they passed very close to Kathryn, now on her second whisky, Lorna leaned over and said, "Did you tell them about Mae West's line. And by the way, how was that ten-inch cock?" Kathryn Horton Wills choked on her whisky and looked very surprised. "How did you get to know about the incident?" she asked very slowly, narrowing her eyes. "Oh!" said Anne, getting her cut in as well, "A little bear told us as he was passing and saw it all!"

Anne linked arms with Lorna and the two of them made their way to the dining room laughing, leaving a very deflated Kathryn trying to escape her friends' questions that were now coming thick and fast.

They sat down at their reserved table and made their choice from the menu. "Now, Lorna! What are the boys really like? I can't believe that Bernard, of all people, has taken a shine to them! If my memory serves, he isn't exactly pro-gay!" "I know", said Lorna. "He's crazy about them! They're now our only conversation at home. And he has this... well, the only way I can describe it... this love for Michael, not like a lover or a father, but like an adoring friend. It's wonderful! When he phoned Killarney yesterday and told Mary he wanted another bedroom made up, he said quite clearly that two men would be sharing the bed. When he hung up, he looked as though he had won the lottery!" "But Lorna, this is splendid! I'm dying to meet them! What exactly is Michael like?" "Michael", came the reply, "has a few social problems, but nothing serious at all. He is very dependent on Paul and obviously loves him dearly and the great thing is, it's reciprocated. Oh Anne! They are both beautiful, but Michael is magic, especially now his hair's growing back." "Good heavens! Whatever happened to his hair?" said Anne, looking alarmed. "At the Institute, they shaved it all off." "Oh, how ghastly!" said Anne. "But his eyes – you won't believe it! – are cobalt blue, with enormous black lashes and olive skin. He's really a stunner! The only thing, Paul tells me, is that he dislikes children." "Well!" Anne interrupted, "In my book that makes him an intelligent and selective genius". She laughed. "But he's also not too keen on women, it seems." "Now there we have a problem", said Anne. "How do you get along with him?" "Quite well. I only met him the once, on Christmas Day, but I felt he was sizing me up, although he was pleasant and created no problems. One big problem he does have is that if someone walks up behind him, he just freezes, and if he's distressed, he covers his head with his hands. Paul said his table manners were a worry, but for me that was no problem at all. I know quite a few people who consider themselves very normal, but have the most shocking table manners." "Oh, don't we all?" Anne replied. "So we are all off to Morton, how wonderful! I must call Colin and see if he's available and then we can make a lovely little group of six for dinner!" "Yes, Anne" said Lorna. "It seems Michael hates, or can't cope with, large groups, especially if they're noisy." "Don't worry, Lorna! I wasn't thinking of opening the ballroom at Bellevue... By the way, what's happening with the ballroom at Killarney?" "Oh, don't speak about it! It's virtually a storeroom for furniture from about eight different houses, and Bernard refuses to do anything about it." They chatted on and, at a certain hour, left the club. Both ladies caught taxis going in opposite directions, since Anne was going on for a drink with some friends who had just bought a new house at Brighton.

Lorna sat back in the taxi as it headed up Collins Street and turned into Spring Street. She was thinking about Anne. They had been to school together and later at Melbourne University, but at university they began to drift apart, Anne instantly seeking and finding a coterie of young gay men, a pattern she had followed throughout her life. She found straight men unbearable. Her parents had been quite old when she was born – her mother was forty-five and her father considerably older– and, as an only child, she was doted on. At the age of nineteen, she found herself bereft of parents. She took over her father's investment and development company and ran it with an efficiency that surprised all who knew her. But her great *forte* was the stock exchange. In this field, her sixth sense earned her a reputation as a brilliant investor. Anne trebled her father's fortune, making vast amounts, and became a very wealthy woman. Her family properties included the large mansion on Lansell Road, Toorak, and Bellevue, at Morton. Suddenly, when Anne was forty-two, she married Edgar Rochester, a man twenty-three years her senior. Edgar Rochester also owned a large investment company, so it was a marriage of equals. Her female acquaintance passed catty comments about her marrying only for money. Her friends remained the same after her marriage and Edgar clearly found no threat in these bright young men whose company and sparkling repartee he enjoyed, just as Anne did. When they married they agreed to sell their respective large homes and purchase a luxurious ground-floor apartment with a garden and swimming pool. This move was one of the few regrets in Anne's life, since as soon as the mansion on Lancell Road was sold – at a very good price – the developers tore it down and built an exceedingly ugly apartment block. She always felt guilty about it, as if she had not taken genuine responsibility for her parents' home.

Anne and Edgar's new apartment was vast: in actual fact, in was two ground-floor apartments knocked into one. Anne got Nigel Storey to decorate it, and his only instruction was that it had to proclaim *chic*, and so it did! Nigel ripped up all the floors, changed walls round, and virtually reconstructed everything. Considering the apartment was barely two years old, it was the top word in extravagance. Black was the dominant colour in most of the entertaining area: glazed black walls, huge glass windows and black marble floors. The furniture was elegant, a lot of it black in the eighteenth century fashion, with gilt bronze mounts. All Anne's gay friends killed to get an invitation for lunch or dinner.

On Anne's forty-sixth birthday, Edgar threw a de luxe luncheon for twenty. Anne was in great spirits, especially after receiving a magnificent pair of earrings, emeralds surrounded by diamonds, which she sported for the day. As everyone arrived, Anne found her guests' coo's and sighs at the sight of her earrings most gratifying. Most of them brought flowers, which was the rule: no gifts whatever the occasion, just flowers.

The day was hot and the guests were invited to use the pool. Edgar sat on a lounger and watched the guests playing and drinking champagne: Anne would drink nothing else. At one-thirty, she called everyone to the table and realised that Edgar was slow in arriving. "Darling, do go and hurry Edgar up!" she asked one of the young men, who returned white-faced and everyone realised something was wrong. Wrong it was! Edgar had suffered a multiple heart attack and died. Anne immediately called the doctor and in thirty minutes, Edgar's body was taken away in an ambulance.

Anne returned to her guests and bade them sit down saying, "He would have insisted on our having a good time. I think it's the least we can do for him!"

But it was a very subdued luncheon party in the circumstances, Lorna remembered, everybody fearing to start what might be an inappropriate conversation. Although Anne was marvellous, carrying on as though everything were normal, her guests felt extremely uneasy throughout the meal.

After Edgar's death, Anne began spending more and more time at Bellevue with her horses and two or three friends, which she found quite sufficient. Then she would feel the need to see all her friends in town, and would return for a frenetic two or three weeks, before going back to Bellevue again.

- - -

Lorna and Paul had arranged that Paul would follow Bernard and the little convoy set off for Morton early the next morning. She had told Paul to pack a dinner jacket, since Anne enjoyed throwing black-tie dinner parties. "But", he said, "Michael hasn't got one and there's no time to get him one". "Oh, don't worry Paul! There must be five or six of them at Killarney. We'll manage something!" They left early, headed for the freeway and on to Morton.

Morton had been developed in the eighteen-forties, when Melbourne had its spectacular building boom, so that in the hot summer months the wealthy elite could move to this higher, much cooler area, where they built large houses in the most eclectic of styles. Time passed Morton by, and the only major change to occur there was in the early nineteen-twenties, when electricity arrived. There was only a local store and two churches and the nearest town was Brunswick, fifteen miles away, where everyone went for supplies, since in the summer holiday period, when people came back to use their country houses.

An hour and a half later, Paul and Michael were following Bernard through a large impressive gateway, its great cast-iron gates standing open, and up a long meandering drive, bordered on both sides by enormous rhododendrons, though not in flower at this time of year. Rounding a sharp curve, Paul was startled by the size of the country mansion before him. He had been to Morton several times, but hadn't realised that such mansions lay hidden at the end of their long drives, protected from prying eyes by a thick forest of trees.

Killarney had been built in 1860 as a rather pretentious Italianate mansion, originally in the form of a giant square, surrounded by a double-storied veranda, its columns on both bottom and top storeys finishing in graceful arches. At the centre-front, the verandas were interrupted by a solid porch topped by an upstairs room and, at ground level, by an extravagant porte-cochere, attached to the large square empty porch, so that in inclement weather one could alight from one's car (or carriage), safe from the elements. Surrounding the entire balustrade above the upper veranda, large urns were placed directly above the columns all the way round. In front of the portico in the middle of the lawn was an enormous Victorian fountain of reconstituted stone, not in working order. In 1921 Bernard's grandfather had an extremely fortunate run on the stock exchange and decided to enlarge the house, building two wings in the identical architectural style, set back fifteen feet and attached to either side of the original building, so that the upper and lower verandas seemed to go on forever. On the left side of the new annex was a vast ballroom, its height occupying both floors and virtually forming a giant cube, behind which was a supper-room and above that the staff quarters, entered from an uncomfortably steep stairway. The other wing mainly comprised bedrooms.

By this time, many of the original rooms had been changed, divided into smaller spaces, or used as staff quarters. The most impressive part of the old house was the entrance hall, with its freestanding Corinthian columns, chequered black and white marble floor and a very grand staircase, directly facing the front door, in the French manner, with white marble steps and bronze and gilt decorative metalwork in place of the traditional wooden balustrade. It had been imported from France in large sections and a master metal-worker and two assistants had laboured for two-and-a-half months in 1860 to fit it all together, making major adjustments so that it integrated perfectly with the white marble stairs that rose to half the height of the room to a wide landing with a tall arched window, whence they divided at 180 degrees to connect with the upper floor.

The other two rooms, to the right and left on entering from the front door were the dining room and yellow drawing room. The dining room on the right on entering had not been much altered since its inception:

a black marble fireplace, surmounted by a large gilt mirror, the great mahogany table and matching sideboard, twelve heavy balloon-backed chairs covered in faded buttoned red leather, an immense carpet and curtains with swags and tassels of a faded tobacco colour, and not in the best of conditions on close inspection. The walls were hung with nondescript beige paper, with a small repeated light brown and gold pattern, covered with huge Victorian landscapes in heavy gilt frames.

On the other side of the hall was the yellow drawing room where most entertaining was done. Like the dining room, the ceiling boasted a large central rose from which a particularly miserable little chandelier was suspended. This room was furnished with the most comfortable bits and pieces, nothing matching. It had faded yellow wallpaper and yellow-cream satin curtains falling from an ornate Victorian carved and gilded pelmet. The ceiling was badly water-stained, with nicotine-coloured marks over a good half of it, owing to constant problems with the two bathrooms directly overhead, which had been badly installed in the nineteen-twenties. Above the white marble fireplace hung the traditional gilt mirror, the cornice above the mirror topped with gilt wood and stucco groups of ferns. The paintings had been collected from various parts, from deceased aunts and uncles, and had literally been attached to the walls by nails, wherever they could be fitted in. Between the two french windows was a grand piano, which Lorna played when she felt in the mood; otherwise it just stood as a memento of past times. The whole décor of Killarney was of roughly the same type.

"Paul!" said Michael. "It's a big house." This was his first speech for twenty minutes. "I think it's very nice!" Paul was genuinely relieved, since Michael had been feeling very unwell, suffering terribly as he did from carsickness, and he was glad that the sight of the mansion had cheered him up. He had been concerned on rounding the last turn in the drive that Michael may have thought it similar to his Institution, but clearly his fears were unfounded.

They pulled up behind Bernard's car, parked halfway through the porte-cochere, half in the shade and half in the full sun. Michael unfastened his safety belt and opened his door to be greeted by Bernard's "Well, Michael, what do you think?" "Cooty, I think it's very nice. I like the room that the cars are in." Bernard laughed, "Come along, I'll show you both around!"

Before they had time to move, however, Mary Ryan opened the front door. "Did you have a good drive up?" she asked. "Yes, thank you!" came the unanimous reply. She shook Bernard's hand and Lorna's and then turned to Paul. "How do you do? I am Mary." "My name is Paul", he replied and, to Paul and Lorna's surprise, Michael chipped in, "Mary, my name is Michael!" It was an instant rapport for both of them. Lorna had phoned Mary and explained Michael's situation, so she was well prepared. She took one of Michael's hands and said, "I know you would like a glass of orange juice!" He looked a little perplexed and said very quietly, "Mary, thank you!" "Why don't you all come into the drawing room and have something to drink?" said Bernard.

Eighteen years earlier, Mary had taken over the whole management of Killarney, and Bernard and Lorna had absolute trust in her, since she had proved to be a very devoted employee. She had originally been recommended to Bernard as a young art student in trouble in her first year at RMIT illustration department: she discovered she was pregnant. Her lover then abandoned her for another and she found herself in a real predicament, with very little money and no idea of what to do. Abortion was out of the question. An old friend of Bernard's, a Mrs. Lacey, heard of her plight and, since Bernard was looking for a housekeeper for Killarney, he was persuaded to offer Mary a one year's trial out of charity. Eighteen years later, Mary was still there. She gave birth to a baby girl, but in her sixth year the child contracted a virus that the doctors were unable to cure and died after just twelve days. Killarney was good for Mary in those terrible months after the death of her child, shielding her from the outside world until she regained her strength and confidence. She didn't live at the main house: Bernard had given her one of the cottages. The other cottage was occupied by Mr and Mrs Barnes: he worked as gardener and she helped at the big house whenever Mary needed her, which was not often since Bernard and Lorna rarely came to Killarney. In fact, this was the first time in two years, so Mrs Barnes had been hard at work with Mary for a week to get the house in some kind of order.

Attached to Mary's cottage was a large double garage, which, at Mary's request, Bernard had restored and floored, with a wall of glass on the side farthest from the big house, so that Mary could have a studio for her drawing and painting. By arrangement with Bernard, she always had Wednesday afternoon free and drove into Brunswick to an artists' club that met on that afternoon. Although not artistically stimulating, it was some kind of company and, as she said, at least she was keeping her hand in.

Paul was overawed by the size of everything at Killarney: the big hall, enormous drawing rooms and the clutter of a hundred years or so of family furniture and possessions.

Mary served chilled wine to Lorna and Paul, while Bernard preferred a whisky, proffered to him on a special little silver salver. Mary also brought Michael his orange juice, circumnavigating the yellow drawing room so that she never passed behind him, remembering Lorna's strict injunctions. Michael sat very straight and looked about him. "Cooty", he said, "what a lot of furniture! I like the plants on the top", and he pointed at the gilt fern fronds forming the decorative top section of the mirror. "Mary", he went on, "Don't you think they are very nice?" "I certainly do", she replied. "Mr Barnes has some real ones growing in the garden." "Come along", said Bernard. "I'll show you the ferns." They stood up and, taking Bernard's hand, Michael accompanied him into the garden, leaving Lorna, Paul and Mary, and Mrs Barnes who had just come in after unloading the cars.

"He likes you a lot", said Paul, as he deposited his and Michael's large bag on the floor of the bedroom that Bernard had arranged for them, Mary following with the two little bags containing shoes and toilet articles. "He generally finds it difficult to talk to people he doesn't know, but with you he seems to have an instant rapport." "He's marvellous and so handsome, and I think he's a little bit magic! And, by the way", she winked at Paul, "he is very lucky to have such a good-looking friend as you!" Paul smiled, "Thanks Mary! I think you're great! Thanks for helping Michael." "I haven't really done anything", she replied, "but I'm sure we're going to be great friends". With that, she put the bags on the table at the end of the bed and silently withdrew.

Paul unpacked the bags and put their clothes in the wardrobe and chest-of-drawers. This generous room was in the old part of the house, and had blue wallpaper with a gold and white stripe. Unlike the rooms downstairs, it was functional and reasonably coordinated. The two large windows reached the floor, so that when the bottom half slid up, by ducking one's head it was possible to step out onto the upstairs veranda surrounding the house on all sides.

Paul had the strange feeling that although he had unpacked everything, something was missing: of course, it was Toby! He turned and made his way along the corridor lined with furniture, its walls covered with paintings, though here they seemed mostly to be watercolours, from very tiny ones to enormous ones in every kind of gilt frame. As he started descending the very grand staircase, halfway he encountered Lorna on her way up. "I think you forgot this", she said, "I saw it on the back seat of your car", and she handed Toby to him.

Having complete confidence in Lorna, Paul said, "Michael doesn't see him as a toy, he sees him as some kind of extension of his friends, so that for him, Toby represents Bernard, you and me". She smiled, "I think we all need a Toby!" Paul said, "I'll just put him on the bed and join you downstairs!"

Michael returned with Bernard, chatting away as though he had lived at Killarney all his life. Bernard had shown him the gardens, which were basically hedges and great thickets of azalea and rhododendron: the soil at Morton was very acid and they loved it!

Dinner was served. It was quite a walk from the kitchens, down a corridor, across the entrance hall and into the dining room. At one stage, they had thought of changing round the yellow drawing room and the dining room, but, as Mary pointed out, you had to cross the entrance hall to either room, so it really made no difference at all.

Mary cut up the meat for Michael into small pieces so that he would have no trouble with it, and she was pleased to see that he ate everything. About an hour after dinner, Paul said he thought they would have an early night and be ready for whatever adventures lay in store for them tomorrow.

The bathroom was across the landing, so Paul said that, as they were guests, he and Michael should use dressing gowns to go back and forth. "Oh!" said Michael, as though he couldn't understand why he had to put on clothes to go to the bathroom, unnecessary at Darling Square, where the bathroom was en suite.

As he lay in bed with Michael's head on his chest and his arm round his shoulder, a great calm, or was it contentment – he wasn't sure which – swept over Paul. He moved his arm and ran his fingers through what was now becoming a beautiful mane of thick black hair. It had grown so quickly, he thought, not even a month since he first saw Michael, a month during which his whole life had changed completely. Michael moved his head onto the pillow and, before going to sleep, he said, "Paul, when we say goodnight, why don't we say goodnight to Toby? We say goodnight to everyone else." "OK", said Paul, and so, on their first night at Killarney, a ritual began that continued every night they slept together: "Paul, goodnight!" to which the reply came, "Goodnight Michael!" and then the two of them in unison would say, "Goodnight Toby!" after which they drifted off to sleep.

Next day, Bernard was busy in the morning going over the administration with Mary and Mrs Barnes, so Lorna suggested that, as it was early, they might go to Brunswick and she would show them around. Brunswick was a large, rambling country town with almost all the major shops on one long street. Most of the old verandas had been demolished in the 'sixties and replaced with new cantilever ones, making the whole street look sad and tired and characterless. Two shops, however, had bearded the local council and replaced their original verandas with thin cast-iron columns and heavy use of cast-iron lacework. The two stores were "Mulberry Menswear" and, two doors down, "Nigel Storey Interiors", Anne's favourite decorator, who had done the Melbourne apartment for her and Edgar. They looked in the shop windows and moved on to a large supermarket, where Lorna said she would get a couple of things for Mary if they didn't mind. "Not at all", said Paul. This was Michael's first time in a supermarket, and he thought it was very like the National Art Gallery Paul had taken him to a day before his initial interview with Bernard. They had gone to the gallery on St Kilda Road. Michael had looked at everything, but passing from one painting to another automatically cancelled the one he had seen previously, so that of the many paintings he remembered practically nothing, except the one with the magic floor. The painting concerned was Tiepolo's extremely large canvas called the "Banquet of Cleopatra". Michael was impressed, not because of the subject, but because of its size, since he had no idea that paintings could be so large. Paul was looking at another canvas, and a small woman in her mid-fifties, wearing a grey skirt and white blouse and carrying a blue cardigan through the straps of a large soft bag, said to Michael, "Can you see the magic floor?" Michael looked at her and frowned and said nothing: His frown, his silence and the slight tilt of his head instantly identified him to the woman. "Watch me!" she said and knelt down on the floor about five yards away from the picture, on the right side. "Come on, you do it!" she said, and Michael obeyed. "Look at the pattern on the floor of the room!" He proceeded to do so, and then they repeated the process at the other end of the painting. "Now, if we walk from side to side, the floor moves with us. Tiepolo designed an interesting perspective with this patterned marble floor and when you stand at any point in front of the painting, it gives you the illusion that the floor goes directly away from you. You seem to be at the centre even when you are at the side!" Paul suddenly realised that Michael was not with him and, in a panic, swung round and saw the woman and Michael standing hand in hand in front of the Tiepolo. "Michael! Are you all right?" Paul asked anxiously. "Paul, the floor moves with me!" The woman explained the optical illusion to Paul, then with tears forming in her very tired eyes, she said to him very quickly, "Look after him! He's very, very special! My late son was very similar. He will need all the love you can possibly give him." With that, she picked up her bag with the cardigan threaded through the long handles, said goodbye and drifted off into the crowd at the other end of the long room.

With a supermarket trolley, Lorna and Paul moved along the aisles, talking slowly. In a short time, Lorna had formed a very strong bond with Paul and greatly enjoyed his witty remarks. Michael thought supermarkets were much nicer than art galleries, because you could touch everything and put goods in your trolley and take them away. The concept of paying never crossed Michael's mind. He was fascinated by anything brightly coloured: tins, jars, packets, goods on the shelves and goods behind refrigerator doors. Oh, it was very exciting, but there were so many things to see. He got separated from Lorna and Paul and, wandering down an aisle, became confused because they all looked the same: different things on the shelves, but they seemed identical.

As he passed a refrigerated unit with small bottles of orange juice and other strange-coloured drinks, he saw a small woman move forward, seize the edge of the unit and then slip backwards and fall to the floor. Whether it was instinct, or it jolted his memory of the Institution and children suffering from epileptic fits, he immediately went and knelt down, placing her head in his lap. She signed to him, her voice having almost disappeared, to open her bag, which he did, and she pointed to a small brown bottle with a red cap, which he pulled out, unscrewing it. He tipped three tablets into her open hand and reached behind himself to take a small plastic bottle of orange juice. He had trouble taking the lid off, but having accomplished it, he drank part of the contents before lifting her head. She put one of the pills in her mouth and let the other two fall to the floor. Michael then put the half-empty bottle to her lips and she drank without spilling any, since half-empty it was much easier to drink from. "You must stay for a minute", he said and she nodded her head. "Someone's passed out near the drinks fridge" squawked an overweight young assistant very loudly.

Lorna and Paul were very close to the drinks section and they looked at each other at once. "Michael!" they both exclaimed. They abandoned their trolley and rushed to the end of the aisle. It was Lorna who gave the first cry, "Anne! Anne! Are you all right? I'll call Colin Campbell at once!" "No, it's all right now. I forgot to take one of these damned pills this morning. This beautiful angel actually saved my life!" "Michael! Oh, Michael!" said Paul, and with Lorna and Michael, he helped Anne to her feet. Paul retrieved her handbag and Anne, somewhat confused, looked at Lorna. "These aren't the boys, are they?" she said. "Oh, how splendid!" "Yes, these are the boys!" Lorna replied. "Oh Michael, you are my hero!" Anne said. Michael didn't understand the word 'hero', but when she hugged him, he grasped the message. "You are a very nice lady", he replied. "I must have a dinner party to say thank you. What about Thursday? About seven-thirty, black tie? I think this calls for a celebration!" Being Monday, there was, thought Paul, time to see what he could do about a black tie for Michael. "Do call tomorrow, Anne, and have a drink with us. Why don't you come for lunch? That would be much better! We shall see you if you're feeling well enough. Give me a call tomorrow morning, and promise me you'll call Colin Campbell the minute you get home. Would you like us to take you home?" she asked. "For heaven's sake, Lorna! I'm perfectly fine now. I just forgot to take that blood pressure pill! Don't worry, I'll give Colin a call! I'm so glad we all met, and I think you're both splendid! Tomorrow for lunch then!" With that, Anne left the supermarket empty-handed and returned to Bellevue.

"Darling", said Anne to Dr Colin Campbell, "I've just met Bernard and Lorna's houseguests. Oh Colin! Two more beautiful creatures you have never seen! Darling, you must meet them! In fact, I'm having a black-tie dinner on Thursday and you absolutely must be there. You'll adore the boys!" "What's the party in aid of?" asked Colin. "Oh!" came the reply, "I passed out in the supermarket and it was Michael, that delicious angel, who saved my life!" " You must be more careful about taking those pills", he said. "There won't always be a Michael around!" "You're wrong, darling! I have this wonderful feeling that Michael and Paul are going to be around for a long, long time!" "Let's hope so!" Colin said goodbye and promised he would be at Bellevue at seven-thirty sharp.

He was tall, Dr Colin Campbell, and very handsome, and he traded on it. Always dressed in the most elegant clothes, the finest shoes – which, by the way, came from Mulberry's – he was the portrait of a successful doctor, married, with no children, and free to move as he wished. But it had not always been so. He came from a lower-middle-class family and was raised in Camberwell. He attended a high-class college in Hawthorn, through the generosity of an aunt who paid all school fees. At a very young age, he became aware that money was all-important, because it guaranteed a certain social stability. He was an all-round athlete, and excellent at all his subjects, but keeping up with his peer group became a difficult game, since his limited funds meant that he had to cut corners. His good looks saved him many a time. When his schooling was complete, he went to Melbourne University to study medicine, which he saw as an avenue to social success. In his second year at university, however, his benevolent aunt died, leaving him nothing since she considered that a good education was quite sufficient. His parents were in no position to foot his university expenses, since he was not an only child (he had three sisters), so for the first time in his life, he had to take up manual work to finance his university studies. He hated his work as a waiter, and felt it demeaning and vulgar, the customers often either ignoring him or treating him like a servant. Even in this field, however, his good looks were a trump card and many a customer was more than generous with the tip, particularly the men.

As soon as he graduated, he looked around for a practice, not an easy thing to do. One evening, at a party with some old school friends, he met Beth Neil. Someone said to him, "She's loaded. Her father owns five clinics in the city and a very large one in the country." So the debonair Dr Colin Campbell began courting Miss Beth Neil. She was quite short, about five foot two, streaky blond hair cut short, and slightly prominent green eyes bulging from between heavily mascara-ed lashes, and a smallish mouth that was generally pulled tight. Even when Colin met Beth, she was carrying a little too much weight, so that when seen together – Colin so tall and Beth so short, they cut a rather comical figure. In due course, the marriage took place. Beth's father paid for everything, in the most luxurious manner. An only child, Beth was spoilt and could be very petulant, but her overriding characteristic was her exceptional laziness. Since his father-in-law was no fool (a good looking young doctor meaning more patients), by agreement Colin and Beth moved to Brunswick after the wedding, with Colin as administrator of the large country clinic. He liked it there, his moneyless past forgotten, and, as his father-in-law had predicted, he was a great success, a doctor in great demand.

The Campbells lived in a large new house, in what was considered to be the smartest part of Brunswick, and to the public eye, everything seemed fine. This was not quite true, however, since Colin's lack-lustre performance as a macho husband rapidly convinced Beth that sex was not all it was cracked up to be, and led to her insisting on a separate bedroom. Colin heaved a genuine sigh of relief, while Beth was now committed to two things: soap operas and eating, and so soon began to put on weight. Colin was completely disinterested and they rarely ate together, since –being in hot demand socially – Brunswick hostesses were not at all dismayed at his habitual reply over the phone, "No, just me".

It was Anne, however, who interested him most, and before long they were always about together, especially after Edgar's death. Colin was not sexually interested in Anne and, on her side, she only demanded social companionship, an arrangement that suited them both. Anne never threw a dinner party without Colin's presence, a fact that gave rise to certain gossip, which worried neither of them, for different reasons. Anne had got to know Colin very well and knew that he did not like talking about his background, making the subject taboo. By watching him carefully over a period of time, she knew why she found him interesting. Anne was an expert on one type of male only, the homosexual, and she saw through Colin almost from the start. He never spoke about it if the subject came up and, at Anne's table, there was always a coterie of single men, into which Colin fitted perfectly. He was constantly flattered and, being conceited, everything went well as a rule. What he did in his very private life, he never said, and Anne was frankly not interested. Her escort was tall, elegant and smart. What else could a wealthy woman need?

When Lorna, Paul and Michael returned to Killarney after the supermarket drama, Lorna sent Mary to find the dinner jackets in one of the many bedrooms. There were four, and Mary left them out in the boys' bedroom to try on. That evening, before they went to bed, Michael started trying them on to see which would fit best. Although the jackets were a problem, the trousers were impossibly short. "Don't worry, darling", said Paul. "We'll sort it out in the morning." Michael got into bed in the safe knowledge that Paul would indeed sort it out in the morning. Paul was not so sure.

Next morning was hot, with no breeze at all. The boys woke and dressed and went down for breakfast, where they passed on their news of no luck in the dinner jacket department.

"Listen", said Lorna, "it's so hot, it seems ridiculous for us to dress up just for dinner in the country. I'll speak to Anne at lunch today". When Anne arrived in her black Mercedes sports car, looking cool and sophisticated in pale blue silk, one of the first things Lorna spoke to her about with Paul was the problem of Michael's dinner jacket, saying that she was not prepared to embarrass Michael as the odd man out.

"Lorna, darling! It's not a problem: Michael and I will fix it directly after lunch", and Anne changed the subject. "Do you know", she said, linking arms with Lorna and Paul, "it's years since I was last at Killarney?" and, looking about as they strolled through the gardens, she continued, "It looks as though Bernard will have to spend some money here". She laughed. "If only", was Lorna's reply. "He's refused to let me spend a penny on the place. Mary's bringing some champagne. I thought we would have a drink on the veranda, it's cooler there." "Where's Bernard?" asked Anne. "He's with Michael. He'll be here in a minute. They will have heard your car."

"Michael was with Bernard, sitting in the yellow drawing room. "I suppose we'd better join them", said Bernard. He noticed that Michael had not moved his head, but was staring at a large photo in amongst the paintings. "Cooty, who is the lady?" The photo was of Bernard and his first wife, Marjory. "She was my wife", said Bernard slowly, and Michael asked, "Where is she?" "She's dead", came the reply. "You must take her away if she is dead. She's no longer here. Paul had pictures of a man that was dead. He took them all away and I felt better. Why isn't there a picture of you and Lorna, Cooty? That would be very nice. Paul can do it for you." He took Bernard's hand and they went out onto the veranda. During the drinks and general gossip, Mary came up and said that lunch was served. Michael went in arm-in-arm with Lorna and Anne. Bernard signalled to Paul to wait, and said, "Paul, please tell me the story of the photos at your house in East Melbourne". So Paul related the story, saying that he had not thought about the photos until Michael had said something. Bernard looked at him and said, "You know Lorna and I are not married. Perhaps we shall be, one day. The photo in the yellow drawing room is of my first wife. Will you do me the favour of removing it and see whether we can repeat here what happened at Darling Square?" "What shall I do with the photograph?" Bernard, who had just opened the door to go in, replied, "Exactly what you did with the one's in your house", and they both went in to lunch.

Right after lunch, Paul collected his digital camera and took about twenty photos of them all. Then Anne said, "Well, it's so hot I shall expect you all at Bellevue in two hours for a swim". "I haven't brought a swimsuit", said Paul. "Darling", said Anne, "I have hundreds at home!" She looked at Michael, "Are you ready for a surprise?" "Oh yes!" said Michael. "Good! You come with me and the others will join us at my house for a swim later on. Is that all right?" "Anne, that's a good idea", he said. She noticed that when he spoke to any of them, he generally prefaced what he was going to say with their first name, as if to be sure they were listening, or perhaps he thought that by so doing he made the person he was speaking to exclusively his own: someone he loved and felt safe with. Anne thought it must be definitely the latter.

So, with that, Anne and Michael hopped into her smart car and drove off down the drive, Michael having first kissed everyone and then returning to kiss Paul again. This was one of the few times during that month or so that Michael had left Paul and gone with somebody else. "Don't worry, darling", Lorna said to Paul, "this is all part of his education, and with Anne he is in the best of hands!"

"Fasten your safety-belt, Michael", said Anne, as she drove through the huge entrance gates and headed in the direction of Brunswick, to a certain store that was indirectly to affect Michael's life. The store was called Mulberry's.

CHAPTER THREE

Mulberry's

CHAPTER 3

Mulberry's

The car pulled up directly in front of Ernest Mulberry's shop with its restored Victorian veranda. Outside it was painted a very dark green, and the front window displayed the name "Mulberry's" in very florid lettering in two tones of gold. The store had belonged to Ernest's father and, on his death, Ernest had taken over the establishment and had immediately started out to super-smarten it up. Ernest was fifty, short and fairly plump, with a ruddy complexion. He ruled his kingdom from a sort of low pulpit in the centre of the shop, accessed by two steps, where he sat with computer and cash register to hand. Always immaculately dressed, his grey coiffure without a hair out of place, he was slightly old-world, with a very fussy manner, especially when kow-towing to someone he was impressed by. He could also be quite off-hand, if he thought that a customer was not really up to his standard. The store was very large, its chic decoration executed by Ernest's best friend, Nigel Storey, who owned the smart interior design shop two doors down, also with a restored Victorian cast-iron veranda. When they were together, Neville – one of the three employees at Mulberry's and the one with by far the sharpest wit, or, as the other two employees, Samuel and Sean, pointed out, the bitchiest tongue, since Ernest was short and fat and Nigel very tall and thin – had described them as Pork & Stork. Since Ernest only stocked what he considered to be the finest quality in everything he sold, he was quite a landmark in this large country town.

Anne linked arms with Michael as they walked towards the double glass doors with gleaming brass fittings, but he removed her arm and held her hand. She smiled at him. They must have seen her approaching, for the door swung open with Samuel standing behind it. Ernest immediately sprang down from his pulpit and rushed nimbly forward. Samuel's eye followed every movement of the beautiful boy in dark blue trousers and a pristine white shirt. His blue eyes, thick, short hair and olive skin were enough to throw Samuel into a state of happy reverie. Samuel was known to the staff as Tarzan and, when he crossed Neville, he was known as Jane. He had, of course, done a lot of bodybuilding and had a mop of soft blond hair. Neville had picked him up many years ago on the beat in Brunswick – the only one that existed – and was greatly disappointed that the well-developed muscles were not matched by development in another part of his anatomy, always saying sarcastically that what Samuel had between his legs was roughly the same size as what he had between his ears. Still, they remained friends and the first vacancy at Mulberry's was automatically filled by Samuel, who indirectly brought many new customers to the store. Although they came on the pretext of looking for new clothes, most were feasting their eyes on Samuel.

Any gossip in Brunswick was first heard at Mulberry's: the staff lived for gossip and in this town they found plenty. Many a guest at a Brunswick dinner party dined out on something picked up at Mulberry's and duly passed it on. The gossip was occasionally malicious and dangerous, in which case Neville was generally behind it, making him a person to be very wary of.

Anne had not set foot in Mulberry's since well before Edgar's death and, had she asked to describe the interior, she would have had difficulty in doing so. However, the moment she stepped inside with Michael and looked about, everything was familiar, the dark polished wooden counters and matching shelving with very imposing pediments, the two tubular display pedestals in the centre, with elegant shirts in boxes, copious quantities of tissue paper, ties in graded colours spread out like large fans, the smallest detail engineered to attract the discerning eye.

The green damask wallpaper with English hunting prints in pairs, and the two enormous brass chandeliers added a certain grandeur that might be deemed unnecessary in a country town.

"Mrs Rochester, how positively charming to see you again!" oozed Ernest. "It has been far too long. How well you look! As elegant as ever! And your charming young friend! How delightful!" "Oh, thank you so much", replied Anne. "It's charming to see all of you again." They had the store's full attention, being the only customers. Needless to say, the three shop assistants came up to say hello to Anne and Michael, but basically to check Michael out.

"Mr Mulberry", Anne started to say. "Oh, Mrs Rochester, do call me Ernest! I would consider it an honour!" "Here we go!" said Neville to the others, at which Ernest swung round and said, "Be quiet, you faded parrots!" – his usual method of silencing the staff. "Oh, Ernest", said Anne, "I'm not sure if I still have an account with you." "But how could you doubt it? Now you have wounded me!" he cried. "Mulberry's without your account would simply not exist!" "Bette Davis, eat your heart out!" was Neville's quiet comment to Sean, the most lack-lustre of the staff. Ernest's faded parrot description suited Sean very well.

"I have a small problem", said Anne. "I need to find a dinner jacket, shirt, tie, shoes, everything, for Michael." "Oh, we have something, I'm sure!" came the reply. "Samuel! Bring me that wool and silk dinner jacket from the storeroom! I'm sure it's the young gentleman's size." Samuel disappeared and in the meantime Ernest took all Michael's measurements: sleeve length, shirt size, shoe size, waist, height, and so on, noting it down in an exercise book under Michael's name. Samuel returned with the jacket. He pushed in front of Ernest and said to Michael in a very quiet voice, "This way!" Without hesitating, Michael followed him. About five minutes later, while Ernest was chatting on with Anne about how delightful it was that she was spending so much more time at Morton and that they must see much more of her, Samuel came out of the dressing cubicle. He pulled aside the green velvet curtain, its big brass rings making a clanking sound, his eyes particularly wide open. Michael followed.

Anne had met Michael only the day before and had thought him beautiful, but dressed in a dinner jacket, shirt with fly collar and black tie, he was stunning, and if *she* thought that, Mulberry's staff thought he was the most handsome thing they had ever set their eyes on. Even Neville whispered to Sean, "He's just fabulous!" It was rare for Neville to pass a compliment, let alone praise!

"Let's see!" said Ernest. "The jacket is perfect, yes, perfect. The trousers are too large. We'll take them in at the waist and shorten the legs." Anne turned the cuff of the shirt to see if it took cuff-links and noted that it had double cuffs. Michael seemed completely unaware of the stir he was creating. He felt the front of the shirt and said, looking at Ernest, "Is it Dior?" Anne gasped. How on earth did Michael know about Dior, or even the name? But that was Michael. At certain times, incidental pieces of information he had heard and stored come to the surface without his being aware of the effect these expressions had on people. Ernest blushed a little and said that although it wasn't Dior it was a very good quality shirt and he was sure that Michael would like it. "Yes", Michael repeated, "it's a very nice shirt".

It was at that point that Mulberry's staff, including Ernest, saw Michael in a certain way that made him their ideal man and customer. Anne said to Neville, who had moved over to her, "Do you have any swimsuits? I mean nice ones, not those things that look like shorts". "Certainly! If you would come this way…". She moved over as he lifted a box down from a shelf and placed it on the centre table. Removing the lid, he said, "Is this what you are looking for, Mrs Rochester?" "Yes, I think so. Michael, come here!" Michael came up, with pins all through the back of the trousers and around the bottom hem. "Which one do you like?" She pulled out of the box a blue pair and a red pair of very small racing-type bathers. He looked at them and said he thought the red. "Are they his size?" asked Anne. "He had better try them on, since there are only these two in the smaller size, and three pairs slightly larger." Michael went back to the dressing room with Samuel to remove his dinner jacket trousers and try on the swimsuit. "Lucky bitch!" was Neville's comment to Sean, as Samuel pulled the dressing room curtains closed.

At this very moment, into Mulberry's came Dr Colin Campbell, who was slightly peeved to note that no one was paying him the usual attention. "Hello, Colin", said Anne. "We are just getting a few things for Thursday evening." "Good afternoon, Dr Campbell!" said Ernest, smiling, but – like the others – looking toward the dressing room. Michael finally came out. If comments like "wonderful!" and "elegant!" had greeted his entrance in his new dinner jacket, the bathing costume produced a very different reaction. There was dead silence. The staff were all now walking two feet in the air, and Samuel, who ignored Colin altogether, was now completely besotted by Michael. During the last month Michael's figure had filled out a little, and the bathing costume clung to every feature, something that Mulberry's customers were destined to hear for months to come. Totally unaware of the effect he produced, Michael, clad only in this tiny swimsuit came up and asked Anne whether they could take one of the larger ones for Paul. "Certainly, Michael. What colour do you think he would like?" Anne suddenly realised her voice was higher than usual, and she cleared her throat. "I like the blue one, with the red one on the side." "Very well!" Her voice returned to normal. "Ernest, may we take these?" "Certainly, certainly!" said Ernest, looking happily confused. "Michael, do go and change!" said Anne. "We must hurry to meet Paul and Lorna! Ernest, do you think you could have the dinner jacket and the rest delivered to Killarney on Thursday morning?" "Of course, absolutely!" he said. "Oh!" said Anne, "we have forgotten the shoes! I would like a nice black pair, with a very fine punched design." "We have exactly what you want! Oh, what taste you have, Mrs Rochester! These are Italian: let's hope we have Michael's size, if I may call him Michael. Sean! This is your department!"

Although while this was happening, the staff were feasting their eyes on Michael, for once in his life Dr Colin Campbell was wholly speechless. It was like a dream. It was as if a male porn model had stepped from the pages of a magazine, three-dimensional in every detail. Colin noted every single detail: the cobalt blue eyes, the black mane of hair starting to grow, the strong jaw and rather full, sensual lips. He missed nothing. Moving his eyes down the elegant slim torso, he noted something even more interesting, then on down to the strong legs with their fine black hair. As Anne had said, he was indeed an angel, but one you could touch, or could you? Aware of the affect Michael had had on everyone, Anne rapidly noted his impact on Colin. She had never seen Colin in such a situation. At parties, he always stayed out of harm's way with women, who adored our Dr Campbell. Although he flirted openly with them, he always went home alone to his wife. But this was a different Colin! The sensual energy Michael emitted shocked Colin through and through. He had never seen anything like this, and seeing practically all of him at once was enormously disturbing to him. Michael's magnetism was working very well!

Back from the dressing room, Sean sat Michael in a green velvet chair to fit his black shoes. Anne said to Michael, "Michael, this is Colin Campbell. He will be at dinner on Thursday". Michael looked at him just as one glimpses at a magazine and then firmly puts it down. He nodded, but didn't say a word. His attitude was quite clear: Colin had just been dismissed! To Colin's conceit, this was very like a rapier blow to the heart. He had never been ignored or rejected, and had always been treated as the bright light on the horizon. But today! The whole staff – and even Anne – were taking very little notice of him and he didn't like it at all.

"Neville", said Anne. "Do be a darling and take all the tags off the bathers for me!" "Certainly! A pleasure!" beamed Neville. Even Ernest looked up: never had Neville been this cooperative. What a beautiful boy! thought Ernest, I hope he stays at Killarney for some time! "May we help you, Doctor?" said Samuel. "Yes. I'm here to collect a pair of trousers that were being shortened." "Oh", said Samuel, not the slightest bit interested, annoying Colin even more. Samuel had always paid him great attention and he liked Samuel… but now, Samuel was in love (not that Colin realised it at once, but he had understood that the dynamics of entering Mulberry's had now changed for ever. "Oh, Ernest! What a lovely shirt! It's exactly the same blue as Michael's eyes!" Anne cooed. "Do you have it in his size?" "Just a moment! Sean! Have we got this in Michael's size?" "Yes, Mr Mulberry, I believe we do!" "Oh, how nice!" said Anne. "Do put it in with the other things for Killarney! You will have everything ready, won't you?" "Absolutely! Samuel will take the trousers up to Mrs Clancy at once. They will be given preferential treatment and be on their way to Killarney tomorrow! On Mulberry's behalf, I should like to offer a little gift, a pair of black silk stockings to complete the splendid outfit!" "Ernest, how kind of you! Michael and I really appreciate it!"

Beaming, Ernest checked that the bathing costumes had been parcelled properly and handed them in a Mulberry's bag to Michael. "We do so hope to see you again soon!" he said, shaking Michael's hand. The staff jostled one another for the same honour, even Neville, who said, ""It's been a real pleasure!" to which Michael returned his usual "Thank you!" making his way toward the door with his bag.

Anne said, "Thank you so much, boys! You were extremely attentive", giving them a knowing smile. To Ernest, she said, "If I telephone you for something for Michael, you now have all his measurements". "Oh yes, indeed!" chorused the three in unison. Ernest shot them a dagger-like look and said, "Be quiet, you faded parrots!" With that, Anne said goodbye to Colin, who was totally ignored by Michael, and they left hand in hand.

The moment the door closed behind them, the staff were unstoppable, even Neville. "Oh, did you see those eyes? Everything?" Colin, who was still in the shop was now annoyed. He had been snubbed by that beautiful boy and now all the staff could do was talk about how splendid he was. He said sarcastically, "I don't suppose my trousers are ready?" "Oh, Doctor!" said Ernest, as though he had completely forgotten about him. "Samuel is taking Michael's trousers to Mrs Clancy, and he will check for you. Remember, Samuel, Michael's trousers must be top priority! Perhaps if you call by tomorrow, Doctor, or perhaps you might prefer to wait for Samuel. He's only going across the street." "I'll call back tomorrow", said Colin haughtily, and left the store. Samuel picked up Michael's trousers caressingly. "Oh, he was wearing these!" he said. "Move it, Sam, or they won't be finished in time for the ball!" "Ha! Ha!" was Samuel's sarcastic reply.

Michael sat easily next to Anne and fastened his safety-belt. "Do you like Mulberry's?" she asked. "Oh yes!" he said. "They are very nice people!" Not all of them, she thought, but they had been super-attentive and she knew she could take him there anytime and he would get top treatment, especially – she noted – from Samuel.

"We have to make one more stop and then home. Goodness! Look at the time! I hadn't realised we were at Mulberry's for so long!" She turned the car into the main road, drove along for two blocks and parked in the central section of the broad street. They got out. It was now very hot and sticky. "We shan't be a minute, come on!" and hand-in-hand they walked into a greengrocer's, run by a large woman with grey hair and a wide smile, wearing the most enormous white apron Michael had ever seen. "Michael, this is Mrs Maisy O'Brien." Michael's sixth sense - or that part of his brain that accepted, rejected, or ignored – accepted Maisy O'Brien without a problem. Like Mulberry's – though dealing in different goods -, she prided herself on quality, and although she was a little more expensive, most Brunswick matrons patronised her shop.

"Mrs Rochester! I haven't seen you for a while. And who is this nice young man?" Michael understood her comment: it was like Mulberry's. They never stopped using the word 'nice', a word he knew and used all the time. He thought Mrs O'Brien was nice. "I'm afraid we're in a hurry", said Anne. "I'm sorry, but Michael is going to meet my horses today, so I thought perhaps a few apples and a few carrots". "No sooner said than done!" She picked up a small red hessian bag and put into in four apples and four carrots. "There we are. What's your name?" she asked Michael, looking at him. "Michael", he replied. "Mine is Maisy. Every time your bag is empty you bring it back to me and I'll fill it up for you. No, no", she said to Anne. "I'll put it on the account." (Sometime later, looking at the accounts with the housekeeper, Anne was aware that she had never charged Michael at all for the apples and carrots collected every week.) Mrs O'Brien said, "Goodbye, Michael" and smiled. He walked over to this large, happy woman with big brown eyes and kissed her saying, "I will see you very soon! You are a very nice lady". With that, they left the shop, leaving behind them a pair of big brown eyes filled with tears, wiped away immediately on that large white apron. "An angel", she thought. "Heaven must be full of them, but I've seen one before getting there!"

So it was that, one afternoon, at Mulberry's and Maisy O'Brien's, conversation turned on a single person: a blue-eyed, dark-haired young man, who in that short space of time had, for different reasons, made himself indispensable to the store-owners. Owing to the public relations they did for him, most of a certain group of Brunswick residents were extremely curious to see for themselves the youth staying at Killarney.

Paul had also been to Brunswick that afternoon, but had purposely not encountered Michael or Anne. He and Bernard selected the photos he had taken and went to have them enlarged and printed. He returned at once to Killarney while Bernard took a nap and Lorna had gone to Mary's studio to look at her latest work. Paul took down the frame and changed the big photo of Bernard and Marjory for an excellent informal one he had taken of Bernard and Lorna. "Not bad! Not bad at all!" he thought. "I captured them rather well!" He also changed four other frames, just by the doorway, as Bernard had instructed, putting photos of them together with Anne. He stood back and looked at his completed work. "Not bad!" he thought. "What a family!"

He went to the kitchen – which was Mary's domain – to get a box of matches, and returned to the yellow room. In the grate of the marble fireplace, he ignited the large photo, which exuded a strange smell as it burnt, a smell of the past. He returned the matches just as Mary and Lorna entered the kitchen.

"Are you looking for something?" asked Mary. "No thanks. I just borrowed your matches for a moment." "Keep them if you need them", she said. "No, it's all done, thanks! Lorna, I think we should be moving or Anne and Michael will think we have forgotten them. Shall I call Bernard?" "No, let him sleep, it's so hot today. He can come over later if he wishes, or else we'll see him at dinner this evening. Come on, let's go!"

The two houses were very close together. A triangular piece of land separated the properties at the front, but they had six yards of common boundary, at the back of the Killarney grounds.

As they drove into Bellevue, Michael saw them and, rushing over, kissed Paul and then Lorna. "I've seen a horse", he said. "Two horses. They're very fine!" He had started using the adjective 'fine' after hearing Anne use it quite often. "Paul, they're very big and they like Maisy's apples and carrots. Anne says I can feed them when I want to. Isn't it nice? We have nice new bathers: mine is red and yours is blue, with a red bit on the side. Oh, come and put them on! You'll look beautiful, Paul! Come on! Anne has a little house where you can take your clothes off." He was very excited and held Paul very tight. "I have a secret, but it's a surprise for Thursday evening."

At the back of the large, weatherboard house that was Bellevue was a pergola with brick columns supporting beams over which white roses had been trained on the right and left of the swimming pool. On the farther side from the house were two small dressing pavilions, to which the boys repaired to change while Lorna and Anne sat down on the side nearer the house, in the shade. There was a large glass-topped table and chairs with green cushions, plus the ever-present bottle of champagne and some orange juice for Michael. "Come on, in we go!" said Paul. "But Paul, I don't know how to do it!" said Michael. "I'll help you", Paul answered and taking him in his arms, slowly let him down into the water.

"One is more beautiful than the other", said Lorna. "Yes!" sighed Anne and started to tell her about their adventure with the swimsuit at Mulberry's. Lorna laughed until the tears ran down her cheeks. "Oh!" she said, "I don't believe it! Everyone in Brunswick will know all Michael's statistics within twenty-four hours. I'll take a bet that the information was circulated in one hour, knowing the boys at Mulberry's. Anne, what about this dinner jacket for Michael?" "It's all organised, darling, don't worry! I've seen to everything". And they watched the two boys playing in the water, laughing and kissing and holding each other. "Aren't they wonderful?" said Lorna. "Bernard's crazy for both of them. They seem to have opened up a part of Bernard that has always been locked away. I don't know what will happen when it's time to leave. I should really like to stay at Killarney for a while. I'm tired of the rush and bustle of the city. What's it all for? I don't really know anymore. These few days here have been wonderful, and Bernard is so relaxed. In this very short time, the boys have become a sort of family, and I can't imagine Bernard without them." "Or you!" said Anne, not looking at her. "I adore them! I've never wanted a family, it's not for me, but they're grown up and so it's a very different kind of family, and one I'm very comfortable with." "It will all work out very well, I'm sure", said Anne. "Between the two of us, we shall just have to arrange it so that the boys stay. I know we can do it!" "I hope so, Anne. I really hope so! Drinks, boys!"

Paul pulled Michael dripping out of the pool. "I like this water, Paul. It's nice! And your bathers are very nice too!" and Michael hit him gently on the bottom and laughed. Michael had changed greatly. He had seen so much in such a short time. He loved the country because there were not too many people at Morton. Brunswick was fine, but only for a short while, and Brunswick – for Michael – consisted of only two shops: Mulberry's and Maisy O'Brien's, and he could cope with that. Now he was talking much, much more and laughing too, which he had never done before. When he laughed, his whole face lit up, his large blue eyes closed a little and his soft lips opened. He had a surprisingly deep laugh, but then, as Lorna said, "He's a man, not a child!" thinking afterwards "Thank goodness!"

Paul put on a shirt over his bathers and Michael followed suit. They had a drink, and Anne said, "Oh, do call Bernard! We'll have an informal meal here tonight. I can't be bothered eating alone". "But, Anne, we're here tomorrow for dinner!" "That's different, darling! We have Colin tomorrow evening." "Tonight we'll be just family!" said Michael, and for the first time in her life, Anne felt a large lump rise in her throat and tears starting to well up behind her eyes. She looked at Lorna, and then separately at the boy. "Yes, darling", she said to Michael. "Tonight we shall be just family!"

Next morning saw a certain rush and organisation taking place, with Mary pressing Bernard and Paul's dinner jackets. By now, Lorna was very agitated at Anne's blasé comment that all would be fine for Michael, when, in fact, it might not all be fine for Michael. She went downstairs to get her reading glasses she had left in the yellow drawing room. She had thought about seeing whether a dinner jacket could be hired at Brunswick. There must be a place that does that sort of thing for weddings and so forth. She walked into the yellow room and realised that something was different. As she turned toward the door with her glasses in her hand, she saw the large frame on the opposite wall now contained another woman with Bernard – herself! She sat on the nearest chair and just stared. Then she turned her head toward the door, to see yet again herself, Bernard, Paul, Michael and Anne, all laughing together in four smaller frames. Paul was missing from two and Bernard from two others, but beautiful Michael was present in them all. She was roused by Mary passing to answer the front door. A courier from Brunswick had arrived with three large Mulberry bags. "These", said the young girl delivering them, "are for Michael." She left them with Mary and departed. Mary turned into the cool hall as Lorna came out of the yellow drawing room. "This is all for Michael", said Mary. "He'll be very pleased!"

Paul came down the side corridor from the blue room, a sad room, badly decorated, which sheltered the television and video set-up, surrounded by an old club settee and chairs and a mixture of furniture that had obviously been put there for some reason and had remained a fixed feature of the room.

Hearing the conversation, he laughed. "What's the noise? Are we under attack?" "Paul, this is all for Michael." "What?" he gasped, "But who sent it?" "Where is Michael? Perhaps he can shed some light on this story." Michael duly appeared. "Oh, yes!" he said. "It's my surprise! It's my black jacket!" He opened up the first bag to produce a box containing his beautiful black shoes all wrapped in black tissue paper, and in another packet were his silk socks. Mary, Lorna and Paul were wholly unprepared for Michael's nonchalant attitude as he unpacked his new outfit. The biggest bag contained his wool and silk dinner jacket and trousers, and the other, two shirts and a black tie in a long black box covered with shiny black paper. "Well! You're going to be the smartest young man at the party!" said Mary. "Let me hang the suit at once, so that it doesn't crease." "I think I'd better call Anne", said Lorna, making for the phone. But she stopped and linked an arm through Paul's, guiding him into the yellow drawing room. "Well!" she said, "the photos certainly look jolly, don't they? Whose idea was it?" she asked quietly. "It was actually Michael's and Bernard's", and he told her the story of the photographs at Darling Square. She looked at the photo of herself with Bernard, then – strangely – she automatically looked at the grate and saw the ashes of the old photo. She kissed him and left the room. "Come on, young man! Let's get these bags upstairs!"

At a quarter past seven, they were all dressed and made their way to the yellow room. Lorna looked wonderful in a long black silk frock, cut very simply, and Bernard's string of Broome pearls. Then came Bernard, looking suitably smart, just as Mary opened a bottle of champagne for them and a bottle of orange juice for Michael. Then in came Paul and Michael. Lorna, who was seated, stood up and exclaimed, "You both look beautiful!" Michael's outfit from Mulberry's was splendid, but he said to Bernard, "Cooty! I haven't got any buttons", and held up his sleeves. Paul said, "We're without a pair of cuff-links". "Oh no, we're not!" said Mary. "Just a minute! I know where I can find a pair", and she disappeared. When she returned, rubbing the cuff-links on her apron, she fitted them into the cuffs. "Who tied his tie?" Lorna asked. "Yes, I know", said Paul. "I can do it on myself, but I have trouble doing it on anyone else." Lorna moved over, undid Michael's tie and in a trice had retied a perfect knot. "Years of practice!" she said, looking at Bernard.

Michael took his orange juice and the others their champagne. Lorna looked at the big photo of herself and Bernard, raised her glass and said, "Here's to our family!" She kissed each of the men, saying, "Throw it down, or we'll be late!" Michael said, "Cooty, we look like statues!" Bernard laughed. "I never thought of it like that, but we really do look like statues, don't we?"

Paul pulled up at Anne's front door at exactly seven-thirty, just as Colin's car followed them up the drive. Paul let the three of them out and parked a little further away on the immaculately raked gravel, leaving Colin space to park as well.

Paul got out of his car and encountered Colin. "How do you do? I'm Paul." "Fine thank you, my name's Colin", he replied rather stiffly. Anne was on the veranda to welcome her guests. "Oh, don't you all look smart", she said and led them into an enormous reception room on the left, well-decorated, but a little old-fashioned, although everything was in excellent condition as the result of Edgar's insistence on maintenance, like the veranda. Originally, it only went across the front and halfway down one side, but he had had it extended so that it now surrounded most of the house. Bellevue also had lots of gables with decorative Tudor designs. When Edgar married Anne, the house was as her parents had left it, with pale green walls and a red corrugated iron roof. Edgar had it painted cream with white trim, and a gleaming black front door. Nigel Storey had been called in to do part of the interior, including the large room into which they were shown. An enormous ceiling rose with a wide outer border and a heavy Victorian cornice complemented the vast space and a large Victorian chandelier was suspended from the centre of the rose. The furnishings were smart, a mixture of antique with comfortable modern sofas and armchairs, old paintings – purchased in Italy on their honeymoon - adorned the walls. Four or five magnificent Persian rugs lay on a highly polished jara-wood floor. Paul's first impression of Colin was that he was stuffy and a little too formal, but was very aware, as was the rest of the company, that his eyes rested on one person only.

Paul adored Anne. Her vivacious springy attitudes were marvellous. They both liked the same ancient and modern artists, and chatted happily together. Lorna spoke to Colin, while Michael and Bernard were totally engrossed on something Michael had elected to speak about. He sat on the arm of Bernard's chair, with his arm on Bernard's shoulder. In their dinner jackets, the two of them were at their smartest. Paul wished he had remembered to bring his digital camera: Ernest Mulberry had done a very good job!

After drinks, they were bidden to the dining room, one of the rooms that had remained from the time of Anne's parents: a heavy room, with a slightly Gothic air, in browns and beige. An enormous Victorian sideboard stood at one end and a brown marble fireplace at the other. With Anne at the head of the table and Bernard at the other end, she had Colin on her right and Paul on her left. Michael sat next to Paul and opposite Lorna. Once seated Michael lapsed into silence, and it was Lorna and Bernard who kept the conversation going. Anne suddenly stood up, went to the sideboard and brought back a parcel wrapped in red paper, with a tiny bow on top. She went and stood beside Michael, having circumnavigated the table so as not to pass behind him, and placed the parcel on his plate. He was not sure what he should do and looked at Paul, Lorna and Bernard. "I think we should open it!" said Bernard. Anne returned to her seat, smiling. Paul helped Michael untie the ribbon, so that he could remove the paper and open his gift. "They are very nice buttons", he said. "Anne", said Paul. "This is far too extravagant!" "Not at all!" she replied. "It's not every day that somebody saves your life!"

Colin was not at all happy at the attention Michael was receiving, for what – in his mind – was after all very little. He started to become jealous.

Bernard stood up and took one of the cuff-links from the white velvet box. "They're rubies, aren't they?" "Yes. 1928 Van Cleef & Arpels. They were the first to develop this kind of invisibly mounted stone." Each link had nine square flat-mounted rubies with no metal support showing, while the back was platinum. "I like them. They're red", said Michael. "It's a happy colour!" Like the others at the table, Colin made a mental calculation as Bernard fitted them into Michael's cuffs. Their value was extraordinarily high.

Paul was most embarrassed, As he turned to say something, Anne put her hand on his, a gesture duly noted by Colin. "Darling, I bought these years ago for Edgar, but he didn't like them, simply because he didn't like rubies. Michael loves red, and hopefully likes the cuff-links as well, so that's that! They have been in the safe here for years. After all, they were designed to be worn, not hidden away!" Paul's mouth closed. He realised he couldn't say very much without confusing Michael and insulting their hostess. "Let's drink to our hero!" said Anne. "This time, Michael, you must try some champagne. It's very nice." She was aware she was using Michael's favourite adjective. They lifted their flutes. Michael, unused to drinking from one, spilled a little down his chin, and looked very worried and embarrassed. He put his glass down and Paul took his napkin and blotted his chin, saying, "No harm done!" "How very stupid of me!" said Anne sharply and rang the bell in front of her. A fifty-year-old woman with red dyed hair came in and said, "Yes, madam?" "Robins, get one of the old type of champagne glasses and place it in front of Michael." "At once, madam", and she returned with a beautiful antique bowl-type glass with a hollow stem, decorated in gold with tiny blue enamel beading. The maid filled the new glass and took the other away. "Now try that, darling", purred Anne. Michael had no problem with this glass and smiled, saying how many bubbles there were in it.

Colin was angry. It wasn't merely that Michael, with two or three attempts, could have mastered the simple art of drinking from a flute, it was this whole *production*, especially by Anne, just to make him happy, or feel special. But Michael didn't feel he was special; he simply accepted what the others decided for him and, since he had complete and absolute faith in them, he had no problem at all.

So that was that. Whenever drinks were served in future, on the silver tray they was always a glass of a different shape that Michael knew was for him. "Do you like champagne?" Anne asked him. "Anne, it's very nice. I like the bubbles: they go up your nose a bit." Anne laughed, "No more orange juice!" The evening continued light-heartedly, and soon Michael was enjoying himself, constantly looking at his new cufflinks, which gave Anne supreme satisfaction.

Bernard and Michael were talking with Lorna about Mary's drawings. "Perhaps you can draw as well", she said to Michael. "Hmm, perhaps…", he said, but he wasn't really sure what drawing entailed. Anne chatted on with Paul, every now and again including Colin, as did Lorna, but Paul still found conversation with Colin a little stilted. He noted that whenever he spoke to Anne, Colin's eyes swerved automatically toward Michael.

The night drew to a pleasant close. Anne again praised the boys on their appearance and insisted that they should come the next day at eleven o'clock for a swim and lunch. Colin would have climbed Mount Everest for an invitation, which was not forthcoming, to see Michael in his bathers. It also crossed his mind that Paul would also be a pleasant spectacle.

As they left, Anne said, "Colin, may I speak to you a moment?" The others piled into the car, and this time it was Bernard who drove home to Killarney. "What is it, Anne? Do you need a new prescription for those pills?" Colin asked. "Come in, darling!" he returned with her to the sitting room. "Open a bottle", she said, and pointed at a gilded side table with a fresh bottle of champagne in a wine cooler. "I don't think I should drink much more", he said, but obediently opened it, poured out two glasses and handed her one. He felt this little talk might not be to his liking, and said quickly, "Is it going to be a lecture?" "No darling, just a policy statement. Don't worry, I'll never bring the subject up again." He gulped more than half his glass, crossed the room and filled it to the brim.

"It's Michael", she said, taking a sip of champagne. "He's so different from other young men in every way. I should be most distressed if, being a doctor, you didn't understand that. He's Paul's lover." She stopped for a moment and looked at him. Their eyes met, but he remained silent. "Do you understand me, darling? I'm aware of the attraction you feel for him…" At this point, Colin attempted to speak, but she silenced him with a look. This was the first time in the several years they had known each other that she had broached this rather personal subject. "Darling", she purred. "With me, it's fine, but Michael's off-limits and that's that!"

"There's no problem!" he said. "He doesn't even know I'm alive!" "Be that as it may", she said, "he's totally in love with Paul." "And, it seems, Bernard too!" he replied sarcastically. "Relax, Colin. In actual fact, he does love Bernard and Bernard loves him, but their relationship is different from Michael's with Paul, and I won't tolerate any interference for a moment!"

There was a deathly silence. It was Anne who broke the ice, Colin feeling uncomfortable and stupid that his infatuation for Michael had been so transparent. "I said I would speak on this subject only once, and now I've finished. Darling, what about that ghastly art gallery opening we're invited to on Monday? Must we really go?" Glad of the change of subject, Colin suggested they should drop in for ten minutes and then go on to a place fifteen miles away, where a new restaurant had opened. "Oh darling! What a fabulous idea. You're always so clever!"

On that note, Colin bid her goodnight and left. But it was a very concerned Dr. Campbell who left Morton that evening and returned home to his wife at Brunswick.

CHAPTER FOUR

A Red Garden

CHAPTER 4

A Red Garden

The night after Anne's black-tie dinner party, Mulberry's was abuzz about the cufflinks. It seems that the woman who worked for Anne, Mrs Robins, had told her son the next morning, and his call to Neville's cell-phone was more-or-less broadcast to the world. "Van Cleef & Arpels! Oh, how appropriate for our Angel! And rubies! Quite my favourite stone! They must be worth quite a lot of money, I should think," said Ernest. "I should think no change out of three hundred thousand dollars", replied Neville. "I'm dying to see them!" "We can organise the dying bit for you", said Samuel sarcastically. "Watch it, Jane, or your leopard-skin jocks might just get twisted! Not that there's a great deal to damage…!" "Be quiet, you faded parrots! We have customers. Good morning, Mr Jones, so nice to see you once more!"

And so the week at Killarney passed swiftly. They then stayed on for another four days, and it was on the second but last day that Bernard took matters in hand and, while Michael was with Mary in the kitchen, he sat Lorna and Paul down with a drink. "Well!" he said, in a very official tone. "I shall come right to the point. Lorna," and he looked at her, "you told me you were sick of the city and would like to stay at Killarney. That doesn't mean you wouldn't stay at St Georges Road whenever you want to." "Bernard! Whatever are you getting at?" "Let me finish", Bernard said.

"Paul, you work three days a week. What are you going to do with Michael? Do you plan to leave him alone at Darling Square all day?" "I haven't quite worked that one out", Paul said, "but I guess I'm going to have to employ someone to look after him, probably Mrs Lamb." "I don't think that's very satisfactory", replied Bernard. "Here's my idea. You work Monday to Wednesday, Paul, and I work Tuesday to Thursday. I'm sure Robbie wouldn't mind changing your workdays to the same as mine – Tuesday to Thursday. That would leave us a four-day break together at Killarney. If Lorna's here, and now Anne is here much more often, Michael could stay at Killarney with Lorna. You know he loves the place. We two could commute; it's only one-and-a-half hours away. You could stay with me at St Georges Road. I think it would work out very well. Why don't we give it a try?" "Bernard", said Paul. "Do you realise that you are asking, or shall I say 'offering', to share not only Killarney and St Georges Road with me and Michael, but also your lives. You may find us quite a burden after a while." Lorna said to Bernard, "Do fill our glasses, dear!" With that she turned to Paul, and Bernard dutifully did what she asked. "Paul, for Bernard and me – and I sure I can speak for Bernard – you and Michael have been a breath of fresh air in our rather staid and stuffy lives. We adore Michael and the thought of not having him with us is just unthinkable. As for you, Paul, in this short space of time you have become indispensable to Bernard and me. You're great company and more than that, our dearest friend". At this point, Paul interrupted. "This is very embarrassing", he said. "You have virtually picked up two strangers and your generosity is extreme. I don't know what to say! I foresee only one or two problems. The question of Mr Robinson's shifting my workdays is not a problem. It's something I had already decided on. But Michael has never been separated from me, especially at night. I don't know what he will think. For me, this is the only real hurdle I can see to your plan, Bernard. I agree he would be much happier at Killarney than stuck at Darling Square for my three working days every week, but I would be with him every night. I must also say I would miss him terribly, as well." "Let's speak to Michael", said Bernard and went to the door, where he bumped straight into Michael. "Oh, I was just coming to look for you!" "Cooty, is something not good?" he asked. "No, no, everything's good, but this is what we were talking about."

Paul felt rather unsure about Bernard's generous plan and, frankly, two nights without Michael wouldn't be pleasant. No beautiful young man to slide in beside and hold..."Oh! This was not going to work", he thought.

"Michael, Paul and I have to work, so we will not be able to see you for two nights and three days, but then we will be back with you for four days and five nights, every week." Michael walked over and held Paul's hand, and just looked at Bernard. "We would leave you at home here at Killarney, with Lorna, Mary, Mr Barnes and Anne, and we would come back to you every Thursday night." "Every Thursday night..." Michael repeated. "Or else you can go to Darling Square and wait for Paul, who will come home to you every night." "Cooty, you told me my home was Killarney." "Yes, Michael, it is and always will be." "Oh", he replied. "Then I want to stay here at Killarney. It's very nice here." "Do you understand", said Bernard, "that Paul and I will not be here for three days every week?" "Three days a week...", he kissed Paul on the forehead, "but only two nights". Paul freed his arm and put it around Michael's waist, as he sat on the arm of the club chair. There was a silence, which was broken by Lorna. "Darling, shall we give it a try, and see how you feel? Remember, you have me, Mary, Mr Barnes and Toby to look after you!"

Michael freed himself from Paul, walked over to Lorna and kissed her on the cheek. "We'll give it a try", he said, and looked directly at Bernard. "Cooty, you promise you will be away only three days and two nights! You promise you will then come back to me!" "I promise!" said Bernard, aware that his eyes had begun to well with tears. Michael saw this too, and moved across to Bernard and kissed him. He put his arms round him and repeated, "Three days and two nights and then you come home". Bernard put his glass down, then turned and put his arms round Michael, who said, "Cooty, I love you!" "I love you too, Michael. You're very special to me!"

Michael seemed content with the arrangement, but Paul was not convinced that Michael had fully understood. Seeing Bernard in this emotional state was a new experience for Paul, but for Lorna, it was as if, in all the time she and Bernard had lived together, she had really not known him. Inside, she was very proud of Bernard for openly stating his love for Michael. "Come on, Michael. Let's go and wash before dinner!" said Paul, thinking this would give Bernard a moment to adjust before they went to the dining room.

The four of them took their usual seats at table. Michael's champagne glass was in front of him, since now he had a glass and sometimes two every evening with dinner. The others drank either red or white, depending on the menu.

"Did you tell Paul about your grandmother?" said Lorna. "Oh, you mean the story about the ballroom?" "Yes!" said Lorna. "And the fountain." "One at a time!" said Bernard. "My grandmother had a great passion for auctions. She simply haunted Leonard Joel's salesrooms in the city. She had heard from a friend that a very large carpet was among other items to be auctioned at one of the big hotels. You must consider that she bought this during the depression, when no one had much cash, so she was able to buy very well without spending a great deal. On the day of the sale, she arrived late and saw her friend on the other side of the hotel reception room where the auction was taking place. She became a little confused with the item numbers and so made a bid for the carpet, which had once been used in the hotel ballroom. Bidding was slow, because such large items required a lot of space, and at this time in history, if you had a large house, every penny was needed to maintain it. Eventually, my grandmother outbid the others and it was knocked down to her. The next item on the list of sale, to her surprise, was – as the auctioneer explained in a loud voice – a Wilton carpet with wide borders, of a beautiful predominantly blue Persian design, from the hotel ballroom, and he gave the dimensions. "Good heavens! What did I just buy for one hundred and twenty-seven pounds?" thought my grandmother. Bidding was opened for the carpet, but there was no offer. Since she had arrived late, my grandmother was at the back of the room, and she cried out, "I'll give you twenty pounds for it!" Since there was no reserve on any of the items, her total expenditure was one hundred and forty-seven pounds. When she finally fought her way through the crowd, a tiny figure in hat and gloves, she asked what she had bought for the large sum of one hundred and twenty-seven pounds. "Weren't you looking at what you were buying?" asked the surprised girl at the accounts table. "Apparently not!" snapped my grandmother. "The sales list states you have purchased a ballroom chandelier and an assortment of six others, two of which are coloured, one red and one green!" My grandmother was so surprised. "The ballroom chandelier!" she thought. She paid her bill and the girl told her that all purchases had to be taken away within ten days. Grandmother told me that she went to the hotel ballroom and gave the employee at the door a shilling to let her have a look at the light fixture. When she saw the size of it, she said she almost fainted. Undaunted, she returned to St Georges Road, telephoned the housekeeper at Killarney – in those days Killarney had a staff of nine – and told her the story. The housekeeper organised three lorries and half-a-dozen men from Brunswick, who were only too willing to take a day's work and wages. The purchases were brought to Killarney. The ballroom chandelier is the one you see hanging in the ballroom here. The rest are still in crates in the old staff quarters above the supper room. They must have hoisted the crated chandeliers up to the upper veranda and in through he window, because the staircase is just too narrow."

"Goodness!" said Paul. "I had a good look at it with Mary the other day. It's enormous! She said when they brought it here, not one crystal was broken." Bernard laughed. "That had quite a deal to do with my grandmother's supervising everything. She was quite a person!" "Cooty! The fountain!" Michael was fascinated by this large structure, directly opposite the porte cochere. It had a sunken basin and from the centre rose three male figures with over-developed chests. But from the waist down they had fishtails, writhing in all directions. In their arms, each held a big shell above his head. It had a deckled edge, so that the water spurting from a stone nozzle then poured over them and into the basin. From the base to the tip of the nozzle, it stood almost ten feet high.

"Don't tell me your grandmother bought it! I thought it was part of the original Killarney!" "No, no!" said Lorna, taking over. "A certain city council had ordered this fountain from England and had it shipped over to place in a newly-developed park. But since it was just after the First World War, it was considered much more appropriate to erect a war memorial instead, so a very monumental marble soldier on a very high pedestal, with the names of the fallen in bronze lettering, was with great ceremony unveiled much to the appreciation of the local voters. As a result, this huge fountain was left in crates – with a large price-tag to be paid. Hearing of this, Bernard's grandmother discreetly offered to take the fountain off their hands at a price that was much in her favour. The council were only too eager to do this, rather than have the ratepayers discover they had paid for a marble memorial plus a fountain! So that was that. It was sent up to Brunswick by goods train, then brought here to Killarney, where it was installed badly. The bottom basin cracked and it leaked extensively, so as it was relatively close to the house, no one wanted problems with the foundations as a result of seepage. So it was turned off and has been like that ever since."

"Lorna, I think it's very nice", said Michael. "It's very big, but the men don't look very happy!" Everyone laughed. "Michael! You're wonderful!" said Lorna.

After dinner they went to the yellow room. It had been a hot day and the evening was still quite warm: everyone was feeling tired. "Tomorrow we'll go to Anne's for a swim", said Paul, still dreading the day after when he and Bernard were to depart for Melbourne. So they went to bed.

In bed with Michael, Paul sought to explain again the ramifications of this turn of events in their lives. Everything was changing so quickly. Michael laid his head on Paul's chest and said quietly, almost whispering, "Paul, for two nights I shall on my own with Toby. Paul, I love you!" Paul thought he was going to cry. Knowing that someone had absolute faith in him was the most wonderful thing that had ever happened, but it was also an enormous responsibility. But then, the day after tomorrow, there would be no Michael for two nights. He had grown so used to him that the thought of not being able to hold him like this worried him greatly.

Next day, Michael and Lorna were waiting for Bernard and Paul, who were in Bernard's library-cum-office, next door to the blue room, where the television lived. Bernard had moved another table into the room for Paul to set up his laptop. Bernard found that Paul's computer literacy was a great help, and often asked him how to do this or that. Although

Paul would do his work for Mr. Robinson at Killarney, three days at the office were essential, since Mr. Robinson had left the administration increasingly in Paul's hands. The library was old-fashioned, but on entering one was immediately struck by the violet velvet curtains that had come from the house of a deceased relative. Their gold braid and fringed pelmets were quite overpowering. Otherwise the room was functional, with one nice Victorian cedar bookcase and lots of hand-me-down furniture, as well as metal shelving. The walls were covered with brown-and-beige floral paper, hung with large engravings of English hunting scenes.

When Paul and Bernard had finished with the computer, still talking about investments, they joined the others in front of the house. Lorna and Michael were having a close inspection of the fountain. "It really is very impressive", said Paul. "Hmm!" said Bernard, and was about to get into the car to go to Anne's when Michael somewhat mischievously slipped his hand into Bernard's. "Cooty! Why can't you make the water work? I'm sure the men would like a shower." Bernard laughed. "So you want to see it working, do you?"

Bernard shared Paul's worry about the following day and they had talked together about it in the library. He thought he would make everything as pleasant as possible for Michael, so he said, "Now listen, my young man! In the next few days while we're away, you and Lorna will have to find a man to repair the fountain so that the men can have a shower." Michael was elated and hugged and kissed Bernard. "Good work, Bernard!" thought Lorna. "Not bad at all!"

At Anne's, a great deal of the conversation was about the fountain. While the boys were in the pool, laughing and splashing each other, Bernard said to the two women that, since the boys loved the pool so much, he should get someone in at Killarney to dig out the swimming pool there. As it also leaked extensively and the water was freezing even on the hottest day, it had rarely been used, and Bernard's father had had it filled in and planted a lawn over it. "Bernard!" said Anne sharply, "listen to me! If you open the pool, I shall never speak to you again! The boys are also part of my family now, and for me to have them here playing and letting me enjoy their company is wonderful. Open up the pool at Killarney and you're in trouble!" "Very well", he said. "Perhaps the fountain will be sufficient."

After this, the chief topic was Michael and how he would adjust without Paul and Bernard for three days. "I'm going to need your help, Anne", said Lorna. "I just hope he doesn't fret!" "He'll be fine!" said Anne. "I shall teach him to ride." Bernard looked most concerned. "You don't think that's a bit dangerous, do you?" "Absolutely not! Goodness! Two or three times he's been to the stables with his bag of apples and carrots from Maisy O'Brien – who by the way is completely captivated by him – and feeds the horses. They don't frighten him at all." "*He* may not be frightened, but *I* am!" said Bernard.

The boys put their shirts on and came up to the table. They sat down to a splendid lunch. It was then that Anne told Michael he was going to learn to ride a horse. Paul looked very concerned. "Darling, leave it all to me", said Anne, seeing Paul's face. "Everything will be fine!" "Paul, I think riding a horse would be very nice!" "Yes", replied Paul, "I'm sure it will be!"

Getting to the city for Bernard to collect what he needed meant a detour first to St Georges Road and then to Darling Square, making it necessary for them to leave at seven, so that Bernard could be at the courts at nine-thirty and Paul at his office in Collins Street.

Next morning, very early, Bernard said to Paul, "Act as though we are going to Brunswick, or Michael will realise you're very nervous". "But I am", came the reply.

The parting went better than even Lorna had expected. There were lots of hugs and kisses. Then, as businesslike as possible, they disappeared down the drive. Paul's last words to Michael were that he would call him at eight-thirty that evening. Michael looked at Lorna. He held her hand, staring at the gravel. "Oh no!" she thought. "Now what?" But nothing happened

Mary came through the main door. She had been told to help them through this difficult period of adjustment. She said, "Michael, you promised to help me bake a cake today! Don't you remember?" "Oh yes, I do!" He looked at Lorna and smiled. With his enormous blue eyes and his thick black hair now getting a little woolly at the side, she found herself thinking that he really looked beautiful. "Mary, I can't do it this morning", he said slowly, "because Lorna and I are going to make the fountain work, aren't we Lorna?" "Yes, Michael. We certainly are. Come with me and we'll telephone a very tall man."

"Good morning, Nigel Storey Interiors", came a deep voice. "Nigel, it's Lorna Mahoney." "Oh Lorna, can I help you?" "Yes, could you come out to Killarney this morning?" "I'll come immediately! My dreary shop assistant isn't here yet. Oh! Speak of the devil! She's finally deigned to appear! I'm on my way", and he hung up. "Nigel will be here in twenty minutes", she told Michael. At that moment, Michael heard his name being called. It was Mr Barnes. "You'd better come and look at something in the garden, when you have a minute." "Mr Barnes, I have to see a man about the fountain." "OK!" said Mr Barnes, "This afternoon will be fine!"

"Michael", said Lorna, "go up and have a shave and shower as quickly as you can, so you're ready to meet Nigel!" Michael was very excited. He put on the blue shirt Anne had purchased at Mulberry's, with dark-blue trousers and his new black shoes. His rolled-up shirtsleeves showed very brown arms with fine short black hair. As he reached the bottom step of the staircase, he saw Mary opening the screen door, saying, "Do come in, Mr Storey!"

Owing to the bright light outside and the shady interior, as Nigel entered, his eyes took a while to adjust, before he distinguished Michael in front of him. Likewise, Michael saw Nigel as a silhouette against the bright light. Nigel became aware that this young man was something very special. He had heard all about him from Ernest, but was surprised. Listening to Ernest rattling on, he had thought Michael must be just another good-looking youth whom the Mulberry set had decided was the best thing in Brunswick. He was totally unprepared for Michael's eyes. He was drawn by his magnetism.

"Hello!" said Nigel. "Lorna telephoned me." "You're here to fix our fountain!" said Michael. "Oh, am I?" said Nigel. "Nigel!" said Lorna, coming down the corridor from Bernard's office. "How good of you to come so quickly!" Nigel Storey was very tall and thin. Although in his mid-fifties, he had the face of a schoolboy, a long face that gave nothing away. He had brown eyes and dark-brown hair, cut like a nineteen-sixties schoolboy: short back and sides. The look was confusing on meeting him for the first time. His voice was extremely deep, and neither his gestures nor facial movements betrayed any emotion at all. He was a brilliant decorator and was known behind his back as being "very damask and tassels". Although extremely professional, he had – when needed, which was very rare – a dry sense of humour and a gravelly laugh.

"It's years since I've been to Killarney. Good heavens! What a state it's in!" he said, glancing through the dining-room door. "But I must say, the entrance hall is fantastic!" "Have you met Michael?" asked Lorna. "Yes, I think so. He's tells me I'm here to fix the fountain." "We have a problem, Nigel, and I'm sure you can see to it for us. Let's have a look at it!" Michael passed by them and opened the screen door, leading them to the fountain, standing in the glaring sun. "It doesn't make water, so the men can't have a shower!" Michael smiled. "He really is the most beautiful thing in the world", thought Nigel. For once, the staff at Mulberry's were not exaggerating. "Well, we shall have to get that fixed, shan't we? What do you want me exactly to do?" He looked at Lorna. "Oversee its complete restoration!" "Very well! I have a couple of stonemasons and a good plumber. I'll start organising things at once! But you should empty all the soil out of the basin now."

Michael left the others for a moment and Lorna took advantage of this to explain to Nigel her concern at having Michael here, separated from Paul, for the next few days. Nigel said, "I'm sure that with you here, Michael will be able to cope with the situation perfectly".

With that, he shook hands with Lorna, got into his car without further ado, and drove off.

Nigel's shop was chic, but business was very slow indeed. He was, in fact, thinking seriously of rationalising his workrooms. Money was not as free-flowing as it had been ten years ago. Things had decidedly flattened out. Perhaps after this fountain was again in working condition, there might be some work at Killarney. As he said to Lorna, he had not been to Killarney for years, and was surprised – although he had only glanced into the dining-room – to find it so shabby.

Lorna went to find Mr Barnes to tell him that the basin of the fountain had to be cleaned out at once. Mr Barnes was anything but pleased and made every type of excuse rather than starting on the task on such a hot day. It was Mr Barnes himself who had filled in the basin, in which he grew pink bedding begonias each year. "I don't think I can start today", he said, scratching his head. "I'll help you", said Michael, "and we'll finish it together!" So that was that. Mr Barnes was well and truly beaten. He might have refused Bernard and Lorna, but could never refuse Michael anything. "I'm not sure about that!" said Lorna. "Oh, well! Up you go and change then!" Michael shot upstairs and returned wearing jeans and a blue tee-shirt, ready for work. "You'd better find him a hat, Miss Lorna. It's pretty hot and we don't want our young man coming down with sunstroke." It was Mary who located a straw hat, and off to work they went.

With two wheelbarrows, it was not, in fact, such difficult work, and when they were full, Michael followed Mr Barnes across the drive, down the side of the house, across the back lawn to the extremely long, low building at the end. It was a weatherboard construction painted a creamy colour, with a high-pitched gabled roof. At one end it housed the garages and the rest of the long space was given over to the storage of one hundred years of pieces that were no longer needed: doors, window frames, drums, boxes, old tiles, bricks, baths, sinks, nothing, it appeared, was ever discarded at Killarney. They wheeled their wheelbarrows to the end opposite from the garages, where a ramshackle gate opened. Then they went down a narrow path behind the building and dumped the soil in a heap.

"What is this garden?" asked Michael. "It was once the kitchen garden", was the reply. The term meant nothing to Michael. "Why would a kitchen need flowers?" he thought. The garden was quite large, one of its walls formed by the service building and the other three, creating a substantial rectangle, were of brick, about six feet high. In one corner, the ivy had demolished the wall completely. The glass in the old cold frames was all broken and weeds and nettles were everywhere. The grass was high. "You stay close to me Michael! I don't want you to be bitten by a snake." "I will stay close to you", he said, a little nervously.

They worked for a couple of hours and by a quarter to twelve had cleared out the whole basin. It was then very obvious why it didn't hold water: a large crack ran down one side of the basin.

Michael went into the house and cleaned up for lunch, but he was still fascinated by the walled garden. He had had no idea it lay hidden behind the service building. Lorna and Mary praised his morning's work.

Late that afternoon, the masons, accompanied by Nigel, arrived to take a look at the problem. Mr Rossi said the basin would have to be underpinned, but that could not be done until the plumber had fitted new pipes and a small pump to reticulate the water.

The day ended; it was still a hot evening, and dinner was to be served in the dining room for just the two of them. Lorna said, "Mary, let's all eat in the kitchen together. I think under the circumstances it would be better for Michael. He won't miss the others so much". "Certainly!" and Mary prepared the table in the huge kitchen for dinner. Michael kept asking Mary, "Is it eight-thirty yet?" waiting for Paul's phone call. "Not quite, Michael. We'll have dinner first." A delicious meal was served, with Lorna insisting to a very embarrassed Mary that she should eat with them. Michael liked eating in the kitchen: it was strange but was full of wonderful smells. The kitchen was the original one, as it was when Killarney was built. Besides replacing stoves and refrigerators over the years, not a great deal had changed. It was painted a pale blue gloss, with a cream ceiling – or, had the ceiling once been white? Two large sinks below a large window overlooked the back lawn and through to the service building, behind which Michael and Mr Barnes had dumped all the soil that morning. The cupboards were also painted pale blue and surfaced with beige laminex. "Not exactly the most aesthetic room in the house", thought Lorna.

Soon everyone was talking. Michael had his by-now-usual glass of champagne in his usual glass, and Lorna joined him using the same type. "You know", she said to Mary, "they're actually easier to drink out of!" and laughed. During dinner, except for constantly demanding whether it was eight-thirty, Michael asked Mary why she wanted flowers in the kitchen. She looked puzzled and said, "But Michael, we don't have flowers in the kitchen." "Mr Barnes said that the garden behind the big service shed was a kitchen garden a long time ago." "He means 'vegetable garden'. Yes, once it was and all the vegetables we used in the kitchen came from there. Up to now, there's only been Mr and Mrs Barnes and myself, so it's not worth the work." "A vegetable garden!" he said aloud, as if some important piece of information had just registered in his mind. The telephone rang. Lorna stood up and walked to where the telephone was in the corridor. She returned quite soon, and said, "It was Anne. She has an adventurous surprise for you tomorrow morning". He smiled at Lorna. Then the phone rang again and Mary looked at the big clock on the wall. "I think this is for you", she said. "Go and answer it, and see if it's Paul!" He got up from the table and disappeared into the corridor. From the excited conversation and rapid laughter and yells, it was clear that he had finally received the phone call he had been waiting for all day.

The two women smiled at one another. Then Lorna, looking about the room, noted a thick sheet of paper pinned to the door that led to the storerooms. "What's that for?" she asked, having seen that 'Michael' was written in bold letters at the top. "Well, Miss Lorna, now that Michael's here full-time, thank goodness", she smiled, "I've noticed that he eats everything and I thought that this is probably part of his institutional conditioning. After all, if you don't eat what's in front of you, you go hungry. So I've been experimenting. I started with lunch today, to find out what he really likes and what he doesn't. It's not easy, as he's such a little gentleman and says everything I cook is nice, but he tasted some sprouts before dinner this evening when he came in to see me, and they definitely go on the 'No' side of the sheet. So, little by little, we'll work out what he really prefers. I'm keeping to Paul's advice, though" – she used Paul's Christian name as he had insisted – "and am keeping him on a high protein and carbohydrate diet until we build him up a bit. He's starting to fill out nicely, don't you think?" "Yes, I do, Mary. How thoughtful of you to do this!" "Oh, it's nothing! He really is the most wonderful young man. I can't believe that someone like Michael could possibly have been left alone and forgotten in an institution. Thank goodness for Paul, and, of course, yourself and Judge Mahoney." Mary took a sip of white wine. "It probably isn't my place to say so, but he loves you both very much." "Thank you, Mary. I appreciate your passing on this kind thought to me. If he loves us, it's totally reciprocated." "I know, I know", Mary repeated.

Michael returned in quite the highest of spirits. Lorna reflected that probably, four or five weeks ago, not only had he spoken very little, but had never used a telephone. "How's Paul?" she said. "Paul is with Cooty at a club. What's a club, Lorna?" he asked frowning. "A club is like a big house and you pay to become a member of it, and then you can go there to eat and drink and meet friends." "Hmm, I must go and see this club one day. Paul says it's very nice. He said he'd be home in two days." He looked a little dejected. "Don't worry", said Lorna, "Tomorrow you have to help me with the men coming for the fountain, and then, Anne has a surprise for you." "Oh yes, I remember". He stopped, finished his champagne, looked at Mary and said, "A kitchen garden... It's very big and the wall has fallen down. When Cooty comes home, I must talk to him about it." "Right!" said Lorna, "Now it's off to bed for all of us", thinking whatever would happen now. But nothing happened. Michael went to bed, tired from a morning's work in the sun with Mr Barnes, and probably from his two glasses of champagne, as well as the happy knowledge that Paul had said 'eight-thirty' and at eight-thirty had telephoned him.

"Anne, where are you taking me?" "It's a secret, darling!" Early next morning, dressed in his dark blue trousers and blue shirt from Mulberry's, he hopped into Anne's Mercedes and they headed off, just as Nigel and the workmen arrived.

"Good morning, Nigel", said Lorna. "Everything satisfactory?" he asked in his deep voice. "Yes, thank goodness! He slept with no problems at all! He said at dinner last night – we had it in the kitchen – that he thought you were a nice man!" "He's an excellent judge of character", Nigel said, with a faint smile. "Lorna, let me get these men going, then I want to speak to you." Fifteen minutes later, he entered the front door, just as Lorna came down the stairs. "Lorna, would you consider it a bore if I ask you to show me over Killarney?" "Not at all! But it's in a pretty shabby condition. We hadn't used it for two years, until this Christmas, but we're getting used to it. It's been used for storing furniture for years." "Yes", said Nigel, "it needs a real overall from top to bottom." "I'm aware of that and so is Bernard. If our arrangement with the boys works out – with Paul and Bernard three days in Melbourne and the rest of the week here – then everything must be done." "But why start with the fountain? It hasn't worked for years." "Nigel, the fountain is being repaired simply because Michael asked Bernard to repair it." "So it's Michael who's doing the organisation", he winked at Lorna. "If you're talking about getting Bernard moving, then the answer's 'Yes'."

Nigel looked over the whole house. "What a pity some of the big reception rooms appear to have been cut up. It really must have been a grand house, and can be again, with a bit of work. The bathrooms, Lorna, are terrible and the ceiling in the yellow drawing room, with all the water stains! Why don't we start on one room and see how we go?" "Which one do you think?" she asked. "Well, the yellow drawing room is the worst, but the two bathrooms above it would have to be ripped out and completely replumbed. I bet the pipes are lead. This is major work. Or else we could start with the dining room. Think about it, and talk to Bernard when he comes back, and we'll start something."

He then left her looking at the house. Although she had always realised the state of it, it was simply used as a holiday home, for a maximum of three weeks at a time, ten days in Spring when the rhododendrons were out, and at Christmas. Now it seemed it was becoming a permanent home after many years of neglect.

Anne pulled her car up in front of a hairdressing salon, which went by the name of 'Janice Taylor Coiffeur' and they entered hand-in-hand. Janice had had Anne on the phone the day before for ten intense minutes of "You can't do this to him – You must do that", until she wondered what Mrs Rochester was up to. She had cut hair for twenty years and prided herself on being an excellent cutter. She had heard – like most people in Brunswick – of this Michael, living with Judge and Mrs Mahoney at Killarney, and was more than curious to see him. In they came. She had a special section of the salon she kept for customers who demanded privacy. Michael was much more striking than she had thought possible. His eyes were amazing. He really was beautiful. "Michael, this is Mrs Taylor." "Call me 'Jan', Michael; everyone does.

Today we're going to cut your hair." A look of fear shot across his face, and Anne at once intervened. "No, darling, not all of it. Just a little on the side, so that when Paul comes back, you'll be looking very nice for him." "Paul doesn't like my hair cut off and neither do I." "Darling, just sit down, and we'll have a tiny look!" He sat in front of a huge mirror, and saw reflected Anne and Jan beside him. Anne grasped his hand as it came toward her. "Jan will have to stand beside and behind you for a little while, but you can see her in the mirror, and I'm here beside you. Do you think we can start, darling?"

Glancing at Anne in the mirror, he asked, "Will Paul like this?" "Yes, darling, I promise!" His hair had grown quickly, but on the sides it sprouted outward and looked most unruly. Jan ran her fingers through his dense black hair. She said to Anne, "Most of my customers would kill for this! I'm going to cut it with a razor. I can do a much better job than with scissors." She sprayed his hair and started work - as Anne had said on the telephone - as swiftly as possible. He showed no emotion at all. He sat bolt upright and watched Jan at work on his hair. Anne directed the cutting, occasionally, to Jan's annoyance. "Well, customer are customers", she thought. The hair on the sides was swept back like raven's wings. The top was left long and the back trimmed ever so slightly. It was the razor-cutting on the sides that changed his look dramatically. Instead of a semi-black mane, the effect now was very sophisticated and elegant. It showed that Anne knew exactly what she wanted, and that Jan was just the person to do it. Fifteen minutes later, it was all over. As she used the hairdryer, Michael seemed not to mind, except for being very rigid. Jan disappeared and returned. "This is for you, Michael", and handed him a special brush and showed him how to use it. He relaxed completely. She said, "So when you wash your hair, you brush it like this, and you'll look wonderful. Now, we're finished!"

Anne thanked her and said, "How much is the brush?" "It's my gift to Michael, my new customer!" "Thank you very much", said Anne, pressing a very generous amount into Jan's hand. "Oh no, Mrs Rochester, it's far too much!" "Not at all, Jan. It looks wonderful!" Michael said, "Jan, thank you!"

They left and walked diagonally across the main street to Mulberry's. It was a lazy, hot afternoon and no one had a great deal of energy. Samuel, standing looking out of the shop window, was the first to see him. "It's Michael! It's Michael!" The shop suddenly came to life. "Oh! Open the door, Samuel!" came Ernest's insistent command. When Anne and Michael – with his new haircut and looking much more tanned – entered the store, he commanded one hundred percent of attention. "How are you?" said Samuel shyly to Michael. "I'm fine, thank you", he replied. "Oh, Mrs Rochester! Such a wonderful surprise", purred Ernest. "How can we be of service to you? It's so nice to see you again! I believe the dinner jacket was a great success!" "Absolutely!" said Anne. "Coming from this store, it couldn't be anything else! Ernest, we should like a black blazer and a pair of grey trousers, but not those very light grey ones. I don't like them." "Oh, nor do I! Far too showy! We have exactly the right shade here", showing her a swatch of fabric colours. "A blazer, hmm! Samuel! Have a look in the storeroom! There should be a black and a dark-blue blazer. I don't know the sizes." Ernest immediately scuttled into his pulpit and, returning with the exercise book, flipped through the pages to the one that said 'Michael'. "Hmm! We need a forty-three. Samuel, see if the black one is forty-three!" Once more floating on air, totally besotted with Michael and his new haircut, Samuel thought "Oh how beautiful!" "Jane! We'd like the blazer today!" chipped in Neville, and a blushing Samuel disappeared.

Ernest said he had something to show Anne and vanished in turn. "Neville", said Anne slowly, "I believe there is another nursery out on Chandlers Road. Who's the proprietor? Is the stock good?" Neville smiled wickedly. "Oh Mrs Rochester, he's a nice-looking guy, but if you want intimate details, perhaps you should ask Samuel. As for the stock, I honestly haven't a clue." "Thank you, Neville. You've been so helpful. I also need a riding outfit for Michael. He's going to learn to ride." "I'm sure he'll look splendid astride a horse", said Neville. Anne pretended she didn't understand the innuendo, and with a smile, answered, "Undoubtedly!"

The black blazer was the right size, and Samuel helped Michael try it on. Ernest returned with a square, dark-green box whose label read 'Da Vinci Fine-Quality Pins'. He opened it and said, "Mrs Rochester, I've had these for years and would consider it a pleasure if you and Michael would accept them as a gift from me". They were gold-plated buttons and, looking very closely at them, you could see an embossed horse's head. Ernest said, "I'll change the buttons on the blazer with these, since there's just the right number of large and - yes! -- exactly the right number of little ones. The trousers -- I'll have the tailor begin at once. Did you say you preferred this shade?" "Yes, the darker one is just right." "I must say, if you'll permit me, that the Cartier brooch you're wearing is just exquisite!" "Thank you, Ernest. How kind of you to notice! I have just spoken to Neville about a riding outfit for Michael." "That's something I'll have to order. I don't carry a range of them, but I hope to have everything for the beginning of next week. I have all Michael's measurements. You obviously want the whole outfit, I take it?" Anne replied, "Yes, boots and all." "A black riding coat or a tweed one?" "Oh, black only!" "Fine, fine! That's that, then!"

"Have you got a white shirt with a very fine blue stripe in Michael's size?" Anne asked. While these arrangements were being made, Michael was looking at the displays on the centre table, especially the ties in their many colours. It was on the tip of Neville's tongue to say something to Michael, but he thought better of it, just in case Mrs Rochester mistook his intention, or -- worse! -- understood it. She was one of the very few he was careful not to offend in any way at all. He was only too willing to give her titbits of gossip, but only if she asked for it.

Sean found two shirts, each with a slightly different stripe, in Michael's size. "Michael, which do you prefer?" He selected the shirt with the finer stripe and it was duly packaged for him by Samuel, who had pushed in front of Sean and taken over. "Pushy bitch!" Sean spat at Samuel, who smiled acidly, then personally handed the bag to Michael.

"Thank you so much for the blazer buttons, Ernest", said Anne. "It's just too gracious of you!" Ernest replied, "Shall we send it all to Killarney like the dinner jacket?" "Yes, perfect!" said Anne. "I shall expect you all for Sunday lunch at Bellevue. Till then, goodbye!"

Michael said goodbye and then walked up to Ernest and said, "Mr Nigel is a very nice man"; he smiled, shook hands and then, with Anne, left the shop, popped into the car and they returned to Killarney for lunch.

"Do you think Michael will be at Mrs Rochester's on Sunday?" asked Samuel, glowing. "Perhaps you can organise a strong vine, Tarzan, swing down over the pool and carry him off into the jungle!" "If only!" and then, looking at Neville, Samuel said "Smart-arse!" "Don't get upset, Jane! We have your best interests at heart. Perhaps you could arrive with the gentleman who has the nursery on Chandler Road, or do you think our dearest Dr Colin may be free?" Neville said sarcastically. "You bitch!" came the retort. "Oh! Speak of the devil: here is your doctor, Jane! I suppose he's here for his trousers. Oh, he's such a bore!" "Be quiet, you faded parrots", came a shrill voice from the pulpit.

"Good morning, Dr Campbell! You have only just missed Mrs Rochester and Michael. He has had his hair trimmed and oh! what an elegant young man he is!" It was Neville who noted the expression on Dr Campbell's face. "Well, there are only two options", he thought. "Either he's also in love with him, or else he's jealous of him. Or, perhaps, even both!" Neville, as bitchy as he was, had summed Colin up perfectly. He was in love with Michael, but as he was so conceited, he was also jealous of the enormous attention Michael attracted so effortlessly.

At Killarney, preparation for lunch were in progress. "Anne, it looks wonderful! Oh, congratulations! I wouldn't have known how to go about it. You say Janice Taylor did it? Goodness, it's a great job! Paul *will* be surprised! Let's have lunch! I'm starving!" Michael had left them, and was staring at the work being done on the fountain. There was soil everywhere and on the lawn were rusty pipes and lengths of new plastic piping that was obviously going to replace the old. The masons had fitted the necessary steel reinforcements beneath the basin and had propped up the broken section. They were ramming cement in underneath to form a strong foundation.

At the end of the day, Michael retired. Lorna was now a little less stressed, but she left her bedroom door wide open in case Michael woke up and needed reassurance, but fortunately, this did not occur.

The third day dawned very hot and slightly humid. Michael woke, shaved and showered and went down to Mary in the kitchen. "Good morning, Michael! Would you like some breakfast?" "Yes, please, Mary! Paul comes back with Cooty today!" "Yes!" she said. "They should be here at about seven o'clock. We're going to have a little dinner party here with Mrs Rochester and, I think, Dr Campbell. Won't that be pleasant for everybody?" "Yes", replied Michael. "Seven o'clock!".

It was a long day for Michael, and as the afternoon wore on, he became nervous. Noticing this, Mary said, "Come here, Michael! Come into the yellow room. Help me turn this big armchair around so that it faces the window. Now, it's six o'clock. You go upstairs, have a shower, while I iron your shirt. If you sit in that chair facing the window, you will see the car when Paul and Judge Mahoney arrive." "Oh, yes!" he said, and he was gone, only to return with the shirt, and then upstairs again.

Mary had not finished ironing the shirt when he returned. He was stripped from the waist up, expecting to collect his shirt. "Just a minute", she said, "I have to finish the sleeves.... There you are! All done!" "Mary, thank you!" He put his shirt on, kissed her and left the kitchen, bumping into Lorna in the corridor, with his shirt still undone. "Oh! We are in a hurry!" she said. "It's near seven o'clock", he said. "Paul and Cooty will be home in a minute." Lorna felt a lump rise in her throat, as Michael headed around the corner doing up his shirt, and made for the big chair facing the window. He didn't have to wait long.

Suddenly, he saw a car coming up the drive and swing in under the porte cochere. He was on his feet and rushed out through the front door, letting the ornate screen door bang behind him, its sound reverberating through the house. Paul was first out of the car and had his arms around Michael at once. He kissed him. "I missed you!" "Paul, I love you!" came the reply.

Lorna and Mary witnessed this emotional embrace from where they were standing at the front door. As Paul released Michael, he dashed to the other side of the car, where he kissed and hugged Bernard. "Oh, Cooty! I'm so glad you're home!" "Thank you, Michael! Oh, look at your hair! Very smart!" "I knew there was something different", said Paul. "It looks really great!" "Anne took me to a lady, and she did it", Michael replied. With all now reunited, Michael was ecstatic and didn't stop talking. "Cooty! Look at the fountain! It's being fixed up!" "Oh, is it?" said Bernard. He kissed Lorna, who said, "Welcome home!" "Thanks!" said Bernard. "Cooty! I found a garden, a hidden garden. It's very nice. I think we should make a garden with flowers." Lorna interrupted, "Michael's talking about the old kitchen garden. He discovered it when he and Mr Barnes moved all the soil from the fountain basin." "They've been working you, have they?" said Bernard, and he squeezed Michael's arm. "Yes, I think your muscles are much bigger!" "Oh, Cooty! They're just the same!" and he laughed with his deep voice. He kissed Paul again. "Toby and I were lonely without you, but now everything is nice again!"

With that, another car came into sight up the drive. It was Anne, who had collected Colin for dinner at Killarney. The first thing Colin noticed was the haircut, and Michael laughing elatedly with Bernard on one arm and Paul on the other and everyone chatting together. But it was Michael who was making the most noise, with his very sensual deep voice. "Come in, everyone! We must have a drink to celebrate the boys' return", said Lorna. At that, they went in and made their way to the yellow room. "Pour me a drink", said Paul, "while I move the car, so Anne and Colin will be able to leave later without my car blocking the way". He disappeared and the car was heard crunching on the gravel. When he reappeared, he was carrying his own and Bernard's briefcases and a cardboard box under one arm. "I'll put your briefcase with mine in the library", said Paul, "and take this box upstairs". When he returned, he said to Michael, "I noticed a little inlaid box on the dressing table". "It's very nice; it's a present from Mary, so I can use it to put my cufflinks in that Anne gave me." "Oh, darling, you're so sweet", cooed Anne. "Now, you're all coming to my little do on Sunday. I've invited some friends to lunch and it's going to be lovely." "We'll see", said Bernard, "but I should think so", not really at all excited by Anne's friends.

Morton was peculiar in that these large houses lay hidden from view, so that each had its own world. It was rare for one owner ever to socialise with any of the others. They chatted on until Mary announced that dinner was served. They moved to the table and took their seats, with

Michael seated as usual between Bernard and Paul. If Michael had got through the three days reasonably well, Paul had genuinely suffered. He had not been separated from Michael in the month-and-a-half since he had collected him from the institution, and the three days had been a real strain. All he wanted to do was to take him to bed and stay with him for the whole night. But that would come later, so he relaxed a little.

Colin had never been invited to Killarney before, and saw this as a great step forward socially. He was surprised at the size of the house, although it was a bit run-down inside, he thought. Still, he was here, something very few of the other locals could boast.

"What did you do in town, Paul?" asked Lorna. "Well, workwise, it was frenetic. A month off! In fact, tomorrow morning I must do some work!" "How convenient!" said Anne, "since Michael and I have an appointment at Brunswick. I'll pick him up at about ten o'clock". "Oh, you're a man in demand!" said Paul to Michael. He turned back to Lorna and said, "I had dinner at Bernard's club on Wednesday. It's very impressive". Brown's was an establishment club, a huge grey Italianate stucco structure, and was *the* place to belong to. Bernard had been a member for years, and was very proud to introduce Paul to his friends. Paul had met Judge Stephen Spender, to whom Michael's custody case had originally been assigned. He was overweight, and had watery-blue eyes; bald, with large, clearly-defined features. Paul declared he was one of the nicest people he'd ever met. He also met the retired Rear-Admiral Amos Watson: six-foot-four, a towering man, solid but not excessively so, an imposing gentleman who listened a lot, but said very little. When he laughed, however, the entire room shook with his deep, hearty voice. Paul continued with his pleasant reminiscences of that evening. Michael took Bernard's hand and squeezed it, at the same time looking at Paul. "Hmm", he said, "you're a man in demand", repeating what Paul had said earlier, and making everyone laugh. Paul kissed Michael. The green dragon of envy rose in Dr Campbell, but he managed to put on a good face. It still annoyed him, however, that Michael drank only champagne from a special glass. "They're all just indulging him", he thought. "It's not the way to handle the problem." But what he didn't realise was that in the closeted world of Killarney, Michael didn't have a problem, just a small group of people who loved him dearly.

Conversation moved on to the Church, another subject that completely excluded Colin. Having been raised a Presbyterian and having attended a Presbyterian school – which was more to the point – he was out of his depth in any discussion of Catholic details. They spoke of how fond they were of Fr. Patrick O'Brien (no relation to Maisy at all), who had been to school with Bernard and Stephen Spender. Bernard recounted some school stories. Fr. O'Brien had been sent to Brunswick nine years earlier, having spent the previous fourteen years in Rome. The Catholic church in Brunswick was dedicated to St Michael, but at Morton, at the bottom of the hill, stood the little weatherboard church of St Mary's and across the road from it, the Uniting Protestant church. Fr. O'Brien came out from Brunswick to say mass at eleven o'clock on Sundays. "Thank goodness he dresses like a priest", said Anne. "My mother purchased most of St Mary's vestments in Rome in the nineteen-thirties, I think. And those lace albs are really so sweet." Colin felt that the language was being used deliberately to keep him out of the conversation. It was Lorna who brought him back into the group by saying, "It's all right, Colin. They're just talking about the costume the priest wears when he says mass. Nowadays most priests wear those hideous polyester Batman outfits, in the nastiest and harshest colours." They all laughed at Lorna's description, except Michael and Colin. Michael did not understand the terms or the concept behind the words that made them laugh, but thought it must be good, whereas Dr Campbell thought exactly the opposite. "I suppose", chirped Anne, "that Michael has been baptised", and she looked at Paul. "I don't know, I've never thought of it." "I don't think it really matters these days", said Colin a little haughtily. Bernard looked at Colin and said very sharply, narrowing his eyes, "I think you will find it depends on what faith you belong to", and there was a deadly silence. Colin realised at once that in future in this house, for him the subject of religion was taboo. Bernard, still put out by Colin's casual remark, said to Paul, "Telephone your brother-in-law and see if he knows. Otherwise, if he's not been baptised, Patrick will baptise him after mass on Sunday." Anne attempted to spark the conversation along, but it was hard work. It was Michael who saved the evening, talking about the kitchen garden and how, tomorrow, he and Bernard would have a look at it.

They moved to the yellow room after dinner. Bernard said en route, "Telephone your brother-in-law now". He was still in a very formal mood. Paul went to the phone near the kitchen. He came back a few minutes later and accepted a coffee. "The answer to your question, Bernard, is, probably, 'No'" "I'll telephone Patrick now", said Bernard, and left the room. Michael felt the undercurrent of the evening, but failed to understand what had been said that had made Bernard cross. Bernard returned and said, "It's fixed. Directly after mass on Sunday!" "How splendid!" said Anne, "I can turn my party into a christening party! Oh, Michael! Won't that be nice!" "I think so", he said, not sure what a christening party was, let alone that he was going to be the centre of attention yet again.

Paul stood up after finishing his coffee and said, "If you'll excuse us, good-night and thanks for a pleasant evening". Michael kissed everyone, but shook hands formally with Colin. Colin thought it was definitely not his night. Paul and Michael then left the room and went upstairs laughing together.

Anne said, "We must be going! I have quite a bit to do tomorrow. I must see Mary for a minute", and disappeared, leaving Lorna to make conversation with Colin, on any subject in the world bar religion.

Anne poked her head around the kitchen door and said, "Mary, may I have a quick word with you?" While she was saying this, she noted, attached to the storeroom door, the large sheet headed "Michael". "What's the sheet for?" "Well, Mrs Rochester, it's things Michael likes and doesn't like eating." "But he eats everything!" said Anne. "He eats everything because, for all these years, the poor darling has been forced to eat everything or go hungry. I've been trying to find out exactly what he likes and doesn't like. We play games tasting things. It's slow, but I'll get there." "I'm sure you will, Mary dear. Would you be so kind as to fax this information to Bellevue? I'd be so grateful! Why I'm here is this: I know you go to Brunswick for the early mass when the family's here, but this Sunday, please don't! Come with us to the eleven o'clock at Morton, then join us at Bellevue for lunch afterwards." "I couldn't Mrs

Rochester, I'd be a fish out of water!" "You most certainly would not! Besides, after mass, Fr. Patrick is going to baptise Michael, so it's your duty to be there and help him through the day. You know he's not just *fond* of you, he *loves* you very much!" When Anne entered, Mary had been washing the last of the dinner things, and she now shook her soapy hands and snatched the corner of her apron to dab her eyes. "He's the nicest person in the world!" "I know, Mary. We all think the same. So you *will* join us! Oh, by the way, Neville will be coming!" "Really!" said Mary. "I shall look forward to some spirited conversation." "Good night, Mary", said Anne, and returned to the yellow room to find everyone waiting. "I've just invited Mary to lunch on Sunday. She and Neville are great friends and she wouldn't miss the christening for the world." They said their goodbyes and Anne sped off down the drive with Colin.

As she entered the road from the drive, she said to a slightly tense Colin, "Relax, darling. They'll invite you back again, if that's what you're worried about. But remember, sweetie, Killarney is a bastion of Catholicism. Either accept it, or bail out. The choice is yours. When Bernard's grandmother ruled the roost – and this was during the Depression – she kept the whole place going with an exclusively Catholic staff, nine indoor and five outdoor. At that time, it must have been a drain on her finances. Look! Bernard will have forgotten all about it by tomorrow!" But deep down, neither of them believed it. "Let's stop at Bellevue and have a drink. It's early! I'll show you my guest list for Sunday. Oh!" she said mischievously, as she turned into her drive, which was all of two minutes from Killarney, "What about the new nursery on Chandlers Road?" "I don't know what you're talking about!" "Hmm, hmm!" she said, pulling the car up near the front door. So in they went for a drink and a gossip.

In this environment, where there was no competition, Colin relaxed, laughed, and the evening finished well.

At Killarney, Paul and Michael had gone upstairs and almost straight to bed, but once undressed, Michael noticed something on the chest-of-drawers that had previously held only the inlaid box that Mary had given him. There they were: all the photographs of the two of them from Darling Square, one beside the other, crammed into the limited space. Michael was overwhelmed. He crossed the room and held Paul in his arms. "Paul, I love you!" "I love you too, darling", and with that Michael pulled Paul onto the bed and rediscovered the exciting sensation of the right person with the right person.

"Bernard! You should relax with Colin! He's really a good person!" "Have it your way!" said Bernard grumpily. "Oh, come on! Life's short!" "I won't have that smart-arse conversation at Killarney. He either accepts everything here, or he can go to hell!" "Bernard! You're over-reacting! You'll just make things difficult for Michael, and especially for Anne!" "OK, OK!" They had stayed downstairs for some time, talking, before going up to bed. While changing into his pyjamas, and just as Lorna was about to change, she turned and said, "I had a long talk with Nigel yesterday and I think it's time we completely renovated Killarney. It's been a holiday home for us, but now we have Michael and Paul, I think we must do some serious work on it. Oh, where did I put my reading glasses? Oh, I remember! Just a moment!" She left the bedroom, crossed the landing, passing the boys' room quietly, and found her glasses where she had left them when she was with Mary earlier, looking through some of the wardrobes. As she walked back on tip-toe, so as not to disturb Michael and Paul, she heard Michael say to Paul, "Paul, I love you! Goodnight!" and the response, "Goodnight, Michael", then, to her surprise, she heard them chorus "Goodnight, Toby!" A lump rose in Lorna's throat and she knew she was going to cry. The words were so simple, but so beautiful. She returned to her room and sat down on Bernard's side of the bed. She put her arms around him and sobbed softly. "What's wrong?" "Nothing, darling!" and she recounted the incident. Bernard held Lorna and said, "I can't imagine life without either of them!" "Nor can I", she said. "We can look at this list in the morning." She changed, got into bed, turned off the light and realised that if she was emotionally involved with the boys, the man lying beside her was even more so.

Next morning opened with bright February sunshine, with a busy Friday ahead for all. Michael was up first, having woken Paul two hours before. While Michael was having a shave and shower, Paul joined him and started shaving. From behind, Michael put his arms round Paul and inside his dressing-gown. "Be careful, Michael, or I'll take you back to bed, and you know what will happen!" threatened Paul. Michael span him around and said, "Paul, it's early! Come back to bed!" The boys arrived late for breakfast, just as Bernard was finishing his toast and tea. Michael entered first and kissed him, "Cooty! Good morning! We must see my hidden garden!" he said excitedly. "Finish your breakfast, and we'll go and have a look. Good morning, Paul! The library's all yours! I finished what I had to do early this morning." "Thank you, Bernard. I must complete this work for Mr Robinson. I must say he doesn't look so good! He's become very slow, I noted." "I saw him at the club for a drink, the night you went to the gym. He has worries about his health and his son." "His son? I didn't know he had one!" "No, he never talks about him. I've only seen him a few times. A nasty piece of work, a smart-Alec. He's also a member at Brown's. I don't know who nominated him. He's not the sort of person for Brown's. But Robbie is a wonderful person!"

"May I come in?" resounded a very deep voice. "Yes, Mr Nigel, come in!" said Michael. "Will it work today?" – referring to the fountain. "No, Michael, but by tomorrow afternoon it should be working. Perhaps Lorna will get out the champagne!" "Excuse me all", said Paul. "I've a bit of work to finish in the library. I'll see you all later! Michael, don't forget your appointment with Anne at ten o'clock!" "Yes, I'll remember! Come on Cooty – and you, Mr Nigel! Let's go and see the hidden garden!" "What hidden garden?" asked Nigel. "Come on! Come on!" said Michael, and they all trooped off across the back lawn to the long service building. Behind it, led by Michael, they beheld the desolate old kitchen garden that had not been used for years and now boasted only a fine array of weeds, from medium to very tall. "It's very nice, isn't it?" said Michael. "Well!" said Bernard, with his hand in Michael's. "I think it needs a bit of work!" "The wall has fallen down in the corner!" Nigel said to Michael. "What do you want to do with this space?" Michael was confused by the word 'space', but he knew what he wanted to do here. "I want to make the centre *down*, and all around *high*, so if you are close you can see the flowers easily." "Oh, you mean a *sunken* garden, presumably!" said Nigel. Michael did not understand the term 'sunken garden', but probably if you asked the people shopping in Brunswick on this Friday morning what a sunken garden was, most of them wouldn't know what you were talking about. "What do you think, Bernard?" asked Nigel. "It's a great idea, but how do we do it?" "Oh, it's simple.

Get Barnes and that man who helps him to clean out the space and get rid of the ivy that's destroying the walls. The two masons that have almost finished the fountain can rebuild the walls."

At this point, Mr Barnes appeared and Bernard and Nigel explained the project to him. "Barnes, get your friend from the bottom of the hill to give you a hand!" "Oh, Judge, it's going to take some time." "The masons will be here next week as soon as they've finished the fountain", Nigel said. "Hmm", murmured Mr Barnes. Nigel continued, "You need a fountain in the middle of this big space". We have another one", said Mr Barnes, "but it's broken." "Where is it?" asked a surprised Bernard. "I don't remember another fountain!" "You sent it up years ago, but they dropped it off the lorry and broke part of it." "Where is it now?" Bernard asked. "In the service building behind the garage." "Well, let's have a look!" said Nigel. "Oh, yes, another fountain, Cooty! That will be nice, won't it?" "I hope so!" said Bernard.

They went back to a side door and entered the dark interior. "I can't see!" said Michael. "Just a moment!" said Mr Barnes and disappeared in the direction of the garage section. Over a high partition, he handed an electric light bulb on a long cord. "Don't burn your fingers", he warned. Nigel took the light and began searching for the fountain. Every kind of outdated garden equipment was stored here. "It's not here!" cried Nigel. "Mr Storey", came the response from the other side of the partition, "There's a big green tarpaulin: it's under that!" In the centre of the shed there was indeed a green tarpaulin, covered with rubbish. Nigel knocked most of the rubbish off and lifted a corner. "Oh, good heavens!" he exclaimed. "Have a look, Michael!" Michael glanced at the shape in the raw unshaded electric light. It didn't make much sense, since it was lying on its side. It was in fact, a large Victorian caste-iron fountain, the base consisting of marine horses and the usual garlands of flowers. It was painted green, but rust could be seen in places. "Which part is broken?" asked Bernard. "All the broken bits are in a sack tied onto one of the figures", said Mr Barnes. Nigel located the sack. "Here, Bernard, hold the light!" He opened the sack, to find four pieces: a decorative spout, in the form of a frog, and three pieces of garland. "Oh, that's not so difficult to fix", he said. "I did one last month for Mrs Ashcroft. A truck had backed into hers while making a delivery. There's a young man who's an expert in re-welding caste-iron – not so easy to do – about fifty miles from here. He's very reliable and he works for a good price. Shall I go ahead with the whole project, Bernard?" "Yes, do, Nigel! Work with Michael, and we'll see how it goes." They handed the light back to a most dejected Mr Barnes, who realised that for the next few days, help or no help, he was in for some work, something he tried diligently to avoid.

As they crossed the back lawn, Nigel looked back and, addressing Michael, said, "How do you enter this hidden garden? You can't always creep around the end of the shed where you dumped the soil".

Michael looked at the site from the lawn side and said, "Cooty, we'll make a tunnel right through the centre of the building, and put a door at each end". Bernard came close to Michael, took him in his arms and hugged him, "You really are wonderful! What a good idea! Nigel will see to it for you!" Nigel was surprised to see Bernard – stiff, formal Bernard – holding a beautiful boy in his arms, and both of them hugging each other. "Wonders never cease!" he thought.

Michael, hearing a car coming up the drive, said he had to go out with Anne and would be back very soon. Bernard doubted it, knowing Anne, but was very pleased that she had taken it upon herself to help Lorna in looking after Michael while he and Paul were in Melbourne.

"He's a very fine lad!" said Nigel, "Very fine indeed! You're a lucky man, Bernard! Now what are we going to do with Killarney? It needs a lot of work done inside", he said in his deep voice, showing no emotion at all. "Well, I don't know exactly. What do you think? I suggest we start with one room and go on from there. Then there are those bathrooms over the yellow room. Lorna and I use one of them, but we could use another bedroom and bathroom." "Well, I'll speak to Lorna. Transfer what you need to the blue living room where you have the television. We'll start work in the yellow room, since it's the worst. And the kitchen, Bernard! It's enormous. I think you should divide it up so you can have a streamlined, up-to-date one and a separate small breakfast room, so that, when you and Paul are not here, Michael and Lorna can use it." Nigel was extremely sharp. He had realised that if he wanted to do anything at Killarney, he had only to include Michael in the plan and Bernard would go along with it, since otherwise, Bernard would hesitate and say he wanted to think about it, or that he didn't want to destroy the past. His excuses were endless, but preface any idea with 'Michael', and you were off!

"Anne, Nigel is going to help Cooty and me to make a garden. It's going to be secret!" He had heard Lorna use the word and understood it as meaning 'private'. No one would be able to see it but Cooty, Lorna, Anne and Paul. This was his definition of 'secret'. Anne said, "How wonderful, darling! I told them all to join us for lunch, so you can have a swim with Paul". "That would be very nice. I like your swimming place, Anne! It's nice! Thank you!" "Let's go first to Mulberry's!"

Anne pulled her Mercedes Sports up right in front of the store, just as another vehicle left. Before the car doors were open, Samuel opened the store's door wide, and with a broad smile welcomed them. "Good morning, boys!" said Anne. "Good morning!" came the response. "Good morning", said Michael quietly. "Good morning, Michael!" chorused the staff. "Oh Ernest, we have a dilemma!" "Mrs Rochester, what can it be?" "The blazer, is it finished? I mean the buttons?" "Oh, but I thought we had made arrangements for it to be delivered next week?" "Well, here's my problem. My party on Sunday is now to be Michael's christening party." "Oh, how lovely! So charming, and on a Sunday, as well! Oh what a wonderful organiser you are, Mrs Rochester!" "Thank you, Ernest. Too kind! But, Ernest, Michael hasn't anything to wear. If we had the blazer and another pair of trousers you have in stock, with a coordinated shirt and tie... Well! What can you do?" she asked. Neville replied first. "The blazer is no trouble. I think the buttons should be on. Samuel can go and check the workroom now. Take a swing on your vine, Tarzan, and see if the buttons are on the blazer!" Samuel shot him a look, narrowing his light brown eyes. To be so close to him and have to leave him to go to the workroom! "Move it, Jane!" Neville spat out. Samuel ran across the street to the workroom on the other side. "I suggest these trousers. Their light fawny cream will look great with black, plus a pale blue shirt and a blue-and-cream or fawn tie." "Perfect, darling, perfect! Have you got all those things?" "Of course we have, Mrs Rochester", chimed in Ernest, "and they'll all be delivered on Saturday. What about shoes?" "Oh, silly me! Of course! I'll leave you boys to select those. You have all his measurements." "We certainly do", smiled Neville. "Very well, then! Thank you all so much! I'm looking forward to seeing you at the christening party on Sunday!"

Samuel got back just as they were leaving. "Two buttons to go, and it's finished! Goodbye, till Sunday!" he said to Michael, who smiled, said goodbye and left. "Action, camera, tears", said Neville. "Great performance, darling! Eat your heart out, Greta Garbo!" "Oh, piss off!" came Samuel's reply. "Touchy, touchy!" said Sean. "Be quiet, you faded parrots! Sean! Get those trousers of Michael's to the workroom at once and tell them they're top priority! Just a moment, I'll write down his leg measurements. There we are now, get going! I don't know, Neville. Do you think the Van Cleef and Arpels ruby cufflinks will look right on that powder-blue shirt?" asked Ernest in a most concerned tone. "Of course they will! Rubies look good with everything, don't they Samuel?" Neville said in a slightly sarcastic tone. "I suppose so", Samuel replied blankly. "He's so beautiful!" "Oh, can it, Jane! Find me a pair of light-brown shoes in Michael's size."

As they got to the car, a boy said, "Good morning, Mrs Rochester!" Anne turned and said, "Good morning", and then realised it was Maisy O'Brien's son. "Oh, we're off to see your mother in a minute!" "I wouldn't! She's in a bad mood. Just think! It's her birthday, and she's as grumpy as can be!" "Thanks for warning us!" Anne laughed. "We have another bit of business and then we'll pop in and cheer her up!" "Good luck!" he said, and picked up his bike and cycled off.

"Michael, we must get Maisy a little bunch of flowers! I know just where to go!" She turned the car in the direction of Chandlers Road, where they pulled up beside the high wire fence of a well-laid-out nursery. Anne was more than curious to see the owner. Right in the centre of the nursery stood an office-showroom, its large gabled roof like an oriental pavilion, surrounded by plants of all kinds grouped together by colour. It was a lot smarter than Mrs Saunders' nursery off the main street, where Snow-White and the Seven Dwarfs in the brightest glossy colours held court amongst pots of flowers. This nursery was called "Chandlers", and its address was the same, making it easy to locate. It was laid out in separate spaces, so one could go from one to another, each according to the different groupings of flowers and plants. As they walked around, they got separated and Michael found himself in the central pavilion where they sold cut flowers. He saw three beautiful little bunches made up, one all white and cream, one cream and pink and the last cream and shades of purple, each with matching ribbon. He was unaware that he was being watched. As he stood upright – since the bunches were displayed on a low table – he was surprised to find someone standing very close to him. He stepped away.

"May I help you?" the man said. He was about thirty-five, and his hair had gone prematurely grey. Like Michael, he had a mane of it. With his green eyes, tanned skin, fine nose, very generous lips and cleft chin, he was altogether a very handsome man. He wore an open-necked white shirt and jeans, with rubber shoes to protect his feet from the damp. "I would like these", Michael said, pointing to the three bunches of flowers and placing Paul's reserve $20 on the counter. The man was just about to say something, when Anne entered. "Oh, Michael! I thought I'd lost you! Good morning! My name is Anne Rochester." "Good morning", came the reply, very sharply with a very clear pronunciation. "I'm Rodney Earl and this, I presume, is Michael." He put his hand out to shake Michael's, but Michael at once moved over to Anne and stood beside her. "I recognised you, Mrs Rochester. I saw you at a restaurant a week ago. Someone pointed you out to me." "Really?" she said, genuinely surprised. "You have a fine nursery here." Rodney stared at Michael, and now knew who they were. The person who had pointed Anne out to him was Samuel, and his description of him could only be this beautiful young man in front of him. "Michael, if you go to the end of this walk here", Anne directed, "you can tell me what you think of the two birds there". Slowly, Michael left the pavilion and went down the path. "May I open an account here", Anne asked. "Certainly, Mrs Rochester." "Anything Michael wants, put it on my account." She opened her Gucci bag, which did not go unnoticed by Rodney, and handed him her business card so that he could open her account. He duly noted her sapphire earrings with diamond surround and her large matching ring. "Anne, Anne!" came a cry from the end of the path, and they both hurried out to see what Michael had discovered. He was squatting down, staring at two life-size bronze Thai geese, one with its head and neck almost parallel to the ground, as if listening, while the other's head and neck were almost vertical, as if snapping at an insect just above its beak. "Anne, they're very nice!" he said. "Oh, but *he* is very nice!" thought Rodney. Samuel had not been exaggerating at all. In fact, he was much better than Rodney had expected. "How much are they?" Anne asked, noticing at once that Rodney's eyes had settled on Michael and not on the geese. "I'm not sure, because the person I'm selling them for is away, but I think they should be quite reasonable. No one here has shown any interest at all. Perhaps I ought to sell Snow-White and her friends." Anne laughed. "Will you hold them for me and let me know. He loves them!" Michael touched the large gander with his bill in the air, "He is a very proud duck!" he said, then stroking the other one.

Anne watched Rodney very carefully and saw that Michael's magnetism was working on Mr Rodney Earl, who was gazing longingly at him. Having regained his confidence, Michael said to Rodney, "Cooty and I are making a secret garden with a fountain in the middle". "What sort of plants are you going to grow?" asked Rodney. Anne noted that his voice was a little higher than before. He cleared his throat and blushed a little. "I don't know, but I think I will have all the flowers red. Don't you think the ducks would like a garden with red flowers?" He stood upright and tilted his head a little to one side. "I think that sounds like a very sophisticated garden", said Rodney, "and I'm sure the ducks would be very happy!" "Michael, we must go, darling! Remember you promised Paul you would have a swim before lunch?" Rodney remembered Samuel's description of Michael in a swimming costume, and felt just a little weak. "Oh, don't forget your flowers!" Michael went with Rodney, who put the three bunches in separate boxes with a window on the front. "Thank you", said Michael. "Now I can see the different colours." Anne asked, "Have these been paid for?" "Yes, they have. Thank you!" said Rodney. "If you are free for Sunday lunch, perhaps you would like to come with Samuel to Bellevue. We are having a little party for Michael. Do come Rodney!" "Goodbye", said Michael as he and Anne left the nursery.

As Rodney picked up the $20 note, he threw the flowers' three little price tags into the waste bin. Each said "$15". "God, it was worth it!" he thought. "How the hell did Mrs Rochester know that I knew Samuel? He mused. "Hmm, Sunday lunch…" and he picked up the telephone and phoned Samuel.

On the way to Maisy O'Brien's fruit shop, Anne said, "Michael, why did you buy Maisy three little bunches of flowers, instead of one big one?" "Oh, but I got one for Maisy; I think the one with the purple ribbon. I got one for Lorna, with the white ribbon, and the one with the pink ribbon is for you!" "Michael, you're so wonderful! It's just what I wanted!" and Anne wondered when was the last time someone had bought her flowers. She stopped near Maisy's shop and looked at the little box of flowers with the pink ribbon. She leaned over and kissed Michael. "Thank you, darling!" They hopped out of the car and, carrying the box and his red hessian sack, Michael entered the shop with Anne. There were two other customers. Maisy looked up, "How's my angel?" she asked. "Happy birthday, Maisy!" said Michael, and pushed past one of the women to give Maisy a kiss, adding, "These are for you!" "Oh darling, they're beautiful, and violet's my favourite colour! How did you know?" Michael just smiled and held her hand. "I like your new haircut! It's very smart! You're quite the little gentleman!" "Can some of us have some service around here?" came a sharp voice, which changed very rapidly when its owner turned and saw Anne behind her. "Oh, Mrs Rochester! How nice to see you again!" beamed the woman, a certain Mrs Beryl Kenworth, whose husband was a retired army man. Taking no notice of the pleasantries between Mrs Kenworth and Anne, Maisy let fly, "Listen to me, Mrs Kenworth! When this young man enters my shop", and she emphasised *my shop*, "he is the first to receive my attention, and if you don't like it, try shopping at the supermarket! Forget about her, darling! I see you have your bag. Give me the empty one and I'll give you a full one!" "Well, really!" began Mrs Kenworth, but Anne quickly interrupted and said, "Michael's with me", with a very hard smile. "Of course, of course!" muttered a slightly confused Mrs Kenworth. "Anne's horses like your apples and carrots very much. They eat them so quickly, they must really like them!" said Michael. "Dearest Michael, thank you very much for my birthday present! It's the nicest gift I ever had!" and Maisy thrust her hand into her large immaculately white starched apron to find a handkerchief with which to dab her eyes. "Mrs O'Brien", said Anne, "what are you doing for Sunday lunch?" Mrs Kenworth, who was an absolute snob, was shocked that Anne, the very, very rich and smartest person in Morton, was about to ask Maisy something on an equal social level. "If you could possibly manage it", purred Anne, knowing the precise effect it was having on Beryl Kenworth, "see if you can come to the eleven o'clock mass at Morton. Directly after will be Michael's christening and then we go on to Bellevue for lunch." "Oh, I couldn't", said Maisy, totally confused, "but it's most kind of you, Mrs Rochester, to invite me!" "That won't do, Maisy! Michael, you must now insist that Mrs O'Brien join us for your christening party!" "Maisy, you must come! Anne said all my friends must come, and as you're my friend, you must be there!" Maisy hugged him and said, "If it's possible, I'll be there!" "Promise, Maisy!" said a concerned Michael. "I promise!" said Maisy, "I promise!" "Well, that's all done, then! How nice!" said Anne. "We shall look forward to seeing you at St Mary's on Sunday!" They said their goodbyes and, with a last hug, Michael left Maisy, as always looking for her handkerchief. With a much sharper tone, Maisy turned to Mrs Kenworth. "What was it you wanted?"

It was getting even hotter as Anne's car drove up to Bellevue. They noted that Paul's car was in the drive. "Out you get, darling! Oh, don't forget the box of flowers for Lorna!" "I won't!" he said and grasped it ready for delivery. They went in to find that Paul had already changed, since they always left their swimming costumes at Anne's, having no need of them at Killarney.

Anne and Michael went through the house and out on to the terrace with the pool at the back. Lorna was sitting there, with a drink beside her. "Hello, you two!" she said. "Another adventure?" "Yes, indeed!" was Anne's reply and, "Oh! Do pour me a glass of champagne, darling!" As Anne went indoors to change, Michael came up to Lorna. "These are for you", he said with a smile. "They are all white and I think they are very nice!" Lorna was very surprised. "Darling!" she stood up. Paul wondered what was happening and came over. Lorna hugged Michael. Not a word was said, but Michael knew that the flowers had been a good idea. Paul said, "That's really sweet of you, Michael!" and, realising that Lorna was quite overcome, "Come on, we'll join the girls in a moment! Let's have our swim first!" Michael kissed Lorna and, with a hand on Paul's shoulder, disappeared into the little pavilion to change before splashing into the cool water.

Anne returned and stared at Lorna. "I know, darling", she said, "With Michael about, I'm now investing in waterproof mascara! Otherwise, one has that perpetual skunk look. He really is wonderful! This morning we went to the new nursery at Brunswick: Chandlers. It's very good. I'm thinking of taking my business to Mr Rodney Earl!" "Oh!" said Lorna, composing herself. "How is Mr Rodney Earl?" "Charming, darling. Very charming! You'll meet him on Sunday, I hope. A very pleasant young man, and very handsome!" At that, she laughed, as did Lorna. "Where's Bernard?" "He's supervising the sunken garden, it appears. I can't believe Michael has got him up and going. Don't forget tomorrow! The big fountain is going to be turned on at four o'clock. If you have time, do pop over! Nigel tells me all is well. Isn't it strange he's so formal, like an overgrown schoolboy? But he and Michael get on like a house on fire!" "Talking of people Michael likes…" They were interrupted by yells and squeals from the pool. "I asked", said Anne, "whether he liked Colin. You know how stiff their relationship is". What did he say?" asked Lorna. "Nothing! He remained absolutely silent, so I changed the subject. I feel Colin isn't managing Michael very well at all. No bedside manner!" With that, Anne cried out, "OK boys! Pop on a shirt! Lunch is in fifteen minutes. Drinks are here!"

If it had been an interesting morning for Michael, discovering two bronze geese and Rodney Earl, the effect he was having at Mulberry's was explosive. "It won't go with the cufflinks", said Neville. "You can't have powder blue, beige, black and red cufflinks. It will just look *so* Brunswick!" "*I* think it's all right!" said Samuel. "Really!" said Neville, sharpening up. "If you had your way, he'd be dressed in a leopard skin jock-strap and you could bound alongside as Cheetah!" "Smart cunt!" came the even sharper reply. "Now, now, now!" said Ernest. "We must resolve this! Oh, what shall we do? What *shall* we do! And we're all invited, as well! If the effect isn't super-chic, I'll just die!" Really?" said Neville. "We'll wait!" "Shut up!" snarled a very nervous Ernest. Sean, the Pale Parrot, looked through the shirt display and said, "I have it! Neville, have we got a black tie with some white and red?" "Not on the table display. I'll have a look in the boxes." He returned with a black silk Dior tie, with fine white stripes and a tiny red square pattern. "Perfect!" said Sean. "Black blazer, white shirt, black, white and red tie, and creamy-white trousers. It completes the look!" "Oh! You've just saved the day", cooed Ernest. At that point, the girl from the workroom entered the store. "Godzilla herself!" said Neville to Samuel, who smiled. She had brought over the blazer and trousers, ready for Michael. "Thank you", said Ernest. As she left the shop, she held the door open for a buxom matron, who pushed past. "Oh, Mrs Kenworth! How are you, on such a hot afternoon?" "Hot! What do you expect?" she retorted. "That's exactly what I want! That blazer is just what I want for Raymond!" Mrs Kenworth had an only son – Raymond, who was overweight and overindulged. Her husband, being a former military man, as she often repeated, she had had this child late in life. The father was basically indifferent to his son, but his mother doted on him. At Brunswick, he was generally considered to be easily led, not very intelligent, and rather sneaky, but for Beryl Kenworth, he was the ideal son.

"The blazer is for someone else", said Ernest. "Get them another!" she replied haughtily. "I like this one with those nice buttons!" At this point, being told what to do in his own shop, Ernest was becoming decidedly sharp, since that was something he refused to tolerate. In his most sarcastic voice, he said to Beryl Kenworth, "This particular blazer is for Judge Mahoney's protégé Michael and he will wear it at a very select and chic party on Sunday at Mrs Rochester's, and besides, your son is far too large to wear this elegant blazer." "Well!" she spat back. "If Maisy O'Brien's been invited, it can't be *that* chic!" "Did your invitation go astray in the mail", asked Neville. She spun around and glared at him, before returning to Ernest. "My husband will be in next week for a dress shirt. I trust you have such a thing?" Like a picador, Ernest was waiting for the thrust. "Only for the right customers", he said, and smiled weakly before returning to his pulpit.

Mrs Kenworth gathered her bag, which she had deposited on the counter, and stalked out, slamming the door behind her. "What an elegant woman is our Beryl", said Neville. "She must be three axe-handles across the backside, and those dykey shoes! We know she's golf-mad, but she really is a mess! And to think she is running for President of the golf-club this year!" With a flick of his hand, Beryl was dismissed.

Saturday arrived, and the whole of Killarney was enveloped in acrid smoke, since Mr Barnes had started a large bonfire five yards away from the kitchen garden wall, to burn the old cold-frames, old stakes and all the ivy he had cut with his whipper-snipper, but using a blade instead of a cord. "We shan't be able to see the fountain at four o'clock. Why didn't he load it all on the truck and take it to the tip? It's such a hot day, and I have to close every window. Really! He's so inconsiderate! Michael, will you help me with the chairs. We'll set them on the veranda, so that everyone can have a drink and watch the fountain playing." "Coming!" came a shout, and in a flash Michael was carrying chairs out to the veranda.

For Michael, four o'clock never seemed to arrive. Michael said to Paul, "Paul, will it be four o'clock soon?" "Yes, darling. Quite soon" But to Michael, it seemed that four o'clock would never come!

Anne arrived at three-thirty, so drinks were served. The morning's smoke had dissipated, but an odd smell remained. Nigel was next to arrive, and that completed the group. "Cooty, make it work! Make it work!" pleaded Michael. Bernard asked Nigel exactly how to turn the fountain on, but much to Michael's dismay, he did nothing about it. Michael consequently grew nervous and unsure of himself. It *should* be working and he couldn't understand why Bernard – and he firmly believed Bernard could do anything – was doing nothing. He moved closer to Paul and held his hand. "What's wrong, darling?" said Paul, and Michael whispered in his ear, "Why isn't it working?" He then stood straight and rather stiffly next to Paul.

Bernard cried out, "Michael! I'm waiting for you to come and turn it on!" Michael looked at Paul and at the others sitting down, and then leapt off the veranda, over the azaleas, and ran to join Bernard. "Shall we make it work now?" he asked. "Yes, turn that switch! That's right! Turn it all the way until you see only red on the dial." He did exactly as Bernard directed. There came a bubbling sound and then the water shot high into the air and cascaded from the top basin over the three male statues and into the basin at the bottom, which was already full of water.

"Hurrah!" called Anne. "Hurrah! The fountain is working at last. Come and have a glass of champagne to celebrate!" Michael and Bernard returned to the veranda, and sat down to watch the water splashing from the fountain. Just at that moment, a courier from Mulberry's arrived

124

with two large bags for Michael. He took them from the girl, who said, "Have a great party tomorrow!" She then looked at the fountain and said, "Wow! It works!" and in a cloud of dust and churned gravel sped off down the drive.

"Michael, what have you been buying?" asked Paul. "Take them upstairs, darling, and Mary will help you to hang them", said Anne. "Anne, you're too generous! You mustn't keep on buying things for Michael! It's just not right!" "Listen, Paul, I'm not short of money, and if Michael's happy, I'm a hundred times happier. He spent all his money this morning to buy flowers for three people he loves, and I'm very honoured to be one of them, so please don't tell me how and when I should spend my money and that I can't have the pleasure of spending it on Michael." Paul stood up. He moved over to where Anne was sitting looking at the fountain and kissed her on the cheek. "I wouldn't presume to tell you how to spend your money", he said, and squeezed her arm, "but you're impossible!" which made everyone laugh. "By the way, Paul", said Lorna, "I was also the recipient of some beautiful flowers this morning, so I'm on Anne's side". Paul smiled, "I must admit defeat, but thanks very much!"

Sunday morning started off very lazily at Killarney, with Paul and Michael still laughing and playing in bed at nine o'clock, when a knock came at the door. "It's me, Mary. Come along you two, or we'll all be late for mass. Breakfast is on the table." Paul started getting out of bed, but Michael grasped him round the waist and pulled him back and kissed him. "Paul, I love you." "I love you, darling! Come and have a shower with me! Hurry up, or we'll be late!"

"It looks funny!" said Michael. "Let me see", said Lorna and re-tied his tie. "That's better. Goodness, you do look smart in that black blazer!" "You look spectacular!" said Paul. "What! New shoes, as well?" "Yes, Mr Ernest said I had to be chic." They laughed. "Oh, the cufflinks!" He dashed back upstairs and came down with them in his hand. He handed one to Paul and one to Lorna. When they were fitted in, he slowly turned a full circle and smiled. "Exquisite clothes!" he said to Paul and Lorna. Bernard had still not come down. "Now I think I look chic. Mr Ernest will be very happy!"

"He'll be a great responsibility and he won't change very much" Paul, now glancing at Michael, heard the echo of his brother-in-law's words of warning. But he now knew without any shadow of doubt that Peter had been wrong. Up to his eighteenth birthday, Michael had lacked understanding and love. Now that both these commodities were in full supply, he was a very changed young man indeed. And the responsibility? Well, that was now being shared with Bernard and Lorna, Anne and Mary, and the responsibility itself had somehow been changed into sharing Michael's love. Michael still saw things in a certain way. He made his mind up at once: something was either good or bad. After their first day and night together, he knew he loved Paul and that was that. When he met Bernard, it was the same, and the rest of his 'family' had followed suit.

"Well, are we all ready?" asked Bernard, as he came down the stairs. "Well, well! You *do* look smart, young man!" Michael smiled. "Today I'm very chic", he said, and laughed.

They all got to St Mary's right on time, and found a large crowd waiting to attend the christening and go on to Anne's afterwards. The staff from Mulberry's, Ernest, Nigel, Maisy O'Brien: all Michael's friends in his safe little world had all forgathered. When they went in together, Michael noticed that Mary sat at the back of the little church, and not with the rest of them. He stood up and, as he was – as always – sitting between Bernard and Paul, he had to climb over both Paul and Anne. Everyone looked at him, not knowing what on earth was happening. He went down to where Mary was seated and, taking her by the hand, led her to the front to sit with all the others. They all moved up to make room for her and Michael returned to his place between Bernard and Paul. Bernard put his arm round Michael's shoulder and gave him a hug, in front of everyone. Mary searched vainly for a handkerchief in her bag, and Anne smilingly handed her a tissue.

When mass was over, Father O'Brien changed into a cope, and Michael and the whole group moved over to the main door where the font stood. The ceremony went off without a hitch. To the surprise, not of Michael, but of Anne, Paul announced that Bernard and Lorna would stand as Michael's godfather and godmother, then halted and continued, naming Anne as well. She was so surprised that she had to dab her cheek at the sudden onrush of emotion in order to remove her running mascara. She would throttle the stupid girl who sold it to her as being waterproof, she thought.

They all congratulated Michael before getting into their cars and setting off for Bellevue for the party. It was a great success. Neville and Mary were great friends, strange for such a brittle and acid person as Neville, who had many acquaintances, but no real friends. In his leisure time, he painted, and when he got stuck with one of his canvases, it was to Mary that he turned for help, knowing she was capable and that she wouldn't make unnecessary comments.

Michael became a little bewildered when people gave him gifts. He knew Christmas was over and gone, but he smiled and said thank-you to everybody. Maisy O'Brien gave him a box with four pots of scarlet geraniums for his red garden; the other gifts were either items of clothing – bought at Mulberry's, obviously – or plants and shrubs with red flowers.

At one moment during the lavish luncheon, Anne took Michael aside and said, "Darling, you'll have to wait for your present. It's a surprise!" "Anne, that will be nice! I like surprises!" She glanced at the ruby cufflinks, smiled confidently and moved on to speak to someone else. She was not the only one to note the cufflinks: Mulberry's staff were equally interested, especially Neville and Ernest. Samuel was content just to gaze at the wonderful young man, a constant sigh accompanying each sip of champagne. Rodney Earl had accepted Anne's invitation and arrived with Samuel. He gave Michael a red camellia bush and told him he would have to wait until spring for it to flower. "Thank you", said Michael, looking straight into his eyes. Like Samuel, Rodney was beginning to fall victim to the magnetism that Michael projected when he liked someone. There was only one incident during that pleasant afternoon. Michael moved to the empty side of the pergola to look at Maisy's red geraniums in their box. He thought they were wonderful, and had told her so.

Anne was more than pleased when Colin Campbell arrived much later than all the others, when the lunch party was already in full swing. He approached Michael from behind and put one hand on his shoulder. Michael froze and instantly put his hands on his head as if to protect himself from a blow. Only two people saw the scene: Anne and Rodney Earl, and since Rodney was much closer, he arrived first. He had learned of the problem through Samuel. He said sharply to Colin, "Go away for a moment! Let me sort this out!" Colin was genuinely shocked at Michael's reaction, and was quite bewildered. He had just forgotten about the problem. He moved away. Rodney knelt in front of Michael and said, "Do you think the geese will like living at Killarney?" Michael's hands came down, and he spun round to see whether anyone was behind him. Then, looking at Rodney, he said, almost in a whisper, "I think they will be very happy at Killarney". "Good!" said Rodney. "Let's go and have something to eat. Do you like fish?" "Oh, yes!" came the reply, and with that the moment of terror or fear passed. "Don't say it, Anne! I don't know why I did it! I'm so stupid!" "Well, that's saved my saying it!" said Anne sarcastically. "You're damned lucky neither Bernard nor Paul saw what you did, since I promise you, you'd never set foot inside Killarney again!"

It was Neville who said to Samuel, "Tarzan looks as though Cheetah has made off with the goods!" and pointed to where Rodney and Michael were helping themselves at the extravagant buffet by the pool. "I've always said 'Never trust a friend when there's a good-looking man about', and that one's the tops. Perhaps, Tarzan, you should strip to your leopard-skin jocks, rush over and smash Cheetah in the teeth, and carry the beautiful one off to paradise up a tree, or something." Samuel glared at Neville and was very close to tipping his glass of champagne over him, but being at Mrs Rochester's, even he realised this wouldn't be wise. "Arsehole!" was his retort, but he felt cheated and wondered whether Neville's words regarding Rodney might not be very close to the truth.

Apart from Samuel's disappointment over Rodney, and Colin's feeling very socially threatened as the result of his thoughtless act, the party was a great success. Anne had invited Police Sergeant Reynolds and his offsider Constable Timms to the event. They had arrived late, but to Anne's pleasure, they declared that this was the most elegant luncheon they had ever been to. Sergeant Reynolds was fifty-eight, solidly built with a slightly red face, blond hair, green eyes, a largish nose and very full lips, and was always laughing or smiling. He was loved and respected by all, with the exception of law-breakers. Constable Timms was the opposite: tall, good-looking, with very dark, almost black eyes and a smouldering look. He had a strong jaw and dark olive skin, black hair cropped very short, and large hands that he always seemed to be hiding. Anne introduced them to Michael, who said "Thank you for coming to my party". Sergeant Reynolds told him that if he were ever in trouble, he should call him and he would come right away. "Thank you!" said Michael. Constable Timms just shook hands, but found it was as though he had got an electric shock on contact, together with an amazingly strong protective feeling for Michael, such as he had never experienced before. His conversation became consequently extremely limited and clipped.

The wonderful afternoon drew to a close, and Michael sought out Paul and held his hand. Most of the guests thought this was charming, but not all. Both Samuel and Rodney felt the onrush of the green dragon of envy. Colin felt envious too, but rather because it was Michael and not himself that everyone took notice of, although he would still kill to get him. Another person was unable to understand exactly the effect of seeing Michael with Paul, and with all its ramifications. This person was Constable Timms, who felt that when he looked at Michael the sensation was like a large drop of oil on water, becoming wider and wider, with all the colours moving about as the oil dispersed.

Next day began with hot clammy weather. Just before lunch, Paul and Michael went to Anne's for a swim, but not before Michael and Bernard had spent some time in the emerging red garden. The broken cast-iron fountain had been set in a basin, and all the pipes for the water system had been set up. They watched a man sent by Nigel, who was re-welding the small broken pieces back into place, using an oxyacetylene torch. "Don't look at the light of the torch, or it will hurt your eyes", said Bernard, very pleased with the result.

The garden was now taking shape. The builders were making a kind of corridor, cutting the long service building in two, and had fitted an old Victorian door with a red etched glass surrounding that had lain on the floor for thirty years, making a little porch. Now the real design of the garden could be seen: raised beds were being brick-walled and, as soon as the plumber had fitted a pipe to drain off any excess water, the garden walls themselves could be re-bricked and the cement coping redone.

"Michael, Michael!" cried Paul, crossing the lawn. "Do you want to come for a swim at Anne's?" "Coming, Paul!" he replied, and for the first time he walked through the new corridor with Bernard, opened the door surrounded by red glass from the porch section, still sheltered by the main roof. They came out onto the back lawn into the full hot sun, thankful for the enormous trees that shaded Killarney all the way round.

"Cooty! Are you coming?" Michael asked. "No, you and Paul go. I'm going to have a quiet day after your party yesterday." Michael kissed Bernard and ran across the lawn, round the side of the house along the veranda and hopped into the car with Paul, waiting under the porte cochere. After exchanging their good mornings with Anne, who insisted they should stay for lunch, they raced to the pavilion to change and then into the water. After half an hour of playing around and generally having a good time, they got out, changed and joined Anne under the pergola, where an exquisite lunch had been laid out and the inevitable champagne glasses waited to be filled. Michael said he wanted to look at the camellia bush that Rodney had given him, which had remained at Anne's. He disappeared saying he would also go and feed the horses with the apples and carrots that had arrived as usual in the red hessian sack via Maisy O'Brien.

"Paul, while Michael's not here", began Anne, "I'd like to thank you so much for your great kindness in making me a godmother together with Lorna. I had no opportunity to speak with you alone yesterday, but, darling, thank you so very much!" "Anne", said Paul, "Michael loves you very much indeed, and it's only right that you and Lorna, who have done so much for him, should stand as godparents together with Bernard and me." "Don't go on, Paul, or this damned mascara is going to run. I'll kill the stupid girl that sold me this waterproof mascara!" "Let me pour the champagne", said Paul and, as he did so, said, "Here's to helping Michael!" They touched glasses. They were on their second glass by the time Michael returned. "Next week, darling, we begin your riding lessons. Won't that be fun!" said Anne. "Anne, it sounds very nice. The horses ate all the apples and carrots. They were very hungry."

"So am I" said Paul. "Then let's start, shall we?" said Anne, as she filled Michael's champagne bowl, noticing that he now preferred it to orange juice. "A great step forward", thought Anne.

Tuesday morning came all too soon, and Bernard and Paul left for their three days of work in Melbourne. It became a pattern for Michael and, indeed, for all their lives. Nigel generally oversaw any work he had been commissioned to do and, as he drove up this morning, he noticed to his satisfaction that the big fountain in front of the porte cochere was playing perfectly. Hearing a car draw up, Michael came out, followed by Lorna. "Good morning, Mr Nigel", said Michael. "Our red garden has a front door now. Let's all go and have a look!" So the three of them set off across the back lawn. "It needs a couple of columns, I think", said Nigel. "It's a bit ordinary like this." He pulled out a pad and wrote something down. The cast-iron fountain was finished, burnt paint showing where the welding torch had re-welded the broken parts. "It's very nice. Mr Rossi says it will be four days before we can put water in the basin. The cement is not ready." Nigel had made this basin very deep, hoping to plant water lilies later on. He had had the welder make a cover of fine netting for the basin, fitted onto a strong metal frame, so that when it was home to both lilies and goldfish, they would be protected from the birds.

Work now was slow, since new foundations had to be sunk where the old wall had collapsed, and Mr Rossi predicted at least three weeks before it would be finished, and maybe even longer.

They returned to the house, to find Mary with Mr and Mrs Barnes upstairs, transferring Lorna and Bernard's bedroom and bathroom furnishings to the other side of the corridor, so that Nigel could begin work, replacing the leaky bathroom pipes that were marking the ceiling of the yellow room, and totally rebuilding and refitting the bathrooms, as well as their large bedroom. Seeing Nigel, Mary said, "I hope we're not going to have a lot of dust!" "Clouds and clouds of it!" said Nigel, with a very straight face. When he spoke, he never moved his lips or head very much: he was like a puppet of a large schoolboy, with his slightly red cheeks and his high forehead, always looking straight ahead. "When we do the yellow room, we'll do the dining room at the same time. I've got just the right red paper. I ordered it for Mrs Bertram."

Lorna interrupted, "But Nigel, Mrs Bertram is dead!" "Exactly, very inconvenient, I'd say! I ordered the paper for her living room. Some idiot made a mess of the order and I got double the amount. Then she died and I had to pay the bill. Still, with double the original amount, I should have enough to finish the dining room and have a bit over. Oh well!" he said in a dry tone. "All's well that end's well!"

So January and February went by, with Bernard and Paul doing three days in Melbourne and four at Killarney. Whenever the end of third day came, Michael would sit in an armchair facing the drive, waiting for Bernard and Paul's car to arrive, when he would bound out, kissing and hugging them, and trying to tell them all the news in one minute, with everyone laughing and putting their arms round each other.

"Cooty, it's nearly finished, and we have a little roof over the door to the red garden, and columns – two of them! It's very nice. There are two big pots with trees that someone cut into balls on sticks! Mr Nigel got them from Rodney. Oh, do come and look, Cooty! Come on, Paul! It's really very nice!"

Both Bernard and Paul were surprised at the progress after just three days' work. "Nigel works his team very forcefully", said Lorna. In front of them stood a large Georgian style porch, with two columns and a pediment, in perfect proportion, with the Victorian door recessed about one yard behind, all ready for a coat of paint. "We can all go in", said Michael, opening the door. The corridor was not complete, but at the far end, the structure of the red garden had been well and truly laid out, the sunken section had been excavated, the little tractor with the scoop now neatly parked outside the fallen walls. These had not been started on, as Michael declared, because the foundations were not yet dry enough. Paul hugged him. "You are becoming an expert garden director", he said. Michael linked arms with Paul and Lorna and said, "I think it's very nice!" They watched Bernard as he inspected the repairs to the cast-iron fountain. "Not bad at all", he announced. "Nigel certainly knows how to organise his team!" "Cooty! Mr Nigel says we can't have grass until spring. Is that very far away?" "Yes, I'm afraid it is, but I think when the masonry is all finished, we might just lash out and get some instant lawn!" Michael had no concept of an instant lawn, but because

Bernard sounded confident, for Michael it meant that they would have a lawn before spring, whenever that was.

They returned to the house to a wonderful meal. Mary had been working all day. When she finished serving the drinks, she went past Michael and said, "Tell them all about our work in the kitchen". But before he could start, Anne's car was heard in the drive. Michael looked through the window, then leapt up to greet Anne at the front door. She gave Michael a special embrace. "Welcome home, boys!" she said to Bernard and Paul and gave them a kiss.

"Tell everyone what you have been doing in the kitchen all day", said Lorna. "Oh! We have a chef, do we?" asked Anne, accepting a glass of champagne from Paul. "Well", said Michael, "I didn't do very much. Mary did most of it!" "That's not true", said Mary, who had returned. "He made a big fish pie, and did it very well. I must say, we put lots of things in it, didn't we Michael? But we will keep it a secret until they've tasted it." "Yes! We'll keep it a secret!" and he laughed with that unexpected, deep sensual laugh. "Let's go in to dinner, so that we can try this wonderful dish", said Lorna. Bernard sat at the head of the table and Lorna sat opposite, with Michael on Bernard's right and Paul next to him, with Anne seated opposite.

Bernard started conversation as the first course was served. Paul had brought with him a dozen bottles of white wine he knew Bernard liked, since he remembered his ordering it at Browns. "The other night at the club, Paul and I had dinner with Stephen Spender." "How is Judge Spender?" asked Anne. "Fine! I've invited him to Killarney next weekend with Amos, but we don't know whether Amos can make it. Stephen can. So Michael, you and Mary will be in the kitchen all weekend!" "Why, Cooty?" "Because Stephen likes eating and drinking", and he laughed. "A perfect occasion for a black-tie dinner on Saturday at Bellevue. I shall be delighted to host Stephen and, hopefully, Amos". "I haven't seen him for years", said Anne.

"Anne, we are going to have early spring grass in the red garden", said Michael. "Really, darling? What is early spring grass?" she asked frowningly. Bernard explained, "I thought of instant lawn, you know. The stuff they roll out and there it is". "Well, Bernard", said Anne, "You must contact Rodney Earl. I'm sure he can do it for you. He really is very clever and very talented. I take all my business to him now. So much nicer not to be welcomed by Snow-White and the seven dwarfs, I feel!" They all laughed. Michael didn't understand why it was so funny, but smiled and held Paul's hand. "Nigel tells me that, talking of ornaments, when he was at Rodney's", Lorna said… Anne interrupted abruptly and spoke of red plants. When she realised that Bernard was speaking and that Paul and Michael were looking in his direction, she reached her hand across the table and touched Lorna's, winking at the same time. She raised her index finger to her mouth to convey the silent message that the subject of garden ornaments was taboo.

All, including Michael, pronounced the fish pie a great success. Every positive adjective was used to assure Michael that he had done very well. He, however, didn't feel it was all his due. He had only done what Mary had told him to do. He said, "It's Mary who did it. She's very clever!" Paul gave him a hug, and with that conversation moved on to foundations in the red garden and the upstairs bathrooms. They moved to the blue room for a drink before retiring. When Anne was ready to say goodbye, Lorna said to her, "Anne, come and see the disaster upstairs!" Halfway up, Lorna, who was more than curious, said, "What's the story about garden ornaments that you hushed me up about?" "Oh darling! It's the geese!" "The geese! What geese?" "Well", began Anne, "Michael and I saw these bronze Thai geese – a bit bigger than life-size – at Rodney's and Michael was entranced by them, so I told Rodney I would like them. But it seems they don't belong to him, so he is waiting to find out how much they cost. This is my surprise gift for Michael's christening!" "Anne, it sounds like a very expensive gift!" "Darling, how often have we been godmothers in our lives? For me, this is the first. I've always refused the challenge before, but this time it's right, so geese it is!" "Anne! You really are impossible!"

They returned downstairs after glancing at the half-demolished bathrooms. "Thank goodness, Bernard, you've got rid of those yellow and blue tiles in the second bathroom! I confess I always hated them. What are you going to replace them with?" "Nigel says he knows a firm in Melbourne that's going bankrupt, and he's getting a large number of twelve-inch marble tiles from them for Killarney, so we'll see!"

"Oh, I forgot! Do fill up my glass, darling", Anne said, looking at Paul. "Bernard, can you believe it? For years I've had all my furniture from Lancelle Road, all the farmhouse stuff from Aunt Mary and the furniture from Edgar's house, stored at a warehouse in Collingwood. Yesterday I received a letter from the company saying very bluntly that they're now going into liquidation, since the site is going to be used for loft apartments. They give me thirty days to remove everything, or else they'll send it to auction and forward me the cash. Can you believe it?" "What are you going to do?" asked Paul. "Well, I have no alternative. I spoke to Nigel, who told me to bring it all here and make a ballroom like you have here at Killarney. When Bellevue is redecorated, we shall have a giant auction in a marquee of the furniture you and I don't need. Oh, how tiresome! Just when I was getting Bellevue organised, and now it's going to become a giant storeroom!" "But, Anne! I think it's a great idea! I've also got some furniture and paintings in storage! Why don't we see what we can use and we can get rid of this burden we've been carrying and paying for all these years!" "I suppose you're right, Lorna, but the organisation of it all!" said Anne in a very flat tone. "Look", said Paul, "I'm in town next week. If you give me all the information in the next few days, I'll see to it for you. It's all catalogued, with numbers, isn't it?" "Yes, it is! Oh, Paul! You are a darling! It's just so much of the past I really can't bring myself to sort out!" "Done then! Give me all the information and next Wednesday I'll have a look at the situation. Yours too, Lorna, if you want me to!" "That would be so kind, Paul. Yes, let's get it all over and done with!"

CHAPTER FIVE

*A Horsey Encounter &
Drawing Lessons With Mary*

CHAPTER 5

A Horsey Encounter & Drawing Lessons With Mary

Anne rose very early in the morning, despite the late evening of the day before. Now she was seeing much less of Dr Colin Campbell after the situation at Michael's christening party, rising early was no real problem. She would take her horse out for a hour's ride around the property and return for a shower and breakfast under the pergola overlooking the swimming pool. Over breakfast, however, she thought the pool was much the poorer without Michael and Paul splashing about.

After her shower, Mrs Robbins gave her a shopping list and said that two gentlemen had telephoned, Mr Ernest Mulberry and Mr Rodney Earl, and would she please call them back. She poured out some more coffee and then phoned Rodney. She was about to hang up, when a breathless voice said, "Hello, Rodney Earl". "Rodney, it's Anne Rochester. How are you?" "I'm fine! How are you? I'm sorry I didn't answer at once, but I was watering at the back of the nursery." "I hope I haven't disturbed you. I can call back later." "No, no, it's fine. About the geese: are they for you or Michael?" he asked. "Well, Rodney, they're my gift to Michael for his christening. As a godmother, I wanted to get him something I knew he would really like, and he loves your bronze geese." "Fine! That friend of mine who's selling them owes me quite a lot of money. Yes, I know we all make mistakes! He gave me the geese as part payment, so I can now sell them. If you'd like to call in the next few days, we'll discuss the price, now I know the geese are going to a good home!" "Very well, Rodney. I'll call in today. Just remember the geese are Michael's, so don't sell them to anyone else. Oh! And I need to speak to you about instant lawn. It's all for Michael's red garden. I'll come in this morning if it's convenient." "It's most convenient, Mrs Rochester! Goodbye!"

"Good", thought Anne. "The geese are ours. Now what could Mr Ernest Mulberry be wanting?"

"Good morning, Mrs Rochester. How delightful to hear your charming voice", purred Ernest. "I thought I should let you know that Michael's riding outfit is ready, and I'm sure you'll be delighted with it. The choice of fabric for the coat is marvellous!" "Oh, thank you, Ernest. How kind! You saw how smart he looked at the luncheon, and it was all thanks to you!" "Oh, how kind of you! He is our favourite customer and he wears his clothes so well! It's an enormous satisfaction for Mulberry's to see our merchandise displayed in such an elegant manner." "I'll be in with Michael today or tomorrow, if that's convenient." "Oh, perfectly, Mrs Rochester. We await your presence", said a very flowery Ernest. "Until later today or tomorrow, then, and thank you so much for your most elegant luncheon. We were all most entertained. So very charming and smart! Thank you so very much. Goodbye, Mrs Rochester!" and Ernest hung up, feeling that today was going to be a good day.

Anne phoned Killarney to find out what was happening, and ask whether she could have Michael for an hour "for a secret, Paul darling, a secret!" "Don't tell me!" he said. "Off to Mulberry's!" "I can't tell you, darling, but can I borrow him, and then you can come with the others for lunch and a swim. The dust and noise from the red garden and the demolition of the bathrooms upstairs must be a frightful ordeal!" "It's not too bad, Anne. After the city it's actually relatively quiet." "Can I borrow Michael about eleven o'clock then?" "Who could refuse to send Michael off with his godmother?" "No one, darling!" came the reply. "And as it's Friday, tell Bernard he'd better come for lunch, since it's all fish and lobster! Oh, does Michael like lobster?" Paul laughed, "I haven't any idea. Let's find out! See you about eleven! He's with Bernard and Nigel, overseeing the famous red garden. Goodbye!"

As he came down the corridor from the library, he saw Lorna moving papers out of the yellow room. "Want a hand?" he offered. "Yes, thanks! I've kept all this sheet music for years in the window seats of the bay window, and now Nigel tells me they've got to go, as they're not smart!" "Do you play?" asked Paul. "Yes, I studied when I was young and took it up again five years ago because I had nothing to do in town." "Do play something for me, please!" said Paul. "The upstairs crew are having a morning tea-break, so there's not quite so much racket." Lorna moved to the grand piano near the window and lifted the lid. Without looking for any music, she sat down and began to play a piece by Chopin. Precisely at this moment, Michael entered the front door, back from the red garden with Bernard. He stood completely mesmerised by Lorna, as he saw it, not playing, but making music. He went closer and saw her fingers moving rapidly up and down the keyboard, and every time her fingers went down on the ivory keys a different sound came out of the piano. He had never seen nor heard Lorna play before, and neither had Paul. It wasn't the music itself that moved Michael, it was the technique used to produce it that had this magical effect. He drew closer and closer. Lorna became aware of him and stopped playing to ask if he liked it, but he thought he had done something wrong to make her stop playing. It took Paul a few minutes, with Lorna and Bernard's help, to convince him that the fact that Lorna had stopped playing had nothing to do with him. When she started again, it was as though he had forgotten the trauma of the music's stopping, and now everything was wonderful again.

Later, Paul told him that Anne would be coming at eleven o'clock, so he would have to be ready. He also told the others of Anne's instructions for lunch, and asked Bernard whether he should invite Nigel. "Why not!" said Bernard. "We can thrash out some more renovation over lunch and some wine." Anne, however, had already been to Brunswick before collecting Michael, to see Rodney Earl. Rodney knew full well that if he played his cards properly, he could do good business with Anne, who had transferred all Bellevue's gardening requirements over to him. He was more than pleased at this, since Mrs Rochester was a customer of some prestige. More than anything else, however, he wanted an opportunity of seeing that blue-eyed young man, under whose spell he was falling deeper and deeper.

"Good morning", he said to Anne. "You were quick!" "Oh, I have some things to do and a few friends coming to lunch. I must thank you for saving the situation with Michael at the luncheon. It was very quick thinking on your part, and I appreciate it so very much!" "It was nothing. Samuel had told me he had a problem when anyone touched him from behind." "Yes", said Anne. "I'm certain he'll grow out of it, but for the time being we must be very careful. Now, Rodney, what about the geese?" she asked in a businesslike voice. "You can have them for one hundred dollars." "Each? Or the pair?" He smiled and ran his strong sun-tanned hand through his thick greying hair. "The pair, Mrs Rochester!" "Rodney, listen to me! The price seems very low. You don't have to do that for me." "But I'm not!" he said truthfully. He was doing it for a young man who filled every moment of his waking life. He could see him on his knees looking at the geese as though they and he had waited all their lives to find each other and be together. "I've had a word to Bernard and as he needs this instant grass, I think you'll find that Nigel will call you to sort out a deal." That grass is damned expensive!" "That's not such a problem, since it's for Michael's red garden. When you have a moment, you must come and see it. Your advice will be invaluable. So far it has turned out very well. They are finishing the walls and the fountain is already in place. But no one seems to know where the fountain came from. Isn't that odd? It has just been lying in pieces on the floor of the shed, just waiting for Michael." "I know the feeling", he thought. "Very well, shall I pay you by cheque now, or shall we put it on the account? No, no!" she answered herself. "I should prefer to pay by cheque, but you must hide the geese away until the red garden is almost ready, if that's convenient to you." "Yes, that's perfectly convenient!" he said, looking at this petite woman, sharper than any other woman he had known, knowing she provided the only access to Michael he was ever likely to have. She wrote the cheque out with her fountain pen and handed it to him, saying, "I've made it out directly to you". The cheque was for two hundred dollars. "Hey!" he said, "I said one hundred dollars for the pair!" "That's fine", she said. "The rest is for your kindness and consideration when Michael was in trouble. You can deliver them, when I phone you", she said, changing the subject. "Thank you very much, Rodney! I'm sure you will be doing quite a lot of business with Killarney!" She shook his hand and returned to Morton to fetch Michael and take him to Mulberry's.

She wasn't stupid: Anne knew one thing very well. Since nearly all her friends were male homosexuals, she was familiar with every move, every halting piece of conversation, the glancing right or left at another person. Thus, she knew that Rodney Earl was much more attracted by Michael than he knew himself. She also knew that if Rodney didn't short circuit socially, Michael was going to become an obsession. This was a pattern she had witnessed time and time again: what you can't have becomes what you must have at all costs.

Anne drove up the drive and under the porte cochere. It was Lorna who came out and they exchanged greetings. "I must say", said Anne, "this huge fountain looks very impressive here!" "You don't think it's a bit pretentious, do you?" said Lorna, laughing. "Not at all, Lorna. I think I must have one put in at Bellevue. You never know, when they bring all the stuff from the warehouse, there may be a fountain in amongst it all!" They both laughed. "Lorna, you're looking very well. Killarney's clearly good for you! You seem so relaxed!" "I love it here with all the boys", Lorna said, with a confident smile. "They keep you going and there's not enough time to think about yourself. That's the right recipe, Anne. Just that!" "Lucky you, darling! Lucky you! But, where's Michael? We have to get to Brunswick and back, or else you'll all be having lunch at Bellevue, while we're still on the road." "I'll give him a call", said Lorna and disappeared inside. In a moment or two, out came Michael. He gave Anne a kiss and smiled. "Do I look good?" "You certainly do, darling! That blue shirt is really you. The Mulberry boys will recognise it at once!" and she laughed. "Off to Mulberry's, Michael, and we'll see how you fit into your riding gear!" With that, she drove down the drive and headed along the main road in the direction of Brunswick.

There was no parking in front of Mulberry's, so they had to walk a bit. As they went past Nigel's shop, they stopped and looked in the window. "Mr Nigel has a lot of nice things!" "He certainly does, Michael! Do you like that table, the gold one with the marble top?" Which one?" he asked. "Oh, let's go in and have a look! Good morning!" said Anne to the assistant, a pleasant woman in her late forties, and very well groomed. "May I help you, Mrs Rochester?" "Oh", said Anne, a little surprised that she had remembered her name. The woman went on, "And you must be Michael. Mr Storey speaks very highly of you!" Michael felt unsure with this woman and sought Anne's hand. "We're interested in the gilt side-table, with the green marble top." "It's beautiful. It's Irish, in fact, one of a pair. Mr Storey is currently having the gilding retouched on the other. It's the carved decoration that makes them special, swags of shamrocks, quite unusual!" "Thank you so much! Michael and I have an appointment at Mulberry's, but do tell Nigel to contact me about the tables", and with that, they hurried two doors further along and entered Mulberry's. "Oh, Mrs Rochester!" exclaimed Ernest, as he nimbly moved across the floor to shake hands with them both. "Ernest, we're in rather a rush. Would you mind if Michael has his fitting at once?" "It's no trouble", said Samuel. "I've got everything ready. Would you like to come this way, Michael?" and he smiled at him. The smile was returned and Michael disappeared into the dressing room with Samuel. To Sean, Neville spat out, "How come Jane is always the one in the fitting room with Michael, sneaky bitch!" "Exactly!" came the reply. Ernest continued his social chit-chat with Anne, until he was called to the phone. "Well, Neville, how's your painting going? Mary tells me your work is very good. Why don't you have an exhibition?" "Thank you, Mrs Rochester, but I don't think the run-of-the-mill at Brunswick would be interested in my work. They would probably see it as an opportunity to criticise!" "Surely not!" said Anne. "If Mary's convinced your work's good, then I think we should organise a show. I'll speak to her. What do you think of a gallery opening?" and she laughed. "Well, the idea's fine, but I just couldn't bear the thought of the likes of Beryl Kensworth and her tribe from the golf club stumbling around in their sensible shoes!" Anne laughed again, "Oh Neville! You are terrible, but very observant!" Their conversation was interrupted as Samuel swept back the green velvet curtain, and out came Michael. "Wow!" said Neville. "Not bad at all! A born fashion-plate, this boy!" He smiled at Anne, who was completely overwhelmed by the image in front of her. She went forward and gave Michael a hug. "You look beautiful, darling, just beautiful!" Everyone in the shop thought the same and would have killed to be able to hug Michael as Anne had done, particularly Samuel. "Everything's perfect", said Ernest, checking details. "Boots: a good fit? Yes! Jodhpurs? Perfect! A shirt, a coat? Yes! Samuel, where is the hat?"

"Oh!" he exclaimed, "it's in a plastic wrapping in the storeroom. Just a moment!" He disappeared and returned in a minute with the black riding hat. Michael tried it on and Neville – not Samuel – guided him to a large gilt dressing-mirror. "Well, what do you think", he asked. Michael gave his deep sensual laugh and replied, "It's very nice. I hope the horse likes it!" At that, everyone joined in the laughter, even Neville.

"Come on, darling! Change quickly, or they'll all be waiting for us for lunch, and we still have to see Maisy!" Into the dressing room, and in two minutes, out he came. Samuel put all the clothes in one bag and the boots in another. "Goodbye, and thank you all!" said Anne, and she left with Michael, whose hands were burdened with the two generous green carrier-bags, with 'Mulberry's' written in gold script on the sides. No sooner had the door closed behind them than Anne found Colin face to face, about to enter the store. "Good morning, Colin! I'm so sorry, but we're so late, and we must rush! Do give me a call tonight! 'Bye!"

"He looks good in blue!" thought Colin, as he entered the shop, only to find the conversation monopolised by the topic of Michael. Knowing he could do nothing about it, he was obliged just to listen to them all chattering on about how beautiful he looked in his riding outfit. He supposed – correctly – that Anne was now taking over this part of Michael's education.

"Quickly, darling! Say 'Hello' to Maisy and swap bags." This was done with apologies for being in a hurry, although Michael did mention he now had clothes to go riding a horse. "You will be very careful, Michael, won't you?" "Oh, yes, Maisy. I'll be very careful!" But he wasn't sure what he should be careful of.

As Anne sped up the drive at Bellevue, she was followed by Bernard's car, with Lorna and Paul. They all alighted together. "Cooty! I have my horse clothes! They're very nice!" "I'm sure they are", he said, and followed up with the fact that the weather forecast had predicted a quick change and rain during the late afternoon. "Oh, I do hope so! This heat is awful!" said Lorna. "Imagine the temperature in town!" said Paul. "OK, Michael. Let's go and change for a swim before lunch." They went arm-in-arm to the changing pavilion, where their bathing costumes were kept, ready for use.

The weekend passed smoothly, and after the rain and a drop in the temperature, it was much pleasanter. So another four happy days went by, and all of a sudden it was already early Tuesday morning. Bernard and Paul headed back to town, leaving a slightly forlorn young man waving from the porte cochere, with a whole three days to wait for their return.

Lorna noted that an hour after Bernard and Paul's departure, Michael was fine, since he had so many things to do at Killarney, especially his red garden and – this morning – his first riding lesson. Lorna did not hide the fact that she was anything but sure that this exercise was a good thing. He changed into his riding outfit and came downstairs, just as Mary, Lorna and Nigel were all discussing the clouds of dust from the demolition of the two bathrooms. "Well, Ernest has done himself proud!" said Nigel. "You look just the part!" "You look wonderful", said Mary. Lorna didn't say a word, but gave him a hug. To Nigel and Mary, she said, "Keep arguing! I shall take Michael to Anne's and return very shortly."

"I don't think the coat is necessary", said Anne on seeing him. "It's far too hot. Give it to Lorna to take home." Anne's stableman had saddled the two horses and the lesson began. "You must only mount, darling, on the right side of a horse, and never walk close behind one, or he may kick you." The stableman helped Michael mount the quieter of the two horses and then they slowly moved off toward the field. Anne noted that Michael was not afraid at all, and was very surprised. "I suppose", she thought, "he has good reason to be afraid of people, but not of horses". It soon became apparent, however, that this was not the horse for Michael, since it was used to a much more experienced rider and soon became a little difficult. Anne was always by his side, and saw the problem. After half an hour, they returned to the stables. She at once telephoned the woman who kept stables and looked after her horses when she was not at Bellevue. Mrs Cynthia Tate, a copy of Penelope Keith, answered the phone. "Anne, darling! How can I help you?" said the tortured voice. "I'm coming over at once. Is that all right?" "Perfectly! I'll be waiting for you." Cynthia hung up, wondering what Anne wanted, and, leaving her office, went to where a group of children were having riding lessons. "Having a jolly time?" she asked a group of three young girls, smiling in a most artificial manner, and walking off before they could reply. Cynthia Tate actually loathed children and if it wasn't for the fact that they brought in good and regular money, she would never have contemplated opening a riding school.

Anne's car entered through the white-painted gates and she parked not far from Cynthia. She and Michael got out. "Oh!" thought Cynthia, in her usual generous manner, "cradle-snatching at her age!" "Darling, you look fabulous!" "Thank you, Cynthia dear!" One was just as insincere as the other. "This is Michael!" "How do you do?" said Cynthia, in her most affected accent. Michael just nodded, but did not reply. He moved very close to Anne, as he was aware of the children's presence. "He's just like you, Cynthia dear! He dislikes children!" "Well, that's two hundred points in his favour!" she replied. "Well, Anne, you're not here for a chat! What do you want?" "Oh, that's easy! I want a quiet horse for Michael." "Oh, do you? I haven't anything to spare at the moment. All the ponies are in use for the riding school." "But I don't want a pony. I want a horse. What about those two?" she said pointing to two horses in a small paddock. "Oh, darling! Don't speak to me about the brown one with the white flash on its right side. Do you know, she also hates children! She's thrown four children headlong into the lake, stepped on Dr. Baldwin's son's foot and broken a bone, and has bitten Sarah Smith's shoulder. Five stitches! The insurance company now say they won't cover this foolish mare! What am I to do?" While they were talking, Michael had walked over to the wooden fence. Then, seeing a group of children coming in his direction, he entered the paddock and walked up to the two horses. The black mare shook her head and moved away to the other side of the enclosure. The brown mare remained stationary, and she and Michael just scrutinised each other. It was at this precise moment that Anne and Cynthia realised that Michael was not with them. Anne felt instant panic, but Cynthia exclaimed, "Oh God! Anne! He's in with that horse that hates children!" She was about to rush into the paddock, when Anne said, "Just a minute! He's not a child. Let's see what happens". The mare rubbed her muzzle against Michael's shoulder and followed him as he returned to the fence. "Saddle her up!" directed Anne, and Cynthia passed the message on to one of the girls who worked at the stables. The horse was made ready. Anne's sixth sense said that this was Michael's horse. "Michael, remember! Mount the horse on the side with the white mark. What's the horse's name, Cynthia?" "Polly, and I can tell you, if this doesn't work out for Michael – and I'm sure it won't – our Polly will be off to the glue factory tomorrow!"

Polly and Michael became instant friends. He walked her around the enclosure twice, before coming back to Anne and Cynthia. "I don't believe it! In all my born days! That beast has never behaved like this!" Cynthia said, "Michael, her name is Polly!" Michael looked at Cynthia. "No, darling", Anne said with a repressed laugh, "the horse is called Polly!" Cynthia's eyes narrowed. "I think Polly is very nice!" said Michael. "So do I, darling! So do I! Well, Cynthia, it look's as though we've saved you from calling the glue factory! How much do you want for Polly?" "Anne, really, as a friend, I couldn't sell her to you, in case she played up again and caused a serious accident!" They watched Michael walk Polly around again. "Do you know, Cynthia, this is only the second time Michael has been on a horse." "He seems very confident", Cynthia replied with her affected accent. "What shall we do? I want the horse and you don't?" "Anne, dear, take the horse. If after a couple of months you still want her, you can name the price yourself. She's no good to me! Five stitches, can you believe it! The drama, a child screaming and a hysterical mother! Please, Anne, take the horse. I'll have her taken to Bellevue this afternoon. You have a spare stall, haven't you?" "Two, actually. Listen, would you do me a great favour?" "Certainly, what is it?" "Have you got a receipt book?" "Yes", said Cynthia, looking quite lost. "I don't understand." "Well, I want you to take twenty dollars from Michael and give him a receipt, saying he has purchased Polly." "But, Anne, it's not really legal, is it?" "It doesn't matter, Cynthia dear. Just do it for me, and make it sound very legal." "I don't understand what kind of game you're playing, but very well!" She turned her head and motioned to one of her assistants to come over. "Get me the red receipt book off the top of the filing cabinet, please." The girl returned with the book and a biro and left them. Michael had been talking to Polly while he was riding, and the horse was reassured by his deep voice. When he got back to Anne and Cynthia, he dismounted and rubbed Polly's chest. As he walked to the gate, Polly followed him, and then put her head over the fence when he rejoined Anne and Cynthia. He patted her muzzle.

"Well, Michael", said Cynthia haughtily, "do you want the horse?" "Yes, please", said Michael quietly, not looking at Cynthia, but at Polly. "She will cost you twenty dollars. Have you got the money?" "Yes!" he replied. She wrote the receipt and Michael gave her the twenty dollars. Polly was now Michael's responsibility, thought Cynthia, thank God for that! No more insurance problems with that dreadful mare! Aloud she said, "I'll have Polly delivered this afternoon. I must rush now and phone to see whether Dr Baldwin's son's foot is better – thanks to Polly! Oh, I do hope Dr Baldwin doesn't get too excited. The last thing I need is a legal battle! Goodbye Anne, goodbye Michael!" And she dashed off to the office to placate a not very happy Dr Baldwin.

"She's very beautiful"; said Michael, on the way home. That was all he could talk about: he had a horse, wasn't that nice! Wasn't that just marvellous! He had his own horse! He must tell Maisy O'Brien! She'll have to put in an extra apple and two carrots for Polly. Oh, how nice life is, he thought.

Polly was duly delivered and next morning Lorna dropped Michael off at Anne's, as she was extremely curious to see the horse. Anne's stableman saddled both horses, Anne's and Polly. "She's a clever horse!" Michael said to them, "because she has a white mark, and I know that is the side I get on". He swung up. Lorna was genuinely surprised. He hadn't any experience and this was only the second day. He walked Polly around the stable yard, while Anne and Lorna watched. Looking at Michael astride Polly, Lorna then glanced at Anne and said, "He's so handsome, and he's so happy! Bernard and Paul are going to have to see this. Oh, by the way, Anne, where's the bill for the horse? Bernard won't let you pay for it!" "It's paid for!" and she recounted the story of Polly, especially the bit where Michael thought Cynthia was called 'Polly'. Lorna almost collapsed with laughter. She couldn't stand Cynthia and her affected accent, and thought her an extremely shallow person. Anne mounted and said to Michael, "Let's go for a trot in the paddock! Are you ready?" "Yes, I'll see you later, Lorna!" He waved to her, and Polly, with Michael astride, set out for what was to become an early morning daily exercise for both horses and riders.

It was at such moments, when Anne and Michael were alone, riding and talking, that she discovered that although Michael's view of the world

149

was relatively simple and he was now leading a very protected life, he was developing a strong personality, founded on his belief that with the support of their little group, nothing was impossible. He loved this small, select group, and was rewarded with all their love and protection, but the centre of his world was Paul. It was on Paul that his whole life pivoted and if the truth were known, Michael was the only person Paul had ever loved unconditionally.

The three days in town were busy with work and Paul's evenings were spent with Bernard, but when he went to bed alone every evening, he knew very well he was missing someone he loved very much.

An hour before they were expected on Thursday evening, Michael sat in the big bay window of the yellow room, waiting for the first sight of Bernard's car coming up the drive. The last hour or so always seemed an eternity. Mary felt sorry for him, just sitting in silence, waiting. But the moment the car turned around the lawn and under the porte cochere, Michael was out there with his arms round Paul and Bernard, talking nineteen to the dozen, as usual. Everyone ended up laughing.

Another car this evening, a few minutes later, came up the drive and parked behind Bernard's. Out rolled a very big man. It was Judge Stephen Spender, whom Bernard had invited for the weekend. Michael held back, and just looked at Stephen, unsure what his response should be. Then Stephen, who knew all about Michael from talking to Bernard at Brown's, came up to him and gave him a hug, saying "You're a very good-looking young man!" Michael looked at him, turned his head a little and replied, "I have a horse called Polly". "Can you ride her?" "Oh, yes. Anne and I go riding together." The ice was broken and Michael accepted Stephen as one of the group, without any problem.

As they went inside, Michael said, "Cooty! We have a lot of red flowers in the garden now and a roll-out lawn. It looks very good! Mr Barnes has to water it two times every day. Come and see!" At that moment, Anne arrived, followed by a truck that bypassed the front drive and continued up to the red garden. "Cooty! Let's have a look!" "Just a moment, boys!" said Anne. "Hello, Stephen darling. How are you? Let's have a drink and then we'll all go to see the red garden before dinner." They went into the yellow drawing room where champagne and other drinks were served. Michael turned his head, from where he was sitting on the arm of Paul's chair, as he watched the truck now departing down the drive. He thought it odd that no one said anything. Generally a strange truck required some explanation, but tonight, nothing! Perhaps it was because Stephen was here, he thought. Michael felt uneasy. Why was everyone so calm and quiet, just talking softly about things he thought were not so important. "Very well, let's look at the red garden", said Anne.

On reaching the back lawn, Michael went ahead, opened the door and continued down the corridor to the now nearly completed red garden. All its walls had been rebuilt and, with its newly rolled-out lawns, cast-iron fountain now painted a very dark green, and raised garden beds around the perimeter, it looked stunning: the beds were filled with lots of bright red annuals Rodney had managed to find for an immediate show. Then, as they all crowded in, he saw them! "Anne!" he screamed with joy, "the geese! the geese! Paul! the geese!" They had all kept it a secret from Michael. He was astounded. When did they arrive? They hadn't been here that afternoon! How was it possible? He was so excited that he kissed Paul and hugged him. The geese had been placed near the fountain, on the broad circle of brick paving that surrounded it. "Look, Cooty! This goose is looking up to the sky, and the other is listening to what is happening under the ground." At that, he embraced Bernard, who ran his hands through Michael's mane of black hair. Stephen was fascinated. Bernard! After all these years, kissing someone he obviously loved, and in public! He had noticed a major change in Bernard since Christmas, but actually kissing and running his hands through Michael's hair! "Isn't it wonderful", said Lorna, slipping her arm through Stephen's, as the rest went down the steps to inspect the geese. "Who would have thought, Lorna, that Bernard could possibly have changed so much in a few months?" "Yes, it's wonderful, and so are the boys! I'll take a bet that Bernard is more than happy about his decision to give Paul custody of Michael." "But it seems to me that you have all taken custody of this handsome young man!" "We have, Stephen, and we would never have it any other way. He is, as Paul is, part of our lives and as time progresses, they occupy an even greater portion." She stopped, as Michael shouted, "Anne! You bought the geese! I know you did! Oh, Anne!" and he hugged her. "Oh, Anne! They're so nice! They'll be very at Killarney! That's what Rodney said to me, that they'd be very happy here! Thank you, Anne!" Then, turning to Paul, he said, "Oh, look at the big one's eyes, Paul! I didn't know geese had big eyes", he said studying the taller goose. Anne moved back to where Lorna and Stephen were standing. "Oh, damn it", she said. "I shall throttle that girl for not selling me waterproof mascara!" and she headed off toward the house to tidy up before dinner.

Stephen was amazed at the happy atmosphere, not at all as formal as at St George's Road: it was a sort of chaotic order, with everyone talking and laughing. Renovations upstairs, a red garden, a horse called Polly, with the promise of very good food and fine wine: the weekend was set to be a very happy one.

Next morning, a joyful and very proud Paul went with the others to watch Michael mount Polly. He set off for a ride in the paddocks behind Bellevue. "He looks wonderful, doesn't he?" said Paul, positively beaming with pride. "He certainly does!" they all chorused. Stephen said, "He looks a very skilled horseman". "He's a splendid all-rounder", said Bernard. Anne had organised morning coffee and Mrs Robbins was seen spreading a large cloth on the table in the shade of the pergola. Soon the four of them sat down, and beside the coffee – to Stephen's delight – there were several different kinds of cake. "Bernard, are you going to renovate Killarney completely?" "Yes, Stephen. It's home for us all now, so it's time to do some major work. I'm sorry for Lorna and Michael, who will have to live all week among the dust and debris!" "Oh, we'll survive", said Lorna. "Michael is wholly oblivious to it. It's just an adventure for him. I don't think Killarney has seen such activity since the two big wings were built." "Excuse me for changing the subject", interjected Stephen, "but while I remember, I saw your employer at the club last Monday. I tell you Paul, he doesn't look well at all." "I know, I spoke to Mr Robinson last week, and asked after his health. He always looks so tired and seems to be carrying the weight of the world on his shoulders. He just smiled and said he was fine. He really is the nicest man. I'm very lucky to be with him. You know, he didn't even hesitate before changing my workdays when I explained about Michael." "We'll organise a dinner at the club one night with him. Bernard or I will always sign you in, Paul, whenever you want." "Thank you very much, Stephen! It's very kind!" "Good heavens!" exclaimed Bernard,

"Paul's always with me", looking at Stephen. "There's no problem about signing him in at all." "Now who's being territorial here", thought Lorna. Bernard had not only Michael, but had also claimed Paul to look after, and, she thought, I've never seen him happier.

They talked on about renovation until Anne and Michael returned, Anne bringing up the rear. Paul stood up and walked over to Michael. "Don't walk behind Polly", said Michael. "Very well!" he smiled and, as Michael dismounted, he slid into Paul's waiting arms. "You look great! Did you have a good ride?" "Yes, I like being with Polly. It's very nice!"

Anne dismounted. "You know, Paul, your charming young friend", she said, giving Paul a wink, "is becoming quite a horseman!" "He looks great!" said Paul. "Oh, let's have a drink!" said Anne. "I mean it! Forget the coffee, it's almost midday." She walked over to the table where the others were sitting. "I don't care what you say, darlings, but you're here for lunch! I'll just have a word with Mrs Robbins. As it's Friday, Bernard dear" - accompanied by a mischievous grin - "we shall not be eating meat!" and she disappeared into the house. Michael came up to the table in his white shirt and jodhpurs, looking so very country-chic, yet totally unaware of it, since he was never conscious of being the right man dressed for the right occasion. He put on whatever Anne, Paul and Lorna bought for him: he liked dressing well, it made him feel part of the group, since they all dressed very similarly. But, being young and beautiful, all unknown to himself, he stood out. It was the same with Samuel, Rodney, and even Colin: he knew they liked him and, in a strange way, he realised it was different, but on an intimate level he never thought of anyone but Paul. Perhaps, in this context, it was his silence that his admirers found fascinating, although it had no effect on Michael himself.

"Stephen, darling, do open the champagne!" and a bottle and silver wine cooler were magically produced. "Bernard, would you prefer something else?" "Yes, I wouldn't mind a Chardonnay!" "Anyone else? Some Chardonnay on the way!" She moved like a sparrow, hopping here and there, Stephen noticed, attentive to her guests' well-being. Mrs Robbins placed a silver tray with glasses on the table. Stephen poured out the wine and Bernard took the single old-fashioned champagne glass and gave it to Michael. It was much later in private that he discussed the matter with Bernard and found the answer to this little mystery.

Lunch was as wonderful as usual at Anne's table: everything was perfect. Just as they were about to leave, Michael went to say goodbye to Polly and Anne reminded them of her black-tie dinner on Saturday. Stephen had been forewarned, and so had come prepared. But for Anne, this dinner party presented a problem: she was two men short to make a table for eight. She had still not forgiven Colin for his stupid behaviour at the luncheon with Michael. Should she just call him, or should she cast her net further afield and see what she could find. She had less than twenty-four hours to find two suitable men.

When they all returned to Killarney, Stephen said he would go and lie down. Paul was helping Lorna move things out of the yellow drawing room, as Nigel had said he could not guarantee the stability of the ceiling, considering the leaks of so many years. Bernard said he had to do a bit of work on the computer, and took Michael with him, on the promise that when he finished they would go and inspect the red garden and check on the geese. As they headed down the corridor, Bernard saw Mary and asked her whether she could bring him a coffee in ten minutes. They entered the library which Bernard and Paul now both used for their work, which Nigel had described as a strictly thrift-shop interior. Bernard had ignored the comment. Bernard turned his computer on, but before beginning, he lifted a potted geranium out of a cachepot on the windowsill and put it in front of Michael, with a sheet of paper and some coloured pencils he retrieved from a drawer in his desk. "See if you can draw the geraniums", he said, and left him to it.

Michael stared at the pot with the plant in it and then opened the packet of coloured pencils. They were arranged like a rainbow, which he liked very much. He took a pink pencil to start on the flowers and found that what he saw and what appeared on the paper were two completely different things. Then he tried the green pencil, for the stalks and leaves. Again, it was not as he saw the object in front of him. He sat looking at his quick sketch and compared it with the geranium. At this moment, Mary entered with the coffee for Bernard and one with a lot of milk for Michael. She was still intent on determining his likes and dislikes, foodwise. After depositing Bernard's coffee beside him, she went over to Michael and peeped at his drawing. "It's very bad! I can't draw flowers, because they have too many numbers." She was taken aback, and couldn't understand what he meant. She persuaded him to tell her about the problem with the numbers. Michael found that, to draw a flower head, you had to count its petals, and you had to count the leaves, which, as well as trying to draw them, was simply too confusing. "I see!" said Mary, very slowly. "I understand. Perhaps we should start with something that doesn't have numbers. I shall have to think about it." Turning to Bernard, she said, "I have an hour or so off tomorrow after lunch. Since you're going to Mrs Rochester's, why doesn't Michael come to my studio and we'll see what we can find to draw without numbers." She gave Michael a hug and left the room.

As she walked along the corridor, she said to herself, "What can you draw that doesn't have numbers?" Lorna overheard her and said in puzzlement, "Whatever do you mean?" "I'm not sure", said Mary and disappeared in the direction of the kitchen.

Friday dinner was a great success and Stephen personally complimented Mary on her fine cooking. The seafood was marvellous. It was often served at Killarney now, because Michael really enjoyed it and always on Fridays, since Bernard demanded it.

Saturday arrived and after lunch everyone disappeared to do something. Bernard went off to Anne's and Paul was working in the library and, since Mrs Barnes was washing up and clearing away, Mary took Michael to the studio. "Well", she said. "Look here!" She had washed the mussel shells from last night's dinner. She placed Michael in her chair with the shells in front of him, and a sheet of paper ready for the exercise. He turned and looked at her confusedly. "Now Michael, watch this!" she said as she sat beside him. "You do the same as I do", and she started to draw the shell. "Look at my drawing and then the shell and you'll be able to do it as well!" she said very confidently. So he began, a look at the shell, a look at Mary's drawing, which she did very slowly, piece by piece, until she had finished the outer line of the shell. He found he could understand using this very patient method and was very surprised at the drawing of a shell that appeared on his sheet of paper. He sat back and looked at his drawing and then at Mary's. "Yours is nicer", he said. She produced an eraser and removed a little squiggly line at the bottom of his drawing. "There! It's almost perfect! Now let's paint them!" With a large box of tubes of paint, she mixed the colour and handed him a brush. He repeated, step by step – or brush-stroke by brush-stroke – her painting of the mussel shell. "Remember, Michael, this side is lighter than the other, because the sun comes through the window on this side." "Yes", he said. "I can see the sunlight on the end of the shell." She showed him how to bring up the highlight using a little white and grey paint. All round, it was a very good, tiny painting of a mussel shell and he was most pleased. "Mary, I think it's very nice!" "It is indeed! Next week, we'll paint some more shells", trying to remember what she had done with a box of them she had kept for years. "What are you going to do with your painting?" Michael looked perplexed and tightened his lips. "I shall give it to Stephen, because he ate so many last night. This will remind him of his dinner!" Mary laughed, "What a good idea! We'll let it dry and I'll cut a little mount and put some cellophane over it. But first you must sign it." With that, she wrote his name and he copied it in a spidery hand in the bottom left-hand corner. "So, you can give it to Mr Spender, before you go to Mrs Rochester's tonight. Don't forget to come to the kitchen and get it before leaving." "Oh, I won't! Thank you, Mary! I like drawing shells", and Michael vanished in the direction of the house to find Paul. He had no idea what a mount or cellophane was, but Mary knew all these things and so it would be all right.

Mary looked at the little painting of the mussel shell and felt certain that with a little – or perhaps a lot – more encouragement, Michael would be able to master the drawing of shells. She thought of what he had said about plants having numbers, something she had never dreamed of, and the fact that some of the objects he saw he equated with numbers, and then abandoned them as being too difficult.

Michael found Paul in their bedroom, dressing for Anne's dinner party. Paul knew immediately that dressing was out of the question, since Michael closed the door and was on top of him, kissing him urgently.

At seven, everyone foregathered in the blue sitting room, since the yellow room had been almost emptied and its contents moved to what little space was left in the ballroom. Next week, under Nigel's direction, the workers would move all the heavy furniture, including the piano.

Lorna and Bernard were down first, followed by Michael and Paul and both of them stood while Lorna knotted their ties. As she was doing so, Stephen entered and, watching this domestic scene, commented that Killarney had indeed at last become a home. They all had a drink and then Bernard pronounced that it was time to leave. "Cooty, no, no! Just a moment!" and Michael ran down the corridor to the kitchen. "I almost forgot", he said, looking a little sheepish, to be greeted by Mary with, "And don't you look beautiful tonight!" "Thank you, Mary! You see, I have my red buttons on!" and he laughed his unexpected deep laugh, showing her his cufflinks. "Very nice, darling! Here is your painting! Have a nice evening!" He kissed her and said he would see her in the morning, and then dashed back down the corridor. He kept the little painting behind his back and walked over to Stephen. Everyone was watching him. "This is for you. I painted it with Mary this afternoon." Stephen was wholly unprepared for this gesture and, for once in his life, found he had nothing to say. He was very grateful that he didn't wear mascara, or he would have the same problem Anne had had the other evening. So he just hugged Michael and said, "Thank you! I shall always treasure it!" Some years later, invited to Stephen's for a drink on their way out to dinner, Bernard spotted the little painting in a beautiful antique gilt frame on his drawing room wall.

On arriving at Bellevue, champagne was flowing as usual. Michael had taken a liking to it, calling it 'Anne's drink' and would now get through three or four glasses in an evening. That was all he was allowed, because if he was already tired, champagne made him sleepy. Moving past the dining room in an elegant burgundy silk chiffon frock with Bernard's pearls, Lorna noted that the table was set for eight and wondered who the other two might be. Colin, of course, she thought, not knowing he was out of Anne's favour, but who else? A little surprise, perhaps.

A car was heard coming up the drive, followed by another, and an exchange of formal greetings, prior to the entry of two men: Colin and Rodney, known to all bar Stephen. Lorna was surprised to see Rodney, whom she had only seen in his work clothes before, bringing one thing or another for the red garden: in a dinner jacket, he cut a very different figure. I now understand what Samuel sees in him, thought Anne and busied herself making introductions.

Michael was aware of a lot of people in a small space and the staff coming and going, and instinctively sought Paul's hand, remaining silent. Paul gently kissed him, "It's all right, Michael, we know everybody!" but Michael stayed very close to him. Stephen was amazed that everyone – and particularly Bernard – accepted Paul's kissing Michael. He was even more surprised when Anne asked Paul to help her for a moment, at which Michael at once moved over to Bernard and held his hand. Bernard acted as though it were the most normal thing in the world, which, in their own closeted world, it was. Rodney also noticed, and felt a little uncomfortable. Sensing this, Lorna drew him into conversation with Bernard and Michael, just as Stephen started talking to Colin. "How are the geese?" Rodney began tentatively. "They're fine!" said Bernard. "I think I like the one with his head up in the air best." "Cooty, why do you like him best?" "Well, the other, with his head near the ground, looks rather sneaky." Michael laughed and gave Bernard a kiss. "Cooty", he said, "I don't think he's sneaky at all!" and his deep laugh sent an unexpected thrill through Rodney's whole body. He smiled. They finished their drinks and Anne led the way to the dining room. The seating arrangements were as usual: Michael sat between Paul and Bernard. Like Colin, Rodney thought it would be a lucky man who could get past those two watchdogs.

The evening went very well. Colin was on his best behaviour, very aware that Anne hadn't called him for a whole week. Rodney got on very well with everyone, the red garden was a good talking point, like travel adventures, but, unlike Colin, he at times drew people into conversation. He also noted that Michael drank only champagne from a special glass, and that no staff member walked behind him. Rodney was also aware of the fact that the way Dr Colin Campbell looked at Michael gave his game away completely.

Colin found Rodney attractive, but was not at all happy when he saw that Michael preferred Rodney's company to his own. Owing to the seating arrangements, Rodney paid little attention to Colin, but, with Paul in front of him, could see why Michael loved him. The little green dragon of envy began to gnaw, although he disguised it perfectly. Now that the red garden was established, Rodney often dropped in after closing, with a few red-flowering plants he had found here and there, leaving them with Mr Barnes or – more hopefully – with Michael, together with instructions for their planting.

At Michael's christening party, Anne had spoken to Constable Timms. She had found out, via Sergeant Reynolds, that he had been in the mounted police division in Melbourne before being transferred to Brunswick. Anne offered Constable Timms the use of her horses whenever he wanted to ride and said that, since she was planning to teach Michael to ride, any help he could provide would be most gratefully accepted, as well as his company. He had blushed and said that he would have telephoned when he had some free time.

Anne said to Michael, "Darling, we have a new friend to go riding with on Tuesday morning". "Who is it?" asked Lorna, very surprised that Anne should share Michael's company with anyone else under any circumstances. "Constable Timms. You remember him from Michael's luncheon party, don't you?" "Yes, I do. He was in the mounted police once", said Lorna. "Exactly! He'll be nice company for us, won't he, Michael?" "Yes", he replied, looking at Anne. Both Rodney and Colin had the feeling that they had been out-foxed somehow or other, and who was this Constable Timms anyway?

The weekend passed smoothly, with Stephen enjoying every moment. On Sunday, they all went to mass and back to an extravagant luncheon. Later on, as Mary was clearing away afternoon tea, she found Bernard and Lorna together and took the opportunity of speaking to them both. She began, "In the past, you have both been very kind and generous to me". Lorna's heart fell. "Don't tell me she wants to leave", she thought. Mary continued, "I appreciate all the free time I have had up to now, but it's the Wednesday afternoons when I go to art classes at Brunswick. I should like your permission to change arrangements". "Certainly", said Bernard. "Whatever you want, Mary!" "I want to use Wednesday afternoons and whenever else I'm free to teach Michael to draw and paint. I know he can do it! Obviously, he needs someone to show him how, but I'm convinced I can!" she said a little breathlessly. "You saw the shell he drew for Judge Spender. I thought it was quite good for a first attempt and I know he found it very satisfying, as – I must confess – did I." She stood as though this speech had taken up all her energy and she was now awaiting their verdict. It was Bernard who spoke first.

"Two things, Mary: first, for Lorna and me, the idea's marvellous, but you must speak with Paul about it. Secondly, where do you buy your supplies?" "At the Brunswick Art & Colour Centre, why?" "Because", continued Bernard, "we shall open an account there for you there. I mean *your* supplies and Michael's will be paid for by me. That's the deal!" "Oh, Judge Mahoney! He would only use such a small amount, and over the years I have built up quite a stock!" "No, Mary, I've told you the only thing I can agree to." Thank you, then. I accept!" It was now Lorna's turn. "If you ever need special time off in connection with this venture, don't hesitate to ask! Remember, Mrs Barnes is here, so we won't be without help. By the way, Paul told us about the shells not having numbers!" and she smiled. "When Paul has a moment, ask him to go with you to the ballroom, where there's a large army box with rope handles that's absolutely full of shells. Don't ask me how it got there! Perhaps Bernard's grandmother added them to her collection of bric-a-brac at Killarney. If they're any use at all, they're yours!" "Thank you so much!" said Mary. "I'll go and ask Paul at once!" With the crockery rattling on the large silver tray, she scuttled down the corridor to the kitchen.

"I think this calls for a large Christmas or birthday bonus. What do you think?" said Bernard. "Absolutely!" said Lorna. "She looks so happy, now that she's at last got her wish, her very own student!"

After tidying up in the kitchen, Mary noticed from the window Stephen, Paul and Michael returning. As it was almost six o'clock, it was nearly time for drinks, as Anne would soon be here and would expect to see the champagne bucket in place, with a chilled bottle bobbing in the ice. Mary went to the blue sitting room to prepare, and on her way back to the kitchen encountered Paul about to go upstairs to change. "May I have a quick word with you?" she asked, and she explained what she wanted to do with Michael. Paul gave her a hug. "Mary! That's wonderful! You must let me pay for any costs." "There are no costs. Judge Mahoney has seen to it! I just need your permission." "Mary, Michael loves you, and he was so proud of his painting, and I must say it was very good! Perhaps you can fit another student in?" "Whenever you want!" Mary beamed and disappeared into the kitchen to get the tray of glasses for the sitting room. She found Mrs Barnes peeling potatoes.

"They're all so wonderful, aren't they?" said Mary. "If you say so, dear!" and Mrs Barnes went on with her potatoes.

On Monday morning, Bernard found he had run out of paper for his printer, and since Michael was busy planting half a box of zinnias in the red garden, Paul and Bernard dashed into Brunswick. Bernard left Paul and went to open an account for Mary at her art shop and on to get the paper for his printer.

Paul went over to Mulberry's. He had heard so much about it, and had met them all at Anne's luncheon, but he was curious to see the establishment itself. As he entered, Ernest looked up from his pulpit and nimbly sped to the door. "Mr Moran! What an honour! How kind of you to call upon our humble store!" There she goes again!" came a crack from behind. "Eat your heart out, Joan Crawford!" Ernest spun round to face the smugly smiling staff. "Be quiet, you faded parrots!"

Paul pretended he hadn't heard anything, but at once recognised Neville's sarcastic tone. "I should like to buy a jumper for Michael." "Oh, anything! Mr Moran. What kind of jumper have you in mind?" "Something for early autumn, if it's not too early to purchase one." "Not at all! Our autumn range is here. It's already early autumn. Samuel, come and help me open the box that arrived with the knitwear! It's in the storeroom. Do please excuse me a moment, Mr Moran!" and he and Samuel rushed to the storeroom. Paul thought he'd fight fire with fire and walked directly over to Sean and Neville and shook hands. "When are you thinking of having an exhibition?" he asked Neville, who was quite taken aback by this frontal approach. "I don't know!" he said, regaining his stance. "The Brunswick *beau monde* are probably not ready for me!" "Come on!" said Paul. "Mary tells me your work is of very high quality and very sensitive!" "She's very kind", Neville replied. They spoke about painting and the fact that Mary was going to give lessons to Michael. "I must join the class", Neville said, smiling. "It's sure to be better than anything this one-horse-town can provide!" They were interrupted by Ernest's return with three plastic bags, each containing a jumper. "These are all Michael's size", he said. "There is, as you can see, no great choice, but these are the best quality available." One was cream, one a mauvey-blue, and one black. "Michael has a black one", Paul said, and then, turning to Neville, "Which do you think would suit Michael best?" "Oh, the cream one, without doubt. He's so dark, it would make a wonderful contrast. Besides, I'm sure Mrs Rochester will buy him the blue one!" He smiled. "Thanks!" said Paul. "The cream one it is!" It was a heavy cable design, but weight-wise was very light. Paul pulled out his credit card. "Oh no, Mr Moran! We'll send the account to Killarney!" "But if you do that, Judge Mahoney will pay it. I wish to pay for it. It's a gift for Michael." "Lucky him!" said Sean. "Don't let that enter your head! I'll open a new account in your name at once and address it to you at Killarney. How does that sound?" "Perfect, thank you!" "Now", said Ernest, "I must ask you a small favour!" "Anything!" came the reply. "That's dangerous!" said a voice from somewhere behind. Ernest shot a dagger-like glance at Neville. "We need your measurements, since poor Mrs Rochester wished to buy you a shirt the other day, and no one knew your size. Just let me get my book…right! A new page", and he wrote down 'Mr Paul Moran'. "Samuel, get the tape!" Paul was measured from head to toe by Samuel and Neville. "That's a very large chest measurement. I think we'll have to have some items made, but a week's wait is no problem at all!" With that, Paul said goodbye and told Neville he would expect an invitation to his opening.

"Well, Tarzan, that's your competition. Not just a great body, but a brain as well! Don't worry! You win some, you lose some… and remember, Dr Campbell is really hot for you!" For once, Samuel did not reply with an expletory, but just took the other two jumpers back to the storeroom, feeling totally dejected.

Paul walked across the street to Bernard's car. Lorna had been right when she described Mulberry's as a nest of vipers.

That afternoon they went for a swim at Bellevue and stayed for dinner, and all too soon Tuesday morning arrived. Very early, while Michael was still in bed, Paul gave him the jumper he had bought for him. He put it on at once and, just having woken up and with nothing else on, Paul decided that the effect was spectacular. After much laughing and twenty minutes of lovemaking, they showered, shaved and dressed, and then joined Lorna, Bernard and Stephen for breakfast. Michael only wore a pair of jeans and Paul's new jumper, without a shirt, creating a really beautiful effect, Stephen thought, his hair now completely grown back into two wings on either side and a wide sweep on top, down to the thick mane at the back of his neck. His enormous cobalt-blue eyes completed the look. Paul was convinced he was the luckiest man in the world, something that no one at the breakfast table would have cared to dispute.

Michael and Lorna waved the others off, Stephen clutching a small mounted painting of a mussel shell in his left hand. "Come on, darling. I have to get you to Anne's. You're going riding with Constable Timms this morning. Go and get changed and I'll get the bag of apples and carrots from Mary. We can't keep Polly waiting, can we?" It all helped to defuse the moment of Paul and Bernard's departure, and was the only moment in the whole week when Lorna felt really sorry for Michael. As a rule, he was happy and full of energy, kissing everyone and having a good time, but Tuesday mornings seemed to steam-roller him, and it took both Lorna and Mary quite a bit of inventiveness to get him over this sad leave-taking.

They pulled up in Anne's stable yard and Michael hopped out. "Here's the bag of fruit, darling", Lorna said, without getting out of the car herself. Anne arrived from the house and came up to the car. "Good morning", said Lorna. "What time shall I pick him up?" "Oh, don't worry, Lorna. I'll drop him off when we've finished. If he gets on with Constable Timms, perhaps he'll stay for a drink. In any case, he'll be home for lunch." "Do come for lunch, Anne! Mary told Michael this morning that she was cooking something special. I've no idea what it is, but do come and try the mystery dish!" "I'd love to", said Anne. With that, Lorna left, crossing an incoming Constable Timms in his dark-blue Range Rover, as she swept out of the drive.

"How delightful to see you!" cooed Anne. "The horses are ready and saddled." "Good morning, Mrs Rochester. This is very kind of you. It's the first time I've been in the saddle for months! Good morning, Michael!" "Good morning", came the reply. Michael wasn't sure what to call him, and 'Constable' seemed a strange name. Anne instinctively knew that names were a problem for him, so she said to Constable Timms, "Since we three are hopefully going to be together a lot, let's use first names. Mine's Anne, and Michael you know. What's your first name? "Patrick", he answered. "Very well, Patrick, let's be off!" He watched Michael mount and said to him, "Keep your leg straight until you swing it over the saddle!" Michael just looked at him and smiled. He felt absolutely safe with Patrick, this good-looking, dark-skinned man with black eyes, and every little piece of dressage information he gave Michael was stored neatly in Michael's mind. Polly was quite happy with a horse either side of her and moved off with Michael patting her and talking to her. The others followed. "Can you get every Tuesday morning off?" asked Anne. "I think so", replied Patrick. "Why is Tuesday morning so important?" Out of earshot, Anne explained that it was very difficult for Michael when Bernard and Paul left for the city and he was left at Killarney. Patrick understood and smiled, "I think we can organise it regularly, and if there's a problem, I'll send Sergeant Reynolds to talk to you!" He laughed, and it was the first time that Anne had seen him laugh, since he was usually so serious and – to her way of thinking – sad. Today, however, he was a different person. He caught up with Michael and the three of them trotted together to the lake at the bottom of Anne's property, where Killarney joined onto Bellevue, giving both estates private access to the lake.

The morning passed very quickly, with Michael chatting to Patrick, who in turn told him all kinds of stories about the mounted police. Michael was fascinated, and Anne was pleased to note that Patrick didn't speak down to him, but conversed normally, although with probably more humour than he was wont to use. She also noticed that he kept his eye on Michael the whole time. "Oh dear!" she thought. "I hope it's all about riding hints!" But she knew that Patrick was really enjoying Michael's company. "Oh well!" she sighed to herself. "Another man for dinner, I suppose!"

During lunch at Killarney, Michael told Lorna that Patrick had been a horse policeman, but then got muddled about what police and horses had in common, and so dropped the conversation. "He's an excellent rider", said Anne, "but I wonder what on earth a trained mounted policeman is doing here in a backwater like Brunswick!" "Is he a married man?" asked Lorna. "He's a man of mystery. I shall have to check with Mulberry's. They'll know!" "Oh, Anne! They're such gossips. They're just terrible!" "Still, they're the only ones that know everything!" Anne didn't finish the conversation, owing to the sound of a dreadful crash. They all rushed to where the sound had come from. "Don't open the door!" cried a workman, who was halfway down the staircase. "I think the whole ceiling has collapsed in your yellow room!" Michael went out onto the veranda and peered through the window. The room was filled with pale grey dust, and where once there had been a stained ceiling there was now a huge black expanse. "Where's Nigel when you need him?" sighed Lorna. "Come on, let's finish lunch! There's nothing we can do." "The dust, Miss Lorna! The dust!" wailed Mary. "Why can't they be more careful?" "I feel this is going to be the pattern, until work at Killarney is complete!"

Mary had forgotten to ask Paul to help her find the box with the shells amongst the stored furniture in the ballroom, so she sought Michael's help. After twenty minutes of climbing over and under furniture, they found the right box and opened it up. "Oh, Mary! There are lots of shells! This one is orange and this one is pink inside!" Their colours fascinated Michael. When they hauled the box out of the ballroom and into the corridor, he noted the very narrow stairs that led to above the supper room at the end of the ballroom. "Would you like to have a look up there, Michael?" "Yes please, Mary!" So up they went. Mary had not been into this part of the house for years. It had been closed since before she came to Killarney; she seemed to remember someone saying it had been closed twenty years before that. The first room had two iron bedsteads, a wardrobe and a dressing table. The next was very tiny, with only a narrow iron bed and nothing else. The third was the largest and housed seven large crates, some taller than others, through the open sides of which could be seen the chandeliers that Bernard's grandmother had bought in the 'thirties. Michael knelt down to gaze through the wooden slats. "Michael! You'll get all dirty! It's so dusty up here!" But Michael was not to be deterred. He slid his fingers in through the slats and touched the crystals, at which the free-hanging ones clinked together. "Mary", he said, looking at another one. "Just a minute! If you want to have a proper look, I'll open the blinds!" As one of them shot up, the room was filled with tired yellow light. "Mary! It's red! It's red, this one!" "Really?" said Mary, and bent down to have a look. "So it is! I thought they were all just plain crystal. It's very pretty, but it's also very big!" He went from one crate to the other. The last was the tallest, covered with a torn piece of sheet. Michael lifted one side and said, "Mary, this one is black!" "It can't be black! I've never heard of a black chandelier! Take the sheet right off and I'll pull up the blind on the other side so we can see clearly." A whining sound was heard as the blind wound upwards. "Oh! It's green, not black! It's green and it's got big wine glasses on it with flowers and gold lines!" Mary, as curious as Michael, got down on her hands and knees. "Oh, it's got storm shades. They used to put candles inside those glass shades so that when there was a draught, they wouldn't blow out. Isn't that clever?" "Yes, I think so!" but he couldn't understand how the candles got inside the shades. Very complicated, he thought, but very pretty.

"Put the sheet back while I close the blinds", said Mary. Easier said than done. She had to enlist Michael's help and with the aid of a chair they managed to seize the cord and draw the blind down again. The room reverted to the dingy grey light that had kept it company for nigh on fifty years.

They descended the very narrow staircase to the corridor and between them carried the rope-handled box through the kitchen and across to Mary's studio, just as Nigel arrived after receiving a sharp call from Lorna to try and solve the problem of the deserted yellow drawing room filled with the finest dust and without a ceiling. "Oh, well! The light fixture was too small, anyway!" he said, and changed the subject to the decoration of the dining room. "At this rate, Nigel, we'll all have to return to the city while you finish this work. It's getting more and more difficult!" "Don't worry", said Nigel, in his driest tone, without moving either head or lips. "It can't get any worse!"

Next morning, Anne paid a visit to Mulberry's on the pretext of buying a jumper for Michael. As she entered, Ernest sped over from his pulpit to receive her outstretched hand. "Dear Ernest, how are you?" "Oh, so much better now that you're here!" he replied. "We have had one of those mornings. Some of the people who live here should really try another store. They're just not the sort of customer we need and they argue so about style and price! Oh, it's simply too much in this hot weather! I wonder when autumn will finally make an appearance." "It's on that point that I'm here. I should like a jumper for Michael." The staff stood back and, for once, there was no wisecrack from behind. "I have just the thing! Mr Moran purchased a cream one, but I personally thought the blue-mauve suited Michael's colouring much better. I'll just go and get it." "Ernest, before you do that, could I just borrow Neville for a moment? I should like his opinion on something in Nigel's shop." "Certainly, Mrs Rochester. Do go along, Neville!" said Ernest, as one would speak to a child. "Waall, thank ya, ma'm!" Neville trilled in a most convincing southern accent, and together with Anne went three doors down to Nigel's shop. She must want something, he thought, and not just advice about something in the shop window. He was quite right. "Darling", she purred, "what do you think of that gilt table with the shamrocks?" "How odd!" he exclaimed, "you're the second person to speak to me about it today!" "Really?" She was genuinely surprised. "Who was the other interested party?" "A certain Mrs Gladys Stoup." Anne, assuming she was also interested in purchasing the side table, asked Neville where Mrs Stoup lived, since she had never heard her name before. "Oh", replied Neville, "under a rock somewhere!" "Neville! You are naughty!" Neville accepted this as a compliment and continued, "She was a maid at Killarney fifty years or so ago." "Good heavens, however old can she be?" "Oh, about two hundred, I should think." With that, Anne started to laugh. "She said that the table was once one of a pair." "It is. Nigel is having it repaired." Anyway", he went on, the pair had large pier mirrors and stood between the windows in the Irish room at Killarney." "I don't think there is an Irish room at Killarney. I've never seen it. Perhaps they destroyed it when they cut up part of it for staff quarters. I don't know." Neville continued, "She said that the ceiling decoration was the same as the side tables and the ceiling rose, and that the two mirrors had swags of shamrocks. It must once have been quite a sight. I believe Nigel is now doing some serious work at Killarney. Pity about the ceiling in the yellow drawing room, though." "You don't miss a trick, do you darling?" Anne said. "On that point, what can you tell me about Constable Timms?" "Well, now! Two must be your number today. You're the second person to speak about the tables and the second to ask me about Constable Timms." Anne didn't say a word, but her glance was sufficient for him to tell her who it was. "Our dear Dr Campbell", he said in a slightly sarcastic tone. "He wanted to know who he was. You know, all Brunswick is talking about you and Michael riding every morning with a police escort!" "Oh, but that's ridiculous! Patrick just enjoys riding with us, and since he is exercising one of my horses, it works all well for all concerned!"

"Now, who can he be escorting?" said Neville mischievously. Anne ignored the comment, knowing very well what he was angling for. "I don't know anything about our mysterious Constable Timms, except that he used to belong to the mounted police. Why he's now in this backwater, heaven alone knows! He has an apartment on Anderson Street, but he's never been seen at any of the haunts, if that's what you want to know. He's a very solitary figure. The only time he appears to be happy, according to the office girl at the police station, is when he returns from riding on a Tuesday morning. Funny that!" he said, raising his eyebrows. "But, believe me, if I find out anything, you'll be the first to know, and not our Dr Campbell, who still appears to be playing cat-and-mouse with Samuel, although we all know that Samuel has eyes for one person only, don't we?" Again, she ignored the very pointed comment. He continued, "Have you met Mrs Campbell?" "No, Neville dear, I haven't", said Anne, suddenly realising that Neville was trying to pick *her* brains. "Darling, do tell Ernest to send the jumper to Killarney. I must pop in here and get them to hold these tables. I'm sure Bernard will be very interested." "But you haven't seen the jumper!" he said. "Oh darling!" she purred. "if it comes from Mulberry's, it must be good!" With that, she opened the door of the air-conditioned shop, and began talking to the shop assistant.

Neville walked back to Mulberry's. "So not even our elegant Mrs Rochester knows much about Patrick Timms!" he thought. "I wonder whether she is interested in him for herself, or is our Patrick interested in Michael? I wonder!" He shut the door behind him and relayed the instructions about the jumper to Ernest, who was most impressed by her comment that everything at Mulberry's was good.

Most mornings after riding – though not all: it depended on Anne's plans – Michael found time to visit the red garden and potter about with Mr Barnes. He was most interested to know what a red zinnia looked like. The previous week, Rodney had left a box with nine of them, but had cut their heads off so that they would produce better flowers, although it was rather late in the season for them to do well. Mr Barnes had been instructed to fertilise them and, within a week, three plants had started to develop buds. "They're very slow", he said to Mr Barnes, "even though you gave them all that food!" He shook his head and his black mane moved from side to side. "I have to go to Mary for lessons to paint shells", he continued. "When I've finished some, I'll give you one." "Thank you very much", came the reply. Michael crossed the lawn, touched the tall goose on its bill, looked at the other and then exited in the direction of Mary's studio.

She began as she had with the first mussel shell. She picked out one whose shape was not too complicated, and they started. She sat beside him, showing him every move on her sheet and teaching him first to look at the shell and then, if he couldn't quite understand, to look at her drawing of the same object. It was slow work, but as he got used to using a pencil and then paint, he grew more skilful and the quality of his production little by little improved. Mary was absolutely gratified. They chatted about all manner of things during these two to three hours, and she noted that he now had no problem with conversation at all. When he felt safe and he liked the people he was talking to, he responded well; when unsure, he remained completely silent.

Anne and Colin were having dinner at Belleville, when Mrs Robbins interrupted, saying that Mr Moran was on the phone. "Excuse me, Colin, just for a moment. This is important!" Anne said, and then, "Hello, darling! Yes, yes, yes!" That was all Colin heard, but Paul was actually explaining to Anne that he had been to the storage depot and was now on his way to join Bernard, Stephen and Amos for dinner at the club. All the items on her check list matched those indicated by the depot, and a delivery van or two – "or two!", Colin heard her exclaim – would be at Bellevue on Friday, bringing an enormous amount of stuff. "Oh well! Thank you darling! I'll see you on Thursday evening. Thanks again! Give my love to the boys at the club! Goodnight!"

She returned to the table. "Sorry, Colin. Two delivery vans! What am I to do with all this furniture? Oh, I shall have to see Nigel tomorrow! Oh bother! Why did they have to close the depot? Colin, do be a darling and open the other bottle. . . Oh, what a nuisance all this is! I suppose all the furniture will have to go into the ballroom. This place is going to end up looking like Killarney!" "Well, at least your ceilings are intact!" Colin said; Anne laughed, "How the word spreads!" and she told him the story about the two tables at Nigel's that had originally come from Killarney. "Now, isn't that strange?" she said.

After hearing from Anne the story of the tables from the Irish room at Killarney and that she had them on hold at Nigel's, Lorna fought her way into the ballroom to see if there were a pair of pier mirrors amongst all the things stored there. After half an hour's pushing and shoving, she thought she saw something in behind a much larger over-mantle mirror. She retreated upstairs and enlisted the help of two of the workmen to move the big mirror: there they were, two gilt pier mirrors, whose sole decoration were swags and swags of shamrocks! "Pull the two tall mirrors out, please and put the large one back. Now put them back on top. Thank you so much!" She heard one of the workmen remark as he was halfway up the stairs, "Have you ever seen so much junk!"

Lorna then phoned Nigel to say she would have the tables, since they originally came from Killarney. In his deep matter-of-fact voice, he asked her whether she was quite sure of that. "Yes!" she replied and told him she had the mirrors that went on top of them. He told her he was coming over to check the work in the late afternoon, and would have a look. Lorna then began looking over the ground floor for what could once have been the Irish room. The only one it could be was the blue sitting room. They must have stripped all the decorative plaster off, or perhaps it collapsed as it did in the yellow room. Who knows, she thought. I wonder what it looked like originally. It must have been quite grand to have had its furniture and ceiling made specially for it.

When she spoke to Bernard about it, he said it was a complete mystery to him. He had never heard any mention of an Irish room, even when he was young. Perhaps it was the blue sitting room: he just didn't know. He was waiting for Paul.

Paul arrived late at the club on Wednesday evening. "I'm sorry I'm late, Bernard, but it's chaos at that furniture depot. They want everyone to take their furniture by the end of the month, and that's only ten days away. Anyway, Anne's things will be off to Bellevue on Friday morning. I don't know where she will put it all, since there's just so much of it! Some are quite nice pieces, too!" "Come on! I'll sign you in", said Bernard. They went into the main lounge and sat with Amos and Stephen. "Drinks, gentlemen?" asked Henry O'Connor. "Yes thanks!" said Bernard, and they gave their order. Stephen said to Amos, "Amos, you're an admiral. Have you got any shells?" "What do you mean 'shells'! I've got one of the finest collections in Melbourne, if not Australia! They've been a passion of mine for years! Oh, come and join us!" This last was addressed to a passer-by. If Amos Watson was six feet two, Major David Keen was just the opposite. On parade, he always stood on a podium, or if that wasn't available, even a box. He was exactly five foot high in his shoes, and was also very rotund. He, Amos, Stephen and Bernard had all been at school together, and had never lost touch. Whenever they got together, it was just like it had been at school: the jokes and gentle jibes never stopped. They accepted Paul as a complete, though younger, equal, not necessarily because he was with Bernard, but because they felt he was one of them. "I've been telling this motley group, Major, that I have the finest collection of shells in Australia. Isn't that so? said Amos. "It certainly is!" David Keen growled back in his deep husky voice. "It's going to cause my divorce, I just know it!" Amos said. "What's the problem?" asked Paul innocently, giving rise to a great deal of raucous laughter from the others. It was Stephen who enlightened Paul. "There are more shells than there is room in the house! They're everywhere! His wife keeps threatening to parcel the lot up and drop them off the pier at St Kilda!" More laughter. "But, on a more serious note. . ." He was interrupted as Henry O'Connor came up to say that their table was ready. As President of Brown's, Stephen had made a lot of changes over his ten-year tenure, having been elected unanimously every three years. He had put the club's finances in order and had worked miracles with the kitchen and wine cellar. The first thing he had done was to fire the then steward and employ Henry O'Connor, which was a brilliant move, as all members agreed. He was efficient and always ready to solve any problem without a fuss. In ten years, the building had been systematically renovated from roof to cellar, and was now top notch.

As they were seating themselves, Bernard said, "As I was saying, Amos, you must have quite a lot of doubles of those shells. Why don't you box some up and send them for Michael to paint? A few exotic ones!" "When is Michael in town next, Paul" asked Amos. "I'd be pleased to show him my collection." "Thank you very much", said Paul, "I'm sure he'll be thrilled to see it!" Bernard went on to say that Mary had a book on shells, but was having a lot of trouble finding their names. She had decided that when the shell had been painted, she would window-mount the shell and cut a tiny, long rectangle in the mount below the shell where she would insert its Latin name in her fine hand.

"I say", said Amos. "Those two seem pretty professional". "Michael gave me his first painting", said Stephen. "I got it back from the framers today. In fact, it's in my bag. Just a minute!" and he struggled out of his comfortable dining chair while the others were finishing their first course and returned with the little guache painting in a small antique gilt frame.

"It's jolly good!" said Amos, being the first to inspect it. "He and Mary seem to have hit on a winning wicket!" "Very good indeed!" said Major David. "I couldn't draw a straight line at school! Absolutely hopeless at art! You weren't too bad, Bernard, if I remember! Yes, a bit of talent!" and he looked mischievously at Paul. "If I was bad, the other two were shocking! I remember Amos painted a footballer once, with fingers like bunches of bananas!" and David roared with laughter. "Michael Angelo Banana!" at which Amos also joined in the hilarity.

Paul was a good thirty years younger than the others, but no one took any notice of that. He was with them, and that was that! Some of their stories they recounted again and again. Paul felt he was being increasingly drawn into this select group, and enjoyed their company. The only company he craved for more was Michael's, but tonight was Wednesday and he would have to wait for tomorrow, for Killarney and Michael.

"You must come to Killarney", Bernard said to David and Amos. "You'll enjoy it. We're having a bit of a fight with renovation at the moment, but we'll get there, won't we Paul?" Paul smiled. Bernard always included him in everything and never excluded him, even from secrets. Paul belonged to him, as did Michael. Bernard loved them differently, but they were his.

"David!" "Yes, Bernard!" "You've been to Killarney before?" "Yes, Amos and I spent some summer vacations there years ago." "Do you remember an Irish room?" "Good heavens, Bernard!" David growled. ""What are you talking about? I can barely remember yesterday, let alone fifty years ago! No, not at all! What about you Amos?" "No, sorry! I remember the beautiful staircase and a yellow room off the entrance hall, and lots of corridors, but that's all, I'm afraid!" "I'm the same!" confessed Bernard, and related the story about the tables and the old woman who had once worked there, giving her description of this mysterious room.

Michael sat on the steps under the porte cochere, his head in his hands, waiting for the car that never seemed to arrive. From the shadows of the entrance hall, Lorna and Mary watched this beautiful, forlorn figure waiting for the two men who anchored his world to the world of reality. Mary whispered to Lorna, "He's just so special! He's beautiful, yes, but there's something else. Do you think he has an Irish background?" "No one knows. He was abandoned when he was about two years old, they think. No one knows anything else, except that on the end of the box that held him was written in texta colour "Michael", and that's all we know." "My grandmother", said Mary, "would have said he had that Irish magic. I never understood what she meant until I met Michael and started working with him, but now I can honestly say I understand perfectly what she meant!"

A crunch from the gravel behind the rhododendrons was the signal for joy, and Michael was on his feet and waving his hands as they pulled up. He kissed and hugged them both. Tonight he was very excited. "Paul", he said, "I love you!" Mary came forward with Lorna to help with the bags, finding a large lump in her throat.

Michael freed himself from Paul and said loudly, "Cooty! You must come! We have three zinnias and they're red! Oh, do come!" "Just a minute!" said Bernard and reached back into the car. He handed Mary two volumes of coloured photographs of hundreds and hundreds of shells, their Latin names written underneath. "Amos gave me the titles of the books and I got them from a dealer in town this morning. They're yours. I hope they help you and Michael. By the way, how's our artist getting along?"

Mary had cleared her throat. "He's coming along very well, thank you, sir", she said. "He's coming along very well thanks to his brilliant teacher", said Lorna. Paul leant over and gave Mary a kiss on the cheek. "Thank you so very much", he said. "When I say it's my pleasure, it's the absolute truth!" she replied.

"Cooty, Paul! Come and see! Come and see!" So, with Lorna between them, they headed off across the back lawn to the red garden to see the three flowering zinnias, guarded by two bronze Thai geese.

Next day, with Nigel, Bernard and Paul inspected the remains of the yellow room, which had been emptied of debris. "You're damned lucky this collapsed!" said Nigel. "Oh, are we!" said Bernard. "How do you work that out? Now I have to pay for a new ceiling!" "Look at the black beam, and the lighter one beside it. They are completely infested with dry rot and could have collapsed at any time, bringing two bathrooms down on top of you all. Tomorrow, the men will replace them and I will have the plasterers in next week to redo the ceiling with a better cornice and a bigger ceiling rose. I've no idea why, in such a grand house, some of the details are so skimpy!" "I have no idea either!" said Bernard, "but see if you can have it done as soon as possible!" Nigel said, "It seems, according to Lorna, that we've lost an Irish room. I personally don't think it could have been the blue sitting room, since the side tables are too big to go comfortably between the windows". "Oh well!" said Bernard. "A mystery it remains!"

On the following afternoon, Michael and Paul went for a swim at Anne's. At about four o'clock, two large removal vans were seen coming up the front drive. "Oh, Paul!" said Anne. "Can you believe it! Two of them!"

In a most orderly fashion, the removers spent the next hour and a half unloading and putting all the furniture in the ballroom. "I don't know where it's all come from!" wailed Anne. "And what the hell am I going to do with it?" Paul left the pool and put on his shirt. "I think Nigel has the only sensible idea", he said. "Finish Killarney, finish Bellevue, have a society auction with all the pieces you don't need, and then retire on the proceeds!" "That sounds feasible! Oh, let's have a drink! Mrs Robbins, will you prepare some drinks out here, please!" Paul said, "I'll go and get changed. He walked back to Michael and said that they had to get dressed. "Just two minutes more!" begged Michael, so Paul took off his shirt and dived in over Michael's head. Peals of Michael's deep laughter rang out. Paul swam up to him and gave him a kiss, which he returned affectionately. Watching from under the pergola with a glass of champagne in her hand, Anne thought, "Who cares about the furniture and the ballroom? These two are just perfect together!" Then another thought crossed her mind and she phoned Lorna on her mobile and said, "We're expecting you here for drinks, darling! Do come over with Bernard! There's enough, if I can convince everyone to stay for an informal meal. Don't you dare say no, darling!"

Michael and Paul changed with a few yells and bursts of laughter. Michael came over and asked Anne if he could take Paul to see Polly. "Of course, of course, darling", she said. On their return they were pleasantly surprised to see Bernard and Lorna sitting under the pergola, having a drink with Anne.

"Cooty! Lorna! Where did you come from?" asked Michael, coming over and giving each a kiss. "We flew over on the backs of the two geese", said Bernard, trying to keep a straight face. "Cooty! Those geese can't fly!" said Michael, and everyone laughed. "I suppose you can get used to a house being a furniture depot, can't you?" asked Anne. "Certainly", said Lorna. "Look at us, at Killarney. It's been like that for fifty years! But now, we're really going to get into it all and get it finished. Paul!" she said, looking at him. "I've got several blocks of apartments and I must get you to check the market to see which I should get rid of: the one with the best price at present, but which may not hold for the future." Paul was surprised. It had never crossed his mind that Lorna had investments. He had assumed that everything was Bernard's. "Of course, whenever you want!" "I'm going to sell one block and just sink all the money into Killarney. I spoke to Bernard the other day, and he's not quite convinced, but I am! If this is to be our family home from now on, it may just as well be comfortable and have everything in working order."

It was to become the family home. For Michael it was his only concept of a home. Whether he thought that everyone lived in houses like Killarney and Bellevue with staff is debatable. If he closed his eyes, he could just recall his years in an institution, but this image was slipping away from him day by day, now that his life was full from morning to evening. His drawing lessons with Mary were a great success. He was completely honest with himself. If he thought that his drawing or painting of a shell or shells was not good enough, he always pushed it to one side and began again. "He's too hard on himself!" Mary told

Paul. "Some of his first attempts do have a sketchy quality about them that's quite delightful, but he prefers the finished work to be as close as possible to the original." He was also learning how to use paint, how to mix it and achieve the right shade. His success in drawing and painting was, of course, one hundred percent due to Mary's patience and encouragement. He liked the work and he loved Mary, a combination that guaranteed perfect success

His plans were changed when Anne went back to Melbourne with Paul and Bernard to have some work done at the dentist's, but she had instructed Patrick Timms that he was to come and take Michael riding as usual on Tuesday morning. Lorna dropped him off and Patrick, who was already there, offered to drive Michael home afterwards. If Michael were asked about the lessons Patrick gave him in dressage, how to mount and sit comfortably, he remained silent, but the moment he saw Polly and the white flash that told him clearly which side to mount, all Patrick and Anne's lessons automatically returned in a wholly natural way.

Riding with Patrick was no problem for Michael, although this was the first time he had been on a horse without Anne present. He accepted people as he found them, and Patrick he had liked from the start and had fitted him mentally into his life, so he felt safe with him. Patrick was very quiet. He rarely spoke unless it was necessary for his work, but with Michael, he found conversation easy. Since Michael's laughter was infectious, they were soon laughing and talking about all sorts of topics. The subjects introduced by Patrick fascinated Michael, because they were completely different from the conversation he generally heard at Killarney or Bellevue. After an hour and a half, they returned to the stable yard where the stable hand took over. Michael had come prepared with his red hessian bag of apples and carrots, so after a good ride, Polly and the other horses got their reward. Patrick watched carefully as Michael stroked Polly and spoke to her. He felt he had become a part of Michael's life, a part that no one but he could share. Riding with Michael was something only Anne could be party to. For the rest, he felt that Michael was exclusively his for this hour and a half every week, and he was surprised how anxious he became as each Tuesday morning slowly approached. When he drove Michael back home, Michael took his hand and led him to see the red garden, which was odd, since he generally viewed the garden as something private, his and Bernard's own little world. Today, however, he was totally confident and held Patrick's hand as he guided him there.

Feeling Michael's strong warm hand, a thrill of intimacy swept through Patrick. They entered the first door and went through the corridor that led to the second. Patrick had heard about this garden, as had all Brunswick, but no one had ever seen it. Having no idea about it, he was totally unprepared for what he saw. It was a little magic world, where Michael was king. All the flowers showed their red faces, the fountain played in the centre and two life-size bronze geese were standing near it. Patrick had never seen anything like it: it was truly beautiful. "These are zinnias", Michael said, pointing at the seven plants Rodney had dropped off, which were finally flowering. "They're very nice!" He looked at Patrick. "It's beautiful, Michael. It's really beautiful!" said Patrick, and gazed about this enchanted garden, where the only sound was the splashing of the fountain. He thought to himself that Michael was an extremely magical person. He felt that if anyone hurt him or made life difficult for him, they would have Constable Timms to deal with first.

On arriving at the police station a quarter of an hour late, he apologised to Sergeant Reynolds, explaining that he had been invited to see the red garden at Killarney. "Whatever you do, don't tell my wife", said the sergeant, "or I'll never hear the end of it! This red garden seems to be something that she and half Brunswick are desperate to see!" He looked at Patrick and continued, "It seems, Constable, that you are a very privileged person!" He spoke slowly, and thought he detected a slight blush on Patrick's cheeks, but he wasn't sure. Patrick moved over to his desk, and started work.

CHAPTER SIX

A Nasty Incident &
Repercussions

CHAPTER 6

A Nasty Incident & Repercussions

So the weeks turned into months, and the hot summer weather gave way to a long and beautiful autumn. The trees began to change colour and the early Tuesday morning rides with Patrick and Anne now required jumper or coat.

It was a Thursday afternoon. The night before it had rained heavily, leaving large puddles and soft muddy sections of ground. Since it was early afternoon and Bernard and Paul were not expected home for another two or three hours, Michael thought he would take the red hessian sack with Maisy O'Brien's offerings for Polly to Bellevue. Anne was out riding by herself that same afternoon, taking the old sand road almost to the end, and was now on her way back. From the front gate of Killarney to the front gate of Bellevue, the walk was at the most 10 minutes. So Michael thought fit to walk down to Bellevue with Polly's apples and carrots. As he left the front gate, he wondered whether he should have put on a jumper, but the sun was shining, so he walked along the side of the road that was still in the full sun. In the distance was Anne with her horse, also making for Bellevue. Michael was almost at his destination when he heard a motorcycle approaching. It had just passed Anne, startling the horse. "Young fools!" she thought, and followed the motorcycle carrying two boys, a thin one driving and a fat one riding behind. They saw Michael and, when they reached him, stopped the machine, hopped off and walked over to him. Anne could see what was happening but was unaware that the person on foot was Michael. Her sixth sense, however, told her that the situation was not harmless, so she used her riding crop and dug in her heels to spur her mount into a gallop.

The thin boy was about nineteen and the fat one about Michael's age. "So you're the retard from Killarney!" spat out the fat youth. Michael froze. He clutched the red bag so tightly that his knuckles went white. Since he made no answer, the thin boy pushed him and Michael lost his balance and fell against the barbed wire fence, ripping his shirt sleeve and making him bleed. He fell sideways and crashed to the ground, hitting his forehead on a stone, which cut it open. Michael was terrified: it was all happening again. For fear of being hit, he cried aloud. At this point, Anne was on the spot and when she saw what had happened and who was on the ground, her defence system geared into full play. She leapt from her horse and went straight toward Michael, but the thin boy stood in front of him. Without a word, like a tiny dynamo, Anne struck the thin boy with all her might across his face with her riding crop. He screamed with pain and a bright red mark began to bleed near his nose. At this, the fat boy yelled "You bitch!" and moved to disarm Anne. As he approached her, she turned half around and then quickly spun back, balanced on her left leg and, with all the strength she could muster, drove the hard toe of her riding boot straight into his groin. She jumped back as he screamed with pain and sank to his knees in a puddle of muddy water. "She's ruined me! She's killed me!" he screamed. Anne glared at him. "Well, Raymond Kenworth", she yelled, "you'll pay dearly for this!" "Come on!" said the thin boy, wiping blood from his face. "Let's get out of here!" "I can't walk!" shouted the other. "Move, Kenworth", Anne screamed, "or I'll butt the *other* boot into your groin!"

The threat was sufficient. He ran, bent in half, and in a flash the motorcycle was heading in the direction of Brunswick. Anne immediately put her arms round Michael, who was still crying in his terror. "I didn't do anything bad!" he said, and kept repeating the phrase, tears mixed with blood running down his face. Leaving one arm around him, with her other Anne pulled her mobile phone from her pocket and called Sergeant Reynolds. Her voice was sharp and steely as she explained the situation. He told her that Patrick Timms must be nearby and that he would call him immediately by radio. Anne then called Colin's office and spoke to the receptionist. "I'm Anne Rochester and this is an emergency", she said. "Please put me through to Dr Campbell at once!" "Yes, Mrs Rochester", came the reply. In the background, Anne could hear an intercom calling for Dr Campbell. In a matter of seconds, he was on the phone. "Anne, what's wrong?" She explained what had happened and added, "Make sure you bring something for tetanus as well. He's bleeding, but I don't think the cut's too deep. For God's sake, get here quickly! I'm taking him to Killarney now!" Before she had time to warn Lorna, a police car came speeding up the road towards them. With a scream of brakes and gravel scattering everywhere, a very white-faced Constable Timms leapt from the car and in a moment held Michael in his strong arms. "I'll carry him to the car and take him to Killarney", he said, "while you bring your horse". "Anne!" cried Michael, "the bag with the apples!" "I'll get them!" she said. "You go with Patrick!" He helped Michael to his feet and then swept him up and carried him, muddy and wet, to the car. Michael cut a particularly sorry sight, the side of his face that had hit the stone covered with mud, as was his hair. Patrick felt clearly that what he held in his arms was the most special thing in his whole world. After settling Michael in the back seat, he put his foot on the accelerator and the police car sped through Killarney's gates, screeching to a halt beneath the porte cochere. Anne was just behind with her horse. "Lorna! Lorna!" she cried, "where are you?" Lorna was upstairs when she heard Anne's hysterical shout and rushed down to the front door, just in time to see, to her horror, Michael being carried in by Patrick.

"Oh, no!" cried Lorna. "What's happened?" Anne explained as they followed Patrick carrying a badly upset Michael to his bathroom upstairs. Lorna and Patrick took off Michael's clothes, leaving only his underpants, washed him down and dried him. He was still crying as Patrick carried him across the corridor to his bedroom and put him in bed. Lorna placed a towel under his cut arm so as not to mark the sheets. Patrick had never seen Michael like this before, terrified, repeating again and again "I didn't do anything bad". Patrick sat on the edge of the bed, holding Michael's hand, very aware of the beautiful, nearly naked boy he had carried across the corridor. Mary was greatly upset, threatening all sorts of punishment for the two boys, and settling finally on death!

A screech of brakes was again heard and Mary hurried downstairs to let Dr Campbell in. After Anne's call, the staff at the clinic had been amazed to see a white-faced Dr Campbell running down the corridor, grabbing all the things he needed from the dispensary and jumping into his car without changing his clothes. He drove as he had never driven before. "Michael! Michael!" he thought. "Oh God! Michael!" When Mary opened the door and told him where Michael's bedroom was, he took the stairs two at a time and burst into the room. Work on the renovations had stopped abruptly, and Nigel told the men that work was ended for the day, albeit an hour early. He stood back, watching the sad scene, and never in his life had he felt so angry and so vengeful. Colin approached the bed and immediately looked at the cuts on Michael's arm and forehead. Then he took his equipment out of his bag and said, "This won't hurt, Michael. It's just a tetanus shot. From the other side of the bed, Patrick turned Michael's head toward himself and held his hand just a little tighter. Colin cleaned the cuts and dressed them.

It was at this point that Mary heard a car, and wailed, "Oh! It's Judge Mahoney and Paul! Oh, goodness! What a terrible situation!"

Paul and Bernard had got away early and had encountered little traffic on the road. They were very surprised to see a police car, with its doors open, plus Colin's car, also open. Aware that something was very wrong, they alighted, leaving their car well behind Colin's. They ran up to the front door, getting there as Mary opened it. Lorna came running down the stairs. "Oh, Paul! Bernard! A terrible thing has happened! Michael has been attacked by two youths." Paul dropped his briefcase and ran, like Colin, taking the stairs two at a time. He rushed into the bedroom to see a bandaged Michael in bed, with Patrick on one side and Colin, who was just moving away. Paul rushed to the bed and kissed Michael, who began crying again, repeating that he hadn't done anything bad. Paul talked to him and calmed him down, although he still kept shaking. Through the doorway came Bernard. Patrick stood up so that Bernard could take his place. "Oh, Cooty!" began Michael. "It's all right now, darling. Paul and I are here." He looked over at Mary and said, "Prepare some drinks for everyone in the blue room. I want to speak to you all". His voice was like stone, with no expression at all. His coldness was frightening. In all the years she had worked for Bernard, Mary had never seen him like this, and neither had anyone else, including Lorna.

Bernard hugged Michael gently, telling Paul to stay with him. As he got up from the bed, Sergeant Reynolds came through the door. "How is he?" he asked and looked at Colin. "He's all right. He's just terrified, but he'll settle down shortly. Unless you want me to, I won't give him a sedative. He's with Paul now, and I think that's better than a sedative." Colin and Patrick looked enviously as Paul put his arms around Michael. "Let's go down", said Bernard, with no expression. His face had lost its colour, and it was difficult to know whether he was upset or angry. In a few moments, they would all realise that it was the latter, which was about to explode.

The little group sat in the blue room and Mary poured drinks. The policemen declined any alcohol while on duty and took coffee.

"It's all my fault!" said Lorna. "I wasn't watching. I should have been more careful! Oh, Bernard! What have I done?" "You haven't done anything", said Anne. "Do you know who these louts are?" asked Bernard. "Oh, yes! Oh, well, one of them." "Who is he?" asked Sergeant Reynolds. "Oh!" he said on hearing the name of Raymond Kenworth, "Was the other tall and thin?" "Yes", said Anne. "I know who he is", said Sergeant Reynolds. "Don't worry, Judge Mahoney, we'll deal with this immediately!" "Oh", said Anne, "you'll find that the tall one has a riding crop slash on the right side of his face, and that cowardly Kenworth hopefully has ruptured testicles from my riding boot!" Bernard stood up and crossed the room. He took Anne in his arms and hugged her. "Thank you, Anne! Thank you very much!" Everyone was very surprised at Bernard's action, especially Anne. "I think, Bernard, you should say thanks, not to me, but to Patrick and Colin." "Of course!" he said, "how stupid of me!" and he shook hands with them both. "Thanks for dashing over here so promptly, Colin. We all appreciate it!" He turned to Patrick. "Thank you, Constable! Your being on the spot probably helped Michael immensely, as he's very fond of you."

Colin had never seen Patrick as competition before, but realised that if he was henceforth one of the inner group at Killarney, so too was Patrick, and he wasn't sure that he liked the idea one little bit. Nigel excused himself and asked Bernard whether the men could go on working tomorrow. "Yes", said Bernard. "We must keep going as we did before. If Michael sees the same rhythm as usual, he'll recover much more quickly, wouldn't you say, Colin?" "Yes, of course!"

Anne said, "I must be getting home with that horse! I'm rather dirty from where I knelt down. Lorna, I'll call you tomorrow to see how everything is. Oh, Bernard! We have a common boundary fence about six yards long, and once upon a time there was a gate which has since been closed. If I send my men and you send Mr Barnes and his offside, we'll reopen the gateway, so in future there'll be no need for Michael ever to use the main road. When he comes to the stables, he can walk down to the back gate. It's only ten minutes!" "Certainly, Anne! It's a brilliant idea. Organise it as you see fit, and I'll cover any expenses." "They'll be no expenses to cover", she said. "I must be off. It's been a long afternoon! Goodbye!"

The police moved to the front door, with Nigel and Colin. Nigel went first, with his stiff, angular walk, got into his car and left. Colin did likewise. "I suppose the whole of Brunswick is going to know about this via the Mulberry broadcasting system!" said Lorna. "There's no doubt about that at all!" said Patrick, and Lorna gave him a hug. "Thank you so much for carrying Michael and helping me clean him up. I'm sure he'll be ready for his Tuesday ride with you!" "Thank you very much, Mrs Mahoney!" and he blushed. "Thank you!"

As the police cars left, and only Bernard's car remained, Lorna took Bernard's arm. "I'm so worried about how Michael is going to get over this terrible experience", she said, and they went indoors.

Michael said he wouldn't come down for dinner, so Mary took him a tray and he ate alone. He had a vacant look in his beautiful blue eyes that Paul was very concerned about.

The others discussed the matter over dinner and were not alone in doing so. It was being discussed by every dining table in Brunswick and Morton. As Patrick had predicted, the wires ran hot from an irate staff at Mulberry's. "I can't believe it! What should we do?" cried Ernest, on learning about it, just on closing time. "It's simply shocking! A wonderful, innocent boy attacked in broad daylight, while going to feed his horse! Oh, it makes my blood boil! Thrown to the ground by those hoodlums! Raymond Kenworth! Well!" he went on, "I'm not surprised with parents like that! I always said he was sneaky!" "I wouldn't kick him in the balls", said an irate Samuel. "I'd take a knife and castrate him personally, the fat bastard!" The conversation heated up and the threats to the two hoodlums became quite nasty. "I think", said Sean, "that since they threw him to the ground and ripped his shirt, it's probably covered with blood". The theatrical attitude of the staff did not help settle the issue, but inflamed it instead. "Why don't we at Mulberry's make a public stand on this and send him a nice new shirt?" Oh, yes, yes!" cried Ernest. "We shall be the very first to show our outrage and distress at this barbarous attack on our favourite customer! Which shirt should we send?" Neville entered the fray. So far he had said very little, but with an icy, crisp voice, he stated that that fucking Raymond Kenworth would pay dearly for this. He went on to say that there was a Dior shirt that someone had ordered, but the size had been wrong, and it happened to be Michael's size. It was white, with a very fine red stripe, barely a thread. "Oh, and it will go so well with the ruby cufflinks. Do get it and pack it up at once. I shall write a card: 'You have our deepest concern and we wish you a swift recovery, from Mulberry's' "'and staff'" the three of them chorused! "Of course! Of course!" Ernest flustered. "Call that courier girl. It must get there tonight!"

So while they were having dinner at Killarney, Mary brought in a large Mulberry bag containing the shirt and the flowery but genuine thoughts of Mulberry's and its staff. Paul said he would take it up to Michael later, and thought the gift extremely kind, as they all did. Paul said he would call and thank them the next day.

Paul went to bed early, and it was a very quiet Michael who laid his head on Paul's chest and held him very tightly until he eventually dropped off to sleep.

Next morning, Rodney, who had heard what had happened from Samuel, delivered a big pot of burgundy-coloured chrysanthemums, saying how sorry he was. As the morning progressed, Mary was several times called to the door to take delivery of pots of red flowers, accompanied by kind, concerned messages written on little cards. Maisy O'Brien also sent a pot of burgundy-coloured chrysanthemums, like Rodney's, with a card saying simply "I love you – Maisy". Lorna said to Paul, "I don't see how Michael could possibly know so many people! There are so many pots of flowers on the veranda!"

That evening, Anne and Colin came to dinner, but again Michael declined to come down for the meal. Just as they were seated at table and the wine was poured, Colin looked at Paul and said, "You realise that Michael has been very lucky. Had he fallen straight and struck the stone head-on so to speak, he could have been killed". There was absolute silence. Paul just looked at Colin and then turned to Bernard. It had never crossed his mind. Coming on top of the shock, the news made him burst into tears. He couldn't imagine life without Michael. He lifted his napkin and covered his eyes. Bernard got up and sat in Michael's place, putting his arms around Paul's shoulder in an attempt to console him. Lorna stood up and quitted the room, leaving Anne and Colin in the midst of a very emotional situation. Lorna rushed upstairs and into Michael's bedroom. "Get dressed quickly!" she said. He looked at her surprised, since she had never spoken to him in this manner. Using his terminology, she said, "Darling, Paul is very bad!" He leapt out of bed with nothing on and climbed into a pair of underpants. Lorna handed him his blue trousers. "No shirt, Michael, just your new jumper that Paul got for you!" As he put on his socks and shoes, she took the jumper out of the chest of drawers for him to put on. "Hurry, darling! He's in the dining room!" Michael bounded into the dining room to see Paul drying his eyes. He went straight to him and put his arms around him. "Paul, don't feel bad! Paul, I love you!" he said, and they hugged each other. "Mary", said Lorna. "Michael will eat with us this evening. Will you arrange it please?" "Certainly! At once", said Mary, smiling. She had been much concerned that Michael might have retreated into a world that would cut them all off from him, but Lorna's quick thinking had saved the day.

It was much later, when alone with Lorna, that Colin remarked, "That was very quick thinking this evening!" She turned and looked at him,

"When you have a family, these things become automatic. The only thing you think of is how to save everyone from hurt and distress, and if you love them, you'll do anything! Look how Anne saved the day with those two thugs. She must be half their size, yet when it was necessary to save Michael, she lashed out and attacked both of them!" "Yes, she was particularly brave", he replied.

From that point on, Michael was exactly as he had been before, except for an adhesive strip on his arm and another on his forehead. The shock of seeing Paul in tears had cancelled his own fear, and his rationale told him that if Paul was now better, so was he.

The gate between the properties was working again, and Bernard had an automatic opening system installed for the front gates, so they were ordinarily always closed, and not open as before.

On leaving Killarney, the police had gone straight back to the station. Sergeant Reynolds said to Patrick, "I'll handle this situation rather than you. You're too involved and I don't want any more problems, although I probably agree with you that a good thrashing would not be amiss." He left Patrick and made his way to 15 Birdwood Drive.

The Kenworth home on Birdwood Drive was the most pretentious house in the street, without even a modicum of good taste. It was a low suburban brick-faced building straddling two blocks of land, and had a semicircular drive with an entrance and an exit. Architecturally, it was a mish-mash of Tudor trim with Georgian columns and aluminium windows. The red clinker bricks and double garage in matching red finished it off. It had been designed by Beryl's husband, Eric, and was his pride and joy. Beryl's pride and joy, on the other hand, was her front garden: she believed people came from miles around to see her display of bedding begonias, so the front fence and gates were less than three feet high to let everyone see her handiwork. The begonias were planted to a chequerboard design using red, pink and white plants, with a standard rose in the centre of one of the same colours. All in all, as Rodney remarked, the whole scheme was hideous and in the worst possible taste. Sergeant Reynolds drove past rows of red, pink and white begonias up to the 'Georgian' front door. He pressed the bell, and a jaunty jingle could be heard from inside. It was Beryl herself who swept the door opened, most surprised to see the police officer. "May I come in?" he asked, without any expression at all. "Certainly!" she said, and let him into a narrow hall with a fake console and mirror on one side and a wooden display shelf directly opposite, suspended on gold cords from a large gold tassel. It held Beryl's prize collection of antique Colport plates, which she had collected over the year and was inordinately proud of. They went into the living room, which was strangely Spartan: a very empty, cold room, probably rarely used, thought Sergeant Reynolds. He was bidden to sit, and she disappeared to return with her husband, Eric. Eric was an aggressive, ex-army man with a chip on his shoulder. He was not very popular locally, since his favourite game was one-upmanship, which most people found boring. A big man, his height and girth, together with his gruff approach, generally kept people at bay.

"What's up?" he said, staring at Sergeant Reynolds. "It's your son", said the latter. "This afternoon he and a friend of his attacked a young man at Morton." "Impossible, you've got the wrong person!" Eric replied aggressively. "I most certainly do not! He's been identified by Mrs Rochester." "What?" cried a distressed Beryl. "Mrs Rochester? What's happened?" Sergeant Reynolds explained the whole story, and Beryl sat down abruptly. "Oh no! Oh no! Are you sure?" "I'm very sure! Now I should like to see Raymond at once!" "You can't!" said Eric, "I'll get a solicitor first!" Sergeant Reynolds was starting to get very annoyed and said sharply, "If you won't cooperate, I shall arrest him and he can spend a few nights in the cells!" "Oh no!" cried Beryl. "What if anyone finds out?" "They will, don't you worry. Being Judge Mahoney's protégé, everyone will learn about this cowardly act in less than twenty-four hours." "But I'm running for club president next week", she wailed. "I shan't have a chance now!" "If you had thought more about disciplining your son than becoming golf-club president, perhaps this might not have happened. Now get me Raymond!"

Beryl rose slowly to her feet, looking totally defeated, while Eric stared straight in front of him, as though nothing were wrong. His only comment was, "He's retarded anyway", at which Sergeant Reynolds was very glad that Patrick wasn't present.

Beryl returned, bringing a sullen Raymond. "Listen to me you worm! How could you do such a thing, and to the protégé of Judge Mahoney and Mrs Rochester of all people? I hope they lock you up for the rest of your life!" "Steady on!" said Eric. Beryl spun round and faced her husband with a look that could kill. "You!" she said, "You've done nothing to guide this boy! Always away at some conference or other! You've done nothing to discipline him!" Narrowing her eyes, she screamed, "Remember, if you want a solicitor for Raymond, you'll pay for it, because I certainly won't!" Money had always been a delicate point between them, as Eric had only a small Army pension, while Beryl's bank account was considerable, due to her well-off parents. She turned back furiously to Raymond. "Not one cent will you ever get from me! Not one cent!" She stormed out of the room slamming the door, leaving Eric, feeling totally unable to cope with this disaster, and Raymond, whose courage deserted him. With tears at the thought of being jailed, he went to his bedroom, very sure that the end of the world was nigh. This should have been the end of the incident, but it wasn't.

The two boys presented themselves at the police station, neither with a solicitor, and were formally charged. Raymond took one look at Constable Timms and had that gut feeling that if they were ever alone together, Patrick would disembowel him, a feeling that wasn't wrong. Patrick's black eyes bored holes through him, and made him sweat out of fear. Sergeant Reynolds told them they were not to leave their homes until the court sat in two weeks, during which time the formal subpoena would be delivered. Raymond was only too glad to have his macho dad drive him home. When they got there, Eric left his yellow jeep in the drive and went inside to collect something, leaving instructions that Raymond was to stay indoors on pain of death. He leapt into the jeep and, after doing an errand, pulled up in front of Mulberry's. He entered the shop with a shirt under his arm. As he swung the door open, Ernest looked up from his pulpit and sprang like a tiger to bar the way. "You wretch!" he screamed hysterically. "Your ghastly son lays hands on our most esteemed customer and you have the nerve to enter my shop!" "Don't get so excited!" said Eric sarcastically. "How dare you speak to me like that!" cried Ernest. "You can take that shirt you have brought and get out!" "I need a new one, just like it" "We haven't got your fitting, and never shall have! Your account here is closed! I'll send you your bill, and if it's not paid within seven days, you'll hear from my solicitor!" "You pack of fags!" spat Eric. At that,

Neville swung into the fray. "Really, Mr Kenworth! What level did you manage at school? All brawn and no brain, that seems to be it! You, of all people, should be an expert on fags, as you so quaintly put it. Look at your son! Have you noticed that he's rarely at home between ten and midnight? That's because he's displaying his fat arse and tiny dick on the beat on the corner of Cromwell Road and Alexander Drive, hoping desperately that some guy will shove a cock up his back passage!" Eric was furious, and moved toward Neville, about to punch him in the face. At that point, Samuel stepped in. "I wouldn't even think about it", he said very slowly. "I promise I'll flatten you!" Eric was a big man, but at sixty-seven, he wasn't about to be rendered senseless by a twenty-four-year-old muscle man. He turned on his heels with his shirt in his hand and left the shop. In a state of fury and extreme agitation, he started in reverse gear, and the bright yellow jeep slammed back into a parked car with two girls in it.

A certain Brenda Cross got out and made her way toward him. Brenda was a very masculine woman, about thirty, enormous, with short red hair, pale green eyes and a very ruddy complexion. She was wearing overalls and a teeshirt. On reaching the jeep, she banged on the door, demanding to speak to "the Creep". For Eric, this was the last straw. Watched by the entire Mulberry staff and a gathering crowd, he waited until she was just far enough away for him to open the door rapidly with his foot and knock Brenda down onto the road. The door caught her full on her mouth, with blood and broken teeth everywhere.

If only Eric had taken the time to look at the side of the pickup he had backed into, he would have seen the wording "Women's Karate and Self-Defence Group" with their telephone number. "Fucking dyke!" he screamed. He should also have noted that there was more than one girl in the pickup. The other was Sandy Smith, and if Brenda was large and tough, Sandy was larger and tougher. Sandy stormed out of the pickup to see her girlfriend with blood streaming from her mouth, and a badly damaged face. Inside the shop, Neville said, "I put my money on the dyke!" "So will I" chorused the other two. Then Ernest saw Sandy make quickly for Eric, still sitting in his jeep. "Oh, he shouldn't have done that!" said Ernest slowly. She wrenched the door open and dragged Eric out, screaming abuse at her.

Beryl drove her powder-blue BMW to the side entrance of the local hospital, as had been arranged with Matron Holt, a great golfing partner of hers, and in due course Eric came out on crutches, bandaged all over and with one leg in plaster, as well as his left arm, assisted by two male nurses. He was helped into the car, and without a word, Beryl drove off. After five minutes of frosty silence, she said, "What happened exactly?" "It was a lucky punch that dyke threw", he answered. "Oh, really!" she said sarcastically, "a broken leg and a broken arm, a broken nose, five teeth missing and severe bruising to the whole body. A lucky punch, was it?" He sat back in pain, sulking. "And where, may I ask, did this occur?" He was silent, not wishing to reply. "Well! Where was it?" she said sharply. "In front of Mulberry's", and his voice trailed away. What?!" she screamed, stamping her foot on the brake. The car behind sounded its horn in indignation at the sudden stop. She gripped the top of the steering wheel with both hands and rested her forehead on them. "I don't believe it! I just don't believe it! All Brunswick will know about this by tomorrow morning! Who were the girls?" Very quietly, he mumbled, "Brenda Cross and Sandy Smith". "Oh how clever of you! An ex-military man attacks two girls in front of Mulberry's!" Her voice was now rising. "Don't you know, you fool, that Brenda Cross's father is President of the Golf Club, or hadn't that crossed your tiny mind? And whatever were you doing at Mulberry's?" "I went to get a new dress shirt for your reception next Saturday week." "Oh, did you get it?" she remarked acidly. "No. They've cancelled our account." At this point, Beryl was trembling with rage. "And those fags said that Raymond is on the beat every night, with his fat arse and tiny dick for all to see." "Well, those two things are obviously hereditary!" she spat back at Eric, who was particularly touchy about mentioning the size of his penis. "Thank God!" said Beryl, "I haven't sent out the invitations to my reception in aid of the Golf Club Presidency vote!" Dead silence ensued. She lifted her head from the steering wheel and looked at him. "I thought I was helping", he said lamely in a whisper. "I posted them all before going to Mulberry's this morning."

This was as much as Beryl could take. "I shall be the laughing stock of Brunswick! Do you realise, you fool, that those invitations you posted included the ones to Judge Mahoney and Mrs Rochester! I've been ruined socially by two fools with tiny dicks!" She burst into tears, while he sat looking in front of him, in the sure knowledge that his whole life was about to change for the worse. Beryl dried her tears and in complete silence drove home.

But another drama had also been played out at Birdwood Drive. When Raymond heard the door chimes, he went to answer the door. To his horror, there stood Constable Timms. He attempted to slam the door, but Patrick was too quick for him and forced it open with a sharp thrust, grabbing Raymond by the throat. Raymond turned white, then red as air stopped entering his lungs. Patrick let go and shoved him against the wall. Raymond was shaking visibly. "If I catch you on the beat, I'll castrate you personally with a razor blade. Mrs Rochester's kick will seem like nothing to that! Do you hear me?" Raymond nodded. "One word about this and I'll get you one dark night and castrate you. You can bleed to death for all I care! If you go near Michael again, you're dead, Raymond Kenworth!" He thrust the copy of the court order into Raymond's shaking hand and left.

Patrick was so angry when he got into the police car and sped out of the narrow drive that he crushed a whole row of Beryl's prize begonias. After he left, Raymond slammed the front door shut and leant back against the wall. He had never been so frightened: those black eyes, that large aggressive form and the very intensity of Patrick's hate were all too much for him. His legs began to give way. On the slippery parquet, the imitation Persian rug slid against the opposite wall. Raymond grabbed behind him for support and seized the suspended wooden shelves that held Beryl's antique Colport plates. The noise was terrific, but the sound of the breaking china and the crash of the shelving was nothing to the gaping hole left by the gold cords torn out of the wall. Raymond sat among the debris on the hall floor. Although he was terrified of Constable Timms, there was another person that could strike special fear in his heart, and she was due home in a moment. In total confusion, he managed to stand up and fled to his bedroom shaking.

When Beryl got out of the car, she went to the front door to call Raymond to help his father, but before putting her key in the lock, she noticed her flattened begonias and a long tire mark leading to the other gate. She let out a scream and again dissolved into tears. Her begonias! Her work of art! Ruined, just like her social life! Everything in shreds.

But her dismay at her squashed begonias was nothing to what she saw when she opened the front door: her prize collection of porcelain in shards all over the hall floor, and a large hole in the wall, where it looked as if someone had wrenched the fixture out. Beryl turned white: no tears now, but anger. She was furious, and the target of her fury was Raymond. In a rather hysterical voice she called him. As he came into the hall, and before he could say a word, she said, "Get your father out of the car!" She stepped over the damage and made for the living room, where she poured herself a large whisky and downed it in two or three gulps, as a bandaged Eric was helped into a chair. "I'd like a drink too", he said. "Get it yourself!" she snapped. Turning to her son, she inquired in icy tones, "What happened in the hall?" "I slipped on the rug", Raymond whispered. "I'm very sorry! Perhaps they can be repaired. . ." "You fool! You idiot!" she screamed. "If destroying my social life, which the pair of you have done so well, isn't enough, now you have decided to destroy my house! My husband", she continued, "beaten up by a lesbian in front of Mulberry's and my son flaunting his little dick and fat arse on the beat every night!" Raymond turned white, and the nausea he felt was very real. How on earth had they found out? What was he to do now?

"Listen very carefully, both of you!" Beryl continued. "Eric! Tomorrow you'll leave for our holiday house and stay there for at least a month. By that time, I shall have worked things out, or filed for divorce. You" she said, waving a finger menacingly at Raymond, "will hopefully be jailed or put into some reform home, after which you can come to some arrangement with your father. Go back on the beat, do whatever you like, but you won't be living here. I never want to see either of you again!" She left the room, slamming the door, and made for her bedroom, from which the sound of hysterical sobbing was heard.

Killarney went back to its usual rhythm, with Paul and Bernard in town for three days and then home again to an excited and anxious Michael. The repercussions of the nasty event were limited, although Bernard, Lorna, Paul and Anne all became extremely protective of Michael. He appeared to have forgotten the incident, but they had not.

Michael continued painting shells, and Lorna had commissioned him to do two shell paintings for her bedroom, which was now nearing completion. Downstairs, the yellow room was being papered and had a new ceiling and cornice and ceiling rose. The dining room was also being done, so there were great changes. "I hate that awful light fixture in the dining room!" said Nigel to Lorna and Michael as they were looking at a sample of red damask wallpaper, laid out on the floor. "We'll move the table and furniture into the hall and eat there until you finish the room", said Lorna. "Mr Nigel, why don't we put the red light in the red room?" asked Michael. They both looked at him. "What red light, darling?" said Lorna. "The one in the big box upstairs." "Where is this box?" "Lorna, Mr Nigel, come with me!" and he led them down the service corridor, past the ballroom and up the very steep narrow wooden staircase. In the end room, he let the blind up, and they gazed at the crates of chandeliers. "Well, Michael, we most certainly will use the red light, and the others!" "Mr Nigel, I like the green one too!" "Nigel, what type are they?" "Well, the red one is Venetian, I think", he said, pushing the straw and paper to one side to see more clearly. He then turned his attention to the larger crate containing the green chandelier. "Oh! It has storm shades!" he said. "They are for candles", said Michael. "How do you know?" asked Nigel. Michael laughed, "Mary told me!" "The green one is a beauty! It's nineteenth-century Bohemian and is engraved and enamelled. It's quite a find! The others appear to be large crystal chandeliers. I'll have them opened up and we'll take a good look, but we'll definitely use the red one in the dining room. Good detective work, Michael!" Michael wasn't sure what a detective was, but he knew he had done something good.

A month went by and as the next set in the yellow room and the dining room were finished. Now Nigel began work on the hall, as well as continuing with the blue sitting room, which he disliked very much. "It's such a mediocre room", he said to Lorna. "I think I'll strip it completely and start again."

During this week, Michael was very excited, as Lorna had told him that Admiral Amos Watson was finally coming to stay for the weekend. Anne and Colin were invited to dinner. Then Bernard phoned Lorna to say that he wasn't coming up as his aunt had died and the funeral was on Friday and he would come on Saturday morning instead with Amos.

The car came up the drive and an excited Michael threw himself into Paul's arms, only to find, with shock, that there was no Bernard. Paul explained that Bernard would be there on Saturday. Michael was rather quiet, but elated at having Paul home.

Anne and Colin arrived for dinner and were most complimentary about the two major reception areas now finished at Killarney. Michael was particularly fascinated by the dimmers and enjoyed nothing more than turning them up and down. After drinks in the almost finished yellow room, they moved into the now complete dining room. Its red silk damask curtains had gone up only twenty-four hours earlier, so it was a new experience for everyone, with their swags and fringe, the paintings, mirrors and a large red carpet. It was indeed a grand room. When they all sat down, Bernard's empty chair produced a confused look from Michael. He took Paul's hand. "What's wrong, Michael?" Paul asked, and Michael burst into tears. Paul threw his arms around him, while they all looked at each other. This was most unlike Michael. "Cooty's lost!" he cried. "He promised me only three days in the city. He isn't here! He's lost! I want Cooty!" and he went on sobbing. Lorna leapt from her chair and went to the closest telephone, near the kitchen. She called Bernard's mobile number and he finally answered. "Bernard, we're having an emergency!" "Has anything happened to Michael?" he asked in a worried tone. "Yes. He thinks you're lost because you promised him you wouldn't be away for more than three days. I'm going to put him on to you. He's in tears. See if you can sort him out, please!" She put down the receiver and returned to the dining room. "Michael, Bernard wants to speak to you!" With that, he stood up and took Lorna's hand and she led him to the phone. She came back to the dining room and said, "I'm so stupid! Paul, please put Bernard's chair against the wall and let's all move up a bit. Why didn't I think about the empty chair?"

Colin thought it was all a bit exaggerated, but he had never realised the relationship between Bernard and Michael: they loved one another, but not on a sexual level. It was a pure form of love between two people. Michael returned to the table and seemed quite settled. "Darling, do have a drink!" said Lorna, and Michael's champagne glass was filled at once. He took a sip and announced that Bernard was bringing him a piece of tortoise furniture on Saturday and Amos was bringing him some new shells. 'Shells' he understood and he knew what a tortoise was, but he couldn't work out 'tortoise furniture' at all, so by Saturday he was very excited about seeing what it was. The others weren't quite sure either about what Bernard meant, so they all had to wait. Anne had planned another of her black-tie dinners and was wondering just how she could arrange her guest list to make the night a great success.

Early on Saturday morning, Michael went riding with Anne for an hour. She was exceptionally pleased with his progress, and he and Polly seemed well-suited. After the ride, Michael took the path to the recently-opened gate between Bellevue and Killarney. He met Paul and they spent the rest of the morning in each other's company.

At eleven o'clock, Bernard's car drove up, and Michael was there to welcome him and Amos. "Cooty!" he said excitedly, hugging and kissing him. "Where is the tortoise furniture?" Amos had never seen Bernard so animated as he was with Michael in his arms, laughing and making jokes. "Michael", said Bernard, "this is Amos". Amos's large frame came round the front of the car and he offered his large hand to Michael. He was exceptionally tall, and his height reminded Michael of the basketball player who had helped him at Christmas. Michael smiled and oblivious to the hand put both his arms around him. Amos was rather surprised, but returned the greeting. Michael's mind told him that he liked Amos and he thus extended his family of friends by a single move. Amos looked at Michael and realised he was far more exotic-looking than either Paul or Bernard had described, and much more gentle. Bernard had told Amos about Michael's problems and he had expected some physical sign of them. What he saw was exactly the opposite: this young man was not an ordinary boy; he was exceptionally handsome. As the others came out to welcome Bernard and himself, it was also easy to see that Michael was well loved.

"Cooty, where is the tortoise?" "Paul, will you get the black plastic bag for us from the boot?" said Bernard. "Oh, Michael!" said Amos and, after reaching back into the car, handed him a box. "This is for you." Michael took the box and they all went into the house, to the yellow drawing room. "My God!" said Amos, looking about. "It's a lot smarter here now! I remember this room two years ago: you have done some work!" "We have a dimmer!" said Michael proudly and, switching on the great crystal chandelier, slowly dimmed the lights. "It's very nice! Mr Nigel had the dimmer fixed for us." "Well, open your box, Michael!" said Paul. Michael took off the wrapping paper and lifted the lid. The contents were wrapped separately in bubble-wrap, which he undid, and placed each shell on the lid of the grand piano. Mary came in with the drinks tray and Michael said to her excitedly, "Mary, these shells are very beautiful!" Mary agreed that they were and that they were unlike anything they had already. It was the last package that caused the most excitement: it was flat and long, and when he opened just half of it, he saw a tiny head emerge. "Paul, look! Look! Cooty, look! It's an animal!" and he finished unwrapping a seahorse. When Amos explained what it was, Michael was very confused. Polly was a horse and she had four legs, but here was a horse that was tiny and only had a funny, curly tail. The seahorse was pinky-grey, and he said to Mary, who was helping him put the shells back into the box, "I think it will be very hard to paint a seahorse". "Michael, it won't be any problem at all! You see, seahorses have no numbers!" It was Amos's turn to feel confused, and Paul explained to him the problem of objects that had numbers. Amos laughed. "I never thought of it like that", he said.

"Now", said Bernard. "Open the plastic bag very carefully." Michael extracted a nineteenth-century Boulle planter. He just stared at it and turned to Bernard, waiting for an explanation. All he saw was a curved box with red tortoiseshell inlay with engraved brass in a very fine ornate design. The rest of the planter was shiny black with a gilt brass frill around the top, and inside a black-painted tin liner with two little handles that folded down to lie flat. Michael ran his finger over the red tortoiseshell inlay, clearly fascinated. Bernard explained that it was used to put plants in, and that the red part was tiny pieces of red tortoiseshell, cut up and fitted in between the brass inlay. Michael returned, as he always did, to sit on the arm of Paul's chair, but every five minutes, he rose silently and went over to touch the Boulle planter. Lunch was served. The finished dining room was a surprise to Bernard, especially the large red Venetian chandelier, which Michael always lit and then turned down low, even in the daytime.

Throughout the rest of the afternoon, they all noticed Michael returning to the yellow room to touch and gaze at the Boulle planter, in which

Mr Barnes had put two pots of red geraniums, with some hemp straw around the top of the pots, so that it seemed as if the geraniums were planted in the Boulle planter itself.

They all arrived, dressed formally, at Bellevue at seven-thirty as bidden. Amos had watched with great interest a procedure he thought must have happened quite often: Lorna tied all the men's ties, after which Michael brought one cufflink for Paul and one for Lorna. When they had been fitted into his cuffs, he pirouetted and said, "Now I am chic!" and laughed with his unexpectedly deep laugh. Everyone laughed with him, and so did Amos.

At Anne's, everything had, as usual, been organised perfectly: it was her trademark. Their car was followed by another three: out of the first stepped Rodney and Samuel; Colin alighted from the second, while the last car held Patrick, who looked very elegant in black and white.

They went into Anne's capacious drawing room. "Darlings, what perfect timing!"

Patrick felt uncomfortable and looked lost, which Michael sensed before anyone sat down, so he went up to him smiling and hugged him, saying, "It's nice you are here!" Although it was a spontaneous gesture, Colin felt enviously that it was improper in front of everybody. The inevitable bottles of champagne were opened and they all relaxed a little. Rodney asked Michael about his red garden. Michael replied, "I now have a little garden in a tortoise box inside, on the piano. It's very nice. The tortoise is all red with brass around it!" Michael now knew what he was talking about, because he had seen it, but the others were now as confused as Michael had been when first introduced to it.

Michael sat between Paul and Patrick, as usual, much to Samuel's dismay, but he joined in the conversation. Amos told funny stories about the Navy that made everyone laugh, including Patrick. Anne felt that ten was a good number for a dinner party: all handsome men, plus Lorna and herself! What could be smarter! It being their first time at dinner with Michael, Amos and Patrick noticed his champagne glass: Amos was fascinated. Although the conversation was light and brisk, it inevitably turned on Michael, whether the red garden, the shells or the shell paintings, or Boulle furniture, it didn't matter! At some stage or other, they all tried out their ideas on Michael, to get his comments. Amos found it interesting that this eighteen-and-a-half, although not saying much, attracted the attention of all. Some sort of magnetism, he thought, realising that he too was waiting to address another comment to Michael.

Samuel asked him when he had had his hair cut. Michael said, "I went with Anne four days ago, and the lady cut it". It looks great!" replied Samuel, and meant it. Michael's black mane was cut exactly according to Anne's instructions and the effect was just what she wanted: beautiful, elegant, and young.

The evening was a success on all accounts. This was the first time either Samuel or Patrick had been invited to dinner at Bellevue, and it would not be long before they received an invitation to Killarney. For most of the evening, Colin sat looking at Patrick, as discreetly as possible. He was a mystery figure, handsome, but a little aloof. Colin realised that there was a bond between Patrick and Michael that went far beyond riding every Tuesday morning, and it annoyed him. It didn't matter how he tried to focus on Michael, there was always someone in between.

Next morning, the boys were late for breakfast, and came down the stairs laughing and joking. "Paul, you are very silly!" said Michael, and was answered by a gale of laughter. As Paul entered the dining room, he apologised for being late, and then turned round to Michael, only to find he wasn't there. He had gone to look at his Boulle planter, as though he thought it might have disappeared during the night.

After breakfast, Michael took Amos to show him the red garden. Paul went to the library, only to overhear Lorna say to Bernard, "Not without Paul's permission. He will have to live with it". "What will I have to live with?" asked Paul as he came through the open door. "I'll let Bernard tell you", replied Lorna, as she settled into a chair. "Well, it's about Boulle furniture. Michael loves it. The piece we have here came from the estate of my aunt who died last week. She left everything to me, so to make amends for the sad night when I stayed in Melbourne and Michael thought me lost, I went and collected it the next day, since I knew it was one of her passions. Do you like Boulle furniture?" "I've never thought about it. Yes, it's extraordinary work", he said slowly. Bernard continued, "My idea is this: to knock the three bedrooms at the end of the corridor upstairs, two down from your room, into one large room, with an adjoining dressing-room and bathroom, so that you don't have to cross the corridor as you do now. I also thought we could put some of my aunt's Boulle in the room, and the rest I'll put up for auction. What do you think?" The idea of a bedroom with its own bathroom greatly appealed to Paul, since it would give him and Michael much more privacy. "Oh, I think it's a great idea!" "Tell him about the bed", said Lorna. "Oh, yes", said Bernard. "Well, my aunt had this very large nineteenth century Boulle bed. Yes, the whole thing is Boulle, and it's enormous, with a half-tester and swags and drapes. When I looked the other day, I saw that most of the drapes and bedspread are torn. You see, she had six Siamese cats, and they did quite a bit of damage over the years to upholstery and drapes. Well, what do you think? We could keep it a secret from Michael until it's all finished. I think I know what I want to do, but no doubt Nigel will have different ideas!" He paused, and looked at Paul with the same intensity as Michael did. For the first time, Paul realised that, although different in so many ways, they were also very similar, especially when they wanted something that involved another party. "Bernard, I think the idea's wonderful and I know, as you both do, that Michael will love it! But the expense! It's not right for you to cover all these costs for Michael and me!" Lorna interrupted, "Paul, please! This is something we wish to do very much and I think it will make you both happy, and if you're happy, then so are we! Killarney has never been such a great place to live as it has since you and Michael made it your home, and for that we're very grateful. So I'm afraid you're going to have to let Bernard realise his fantasy of being an interior decorator, and your Boulle bedroom will become a reality!"

For Nigel, the Boulle bedroom became a nightmare. Bernard interfered from start to finish, and sharp words were often exchanged. Nigel stored the entire collection of Bernard's aunt's Boulle furniture at his workrooms, so it could be put in place at the very last moment. Some restoration had to be done on two or three pieces, minor work where the engraved brass had lifted. In all, there were seven large pieces, but the bed was the largest by far. They assembled it at the workshop, and Nigel's seamstress began the difficult task of renewing all the plain silk and matching the silk damask with a pinky-red shade. The bedhead was covered in Boulle, with fairly large gilt putti on top on the right and left, repeated at the foot. The half-tester had a pleated silk ceiling and was surrounded by swags of silk and red cords with large gold and red tassels. Bernard agreed that the bedspread and curtains should all match. The women working for Nigel felt this well beyond their call of duty and complained bitterly when Nigel insisted on some parts being done again because they didn't hang properly.

After a week of arguing, Bernard and Nigel finally decided on a design for the room. Since the three rooms formed an L-shape, an opening was knocked in the wall between the two parallel to the front of the house and columns were placed on either side to give a grander effect to the bed, when it was finished. The last room, opening off the area where the bed was to be, became a large bathroom-cum-dressing room.

Michael knew that work was being done down past his bedroom, but as Bernard had asked him to stay away from the area until it was finished, he was happy to obey and never went near it. In addition, it was locked every evening.

It was Nigel who discovered that the flooring on the upper veranda outside the Boulle bedroom was totally rotten, owing to a leak in the roof, so what started as a bedroom-bathroom restoration became a much larger job, with workmen from morning to evening. For Nigel, the work in the rest of the house had been straight forward and he had virtually been given carte blanche to do as he wished and use whatever furniture in the ballroom best suited his designs. But this was not the case with the Boulle bedroom: since it was for the boys, Bernard decided that he knew best. The wall finish was the real tussle: rag-finish, wallpaper, plain colour wash, painted or striped. The battle went on for weeks, and Bernard thought of nothing else.

Anne, too, was fascinated with the project and whilst in Brunswick one afternoon popped in to see Nigel – having phoned earlier – to see the results of the work. To say she was surprised was an understatement! The incredible richness and decoration of the bed was so theatrical and sensational that she said to Nigel, as a joke, but with a straight face, "Nigel darling, I must have one exactly the same!" He lifted his eyebrows and said in his deep voice, "If you'd like to wait ten years, I'll see what we can do!" "Nigel, have you got enough of this furniture to furnish both rooms?" "Not really", he replied. "The floor area is extremely large, and apart from the bed. . ." Anne just stared at the huge structure, now all assembled, with the women fitting all the side curtains. "Listen", she said. "When my furniture came back from storage in Melbourne, I discovered two pieces of Boulle, a large salon table and a credenza. Come and get them! The credenza has a broken slab of marble on top. Perhaps it can be repaired, I don't know. But don't say anything to anyone! We'll keep it a surprise!"

"Bernard's being very difficult", Nigel said. "I could strangle him! I've never known him to interfere all the time! It's slowing the work down." "Oh, Nigel! You know he wants the best for the boys, and you also know he can't do it without you! So I'm afraid you'll have to be patient!" "'Patient'!" he boomed. "Do you know we finally decided on the bathroom only after I asked Paul to intervene. Bernard was determined to put in a bath, but we've managed to convince him that a double shower would be much better for the boys. A bath indeed!" "Nigel, you're fantastic! And Killarney is looking great now." "Thanks, but there are seven or eight rooms to go yet, that hideous blue room with the television, and some of those guest bedrooms that look like a youth hostel!" "Don't worry, Nigel dear! The moment you finish at Killarney, you must start at Bellevue." "Thanks for your vote of confidence!" he said. "No! No!" he yelled at one of the women. "The cord must be the red and gold woven together!" The woman snatched the offending cord down, found the right colour and went back up the ladder to the half-tester, giving Nigel a black look.

The whole of the smart set in Brunswick, as Ernest would have said, were talking about this bedroom to be built and decorated at Killarney, and the boys from Mulberry's had trooped to Nigel's workroom to catch a glimpse of the fantastic bed that was the talk of the town. Even Neville was overwhelmed. Samuel just stared in total silence, his eyes roving over every piece of decoration. He had never in his life seen anything like it. "Just imagine Michael in that, Tarzan!" Neville murmured. Samuel ignored the jibe. He just moved closer to the huge structure and ran his hand over the Boulle-work. "Don't touch anything!" screeched one of the women working on the pelmet swags. "This bed is a nightmare!" "I think it's fantastic!" Samuel replied. "I've never seen a bed so large!" "Oh, come on, Jane! You've been in and out of so many beds, I'm surprised this one overwhelms you!" "Bitch!" came the reply. So the staff at Mulberry's could now impart first-hand knowledge about the Boulle bed soon to be installed at Killarney, but only to customers they considered important. Neville teased Dr Colin Campbell about it, and Colin became very abrupt, which encouraged Neville to continue. "Perhaps, Doctor, you'll be able to see it when you do house calls", he said sarcastically. "I'm not interested in this bed", said Colin. Neville now had the devil in him. "Oh, well! What about the person who's going to sleep in it?" "I don't know what you're talking about!" snapped Colin, getting angrier and realising that Neville was drawing him onto a subject he didn't wish to become involved with.

And so a very weary Nigel continued the decorating battle with Bernard until the work was almost completed, at which point Anne stepped in to aid Nigel. "Lorna", said Anne. "How long is it since Michael had a dental check-up?" "Good heavens, I have no idea. I must ask Paul!" "I think it would be a good idea to have a week in town. I could take Michael to my dentist, who is just the right man for the job, and that would give Nigel free rein for a week to finish the bedroom." Although Anne and Bernard did most of the organising, the other seemed to fit in with the arrangements quite happily. There was no jealousy or competition at all: Michael was the fulcrum around which they arranged their lives. After Lorna talked with Bernard and Paul, the staff at St George's Road were alerted and this time, when Bernard and Paul left for Melbourne, Michael and Lorna went with them. Michael looked on curiously at all the packing and organisation, listening to comments such as "Anne's sure to have a black-tie evening! Oh, and what about the Club? That means a blazer and dark grey flannels", and so on.

On the morning of their departure, just as the car was about to start off, Michael yelled, "Cooty! Just a minute! I've forgotten something!". As he ran up the steps to the front door, Mary opened it and handed him what he had come to look for: Toby! So, with Toby sitting between Paul and Michael, Bernard drove down the drive, with Mary waving from the top step. Michael had a strange feeling that he was leaving part of himself behind. He had never had a home before, his only memory was that of the Institution, but even those hard times were beginning to fade. Killarney had become the basis of his life: he lived in an extremely sheltered environment where everything and everyone revolved around him. Even when Paul and Bernard were not there, they now phoned Michael every evening.

After a little more than an hour and a half, Bernard halted at the Law Courts and got out, together with Paul who worked not far from there. Lorna took over the driving, with Michael seated beside her. "I'll see you tonight!" Paul said, smiling. "Yes!" came the answer and a smiling Michael waved goodbye. Lorna drove to St George's Road. Michael had never stayed at St George's Road, although he had had Christmas dinner there many months before. With Toby under his arm, he followed Lorna to Paul's room, which was the second most spacious suite in the house. In the small sitting alcove, the first thing Michael noticed were photographs of himself and Paul at Killarney, in silver frames standing on a small table. Then Michael exclaimed, "Lorna! You're here too!" and held out a photo of the four of them, all laughing. Lorna looked hard at the photo: it said it all! There they were, all four of them, with Michael sitting between Bernard and Paul and Lorna herself standing in the middle behind Michael. She had completely forgotten when the photo had been taken, but seeing it now in the boys' bedroom gave her a wonderful feeling of continuity, the sense that they now had a past together, and that the future that stretched ahead was, for the first time, a predictable, pleasant adventure in waiting.

Anne's social skills went into top gear. She and Lorna organised a whirlwind week of smart social events to keep them all amused. Anne had come down to Melbourne three days before the others, so she had arranged the dental appointment. A very worried Paul kept asking Anne whether he should accompany Michael to the dentist. "No, darling! Leave it to me! It will be fine, just like the hairdresser. Michael and I will sort it out. The appointment is for five-thirty, so we'll join you all at the Club afterwards for drinks and dinner." So that was that.

The dentist proved not to be a drama. Michael thought he was very nice. He was a good friend of Anne's, said he thought Michael was delicious and asked whether he was available. The negative reply did nothing to dull his admiration for this beautiful young man. A filling without an injection followed and an appointment was made for the end of the week for another filling. The dentist gave Michael a hug and told him he was a fabulous patient, meaning every word of it. He had come in, dressed in blazer and tie, and the combination of black blazer, black mane of hair, and electric blue eyes seemed almost too much for the dentist. He said quietly to Anne, "I'd kill for him!". She laughed and said, "Darling, so would many others! Come on, Michael! We have to meet Paul, Lorna and Bernard at the Club!". With that, she whisked him downstairs and into her car, and twenty-five minutes later they were walking up the front steps at Brown's.

Michael was most curious: so this was a club, a sort of house, he thought. Big double glass doors with designs etched into the glass, leading into a reception area, where Brown's Manager, Henry O'Connor, came forward. "Mrs Rochester, how nice to see you again! The others are waiting for you both. You must be Michael: how do you do?" Michael suddenly felt ill at ease and clasped Anne's hand, not knowing what to reply. Anne squeezed Michael's hand as if to say, "It's all right. He's one of us". With that, Michael said, "It's very big, your club!" Henry smiled, "Thank you Michael. Let's join your friends!" and with that he led them across the lounge to a red leather club sofa and four armchairs grouped together. Bernard stood up. "Cooty!" Michael exclaimed, "I saw a dentist man. He was very nice", and he gave him a kiss and a hug. Henry stood back and watched with interest the effect that this youth had on everyone. Paul embraced Michael. "No pain?" he asked. "No. I must see him again on Friday morning." Amos stood up too, as Michael kissed Lorna. Amos said, "Do you remember me?" Michael smiled and went up and hugged him, just as he had when they first met, but this time Amos hugged him back, and asked how the shells were. "They're very beautiful", Michael said, "but the seahorse is very difficult. He has a funny nose." Amos laughed, "I'm sure you and Mary will do a beautiful drawing of him!" "Does he have a name?" "Only a Latin one and it's very difficult!" "Oh, Amos! What a poor horse!" said Michael, at which everyone laughed.

Anne noticed that Bernard seemed so proud of his two boys. She was not the only one to see a different Bernard. Champagne was served for those who liked it and on the tray, brought by Henry himself, was an old-fashioned champagne glass for Michael. "Michael, I want you to meet a good friend of ours", said Amos. "This is David Keen." A short fat man stood up and shook Michael's hand. "We've heard a lot about you, young man. I believe you and Anne go riding." "Yes, we do", Michael answered very chirpily. "And on Tuesday mornings, Patrick comes with us. It's very nice." "I'm sure it is. It's been years since I've been on a horse. If I were to mount one now, he'd have to be very stout to support me. Did you ever ride, Amos?" With a twinkle in his eye, Amos looked at Michael and said, "I only ever rode seahorses", making everyone laugh. "Amos! You're too big to ride a seahorse. They are very tiny!" "Why so they are!", laughed Amos. They finished their drinks and went on to the dining room.

Michael was surprised to see other tables and other people. His concept of a dining room was a single big table, as at Killarney or Bellevue, but in this strange club there were many tables. Henry himself sat Michael against the wall, so that nobody could pass behind him, and every other instruction Bernard had given Henry was carried out to the letter. They were just seated, when Stephen Spender entered the dining room. "What an illustrious group we have the honour of hosting this evening", he smiled. "Hello, Michael! Do you like the Club?" "Stephen, it's very nice. I like it very much!" "Will you join us?" asked Bernard. "There's no problem; there's heaps of space." "Oh, you'll need the space for him!" said Major David Keen, and winked at Stephen, since they were both fairly rotund. Henry arranged the extra place and an enjoyable evening was had by all. Henry O'Connor was fascinated watching Stephen, the President of Brown's, Admiral Amos Watson, Major David Keen, Judge Bernard Mahoney and Lorna, Mrs Rochester and Paul Moran all include Michael in their conversation, as though he were an equal and someone they had known for years. Stephen had instructed Henry that should Michael ever come to the Club alone, for any reason, he was to be automatically admitted in his name.

On Wednesday, they all met for lunch at Brown's, but in the morning, after Bernard and Paul had left for work, Lorna took Michael to the zoo. He was enthralled. It was as though a book on animals had become three-dimensional. The sizes of the animals fascinated him, from elephants to tiny monkeys. There was the butterfly house and an enormous aviary where you could walk through three different zones, each with different birds and plants. Climbing some steps and walking along a long bridge in the air, he looked over at the lions below. Melbourne Zoo was a wonderland for Michael, and was the first time he had seen anything so exotic. After an hour, they had a break and, while having an orange juice at the café, a peacock strutted by, while a pair of guinea fowl scurried under the tables, looking for crumbs. The late autumn morning was fresh, but the sun was shining, and all the animals seemed content. On reaching Brown's for lunch after their visit, Michael couldn't speak of anything but the animals he and Lorna had seen. "I hadn't been to the zoo for years", she said to Paul. "It's really very good. They've made so many wonderful changes!" "I like the elephant, Cooty! He was so big and he was all grey. But I didn't like the snakes. I don't think they're very nice at all, but the elephant was very nice. Cooty, do you think we could have an elephant at Killarney?" Bernard looked a little surprised, at which Michael reached over and hugged him. "Cooty, even I know he is too big for Killarney!" and gave his deep soft laugh. It crossed Lorna's mind – and Paul's too - that if Michael had asked Bernard for an elephant, Bernard would have bought him one, if it were at all possible.

Anne was a little late in joining them. "Darlings, I've got the most fabulous news! Bernard, that big triangular plot of land between Killarney and Bellevue is up for sale. I've put in a bid. We can go halves if you want. Oh, isn't it exciting! At last, they've decided to sell!" Michael looked at Anne and said, "Will we put up a high fence?" "I don't know, darling. Do you want a high fence?" "Cooty, we saw some animals – I forget their name – and they have big horns growing out of their heads and they're brown with spots on their backs. They are very nice. Could we put some in the new paddock?" Lorna explained, "Michael is talking about the spotted deer. He thought they were very chic". She smiled. "Well dear, they'll be easier than elephants!" said Bernard. "Bernard, what on earth! Do you want to put elephants in our new paddock?" "Don't you think they would look exotic, Anne?" he teased. "Oh, I don't know, Bernard, but I'm sure twelve acres is a bit small for a herd of elephants! Oh, well! What else did you see, Michael?" Michael told them about the peacock, which wasn't at all frightened of people. When he opened his tail, it became very large and it was green and blue, and at the ends it was very nice, he said.

Michael loved his week in Melbourne, but especially the fact that every night he could sleep with Paul. This was exceptionally very nice, thought Michael.

Earlier in the week, Paul had received a call from his brother-in-law Peter, asking how everything was going and whether, now he was living at Killarney and St George's Road, he was interested in letting his terrace house in East Melbourne. Paul invited him to St George's Road for a drink to talk about it on Tuesday evening, before going to Anne's for dinner. Prior to Peter's arrival, he took Bernard and Lorna aside to discuss the issue. Bernard was quite firm, "Lease it by all means!" he said. "You'll never use it again. You have this place and Killarney, so you don't need it anymore!" That was that. Bernard made this decision about Paul's life and all his financial investments, such as his house. For Bernard, Paul was *his* as much as Michael was, and if anyone had suggested otherwise, he would have been genuinely surprised.

Peter arrived punctually and was shown into the large sitting room where he introduced himself to Lorna and Bernard, who were dressed to go to Anne's – black tie of course! "I hope I haven't come at the wrong moment", he said. "Not at all!" said Bernard, still in his shirtsleeves, "We have three quarters of an hour before we need to go. May I get you a drink?" "Yes thanks! I'll have a whisky." "Good! I'll join you." Paul entered and shook hands with Peter. He helped himself to champagne and asked Lorna if she would like some. "Yes, thank you!" came her reply, and they all sat down. To make conversation, Lorna said, "Michael and I spent the morning at the zoo. We had a great time! I hadn't been there for years!" For the first time, Peter realised that Michael was very much part of Bernard and Lorna's life as well: it hadn't occurred to him. Bernard went on to say that Michael was painting, had designed the red garden and was riding very well now. Peter was muddled and showed it. "Don't worry, Peter", said Paul. "Michael is a very different young man from the one you last saw." With that, Michael bounded into the room in his dinner jacket, his tie ready for Lorna to knot and his cufflinks for them both to insert in his cuffs. He stopped short when he realised that somebody else was present. Peter stood up and just stared at him.

"Michael!" he said, in a most uncertain voice, "is it you?" Michael moved toward Bernard, who was closest, and sat on the arm of his chair and put his arm round his neck. "I can't believe it! Good heavens! What have you all done to him? He looks amazing!" "Sit down, Peter", Paul said. "He's changed a lot, probably more than you would have thought!" "Come over here, darling", said Lorna. Michael went to her and she knotted his tie. As usual, he put out his arms and Paul and Lorna each inserted a ruby cufflink. The look was complete! Peter was wholly lost for words, and watched Paul proffering champagne to Michael in an oddly old-fashioned glass. Peter thought, "This really is a happy ending, but – my God! – look at him! He's so handsome".

"Peter, we have decided to let the terrace house in East Melbourne. You can give me all the details this week and we'll start arranging leases and so forth." But Peter was only half-listening. He watched Michael move like a cat back to his place between Bernard and Paul. Michael was watching him, too, since for him Peter represented the past, and Michael wasn't interested in remembering it. For Michael, it was becoming a hazy dream now, albeit a bad one: the institute, the noise, the other children hitting him. It was a dream he could now dismiss completely, but Peter was the only living link to that past. Whereas Michael thought only for a moment about the past, Peter saw not only Michael's present status, but also his future. Peter found Michael fascinating to watch: elegant, calm and handsome. Was this really the boy he had foisted on Paul all those months ago? How had this radical change taken place in such a short time?

They chatted on for half an hour, and then Peter said goodbye. Before leaving, he said to Bernard, Lorna and Paul, "What you have all done is a miracle!" "Oh, but you're wrong!" said Bernard. "It's what Michael has done for us that's the miracle!" and he put his arms round Michael. On that note, Peter left. Driving back to Camberwell, he just couldn't get it out of his mind. How could that skinny youth with no hair and cuts all over his face have been the cygnet who had turned into this dazzling swan?

"You wouldn't believe it!" he told Janet, overwhelmed by the change. "You'd think he was the owner of St Georges Road. He paints, he's a garden designer, and he rides! Can you believe it!" "Well, you see what

211

love can do!" answered Janet. He looked at her and became strangely silent. "So it seems not only does my brother-in-law love him, but the Mahoneys as well!" "Well, with a support team like that, Peter, how could he fail to be a success?" "But you should have seen him!" he started again. "It's unbelievable! They were all going out to a black-tie dinner, and he looked just fine! What can I say?" "Gorgeous!" Janet teased. "Don't tell me you fancy the handsome young man my brother's in love with?" "Oh, don't be stupid!" Peter retorted. "But I'll tell you one thing: if I had to sleep with any male in this world, it would be" - and they chorused together - "Michael!" They both laughed. "Pour me another glass of red, darling! I really am proud of you! If you hadn't forced the issue with Paul, I wonder what Michael's fate might have been at the other institute!" "I dread to think", Peter said. He sat without moving, his mind racing ahead. How was it possible that Michael had been diagnosed as having no possibility of great change, when in fact his physical change was extraordinary and his confidence and coordination skills had clearly improved to such an extent that, according to Paul and the Mahoneys, he was now able to design a garden, paint and draw, and ride a horse, as well as many other skills? Why had the diagnosis been wrong? Or might it also have something to do with the environment? Here he was, protected by four people, one his lover and the others just as important in their own way, and this assistance and love had enabled Michael to bloom. "What's wrong, Peter?" asked Janet. "Oh, nothing! I was just wondering how many other Michaels remain in institutions all their lives, without any possibility of change!" "Listen, Peter, you've given a young man a new life, not to mention Paul. I think that calls for us to top up our glasses! As I said before, I'm very proud of you!" With that, she kissed him on the forehead. The noise of their three children arguing about a television programme in the family room next door made them both move in that direction, arm-in-arm.

Paul drove them all to Anne's for dinner, where they found they were not the only guests. Once again, Anne had filled her dining table with ten men, plus herself and Lorna as the only female representatives. It took Bernard and Paul two seconds to discover the common denominator of all the other men. Michael stayed very close to Paul and at table sat between Paul and Bernard, with Anne at one end and Lorna at the other.

One of the guests opposite Michael attempted to engage him in talk, but without any notable success. Michael answered questions politely, but did not extend the conversation. Paul was well aware that Michael was the focal point of the party. One young man on the other side of the table asked Michael about his cufflinks. He raised his arm to look at them and said, "Yes, they are very beautiful. Anne gave them to me". From her end of the table, Anne heard his reply, and a surge of pride swept over her. Michael was always kind about situations or persons he believed in, and Anne found his gentle comment extremely flattering. The evening passed well, owing to a splendid meal and interesting talk, but not one of the guests forgot the quiet young man with the black mane of hair and the electric blue eyes.

On Friday morning, Anne collected Michael for his dental appointment, after which everyone was to have lunch at St Georges Road, to decide when to return to Killarney.

The dentist again declared that he was crazy for Michael, drawing laughter from Anne, who reiterated what she had told him about Michael's many suitors. If he didn't behave himself, she teased, she would have to find a new dentist. "Anything but that!" was his reply.

As they went down the stairs, Anne's mobile rang. She searched for it in her handbag and answered, "Good heavens, Claire! How did you get my number after all these years? Yes? What, now? Very well, but only for a few minutes, since we have a luncheon engagement. Yes, dear, *we*!" She closed the mobile and said to Michael, "Do you mind if we stop off at a friend's for ten minutes?" "No", he replied. "Great! Let's go! I went to school with the woman", said Anne. "She wasn't really a great friend, but her parents and mine were." She pulled her car out into the traffic and headed toward Malvern, where she drove down a street lined with plane trees now dropping their leaves. The large leaves floated down, covering cars, rubbish bins, the pavement: everything was covered in a yellow-brown mantle.

They went up to the front door of a very large house, and Anne rang the bell. She had to ring a second time before it was answered. "Anne, darling! How are you? Oh, and who, may I ask, is this?" said the woman, looking straight at Michael, who felt uncomfortable and took Anne's hand. "Claire, this is Michael." "Well, I must say, Anne, you have exceptionally good taste!" "Thank you", said Anne, playing the game. "Come in!" "Good heavens, Claire! Are you moving out? Why?" "No, I've just decided to get rid of all my parents' stuff and start again. It's like living in a mausoleum!" There were crates, boxes, rolled carpets, paintings, just everything, stacked everywhere. "The auction people are coming this afternoon to take it all away, and I shall be free of this burden at last! But do come through! There's a small space where we can sit down." They threaded their way between boxes and stacked up objects. "I got your number from Lorna. I saw her yesterday. It seems you two are becoming country girls. Who would have thought you would be living side by side at Morton? I do envy you!" "Well, darling, buy yourself a house at Morton! With all the stuff you're selling, you'll be able to manage it!" "If only! With two girls at school, it just isn't possible *yet*", and she emphasised 'yet'.

Michael was behind them, looking at everything. In a curious way, it was just like the ballroom at Killarney, he thought; everything piled on top of each other. Claire whispered to Anne, "He's beautiful!". "Yes, isn't he?" purred Anne, not giving the inquisitive Claire any more information than necessary. "Anne, Anne!" said Michael, with urgency in his tone. "Look, it's Polly!" Both Claire and Anne turned and looked. Through an open door, in a room with boxes everywhere, leaning against the fireplace stood a large painting in a heavy gilt frame. It was an equestrian scene, and the horse did look like Polly, right down to the white mark on her flank. "Why, darling, so it is! What are you doing with this painting, Claire? Are you going to sell it?" Michael was on his knees, staring at the horse. "It *is* Polly", he said. "It's very nice!" "The painting", said Claire, "is a fake".

"A fake! What *do* you mean?" asked Anne. "Well, my grandfather paid a fortune for it. He purchased it as being by Landseer, but the experts told me a couple of days ago that it's a copy. It needs cleaning, and it has a rip at the bottom. The auctioneers say it will probably be bought for its frame, but I don't know who has a house nowadays big enough to take a painting that size! It's seven feet by four! So what I thought was going to net me a small fortune is actually worth nothing! Oh well! You win some, you lose some." "How much do you want for it?" asked Anne.

"Anne, you're surely not interested in it, are you? I told you it's a copy!" "How much, Claire?" Claire tilted her head to one side and smiled an evil smile. "This couldn't be a gift for your young friend, could it?" "It could!" said Anne, returning the smile. "Anne, if it makes your man happy, take it! I'll get nothing for it at auction, and your young man is obviously enthralled by it!" Michael stood up and looked at Claire. He smiled and looked back at the painting. "Darling Claire! You must let me do something for you! This is so generous!" said Anne, just a little superciliously. "Don't worry, Anne! If I run short of beautiful men, I'll give you a call!" They both laughed. "I'll organise a courier right now", said Anne and pulled out her mobile. She spoke to a painting restorer she knew. It seemed he could send someone to collect it immediately, as for Mrs Rochester nothing was too much trouble. Anne gave him the address and told him she would call tomorrow to make arrangements for its repair and cleaning.

"I'm off to Brown's this evening", said Claire. "Oh, so are we! It's Stephen's birthday. So I'll see you there!" "Oh, what fun! Will Lorna be coming?" "Oh, yes! We'll all be there!" "We?" said Claire curiously. "Yes, darling. You'll have to wait for this evening to see what I mean." With that, they were shown to the door by a rather confused Claire, wondering who exactly "we" might be. Don't tell me, she thought, that Anne's got yet another boyfriend! After all, Michael's so cute and so very young. . . Anne is certainly moving on!

Michael bounded into the sitting room at St George's Road, crying out, "Paul! Cooty! Lorna! We've bought a giant painting of Polly!" Since Anne and Michael were a little late, the painting was clearly the reason. "How big?" asked Bernard. "Where shall we put it?" "Oh Bernard!" said Anne. "You have tons of space at Killarney! Don't worry! When it's been cleaned, I'll have it sent up." "Oh, will you!" he said rather dryly. "Cooty! It's Polly! It's a very big picture of Polly", said Michael, clearly excited. He hugged Bernard. "Oh, Cooty! It's very nice!" "I'm sure it is!" said Bernard, won over without much trouble by Michael's enthusiasm.

"Let's have lunch", said Lorna, "or else everything will be cold!" "Don't forget", said Paul, "that we have an appointment on Sunday afternoon to see Amos's shell collection". "Oh, I'd completely forgotten!" said Anne.

"At what time?" "I don't know, but we'll see him tonight at Stephen's birthday party, and we can sort it out."

After lunch, Paul and Michael disappeared, and the other three returned to the sitting room, overlooking the front lawn. It was Lorna who said, "Talking of birthdays, when's Michael's birthday?" They all looked at each other. "I don't know. I suppose Paul knows. I just haven't asked", said Bernard. But when, much later, he did ask him, Paul replied that he had no idea and would have to find out through his brother-in-law. He phoned Peter half an hour before they had to leave for Brown's, only to be told that because Michael had been abandoned, he had no exact date of birth or official surname. Peter said he would check again, but was certain that what he'd told Paul was right.

Paul went to the sitting room, where Lorna was knotting Michael's tie. Paul said he was going to see Bernard for a moment in the library and asked Lorna to put both Michael's cufflinks in. Paul repeated to Bernard what his brother-in-law had told him. "Never had a proper birthday!" said Bernard quietly. "Listen, Bernard, every day with you and Lorna has been a birthday for Michael! He's caught up!" "Thank you very much", said Bernard, "but from now on, if it's all right with you, he'll have his birthday on September 29th, which is St Michael's day. What do you think?" "That's fine! It's a very good idea, Bernard! Come on, let's go! They'll be waiting for us!" As Paul made for the door, Bernard put a hand on his shoulder and, as he turned back toward him, took Paul in his arms and hugged him. "Since you and Michael entered our lives, every day has been a birthday for Lorna and me." Paul could see tears brimming in his eyes and returned the hug. "Come on, or we'll be late!" he said, and arm in arm they joined Lorna and Michael.

They reached Brown's exactly as Anne's taxi drove up. Anne looked extremely elegant, all in black and dripping with diamonds. They greeted one another and, when Paul returned from parking the car, they swept into the reception room. Bernard led with Lorna on his arm, while Anne made her triumphal entrance with Paul and Michael on either side. Claire crossed the room to greet them. "Darling!" she exclaimed, glaring at Anne's diamonds. "Aren't they beautiful!" In fine form, Anne replied, "Aren't they just! They're the two best-looking men in Melbourne!" Claire looked a little taken aback and said, "Of course, darling, of course!" With her escorts, Anne crossed the floor to greet Stephen and wished him a happy birthday. The others all did the same. Michael, unsure amongst such a crowd, simply hugged him. Stephen whispered to him, "That's the nicest gift I've had! Thank you, Michael!" Michael smiled in return.

Henry O'Connor supervised the reception like a hawk. The waiter who served the champagne for Anne and her group also brought one old-fashioned champagne glass for Michael. Henry forgot nothing. As a rule, Anne hated this kind of reception, especially if there were lots of ladies present. She found their conversation trite and her retorts were generally sharp and accurate, so it was no wonder that most of the other women thought Anne was a real bitch! But tonight, with Paul and Michael, she was having a good time. A magistrate's wife came over and said, somewhat insincerely, "Anne, you look simply radiant!" "Of course! It's the company I keep!" she replied and kissed Paul and Michael on the cheek. The woman smiled and realised there was no winning this conversation. She excused herself and left, saying later to a girlfriend of hers how impossible Anne had become.

Michael was happy to see Amos and David and even happier when he found they were seated together at table. Anne was determined that Michael should get used to large groups of adults – not children, since she loathed them – and he was in fact beginning to cope, now seeing individuals instead of a large group as a whole. Tonight, Michael was quite chatty, which pleased Anne very much, and at the table for ten he was the centre of attraction as usual. Amos paid him great attention, drawing him into every corner of the adult conversation, and Michael was holding his own. Paul was particularly proud of him. Michael told Amos that the seahorse he had given him was not so easy to paint, but Mary was going to help him finish it when they went home. Bernard looked at Lorna: it was the first time Michael had used the word 'home'. Bernard felt that somehow, Killarney and Michael were becoming one.

Anne excused herself, left the table and went down the thickly carpeted hallway, hung with nineteenth century landscapes in large gilt frames. A set of basket chandeliers lit the way to the Ladies Room. Anne entered the old-fashioned pink and beige room and wondered why it had never been renovated, thinking she must have a word with Stephen. While she was redoing her makeup, two ladies entered, chatting loudly. They fell silent on seeing Anne. In the mirror, Anne saw that one of them was an old school companion she had loathed, and time had only strengthened the feeling. "How are you, Anne?" said Marian Rains. Anne continued with her makeup before answering, "Fine, Marian! And yourself? A little worse for wear, I see!" Marian had married a famous tennis-player some years before. As a result of his great passion for gambling, especially at the races, he had managed to squander a fair amount of Marian's fortune. Marian was extremely jealous of Anne's collection of famous jewellery, and never missed an opportunity to say something sharp about it. "Anne, don't you think you are really overdoing the diamonds tonight?" "Not at all, Marian! When they're Cartier, I just don't see how you *can* overdo it!" Marian's friend excused herself and left the two of them alone for a moment. "And by the way, what's happened to your jewellery, Marian?" Marian made no reply, knowing full well that Anne knew she had had to sell most of it to pay her husband's debts. "I think a simple string of pearls like you are wearing is probably very suitable, considering your circumstances", smiled Anne. Realising she couldn't win on the jewellery issue, Marian quickly changed topic. "Really, Anne!" she said cattily. "Cradle snatching at your age!" Whether she meant Michael or Paul was uncertain, having seen Anne swan in earlier, looking very glamorous, with one on either arm, much to Marian's annoyance. "Oh Marian! How little you know about beautiful men! And for a woman of your senior years!" By this time, Marian's friend had returned, in time to see Marian about to burst with anger. Anne stood up and adjusted her large Cartier diamond necklace. "Marian, at your age, you should be using better quality makeup: you might even look a year or two younger!" Marian was furious and swept her hand from her bosom to the side of her hair, but in the process caught it in the string of pearls. To free her hand, in her anger, she broke the string and the pearls bounced all over the pink marble floor. As quick as a flash, Anne glanced at the distressed Marian and said sarcastically, "Pearls before swine!" and walked out, leaving Marian on her hands and knees collecting her scattered pearls.

Mr. Robertson, Paul's employer, was also a member of the club and an old friend of Stephen's and Bernard's, a true gentleman, but seemingly in rather poor health. Stephen had invited him and his son to his birthday party, despite the fact that he disliked the son immensely. The son had been 'interstate' for some years, but was still a member of the club since his father paid his dues. Mr Robertson came over to the table and said hello to all, and Paul gave him his seat. He looked at Michael and said, "So finally I have the pleasure of meeting you. I've heard so many wonderful things about you from Bernard and Paul!" Michael smiled, but did not reply. He saw a man who was very worn out and tired, and thought he was very sad. Mr Robertson stayed for fifteen minutes, catching up with the news from Amos and David. He said he couldn't remember the last time he has seen Anne and Lorna and apologised for letting his social life slip a bit. He then left, wishing them all a pleasant evening, but not before shaking hands with Michael.

Michael was fascinated when, at a certain point in the evening, Henry O'Connor wheeled in on a trolley a large cake decorated with white leaves and flowers. Stephen appropriately cut the cake and everyone sang "Happy Birthday" and filled up their glasses. Michael didn't or couldn't understand what the cake was for, but he thought it was all very nice. He very much liked the piece of brandy-rich fruit cake he was given, and thought that birthdays were very nice. It never crossed his mind that he should also have a birthday, since he had never had one, so he assumed that it was something like his christening party. The evening ended calmly and Paul overheard Stephen saying to Bernard, "Mr Robertson's son is back in town, I'm told. What a nasty piece of work! Thank goodness he didn't bother coming this evening! As Chairman of Brown's, I should check up on him. He seems to be involved in things that do not become a member of this Club!"

Back at St George's Road, snuggled up beside Paul in bed, Michael said he liked birthday parties, and especially the cake. Paul hugged him, but didn't elaborate. He thought, let's wait and see what happens for Michael's birthday party. Bernard had left his reading glasses downstairs. On passing the boys' room, he heard for the first time what Lorna had heard. "Paul, goodnight!" "Goodnight, Michael!" and the two chorused together, "Goodnight, Toby!" Bernard felt a swelling sensation in his chest, a feeling of pride, since he had given Toby to Michael, but also a special pride in his new family, which had now become the most important thing in his life.

During the week and a half since they had all been in Melbourne, at Killarney Nigel had been working much more easily, without Bernard's interference, and the Tortoise Room – as it was about to be called – was almost finished. The bathroom was of soft terracotta-coloured marble with a large double shower, giving directly onto the dressing room, which in turn gave onto the bedroom, with its own private sitting room though the columns. With the Boulle furniture everywhere, the effect was quite theatrical, but the enormous bed was the main feature of the suite, its curtains, half-tester and gilt cherubs were all quite sensational, thought Nigel, knowing he would never have the opportunity of doing a room in Boulle again, and happy that it was all over the top. "Very sensible indeed!" he thought.

He had emptied out the blue sitting room, cramming its contents into the ballroom, and began reworking the 'miserable room', as he called it. He ripped out the little, narrow cornice and replaced it with a heavy ornate Victorian one, contemporary with the house. He also fitted a large new ceiling rose and new high skirting boards. He couldn't understand why a house as grand as Killarney was outside should have been finished so miserably inside. Only the grand staircase was worthwhile, he thought, the rest would have to be totally remade. By this stage, the ballroom looked like an enormous furniture warehouse, with furniture of all kinds – good, bad and indifferent – stacked everywhere. It was now almost impossible to cross the room without having to climb over something.

Whilst they were in Melbourne, Patrick Timms was missing Michael very much. This was the second Tuesday morning with no Michael. His horse saddled, Patrick rode out into the cold autumn fog, greatly missing his riding companion. Patrick was a solitary person: he worked efficiently, but his private life was a mystery. Goodness knows, the boys at Mulberry's had tried hard enough to find out about him, but the only person he seemed to relate to was Michael, and he felt genuinely lonely without him, this special boy who needed Patrick to protect him. He wasn't sure whether this might not be conceit on his part, but he felt that their rides together were the only real thing – or the only important one – in his life at present.

Back in Melbourne, towards the end of their stay, a little drama occurred among the lunchtime crowds on Bourke Street. Michael got separated from Paul and Lorna and realised he was in trouble. He put his hand into his shirt pocket, only to discover that he hadn't got his card with all his addresses and telephone numbers if he needed help. All he had was the twenty-dollar note that Paul insisted he should carry with him. He stood still, jostled a little by people rushing by, doing as much as possible in the shortest possible time. There was a seat in the mall, so he sat down and tried to think what he should do. Then, at the end of the mall, he saw a taxi rank. He had used taxis with Anne and remembered that if you sat in the back and told the man where you wanted to go, he would take you there. But where was he to go? He didn't remember the number or even the name of St George's Road, or the suburb. He stood up and headed for the taxi. Strangely, he wasn't afraid. He didn't like the jostling of the crowd, but he could manage. He got to the taxi and told the driver "Brown's Club". In seven or eight minutes, the taxi deposited Michael on the steps of Brown's. He handed the driver the twenty dollars and received his change. As he opened the large glass door, another man pushed him aside and went in ahead, which worried Michael a lot. From just inside the door, Henry O'Connor had witnessed this unseemly behaviour of a club member barging in front of someone, or in his mind "behaving like a ruffian".

"Michael, how nice to see you!" said Henry, looking daggers at the other man. "Do come in! May I help you?" "They've lost me", Michael said very quietly. "No problem at all! We'll find them all immediately!" said Henry. "Come with me!" He sat Michael down in the lounge. As soon as he sat down in the large leather armchair, Amos entered. Michael immediately flung himself into Amos's arms. "I'm lost!" he said. "I lost myself!" Amos held him tightly. "Henry, I think this young man would like a glass of champagne. Would you please phone Bernard at once and tell him that Michael is here!" "What a fuss about nothing!" came the sarcastic comment from the man who had pushed Michael out of the way. "Hold your tongue!" said Amos very sharply. "He's probably not even a member. Soon we'll be letting any stray dog in!" "He's my guest!" said Amos, his eyes narrowing. "If you wish to make an issue of it, I think Judge Stephen Spender will be able to sort the matter out!" Henry returned and said, "I've contacted Judge Mahoney and he'll get in touch with Mr Moran and Mrs Mahoney". "Thank you, Henry!" said Amos. The youngish man with yellow-green eyes, who, in Henry's terms, had acted like a ruffian, was in fact Mr Robertson's son Philip, who was now back in Melbourne and making his presence felt. Not even fifteen minutes later, Paul and Lorna came in, together with Stephen, who had arrived for lunch. "What a happy coincidence!" said Stephen. "Well, it's not quite like that", said Paul. "We somehow got separated from Michael, who felt lost, caught a taxi and ended up here. Henry telephoned Bernard, who called us, and here we are!" "He's a clever boy! He knows this is a safe haven and if he's ever in trouble, he'll always find help here!" "Thank you, Stephen", said Paul, feeling he would like to hug him. That awful feeling when they found Michael was lost had been devastating for him and Lorna.

Stephen signed everyone in and they had a late lunch. Sometime later, when they had gone, Amos and Stephen called Henry over and they discussed Philip Robertson's bad behaviour. "How did he ever become a member?" Amos asked. "Well", said Stephen, "his father decided that his only son should be a member, so when he turned eighteen he was nominated and, since there were no objections, became a member. His father pays his dues, so that's that, or so it appears! I've never liked him. He's so arrogant and rude to his father in public. It's really not on! I should do a check on him". "Well, as far as I'm concerned", said a very determined Admiral Amos Watson, "if he thinks he can just push Michael literally aside and pass uncharitable remarks, he can go to hell!" Amos had drawn the line: anyone who gave Michael a hard time would have to answer to him!

"Run a check on him, Stephen, and see what comes up! I'll take a bet it won't be anything good!" "I'll see what I can do", said Stephen. "Henry, thank you for handling the situation with Michael so well today. He feels very safe with you. If anything like that should happen in future, I'll leave you a proxy signature to use in case anyone here gets excited! Remember that Amos, myself, David and Bernard will all cover you." "That won't be necessary, gentlemen", said Henry. "No one here at the club would know that he's not a new member. So far as I'm concerned, and with the Chairman's permission", he said, smiling at Stephen, "I think we'll handle the future without any problems at all!"

"Cooty, getting lost wasn't really bad", Michael told a slightly nervous Bernard at St George's Road over dinner. "Mr Henry gave me a glass of Anne's drink and Amos was there. We're going to see his shells tomorrow. Will you come, Cooty?" "I can't. I have to work, but Lorna and Anne will take you, I think."

After dinner, Michael walked over to Bernard and sat on the arm of his chair. He put his arms round his neck and said very quietly, "Cooty, when can we go home?" Bernard turned in his chair and put his arms around him. "After you've seen Amos's shells, Lorna will take you home and we will come up the next day. Is that all right?" "Cooty, do you promise to come up the next day?" "Yes, Michael, I promise!"

Amos was very much the seaman, everything shipshape and on time. So, punctually at 10 o'clock, a knock was heard on Admiral Amos Watson's front door. He opened to a beaming Michael, who gave him a hug, and to Anne and Laura, who followed suit.

"Goodness, this is my lucky day!" he said, laughing. They moved into the plain, ordinary sitting room of a large 1910 house. Its big rooms had lots of arts and crafts features that didn't ring quite true: the house lacked character. There were some nice pieces of antique furniture, but the various ornaments looked like souvenirs. Amos took them upstairs to what must once have been a bedroom, part of the ceiling sloping under the eaves. It was here that Amos was most at home, the walls were lined with fitted glass-fronted cases containing thousands of shells of every colour, shape and size, all clearly labelled in Latin. Michael was fascinated, as were Lorna and Anne, neither of whom had ever visited this Brighton address before. As usual, Mrs Amos was not around.

The collection was not merely impressive, it was marvellous: the shape and colour of each shell seemed to give it a separate personality. They all seemed to say, 'Look! Look at me! I'm the most interesting and the most beautiful!' Amos was very proud of his large collection. It had taken him years to amass this wonderful spectacle, and the fact that Michael was transfixed by everything he saw gave Amos a satisfaction he had never known before. Michael looked at every shell, but toward the end of the cases, he stopped dead. There it was! "Amos! Amos!" he cried, "Look! He's all red! He's very nice, isn't he? Look Lorna, Anne! Look! He's all red!" On a little stand stood a bright red seahorse. "Oh, Amos! He looks very happy!" said Michael, and his comment made Amos burst into great gulps of laughter. "Do you really think he's happy?" he asked. "Amos! I'm sure he's happy! He's all red!" As a sign of approval, Amos linked arms with Michael and said, "You're a fine young man, Michael", at which Michael swung round and hugged him. Lorna smiled at Anne, in the realisation that Michael's magnetism, which affected anyone he loved or felt safe with, had trapped a very wily old Admiral in his strong young arms.

Next day brought a great dilemma for Bernard, since he wished to be at Killarney when Michael and Paul saw their new bedroom suite for the first time. "Do you think you can keep Michael from seeing his room until we get there tomorrow evening?" he asked Lorna. "Of course! Relax, Bernard! Michael won't go there if he's asked not to!" "But what if he stumbles into the room by chance. . .? I do hope Nigel's made the pelmets match the curtains properly. And I hope the furniture's all ready!" "Bernard, please! You'll have a heart attack! Don't worry! We'll all wait. I'll arrange a dinner party, and at a certain moment, we shall all go up and have a look at Nigel's extravaganza." "Well, he didn't do all of it!" said Bernard sharply. "Remember, I decided on the colour for the marble in the bathroom! Oh! You do think everything is working, don't you? I mean this new heating system that Nigel has had installed." Bernard went on, concerned only that tomorrow evening should be something very special. "Don't worry, Bernard! I've telephoned Mary and everything will be fine! It's Friday: fish, white wine and champagne. What more could you want?" "Do you think Mary could procure some lobsters? Michael likes them, I know." "Bernard! If you don't stop it, there'll be trouble! Do you understand?" "Yes, Yes!" said a totally unconvinced Bernard. "Of course, Lorna, of course!"

Lorna left early next day with Michael; Anne left in the late afternoon. Michael was so excited to be back home at Killarney that he rushed everywhere, hugged Mary, who cried, then ran off to the red garden to see how his bronze geese were.

Now it was autumn, Rodney – with Bernard's permission – has started to plant out a spring garden, so Michael discovered large empty spaces of brown earth with no plants and couldn't understand why there were not many red flowers. Rodney had planted two hundred and fifty red tulips for the following spring. He had also started redeveloping the other garden, which, being only rhododendrons and azaleas, had made it an easy life for Mr Barnes. This meant that for the greater part of the year, there was no colour at all. So Rodney began to design a whole new system that would provide colour for most of the year. Although happy that someone else was organising and doing some of the work, Mr Barnes saw inevitable maintenance looming ahead and tried to block several projects. But Rodney went ahead, despite wails and complaints from Mr Barnes, knowing full well that Bernard, who was his employer both directly and indirectly as a supplier, would see a great change in the gardens at Killarney. He also hoped desperately that Michael would appreciate the change, since it was really for him that he was performing this miracle, and not necessarily for the man who was paying for it.

"Where, oh where can I find lobster for eight people at one day's notice?" "Oh, Mary! Just do what you can! Bernard is being a little hysterical about the bedroom. If we can't have lobster, then that's that!" "I'll phone Mrs Harold at once", said Mary, and rushed to the kitchen, where she found Mrs Barnes. "It's black tie and lobster, it appears!" "Really!" said a complacent Mrs Barnes. "I suppose that means the big white damask cloth for Friday night. It's such a bore, ironing it without any creases!" She went off, moaning about the work of starching and ironing the big white damask tablecloth without leaving creases.

Bernard and Paul arrived late on Friday afternoon, to be greeted by an excited Michael. "Paul, we're having a black jacket night!" he beamed. Paul kissed him. "Sounds great!" "Cooty, I've seen the geese. They seem very happy, but we have holes in the garden where Rodney has put things in for springtime." "I'm sure Rodney knows what he's doing!" said Bernard, his arms around Michael. Michael held him very tight and said, "Do you like being home, Cooty?" "Yes, I do, Michael! I like being home!" Bernard felt sentiment pulse through his whole body, bringing him very close to tears. "Let's go inside and see what Lorna and Mary have organised for us." Michael still had no inkling about the 'tortoise bedroom' upstairs. It had been kept a tight secret, and he merely assumed that Nigel was doing some more renovation, and nothing else.

"Come on, boys, get moving! Everyone will be here in an hour! Go up and shower and change!" With that directive, everybody disappeared into one bedroom or other. Having showered, Paul and Michael found they had half an hour to themselves, of which they took full advantage, but they were ready just on time for Lorna to knot their ties, and to fit the ruby cufflinks into Michael's cuffs. No sooner was the last tie knotted than a car was heard coming up the drive. Mary welcomed Rodney and Samuel, and showed them into the yellow drawing room. Bernard found Rodney an easy-going and straight-forward man to work with. He was humorous, but efficient, and could talk on any subject without being pretentious. Bernard immediately started speaking about developing the gardens, to which Rodney, in a devilish mood, suggested that the only thing missing was Snow White and her seven dwarfs, cement-cast, painted in electric primary colours. This brought gales of laughter from all but Michael, who didn't quite grasp who Snow White was, let alone her seven dwarfs.

Anne and Colin were ushered in shortly afterwards. Samuel said very little, but his eyes rested on Michael like a weary traveller for most of the evening. Although the rest of the company interacted, everything pivoted around Michael. The only person Michael never spoke to was Colin: he never related to him at all, and, innocent as this was, it kept Colin on his toes the whole time. Rejection was not a word Colin was familiar with: it was just impossible, yet here it was! What on earth was wrong, he thought, in his usual conceited way. He was sure that with a little effort, he could manage Samuel, and perhaps Rodney, , but Paul and the beautiful Michael were forever off-limits, and that annoyed him.

They were soon bidden to the table, which was laid out in great style. Finished only about a week before, the room looked wonderful in the evening light and its red colour made it a safe warm haven against the cold outside. The menu was splendid. Mary had managed to procure lobsters, and everyone enjoyed every mouthful. After the main course, Bernard stood up and said there would be a break before the sweets, and would they all follow him. He started toward the door and up the staircase, followed by the rest, all chatting about this strange adventure before their dessert. They passed Paul and Michael's bedroom and continued down the corridor, only to stop before a closed door. "Well, here we are!" said a triumphant Bernard. "Come here, Michael! Now, just open the door! That's right! Now turn on the light!"

Michael was dazzled by what he saw. They all crowded in to the sitting room end of the bedroom, which was like a huge stage set in strawberry with burgundy and gold. But, oh, the bed! Its half-tester was draped and swagged with tassels and cords and silks, all matching the window curtains. And the vast quantity of Boulle furniture! There was complete silence. Bernard said nervously to Michael, "Do you like it?" "Cooty", said Michael, "it's very, very nice. Look, it's a tortoise bed!" Everybody laughed. "Yes, this is your new bedroom!" Michael hugged Bernard. He was so excited that he hugged everyone else and, for the first time, Colin felt the physical contact he had always previously imagined. Anne was overwhelmed by the effect of the room. "Oh, Bernard, it's breathtaking! It's marvellous! I must have Nigel start at Bellevue at once!" Samuel was astounded. He had seen the bed under reconstruction in Nigel's workrooms, but the whole room seemed to him like a movie set of a de luxe palace, and it had all been created for the most beautiful boy in the world.

Michael walked around fascinated, looking at everything. He returned to Paul. "Paul, Toby will like this very much, don't you think?" "Yes, he will!" said Paul, looking round the room in amazement, wondering whether he would ever get used to such an extremely ornate room. Michael took Paul to look at the dressing room and bathroom. It was a private world, thought Rodney, an exotic hideaway from all the troubles and unhappiness of life, a cocoon, a de luxe cocoon of silk and damask and Boulle. He was quite sure there was nothing in the world quite like this and it crossed his mind that a total exotic adventure with Michael could only take place in such a setting.

After praises and gasps and inspections of every part of the suite, they finally returned to the dining room for their dessert and had a glass of champagne to toast the tortoise room.

While dessert was being served, Michael leant over and said to Paul, "Can we sleep in the tortoise room tonight?" Paul replied, "You'd better ask Bernard". "Cooty, can we sleep in the tortoise room tonight?" Michael reiterated. "Yes, Mary has arranged everything. Do you really like it?" Michael stood up, lifted Bernard out of his chair and put his arms around him. "Cooty, it's the nicest bedroom in the whole wide world! Thank you!" and he kissed him. For Bernard, this was the supreme reward for all his work: this public thank-you. Led by Anne, everyone applauded.

Conversation spilled over with happy and chatty subjects and anecdotes for the rest of the evening. After the guests had been sped, Michael raced upstairs to his and Paul's new bedroom. They all said goodnight on the landing and then he scampered down the corridor and into his new domain. The large crystal chandelier on the dimmer just gave sufficient light to create a very private space, and in the middle of the bed sat Toby. Mary had thought of everything: their clothes had been transferred to their new dressing room, even their photographs had been placed about the room. Everything was in place, including two of Michael's shell paintings, framed and hung, one above the other, between the windows.

Paul arrived to find an exceptionally happy young man wandering about the room half-undressed. He immediately drew Paul into his arms, whispering, "Paul, it's very nice, isn't it!" "Yes darling. It's splendid, and it's just for you!" "Oh no, Paul! Cooty made this tortoise room for you and me! It was made for us!" he said with an innocence that brought tears to Paul's eyes. "Michael, you're wonderful", was all he managed to say. "So are you", came the answer. "Come on, come and get undressed and we'll try this Boulle bed!" "Oh yes!" said Michael, "I'll be in first!" He laughed and removed the rest of his clothes, which he draped over a chair. He put Toby on the bedside table and disappeared under the thick warm blankets that Mary had so carefully prepared.

Well rugged, Anne left with Colin and arrived at Bellevue in exceptionally high spirits. She insisted Colin should come in for a drink and, after removing their coats, they went to the sitting room. "Darling, open a bottle!" said Anne. "I know!" he replied, "While you change the diamonds!" "Exactly!" Anne said. "I'm glad you had a good evening!" He opened a bottle of champagne and poured out a couple of glasses, before sitting down in a comfortable chair. In a moment, a refreshed Anne returned. "Darling, what a fun night! And what about the lobster? How does Mary manage it? When I try, they never have enough of them. She really is a saint! And the bedroom, what do you think? I love it, in fact I may get Nigel to do something in that vein for me!" "I think it's a bit over the top", said Colin. Anne, now in the highest of spirits, felt the urge to bait Colin. "Darling", she purred. "Imagine yourself in that bed, with the drapes and tassels and whatever, and someone else! Divine, don't you think?" "I suppose so", came the slow answer. "Now I wonder who it could be that would catch your attention long enough to drag you into paradise?" "Anne, you've had too much to drink, and you're being very foolish!" "Oh no, darling", said Anne, settling back with her feet folded under her. "You really must get organised, Colin. Look at Samuel and Rodney, both charming young men! Don't be slow, darling! Time waits for no man: I believe that's the expression!" "Ho! Ho!" he murmured sarcastically. "Very funny!" "Colin, you're a handsome man and unfortunately what you want is strictly off-limits. But keep your eyes open. You never know what you may see!"

When the bottle was empty, Colin donned his coat, gave Anne a kiss and wished her goodnight, and went out into the chill autumn air. He was not happy as he drove home to Brunswick. He was cross that Anne, as usual, like Michael, always ended up as the centre of attention, and he had to suffer the consequences over a bottle of champagne later. He very much disliked Anne's making fun of him about Samuel or Rodney as possibilities. If truth were told, either would suit him fine, but to be told constantly that Michael was strictly out of bounds angered him greatly. Of course, he was more than interested in Michael and believed that he would be much the better without all this cosseting. But Colin didn't understand that Michael couldn't relate to him, simply because he didn't love him on his own terms. Michael saw black and white: no shades of grey entered his existence. He loved because he felt safe, and that was that. Colin's approach, aloof and sophisticated, meant nothing to Michael: he just couldn't understand it, nor did he feel secure when with Colin, with the result that in public he always remained close to the others, to Colin's annoyance. It also had to do with Colin's conceit, for which he was now paying the price, not Michael.

CHAPTER SEVEN

Danger For Paul &
The Irish Room

CHAPTER 7

Danger For Paul & The Irish Room

The months went calmly by and the pattern of leaving and returning to Killarney continued all winter. Michael still went riding at least twice a week with Patrick, even in bad weather. Of all Michael's acquaintance, Patrick was the closest and he spoke openly to him on any subject. Patrick very much wanted to share his thoughts with Michael, and it was only during these two or three hours each week that he could relax and feel complete. He was very proud of Michael's riding prowess, and when Anne join them one foggy morning, even she had to admit that Patrick's soft handling of Michael had paid off.

They cantered across the field and down toward the pond at the bottom. "Well done, Michael!" said Anne. "You're doing very well!" He looked splendid in his black coat, hat and jodhpurs, breathing heavily after the ride and producing puffs of vapour from his mouth and nose. "Polly likes going fast!" and he laughed with his infectious deep laugh. Patrick felt truly proud of him: he had listened to and remembered every instruction. Patrick never confused him: his instructions were logical and short and Michael grasped them easily. It also had a great deal to do with the fact that this dark-eyed, handsome instructor was someone with whom he could relate completely.

"Patrick, before we came out this morning, I spoke to Sergeant Reynolds and told him I was holding you hostage for lunch. He agreed, so that's that! You and Michael are my guests." "Oh, Mrs Rochester!" began Patrick. "That has to stop at once, Patrick! It's Anne to you, not Mrs Rochester! I consider you a great friend and my horses – not to mention Michael – couldn't get along without you!" Patrick felt that the swelling sensation inside came close to bursting. "Thanks!" was all he could say. "Anne, that will be nice! Can we have Patrick at lunch every Tuesday?" "I hope so, darling! It will probably take a bit of organising with Sergeant Reynolds, but nothing's impossible! Oh! That reminds me, Patrick! I'm having a little dinner party tomorrow. You will come, won't you? Michael and I would be so disappointed if you were to say 'no'". Patrick realised precisely the situation Anne was setting up with Michael as bait. It wasn't that he didn't want to accept, for heaven's sake, he would have killed for the opportunity to be with Michael, but he was most unsure as to why Anne was being so insistent. So, taking his courage in both hands, he accepted the invitation. They returned to Bellevue and had an excellent lunch in the small dining room, with a blaze in the black marble fireplace. Patrick was a little nervous and was surprised at Michael's familiarity with Anne's house, removing his boots at the front door and entering confidently in his woolly socks. "Do the same, darling", she said to a surprised Patrick, who followed suit.

Conversation was light and amusing, but Patrick was aware that Anne was seeking something, and that something was his past. He was clever enough, however, to sidestep any awkward moments. Anne found Patrick fascinating, darkly handsome, almost exotic. In her mind, his great love of horses immediately entitled him to be less formal and more relaxed: but for all that, he remained the mystery man. The only person he really relaxed with was Michael. "Patrick, you must come to Killarney", said Michael, enjoying his fish, "and see my tortoise bedroom. It's very nice, isn't it, Anne?" "Yes, darling, it's fabulous!" "Anne gave us some tortoise furniture for the room. You'll like it, Patrick!"

Patrick felt he was being drawn into a world that was padded with felt: everything was beautiful, with plenty of champagne and good food, and people lived in palatial homes, of which the centre was Michael. He was so natural and spontaneous with Patrick and over lunch, Anne thought that Colin could never have taken Patrick's place today: the substitution would have produced an effect as cold as the weather outside. But with Constable Timms, everything made for happiness and warmth.

After lunch, as he was leaving, Patrick fell over on the veranda while putting on his riding boots, making Michael burst into laughter as he helped him up. Taking his leave of Anne, Patrick summoned up all his courage and said, somewhat sheepishly, "Thank you very much, Anne! It's the nicest lunch I can remember!" "Well, we must do it again! It was fun! Goodbye!" She kissed him and said, "Remember tomorrow night, Patrick! About seven. We can relax with a drink before dinner". "Thanks again!" he said, then, "Come on, Michael, we must get you home!" They got into Patrick's car just as a light rain commenced. "Oh, well!" said Patrick. "The rain will be good for the garden!" "Patrick, I'm sure it will!" said Michael. Patrick had got used to Michael's way of speaking, always prefacing the message with the name of the person to whom he was speaking, as if to gain their attention.

They pulled up under the porte cochere at Killarney. Michael hugged Patrick exactly as he did with Bernard, but the effect on Patrick was very different. He held Michael for a split second, but that was enough for him to realise that his young riding companion was really much more than that to him.

Driving back to Brunswick in the light rain, Patrick felt that at any moment he might levitate effortlessly. His heart felt as though it were six or eight inches higher in his broad chest, and he felt wonderful. All he had to do was wait until tomorrow evening to start all over again. Life wasn't so bad, after all, he reflected. After changing from his riding gear, he went back to the office, where his happy countenance was remarked by all, especially the secretary, who was a friend of Neville's, and Sergeant Reynolds. "Thanks for letting me stay for lunch!" he said to Sergeant Reynolds. "Did you enjoy it?" came the query. "Yes, it was very good! Thanks again!"

Having finished some work for Mr Robertson, Paul took the sheets in to him and immediately noticed that he was not well. "Listen", he said, "I can finish this work. I think you should go home and call the doctor. I'll take you if you like. I'll come back and finish the work afterwards." "I don't feel well at all", said Mr Robertson, and let Paul help him from his chair and down the corridor to the lift. Paul was very worried. "I think we should stop off at the hospital for a moment. You have become very white. Do you feel any pain?" "Yes, in my chest", he replied very slowly. Paul accelerated. He went through two red lights, with horns blaring, and pulled up at the hospital's emergency section. Paul helped Mr Robertson out of the car and took him in. Having given the staff the name of Mr Robertson's doctor, he rushed out to park his car. While waiting for a doctor to give him some news, he telephoned Bernard. "I don't think he's very well. He looks terrible! Can you get me his son's number from the club? He should be informed at once." "I'll call Stephen immediately", said Bernard. Five minutes later, he rang Paul back with the number, and Paul called Philip Robertson. "Your father's very ill and is at the hospital. I'm here. I think you should come at once!" "I'll come when I decide", came the icy reply, "and not when an employee tells me to." "I've given you all the information", said Paul. "Good afternoon!" and he hung up. The doctor came out. "He's in very bad shape", he said. "Why didn't he seek medical advice before?" "I don't know", replied Paul. "Why? What's wrong?" "It's too early to say, but he seems to be in great pain, and has been for some time." "You don't think it's really serious, do you?" asked a very worried Paul. "I most certainly do think it's very serious. Does he have any relatives?" "Yes, I've already called his son. Hopefully, he's on his way." "Good! Well, there's not much you can do here. If you call in the morning, someone will give you a bulletin."

Paul walked slowly down the corridor, though the foyer and towards his car. Mr Robertson had always been a very special person in Paul's life, someone who had supported him in every way: Paul was bright, and together, this investment company had grown from a medium to a major enterprise. Mr Robertson had appreciated Paul's potential and had given him every opportunity, for which the Company had been amply rewarded. Their relationship was based on complete trust and understanding, and even when Mr Robertson had to hold his breath at some of Paul's daring short-term investments, they had always come through. He was far closer to Paul than to his son, Philip, who was an extreme opportunist, but not a good investor. He had been working with the firm when Paul started, but had left for greener grass in Sydney, leaving Paul to take over his post in the firm, where he was respected and well-liked. When he had spoken to Mr Robertson, at what now seemed a hundred years ago, about altering his work schedule because of Michael, Mr Robertson had had no qualms. "Certainly, Paul! Anything you wish!" He was a person who understood someone's needs, as well as appreciating Paul's work for the firm. And now he lay in hospital, seemingly not in a good condition. What exactly was wrong, Paul mused? Why hadn't he sought medical help before? Bernard called Paul on his mobile to find out how Mr Robertson was, and Paul replied in all honesty that he didn't really know. He arranged to meet Bernard for dinner at the Club at eight-thirty, which gave him time to return to the office, organise the staff, and rush off for forty-five minutes at the gym.

Bernard was exceptionally possessive about Paul. Paul didn't find this disagreeable, just occasionally a little difficult logistically, but they always managed. He was half-an-hour late as he climbed the steps at Brown's, only to meet Henry O'Connor at the door. "Oh, Henry! I'm so late! Have they all been waiting for me?" A wink and a smile from Henry suggested that all was not lost. Paul entered the lounge and Henry brought the book for Bernard to sign him in. Stephen, present with Amos and David, were most concerned about Mr Robertson's health. "How is Robbie?" asked Bernard. "Well, in all truth", said Paul. "I don't really know. I hope it's just overwork or something like that. I really haven't got a clue until I speak to the doctor tomorrow morning. I spoke with his son Philip, but he wasn't at all receptive. In fact, I think I was probably not the right person to give him the news." "He should be grateful that someone else had taken over the responsibilities he had refused! A nasty piece of work, if you want my opinion", said Amos. "I never liked him. He has an overrated opinion of his own limited importance!" "Hear, hear!" said David. "I can't really understand how he could still be a member of Brown's. It seems so very strange! Not the sort of person one would ever want to know, but Robbie is such a gentleman! I've known him for more than forty or fifty years. We were all at school together. And to produce a rodent like that! What a shame! So much effort for so little reward!" They all variously agreed that Robbie deserved a much better son. They then moved to the dining room and spent a pleasant evening, it having been tacitly decided that nothing further would be said about Robbie until the doctor's report in the morning.

Next morning at St George's Road, Paul had breakfast with Bernard. "Do you think it's too early to call the hospital?" he asked. "Oh, why not!" said Bernard. "They're twenty-four-hour institutions!" With that, Paul got up from table and picked up the phone. The reply regarding Mr Robertson's condition was brutal and direct: during the night he had had a stroke and was very poorly. No other information could be given over the phone. Paul was stunned. "They say he's had a stroke!" "You'd better take over the running of the firm for a while. I'm sure that's what Robbie would want", replied Bernard. "Why is it always the nice guys that end up in trouble?"

Paul drove Bernard to the Courts, then made for his office, two blocks away. As usual, he organised the staff schedule, but now there was no Mr Robertson. So the week went by, and on Thursday a very concerned and worried Paul left with Bernard for Killarney, knowing that he would be back at the office on Tuesday to solve any problems, and that the staff could reach him on his mobile if they needed to.

This pattern continued for four weeks, with Paul calling at the hospital every morning or evening to see how Mr Robertson was faring. He didn't seem to get any better or worse, and this limbo-like state worried Paul greatly. Philip never called and was never available when needed. Only when he put a cheque through for a large sum of money and Paul put it on 'hold' did they hear from him, screaming, "How dare you refuse to cover my cheque! I'm the owner of this company! Clear it at once!" Paul instructed the staff member in charge of payments not to clear the cheque and if Philip were to phone to reroute his call to Paul's office. Silence ensued. Philip was clearly uncertain as to what powers his father had left in Paul's hands.

After four weeks, Mr Robertson left hospital, extremely thin and ashen-faced. He managed to come to the office one day a week only – on Mondays – and everything was handed to Paul. So they went on throughout the winter and beginning of spring, when a jarring incident occurred that changed Paul's life.

One Wednesday morning, Paul breakfasted with Bernard and dropped him as usual at the Courts. He made his way to the office, glanced at the worksheets on his desk and began to sort through them. About half an hour later, Philip made one of his rare appearances. He stalked into Paul's office and said, "I want a staff meeting called at once!" "Why? Can't it wait until work's over?" "Call the meeting now!" Philip screamed. Paul called his secretary and in ten minutes the firm's not inconsiderable staff crammed into the conference room, everyone expecting a health bulletin about their employer. After fifteen minutes talking and exchanging pleasantries, Philip entered, swept to the head of the long board table and sat down. Most of the staff remained standing as there were not enough chairs.

"I'll make this brief!" said Philip. "My father has finally signed everything over to me, as his only son, and I am now Managing Director of this firm. My first act is to fire Paul Moran. He's a homosexual with a retarded lover and it won't do for the Company image!" This statement was followed by a deathly silence, all waiting in the expectation that Paul's sentence would fall on all of them. No one moved. The electric atmosphere even affected Philip, who stood up and said arrogantly, "You are paid to make money! Do it, or I will fire the lot of you!" He then turned on his heel and stalked out of the conference room.

Nobody said anything. Someone offered Paul a chair, but he said 'No thanks!' and walked back to his office. His head was spinning. He sat down. He was unemployed: his future, Michael's future! What was he going to do? It all felt so unreal, like walking and not using your feet, or breathing, but not using your mouth or nose. He was absolutely stunned. 'Fired' was the word Philip had used, 'fired'! Paul picked up the phone and dialled Bernard's number. He explained the situation, feeling that Bernard seemed not to grasp how serious it was. "Paul, stay by your phone for ten minutes. Don't move! It's very important!" "But Bernard, you don't understand!" "Paul, do exactly what I say! Don't move for ten minutes!" and Bernard hung up. He then called Lorna, who in turn put a call through to a large investment firm only two buildings away from Paul's office: Ryan & O'Farrell, one of the most important in Melbourne. Lorna asked to speak with the director, Kevin Simms, and was put through immediately. "Yes, Mrs Mahoney! Of course, Mrs Mahoney! How very kind of you to think of my problem! Very kind! Yes, in the big office. I have the spelling. In how many minutes? Very well! The girls can do a temporary one on the printer in five minutes. Yes, not a word. You will call that number in twenty minutes and we will have it put through at once." Kevin Simms hung up. He paged his secretary and gave her instructions to be carried out at once, and to inform all the staff immediately.

In his office, Paul felt the world was closing in on him: his independence, keeping up with Lorna and Bernard, supporting Michael – although this was not such an expense, shared as it was with Lorna and Anne. Michael wanted for nothing in fact. Paul often felt he was over-indulged, but, considering his background, he could begrudge him nothing. What could he do? He just couldn't think. Fired, for being homosexual. It was crazy! And making a comment like that about Michael! If he had not been so shocked, he was sure he would have struck Philip. He went through a moment of extreme despair, followed by a moment of extreme rage. It just wasn't fair! He had worked for Mr Robertson for more than fourteen years, and their bond was one of trust. Paul knew he had made a great deal of money for the firm. And to be thrown out like an old sand-shoe! Whatever shall I tell Michael? Horror swept through him. All those people, now passing comments: 'Oh I am so sorry', 'Oh what a pity'!

He started to get up, but then remembered his promise to Bernard to stay by the phone for ten minutes. "Oh, surely the ten minutes is up!" he thought impatiently. "The staff are going to think I'm hiding, that I'm afraid of that rat Philip!" At that moment the phone rang and it was Lorna. "Lorna, do you know what has happened?" said a very distressed Paul. "Listen to me carefully!" said Lorna, in a very businesslike manner. "Leave the office, and go two doors up to the offices of Ryan & O'Farrell, right now! It's extremely important! You know where it is?" "Yes", said Paul, with the sensation that no one was listening to him or understanding his dilemma. "But, Lorna, I've been fired!" "Paul!" retorted Lorna sharply, "Do this for me, at once please!" "Very well!" said Paul. He left the office and went out into the brisk Melbourne spring morning.

Two buildings up stood an imposing modern structure, with the name of Ryan & O'Farrell in large brass letters at the entrance, unmistakably denoting proprietorship. Like a zombie, Paul took the lift. He felt nothing; he wasn't even confused, but he felt completely empty, drained. ?'Fired! Fired!' was the only voice echoing in his mind: homosexual! fired! The lift took him to the eighteenth floor and he walked over to the receptionist. As she took his name, she pressed a key on her computer that alerted everyone that Mr Paul Moran was now in the office. Paul had the uncanny feeling that all was not well. "This way, Mr Moran", said the receptionist and led him to another young woman, who said, "I'm your personal secretary, Mr Moran. We're so glad to have you aboard!" Paul looked at this very attractive corporate-dressed young woman and said confusedly, "I don't know what you're talking about!" "Come this way please, sir", she said and he followed her like a child, not knowing where he was going or why. The de luxe office space and surroundings spoke of a very successful business. He followed the girl to the end of the broad, thickly-carpeted corridor, with large prints on the wall. There, he stopped dead, as though someone had hit him from behind. His head spun; he blinked and looked and blinked again, then looked at the girl. "But. . ." he began. "We're so sorry, Mr Moran", she replied. "We'll have a more professional sign up by the end of the day." There it was, in large computer print: "Mr Paul Moran, Managing Director". He felt as though his feet had been nailed to the floor: he couldn't move forward or backward. "Do go in, sir", said the girl. "By the way, my name is Jenny. It's going to be a pleasure working with you, sir! I have your first message: a call will be put through to your desk in about two minutes. I shall return after you've received your call."

She left and Paul entered the large room, unlike any office he had known. Everything was decorator-smart and tasteful: its beige carpet with tiny burgundy triangles; the antique desk and beautiful Georgian bookcase. The rest of the furniture was modern, of the highest quality: a set of beige chairs and a black leather chesterfield. Modern master prints hung on the walls and the curtained windows overlooked the whole of the Yarra River development and far beyond, to the sea.

Nothing, absolutely nothing, made sense to Paul. The phone rang and he crossed the large carpeted space and picked up the receiver.

"Darling, how do you like your new office?" asked Lorna. "Lorna! What's happening? I don't understand! I've just lost my job and yet I find on the door of this fabulous office that I'm Managing Director! What's happening?" "Paul darling, don't worry! Everything's fine! Go and clean out your old desk and take what you want. Get rid of the rest. Kevin Simms will explain your new job as Director. By the way, Paul, be at the Club punctually at twelve-thirty, since Bernard is having a special lunch for you. He'll tell you everything. We're looking forward to seeing you on Thursday evening! Goodbye, darling!" With that, Lorna hung up, leaving Paul none the wiser as to what was happening. Jenny came in and asked him whether he needed anything. "Yes", he said, "I need to see Kevin Simms". "Right away, sir! I'll contact his office!" "Oh", he said, interrupting, "please call me Paul. 'Sir' makes me feel a hundred years old!" She laughed. "Very well, Paul! I'm sure we going to get along!"

Less than five minutes later, a very thin, and not so tall, man, with receding sandy hair, glasses, and a narrow face, dressed in very smart attire, entered Paul's new office. Paul stood up. "Do sit down", the man requested quietly. "I'm Kevin and you're Paul. I'm so pleased to meet you and welcome you to the firm. Personally, I'm glad you've joined us. I'm sure the two of us can make both our own lives and this business work more smoothly." Paul looked at him in wonder. "Where am I?" he thought. "Who is this man?" He said, "May I ask you something?" "Certainly", said Kevin. "Whatever you like." "What am I doing in an office that says 'Paul Moran, Managing Director' on the door? Would you please explain?" "Oh, that's easy!" said Kevin. "Ryan & O'Farrell's and - I might add – the entire building is the private property of Lorna O'Farrell." If Paul felt weak before, he now felt as though his legs might give way, and he sat down heavily in his chair. "Didn't you know?" asked Kevin. Paul didn't answer, he simply shook his head slowly. Then, with an attempt to pull himself together, he said quietly, "This is Lorna's company?" It was both question and statement. He just couldn't believe it. Neither she nor Bernard, nor even Anne, had ever said a word about Ryan & O'Farrell's. He remembered she had said something some time ago about selling a block of apartments, but Ryan & O'Farrell were the most important investment brokers in Melbourne, if not Australia, and had assets everywhere. "I'm so glad you are here to help me out", said

Kevin. "I believe we can now organise our time more rationally. If I'm not mistaken, according to Mrs Mahoney, you prefer working from Tuesday to Thursday, which is excellent, because it leaves me Mondays, Fridays and the weekend to spend with my son." "Your son?" said Paul, nothing making any sense at all now. "I didn't marry until quite late, and at fifty-three I find myself with a four-year-old son who suffers from a rare viral disease. The doctors give him five or six years, and I should like to spend every minute possible with him. Mrs Mahoney has been wonderful, allowing me time, but now that you are here as Managing Director, we can share time. I don't think you know how important it is to be with someone who needs you completely." "I'm afraid I do", said Paul very quietly, "and it's for this reason that I spend as much time as I can at Killarney." He stopped short, aware that at nine-thirty that morning he had been fired for being homosexual. He wasn't looking for another run-in before lunch. "It's quite all right", said Kevin, standing up. "Mrs Mahoney has explained everything and I am personally very proud to work under you as Managing Director." "Listen", said Paul. "We will and must work together. I'll need you to show me the ropes." "It will be a pleasure. Mrs Mahoney was right. You will be a great asset for Ryan & O'Farrell!" "Thank you very much, Kevin! Lorna tells me I'm to meet Bernard at twelve-thirty at Brown's." "I'll call a taxi now, since it's already ten past. You'd better scamper! You don't have to start here unless you want to until next week, by which time I promise that the nameplate on your door will not look so temporary!" Kevin laughed softly as he left Paul's new office. Wow! Thought Paul, I can't wait to tell Michael. Why did Lorna and Bernard keep all this a secret? I just don't understand.

The taxi drew up in front of Brown's. At the entrance he was greeted by Henry O'Connor, who said, "Congratulations! Well-deserved!" "Thank you, Henry, but I haven't done much to earn it!" "Oh sir, you're just being modest. This way please. The gentlemen are waiting." He followed Henry across the hall and into the lounge. It was Bernard he saw first, before Stephen, Amos and David. He was going to say something, but all of a sudden no words were needed. He went to Bernard, looked into his eyes and put both his arms around him, holding him tight. It was as though he were passing energy to Bernard, or perhaps, by holding

Bernard, the whole unreal situation of the day would disappear and everything would return to normal again.

"Well! Don't we all get a hug from the Managing Director?" said Amos, his large, tall frame moving toward Paul as he let go of Bernard. Paul whispered to Bernard, "You should have told me!" Bernard smiled, "But we couldn't. We would have destroyed your independence." They exchanged smiles, and Paul was most grateful for Amos's hug, because tears were not far away. "Jolly good!" pronounced David. "You'll be a great asset to the Company. Jolly good!" "May I offer you a drink?" smiled Stephen. "I've a feeling you'll need it after a day like this!" "Yes, Stephen, thanks! I could do with a drink!" Stephen called Henry, "Let's have a good bottle of champagne! We all have something to celebrate!" "At once, Judge Spender!" said Henry, and was gone.

Paul said, "If you'll excuse me for a moment, I'll just go and wash my hands, and I must phone home again". Paul disappeared down a well-trodden corridor at the same moment that Philip Robertson appeared with a glass of whisky in his hand. He noticed the four men together and Henry opening a bottle of champagne. "Something to celebrate?" he asked sarcastically. "Oh, lots!" said Major Keen. "Really!" said Philip, in an offhand manner. "I'm the one who should be celebrating, not you old lot! My father's now given me complete control of the firm. I plan to revitalise the whole operation", he said arrogantly. "Stay calm, Bernard!" said Amos in a whisper. "We'll have some fun here!" Philip went on, "I've fired Moran and now I'm in charge. No idea why my father ever employed that homosexual. I believe his lover's retarded. Such taste!" This time Bernard did have to be restrained. He moved forward with a more than threatening look in his eye. "Careful, it's not worth it!" said Stephen. "So you fired him because he was homosexual?" said Amos, and looked at David. "Chloe, what do we think of that?" "Oh!" said David, quick as a flash. "I don't think we like it at all, Daphne!" Philip was shocked that his comments had been short-circuited by Amos and David, who continued, having great fun. "Daphne, do pour me another glass of champagne, dear!" "Certainly!" boomed Amos in a loud voice. "A pleasure, Chloe dearest!" "I'd fire the whole lot of you poufs!" said Philip, in a voice that was now taking on a hysterical quality. "You'll not be firing anyone, and certainly not in this club!" said Stephen. "In

244

fact, you're just having your last drink here!" "What are you talking about?" asked Philip, swinging round to face Stephen. "Membership of this club is for gentlemen, which doesn't fit you, for a start! But be that as it may, no Club member may have a criminal record. Why don't you tell us about yours?" Philip blanched. He knew he was now on thin ice. "You don't know what you're talking about!" "Oh, but I do!" came Stephen's sharp reply. "If you are under any illusion that just because your father is a great friend of ours it will shield you from the truth, you are very mistaken. I ran an interstate check and you have one conviction in Adelaide and are awaiting trial in Sydney. The conviction was for assaulting an underage girl, and the charge in Sydney is very similar. In Adelaide they gave you eighteen months in prison. Being the Chairman of this Club gives me the power to cancel your membership immediately, without waiting for the other members to vote on it. I think you will find that Mr O'Connor is ready to show you to the door." "You can all go to hell!" shouted a hysterical and white-faced Philip. He threw his glass to the ground, smashing it and scattering ice everywhere, before making for the main door as quickly as possible, since he could see Henry and four burly waiters coming in his direction.

Paul returned, unaware of the drama, but he found the conversation between Amos and David very peculiar. "Why Chloe, you could have called me something a little classier!" "Like what?" "Well, 'Anastasia Alexandra', whereas I don't like 'Chloe' at all!" said David. "Terribly unsmart!" "Well, what about me?" complained Amos. "'Daphne'! Straight out of the film 'Some like it hot'. Where's your imagination? You could have said 'Marlene or Greta, but no! Just tired old Daphne. I'm not sure I should sit with you at lunch. I might move to another table and see what I can find!" By this stage, the joke had gone too far. No one could keep a straight face and shouts of laughter came from all four men, leaving Paul feeling completely out of it – not for the first time today. But at least he now had a drink and, as Daphne and Chloe's behaviour was explained, it was Paul's turn to laugh, laughter that released all the tension that had accumulated during the morning.

"I'd better get back to my new job", said Paul, standing up. "I'll see you at St George's Road about seven o'clock, Bernard!" and, after thanking the others, he left. "Well! What a day!" said David. "By the way, I was thinking 'one out, one in', if you get my drift". "What are you talking about?" said Amos. "Well, since we have got rid of Robertson, I see no reason why we shouldn't nominate Paul as a member. What do you all say to that?" All comments were definitely affirmative. "I should like to nominate him", said Bernard. "There's no problem with that, and I'll second the nomination", said Amos. "And Daphne and I will be guarantors for him, shan't we?" "Certainly, Chloe!" After a great deal of laughter, Stephen said, "A fortnight ago, Henry and I were sorting out all the records and preparing them for transfer onto the computer, when Henry came across a document and said he thought it was particularly relevant. I glanced at it and it took me a minute or two to grasp why Henry had handed it to me. It concerned a member who, in 1923, wished to nominate his son as a member, but it appears that the son had several problems – limited reading and writing skills. He was made a member extraordinary, and when I checked this out with some of our older members, they said they remembered him as a very quiet young man, who was killed in a motor accident, but had been a worthy member of the Club." They all looked at each other and, as though it had been rehearsed, they all chorused "Michael!" "Exactly! Now there's a precedent, or else we can elect him as an ordinary member. Either way, he's totally covered. What do you all think?" "I'd be more than proud to nominate him", said Amos. "Let's go ahead with an ordinary nomination, and if there's a problem at the general meeting next week, we'll switch to the other kind. Personally, I don't think there'll be any problem at all. David and I will do a bit of lobbying among the other members of the executive committee." "Henry will be very pleased. He's very fond of Michael", smiled Stephen. "Well! Now all that's sorted out, we may as well have another drink!"

The new job suited Paul down to the ground. It was a prestigious company, and Paul found working with Kevin very rewarding. They used each other to bounce ideas for their clients' investments, and many clients were more than pleased at the consequent increase in their dividends.

About a week later, when they were all at Killarney, just about to go in to dinner, Mary told Bernard he was wanted on the phone by Judge Spender. Bernard returned quite quickly. "Paul, Stephen wants to speak to you." Paul went to the hall phone. "Good evening, Stephen", he said, "is anything wrong?" "Hello, Paul! Well, not exactly. . . Both your nominations went through without a hitch, but I've a problem with Michael's surname." Paul replied, "He doesn't seem to have one. Michael doubles as both Christian and surname." "Listen, that's silly! Why don't you give him your surname, or let him use Bernard's. I can get it altered by deed poll. You and Bernard talk it over and let me know tonight, and we'll get going on it." Paul added a few words and hung up.

Paul returned to the yellow room and he and Bernard looked at each other. Then Paul said, "Come here, Michael. I want to ask you something very important". As usual, Michael was sitting on the arm of Lorna's chair. He stood up and walked over to Paul. "Michael, you need a surname." Michael looked straight at him, tilting his head a little and moving his mane of hair. "There's no point in your taking my name, since it would make us seem like brothers. I want you to ask Bernard if he will let you use his." The silence in the room was electric: everyone stared at Bernard, who appeared to be holding his breath. Lorna went over to stand beside Bernard and held his arm. Michael turned to Bernard and said softly, "Cooty! Will you let me use your name?" Bernard said nothing, but embraced Michael, who wasn't quite sure why, but worked out that it meant an affirmative. Michael felt Bernard's wet cheek against his. "Cooty, do you feel bad?" he asked. "No, Michael. I feel very, very fine." "Let's go in to dinner", suggested Anne, and they all moved towards the dining room, across the hall. Bernard and Paul were the last to leave the yellow room. "Thank you very much, Paul. I don't think you know what this means to me!" "I think I do, Bernard, and when Michael works it out, he'll be as happy as you are!" Bernard put his hand on Paul's shoulder and they went into the dining room together, to join a smiling Anne and Lorna. "Don't forget, Paul! You have to phone Stephen." "I don't have to", Paul replied. "I told Stephen I would only call back if Michael was not Mr Michael Mahoney!" "Hooray!" said Anne. "Let's drink to Mr Michael Mahoney!" and she looked at Michael and said gently, "That's you, darling! You have a new name! Isn't that wonderful?" Michael smiled and looked at Bernard beside him. "Cooty, thank you for your name: now we are the same!" Everyone laughed. Bernard was bursting with pride: now he had Michael for life; he had his name and that made him officially his. He could love him no more than he had, but for Michael to bear his name was like having a son, plus a friend, all rolled into one!

The following weekend, since the guestrooms at Killarney were being totally overhauled and redecorated by Nigel's careful hand, David and Amos were Anne's houseguests. She was delighted and rose to the occasion of being the *hostess with the mostess*, providing lunches and dinners of the most extravagant kind. The big dining room at Bellevue had never known such laughter and joking. Patrick joined them, as did Colin, one evening and a great time ensued, with Daphne and Chloe gently insulting each other the whole time. Patrick wasn't quite sure about the humour, but as the evening wore on, he was also seen laughing with the rest.

The group from Killarney and Bellevue attended the little church on Sunday morning, and then they all went back to Killarney for a special Sunday lunch, to which Patrick, Colin, Rodney and Samuel were also invited, with David and Amos. Bernard had softened toward Rodney a lot: he realised that he was not – or at least didn't appear to be – a threat to Michael and Paul's relationship, and had given him quite a lot of work redoing the gardens. During the meal, Bernard asked Anne whether, since they were now co-owners of the piece of land that had previously separated them, he could use the plot nearest to Killarney. "Of course you can, Bernard! You can have the whole lot if you want!" "No, I just want enough for a croquet lawn." "What!" exclaimed Anne. "Bernard, I never knew you played croquet!" "I don't", he replied, "but yesterday, Michael and I found my grandmother's set of mallets and balls and hoops. They are quite beautiful and can be used even at night!" "Really?" said Anne. "I've never thought of it as a night game!" "The hoops", began Bernard, "will have to be repainted, and two are broken. They are made of cast-iron and each of them has a candle in a glass shade on top, plus a little bell in a decorative space just below, so that if you play at night, the light will guide you and the bell will ring if you manage to put the ball through the hoop. They are very decorative." He looked over at Rodney. "Will you lay it out and put in plants and hedges?" Rodney gulped, "I haven't any experience in laying out a croquet lawn, but there's one at Brunswick. Yes, sure, I'll see what I can do". "Excellent!" said Bernard. "Oh, Bernard!" said Anne, "I knew I had something to tell you. The old Wallace house has been sold and they're going to pull it down and put up eight villa units! Can you believe it! Where's the National Trust! The Wallace mansion is a beautiful old house." "What about the conservatory?" "I haven't a clue. It's been years since I've been there." "I remember it", said Amos. "Don't you remember, Bernard? We went there when we were here on school holidays." "That would make it about 1850, wouldn't it", said a laughing David. "Careful, Chloe, or you'll be in trouble! I remember because Bernard hit a cricket ball through one of the panes of the conservatory. I can still hear the sound of smashing glass." "An accident, I think", said Bernard gruffly, as he stabbed at his plate. Then suddenly, as though he had received an electric shock, he sat bolt upright. His movement was so sudden, that everyone fell silent. "Anne", he said, "are you sure the Wallace place has been sold?" "Well, I think so. Someone told me the other day when I took Michael to have his hair cut. Why?" "Just a moment", said Bernard, and he stood up and left the room. "Oh, I don't like this at all!" said a worried Lorna. "I know that look Bernard has in his eyes!" Ten minutes later he re-entered the dining room humming with chatter and sat down without saying a word. Most of the guests assumed that Bernard had been to the bathroom, except Lorna and Anne. "Well?" they both chorused. "It's not sold, and Teddy Wallace said that the papers will be signed next Wednesday." "What a shame!" said Anne. "It's a solemn sort of house, but it has its charm." "Bernard, what have you been doing?" demanded Lorna sharply, causing a silence to fall over the table again. "Michael", said Bernard, with a twinkle in his eye. "Do you know what we are going to have in the garden?" "Cooty, I don't know." "Well, Michael", said Bernard, enjoying the moment, and taking a sip from his glass, "we are going to have a conservatory!" "A what?" cried Lorna. "I've just purchased the conservatory from Teddy Wallace." "Bernard! Where on earth will it go? I remember seeing it only once, about twelve years ago: it's an enormous structure!" "Well, we can't have it near the croquet green", said Amos. "I can just see Chloe shooting her ball straight through the glass!" "Ho! Ho!" came the sarcastic reply from David.

Patrick said he had seen it only three months ago, because there had been a break-in at the house, and some furniture had been stolen.

"You're right", he said, looking at Lorna. "It's very large, but a lot of the glass is broken. It has a beautiful floor of black and white marble, and a fountain at one end inside. How are you going to remove it?" he asked, looking in Bernard's direction. "Oh, that's not a problem! I'll phone Nigel this afternoon. He'll be able to sort it out. It will have to join on to the blind end of the ballroom, and it can be connected with a doorway behind that little narrow staircase. Oh yes! It will be a great asset. It's not too far from the kitchen, so perhaps we could dine there on summer evenings. It's a splendid idea!" he said, congratulating himself. "Poor Nigel!" was Lorna's only comment.

The meal proceeded as though nothing had happened, as though it was, after all, quite usual to buy a huge conservatory during luncheon. This attitude annoyed Colin. How irresponsible, he thought. Who needs a conservatory? Thoughts of conservation never crossed his mind, dominated as ever by the young man seated safely between Paul and Bernard. Now that he bore – or would shortly be bearing – Bernard's family name, it seemed to Colin that something he wanted very much was being pushed further and further from his reach. What he found even more galling was that Patrick was the only other male, apart from Paul and Bernard, to whom Michael spoke without any apparent problem. Patrick seemed to have no difficulty in finding subjects that he, Michael and Paul could share and laugh about together.

Samuel was wholly besotted with Michael and he could do nothing about it because he was so obvious in a charming but forlorn manner that it never bothered anyone, except Colin, who saw him as another competitor. Rodney was far more sophisticated. He charmed them all, especially Bernard, but his long-term intentions were totally opaque. Anne found the whole occasion splendid and, later, alone with Lorna, said she wouldn't dare miss another Sunday lunch party with so much electricity!

But the person most unaware of the dynamics was Michael. He loved Paul and that was that. This love was totally reciprocated, which in Michael's mind made black and white, without even a hint of grey. He liked attention, but was unaware of his attraction. Even though he and Patrick had a very special relationship, the thought of not being with

Paul, or of sleeping with another man, never entered his head. This could not be said of the other guests that afternoon at Killarney.

After lunch, they returned to the yellow drawing room for coffee, drinks, or both. At a certain point, Michael stood up and said to Patrick, "Patrick, come with me! You too, Paul. I want to show Patrick the tortoise room. The three of them left the room, much to Colin's annoyance. He saw this as a calculated move to show that Patrick was preferred above the others, whereas it had been a promise made by Michael when they were out riding some days ago. Michael took Paul, not because he needed an escort, but because it was the room they shared together. If Paul and Michael had been overwhelmed when they first saw the tortoise room, Patrick was quite unsure of what he was seeing. It was like a film set, a magic scene from Harry Potter, quite unlike anything he had ever seen before.

"Come in!" said Paul, smiling. "Yes, it's quite a room, isn't it?" "It certainly is!" said Patrick, walking into the middle of the sitting room part. "It's beautiful! I couldn't even imagine a dream room like this! It must be wonderful to wake up in it every morning!" "It's not bad: you get used to it, but you do miss it when you're not here. I think this opulence is too much, but Michael loves it, so I've come to like it too." "It suits you both", said Patrick, shyly. "Come on! Let's go down and join the others!" Michael turned the dimmer down on the big crystal chandelier. "I like it like this", he said. "It's nicer." "Come on, Michael! You can one more glass of champagne, and that's all!" "Patrick", he said, "let's have a glass of champagne". They returned to the yellow room, where Bernard and Rodney were discussing plants for the new conservatory.

Sunday lunch was deemed a great success by all. On Monday morning, Mulberry's was agog, waiting for Samuel to appear and provide a detailed description of what had happened. He was very reticent in answering Neville's leading questions, but as the day wore on, he filled them in on all the details, what everyone was wearing, and so on, especially Michael's blazer with the antique gold buttons. He commented that Patrick was obviously in favour, which Neville recorded, computer-like, for future reference.

Lorna was absolutely right: Nigel was shocked at having to erect the vast cast-iron conservatory from the old Wallace mansion, against the blind wall of the ballroom and at having to do it so quickly. He had to obtain a council permit to transport it, as well as to re-erect it, but as usual he knew someone who could do the work, once the permits had arrived. The new foundations for this enormous airy structure began to be laid. The biggest problem was that the original nuts and bolts had been welded together by rust and had to be drilled out, so that it took much longer and needed many more men to dismantle and reassemble it.

Michael was drawing a picture with Mary, making very good progress, and was otherwise occupied riding with Anne or Patrick. After lunch, when Paul and Bernard were in Melbourne, Michael would sit for half an hour at the grand piano, where Lorna taught him to play Chopsticks as a simple duet together. As with riding or painting, if everything started well, he was fine. If he made a mistake to begin with, he developed a mental block, and found the exercise very difficult. In time, he found it easier if Lorna started a split second earlier, after which he would follow and they could complete the duet. His riding was also making progress, and on Tuesdays Patrick was teaching him to jump small hurdles. His instructions were extremely sharp: lean forward; now back; do this, not that! But Michael believed in Patrick, and he felt his instructions were to help him, not to discipline him. One day, as Polly was taking a jump, Michael fell off and rolled on the grass. Polly was the first to reach him, rubbing her wet muzzle against his face. Patrick was not really close to him when he fell, and when he realised what had happened, he turned his horse and galloped back, fearing the worst, only to find Michael laughing at Polly. Patrick dismounted and took Michael in his arms. "Are you hurt?" he asked. "No, I did something bad and leaned the wrong way, but Polly came to help me." Patrick was quite white with fear that Michael had been hurt. "Well!" he said, releasing him. "Back on Polly, and let's do it again!" This time Polly and Michael cleared the hurdle without a problem. Patrick finished the morning ride with Michael, and returned to his office after receiving his usual hug. He could still feel him in his arms as he drove toward Brunswick.

Not only was Nigel overseeing the conservatory, but had almost finished the blue sitting room, the room he most disliked at Killarney, with its new Victorian cornice and pale Prussian blue hand-blocked wallpaper, and furniture rescued from the ballroom. He altered the inside of a large early nineteenth century black lacquer cabinet to hold the television, video and DVD equipment. When its great doors, inlaid with soapstone, were closed, all these appliances disappeared from view. The new curtains with their heavy valences gave the room a look that was now taking over Killarney: very much damask and tassels, but at Killarney it seemed wholly appropriate.

One morning, Michael was with Mary in the kitchen, when she asked him to help her carry some large pans to the storeroom, a place he had never been to before. The door bearing the chart showing Michael's eating likes and dislikes opened onto a low windowless passage that led beneath the main staircase landing. Mary turned on the harsh electric light and they carried the pans to another door at the end of the gloomy passage. Mary pushed the door open and switched on the light. The glare showed Michael a large room, filled with old kitchen utensils, stoves, refrigerators, and shelving filled with bottles and old saucepans and boxes of old preserving jars. The room was simply packed with things deposited here over sixty years, some never even used. The one window had been cemented up to two-thirds of its height, leaving a fixed pane with iron bars on the outside, making the room smell of mould and damp. Michael looked around in amazement at the confusion in the merciless glare of the unshaded light. High above the wooden shelving, he saw something, creeping all around on just three sides of the cracked and rotted ceiling. "Mary, look at the plants! What are they called?" Mary gazed upward, but the glare made it difficult for her to see what Michael was talking about. "Just a moment", she said, and returned with the kitchen broom, which she used to push the suspended light bulb to one side in order to see more clearly. "Good heavens, Michael! You're right! They're shamrocks." And there they were: on three sides the cornice was covered with shamrocks that crept out onto the damaged ceiling, but on the far side there were none, but in the centre where the blank wall joined the ceiling was half a ceiling rose, with the same shamrocks trailing out from it.

"Michael, darling, we've found the Irish room. I can't believe I've never noticed the decoration before! Go and get Mrs Lorna and Nigel at once!" Michael was so excited at having found the Irish room, although he wasn't sure what an Irish room might be, but anyway, he had found it.

"Lorna, Lorna!" he cried as he ran through the kitchen and into the blue room, where Lorna was writing. "Come quickly, we've found the Irish room! Come quickly!" Lorna was taken by surprise. "Where?" she asked. "In the kitchen", said Michael. "I must get Nigel." Lorna dropped her pen and went quickly to the kitchen, where she found the door to the passage open, and raced through to the storeroom. "In here! In here!" called Mary, hearing her footsteps, and Lorna entered. "Goodness! I haven't been in here for years! What a shocking smell! Perhaps the floorboards are rotten. Well, where is this Irish room?" "This is it!" said Mary. "What are you talking about?" replied Lorna. "Just look up at the ceiling a minute. I'll move the light with the broom." "Good heavens, Mary! It's the same decoration as on the consoles and mirrors that are now in the ballroom!" "What have we found?" came Nigel's deep, booming voice. "Oh!" he exclaimed, straightening up and gazing at the ceiling. "It's the same decoration as those consoles you bought from my shop. Push the light in the other direction! That's right! Oh, I see! This is only half the room. What's on the other side?" "The old staff rooms: two bedrooms and a little corridor and a bathroom", said Lorna. "So you think, Nigel, that it was once one large room?" "Of course! As you can see, we have half the ceiling rose and this dividing wall cuts it in half. The other half was probably smashed, or do the staff rooms have false ceilings?" "I haven't a clue! We shall have to look", said Lorna.

"Well, what shall we do with half an Irish room?" asked a straight-faced Nigel. "Lorna, let's make an Irish room. I think it would be very nice." "Are you sure you want an Irish room?" asked Lorna. "Yes", said Michael. "Mr Nigel, don't you think it would be very nice?" "I certainly do!" he replied. "Since the trucks are bringing the conservatory over, they can take away all this rubbish, plus the walls we knock down, and they can dump it all at the tip. It's more or less on the way. I'll get my men to smash out this cemented-up window, and everything can be taken out through there. Gosh, the smell is bad in here! Mary, take out just the things you use, nothing else. The rest is just junk, and we'll get rid of it all before Bernard gets back tomorrow evening!" "What a good idea!" said Lorna, and they all left the room in search of fresh air.

When Lorna, Michael and Nigel looked over the old floor plan of Killarney, it was clear that this large reception room had at some time been divided up for staff quarters. That same afternoon, the cemented window was smashed open, and the pane and iron bars removed, allowing the stale air and smell of decaying wood to drift out into the late winter afternoon.

On Thursday evening, Michael was at his usual post, gazing out into the dark and waiting for Bernard and Paul to come up the drive. When he finally saw the lights, he was at the front door in a flash. Before Bernard and Paul alighted, Michael was in Paul's arms and then Bernard's, telling them all about the Irish room, with all the plants around the top of the walls. Bernard and Paul were then greeted by Lorna, who said, "Well, boys! We have a tortoise room, so an Irish room should be easy!"

They followed her through the kitchen and the passage and into the Irish room, where the smashed-out window had been replaced by heavy plastic, nailed onto a frame. Nigel had put in more lighting, so it was now easy to see the moulded decoration in what was now a completely empty space. "What has happened to everything?" asked an amazed Bernard. "With Nigel's help, I've got rid of everything we never use or are likely to. Besides, Michael is very keen on an Irish room!" Bernard crossed the space and looked through a huge hole that had been knocked through into the old staff quarters. "Lorna, the space is about the size of the ballroom! It's vast!" "It looks as big, but it's only four yards longer than the yellow room. Nigel seems to think that renovation shouldn't be too difficult. The space in the centre of the wall opposite the windows had once held a fireplace, and the spaces between the three windows had held the consoles and long pier mirrors. Nigel said that Mr Rossi would take down the ceiling rose, or half of it, and recast the other half from it. We don't know how much of the original cornice still exists on the other side, until the false ceilings are taken down. The room was originally accessed by two doors, one on either side of the fireplace. It's all quite exciting! I can't wait to have it finished!"

Bernard looked at the shell of the room and, turning, said to Michael, "So, young man! You want an Irish room, do you?" "Cooty! I think it would be very nice!" he replied excitedly. "Cooty, look at all those plants around the top of the walls. There are hundreds of them!" "Yes, so there are! Come on, let's have a drink. I'm starving this evening! How about you, Paul?" "Yes, it must be the cold weather! How's the conservatory coming along?" "Quite well", said Lorna. "Nigel seems to have an army of men working for him. I have no idea how much this is all going to cost! By the way, Paul, have you worked out which apartment blocks I should sell?" "I have, but I think it would be best to sell only one block and cash in some of your smaller investments." "Good! That should pay for the Irish room." "But Lorna", began Bernard. "We're not short of ready cash!" "I know, but I'm doing this because I want to finish everything here. What good are all these apartment blocks if I can't spend the money as I want?" "As you wish", said Bernard, and made for the narrow passage and some clean fresh air. "Mary", he said, as he passed through the kitchen, "I'm starving!" "Thank goodness for that! I've prepared something very special and I've been hoping that everyone's got a good appetite!"

After their usual pre-dinner drink, the four of them moved to the dining room, with Michael still nattering on about the Irish room. "Cooty, Mr Nigel says that if it's an Irish room, it must be green. Why?" "Because, Michael, green is the national colour of Ireland, and also because it always rains so much there that everything's green!" "Oh, it rain's a lot!" He seemed to be digesting this information as Mary swept in with her special Thursday dinner, everything French! It was a great success with everyone, and even Michael, who was not a big eater, asked for seconds. "Cooty, if the Irish room is green, then we must use the big green chandelier in the box upstairs." "Of course we must", said Bernard. "Hmm", came Michael's reply. He appeared to be entirely absorbed by this room and, although he had no concept of Ireland, the idea of an Irish room was something very concrete. "Cooty, do other people have Irish rooms?" he asked. "I don't really know. Have you ever seen one?" Bernard asked, looking at Lorna. "No", she said. "Have you, Paul?" "You mean a room filled with Irish memorabilia? Well, sort of, but not like this one, with plaster shamrocks all over the ceiling. My grandmother had two cabinets filled with 'Bellique' china and lots of

Limerick lace, but that's as far as I go, I'm afraid. Perhaps Killarney is the only house in Australia with an Irish room. Who knows?" "I think this is the only house in the world with an Irish room", piped up Michael, "and I think it's very nice! Yes, it's very nice!" His reaffirmation of what he thought was right made everyone laugh. "Michael, you're wonderful!" said Paul. "Cooty!" Michael said abruptly, "I forgot. Mr Nigel said that you have to find the fireplace for the Irish room". "Good heavens!" replied Bernard, "I have no idea where the old one is. Perhaps it's at the back of the service building, in front of the red garden. You and I will have a look tomorrow". With this reply, Michael was quite content. After a splendid meal, everyone decided on an early night.

Several months before, Paul had told Mary that he would leave his cell phone on during the night, so that if any problem arose she could phone him without disturbing Bernard and Lorna. When his mobile rang at seven-thirty on Friday morning, Paul was rather surprised. He rolled over and picked it up. "What's wrong, Mary?" he asked. "Paul, there is a truck down here at the front door with two men insisting that Michael has to sign a receipt for a huge box." "OK", said Paul. Give us five minutes." He hung up. "Michael!" he said severely. "What did you buy?" "Paul, nothing. The twenty dollars are still in my jacket!" "Get dressed quickly! A big box has arrived for you." They scrambled into some clothes and made their way downstairs. Paul was overwhelmed at the size of the crate, which was seven feet by four and one-and-a-half feet thick. "Michael", said Paul. "What have you bought?" It crossed his mind that the crate alone probably cost more than twenty dollars. "Sign here", said one of the men. "Where do you want it?" "It had better be squeezed into the ballroom for now. Follow me", said Mary, taking over, and the two men lugged the huge crate into the hall and up the corridor to the ballroom. "Put it anywhere it will fit", said a forlorn Mary. Meanwhile, Paul had written Michael's name onto a piece of paper and he had copied it on the dotted line of the receipt. Paul was quite surprised at Michael's nonchalance about the whole business. After thanking the two men, who seemed totally disinterested, they drove their truck off down the drive.

"Now, Michael, what's in the box?" asked Paul sternly. "Do you know?" "Oh, yes Paul! It's Polly!" "It's what?" "It's Polly! Come on, let's go and have a shower!" "Michael", said Paul, "you're impossible! I'm not going to have a shower with you until you explain what's in the box!" "Paul, it's Polly! Anne and I saw her in a big gold frame, and Anne had the hole made good. That's what's in the box." "You mean that there is a painting in the box? Good heavens, Michael, it's enormous! Where are we going to put it?" Paul asked desperately. "Paul, we'll put Polly in the Irish room" said Michael in a matter-of-fact manner, making Paul feel that he must have missed something in the conversation. Michael put his arm around Paul's shoulders and they went back to their bedroom.

At eight-thirty everyone was down for breakfast and the story about Polly in the box prompted Lorna to call Anne in order to clear up the issue. She returned from her call and said, "He's absolutely right! There's a large painting of a horse in that box. It appears to be a copy of a Landseer. Anne had it cleaned and a hole repaired and here it is! Michael darling, where shall we hang it?" "Lorna, in the Irish room there's a lot of space." "I suppose there is", she said pensively.

When Nigel arrived, he was very anxious to see the painting, and called two of the men working on the conservatory to pry open the front of the crate. They were all overwhelmed. It was Michael who piped up and said, "Yes, it's Polly! You can see the white mark on her side! Yes, it's really Polly". Nigel inspected the canvas very closely and said, "Is it a copy, or is it the real thing?" "I presume it's a copy", said Paul. "Well, I wouldn't be so sure!" boomed Nigel, and with that they put the front of the box back on, and went to see what the Irish room looked like in broad daylight.

It was a very sad space, with a terrible, pervasive smell of damp. Since it was still winter, the effect of the grey day on the half-demolished room was very bleak. The men had torn down the dividing walls in two hours and above the false ceiling they found a large amount of the original cornice. But, as Bernard had said the evening before, it was an extremely large room. "Bernard, where's the fireplace?" Before Bernard could reply, the plumber's voice was heard from beneath the floorboards. "Two pipes are leaking down here, which is why there's water everywhere. What a mess!" "Ah well! At least we've found the problem!" said Nigel. "It will probably take until summer to dry the whole lot out. Oh, I was saying, Bernard, where's the fireplace?" "I haven't a clue. I'll take Mr Barnes and the boys here and we'll have a look at the back of the service shed. If we can't find it, I suppose we'll have to buy one." Oh, talking of buying, I've bought a croquet pavilion for you. Rodney thinks it's just right", said Nigel, walking away to supervise what was going on at the conservatory. "What, may I ask, is a croquet pavilion?" said Bernard, "and do we really need one?" "It seems we shall have to ask Rodney, as Nigel doesn't appear to be very concerned about it", said Paul. "Hmm, I suppose we will. Well, let's see if we can find that fireplace."

Outside, they were confronted by a vast cast-iron structure that was starting to take shape. "It really is quite large. I had no idea that ordinary private conservatories could be so big!" "No, nor did I", smiled Bernard. "Let's see what's in the shed! Mr Barnes! Mr Barnes! Over here!" The noise from the erection of the conservatory and the continuing demolition of the partition walls in the Irish room was deafening. "I don't remember any fireplace", said Mr Barnes. "What's it made of?" "Marble, I suppose, like the others inside." "There's nothing in marble, except those old shelves at the back of the garage." "What shelves?" "Come and have a look. They're wrapped up in old canvas." They followed him to the back of the garage. "I can't see a thing", said Bernard. "Isn't there a light here?" "Just a minute, Judge, I'll get the extension lead." In due course, Mr Barnes produced a light, Michael and Paul unwrapped the canvas to discover a dark-green marble fireplace, in six or seven pieces. "Well, it looks as though we've found it! I've no recollection of ever seeing it in my whole life. I hope they can put it back together!" said Bernard. With that, the three of them headed for the red garden, to see whether any of the one-hundred-and-fifty red tulips that Rodney had planted were breaking through the soil.

After much indecision, the croquet pavilion finally arrived on a large truck and was settled temporarily on four 40-gallon drums. When Bernard finally saw the so-called pavilion, he was quite perplexed. It looked rather like a very large and ornate bus-stop, with rooms either side, and in very poor condition on the left side as viewed from the front. "I hope this has not cost me a fortune", he said to Nigel, as they viewed it together. "Don't worry, Bernard", he said in his deep voice, "all you have had to pay for is delivery and restoration. It was free, so I got it for you. You need somewhere to sit out of the sun, while the others are playing." "Hmm, I suppose you're right!" said Bernard rubbing his head, and walked off, leaving Nigel and Rodney to decide exactly where it was to be sited and how to landscape the surroundings, as well as to work out who was going to do the restoration, since a lot of the decorative woodwork was in pretty poor shape.

As spring arrived, Killarney's azaleas and rhododendrons came into their own: their colours were spectacular and since no rain fell, they kept their blooms for a long time. Everyone continued to follow the established pattern, and life was calm and peaceful. This could not be said for Raymond Kenworth, who was summoned to appear before the magistrate. Anne was called as a witness, as were Patrick and Colin, but Michael was not present. Having heard the case, and realising that Michael was Judge Bernard Mahoney's protégé, the magistrate passed sentence on the tall thin boy who had pushed Michael to the ground, giving him six months in prison, since he had three previous convictions for assualt. Since Raymond had not touched Michael physically, he only got three months' community and social work. After the sentence was read out, to the surprise of everyone, including Raymond, not to mention the magistrate, Beryl rose to her feet and stated that for her, as Raymond's mother, the sentence was far too lenient and a year in prison would be much more appropriate. Everyone turned to look at the stony-faced Beryl, who gathered her capacious handbag from the seat beside her and stalked out of the court. Raymond looked across at Patrick and felt a sense of nausea and began to perspire. What, he thought, if I have to report to him every day. He took a handkerchief from his pocket and wiped the sweat from his forehead.

Raymond's worst fears were realised: he had to report to Patrick every morning, six days a week, for three excruciatingly long months. Patrick showed no pity whatever, and made sure the tasks Raymond was set were properly carried out.

It was now that Beryl realised that she had been playing the wrong game all her life. Her relationship with her husband was practically null: no love, no sex, only constant requests for funds; her son had turned into a fat, lazy bully. She mentally divorced herself from them both and, in the near future, would do so legally, with the support of a most unlikely friend. After her exit from court, Beryl drove to a large run-down house in what had once been a good part of Brunswick, now moving up real-estate-wise, but still a bit forgotten. She pulled up in front of 33 Hatfield Road, left the car, opened the damaged front gate and walked up the path to the front door of her childhood home.

Her grandfather had built this large weatherboard house, with verandas on both sides interrupted by a projecting room in the middle at the front. A commodious Edwardian house, it was roofed with orange-red tiles, and the weatherboarding was painted a horrid faded duck-egg blue, and all its features – windows, decorative fretwork and veranda posts – were picked out in sun-yellow. She had lived here all her unmarried life and, as an only child, had inherited it. She couldn't remember why they had bought the block of land on Birdwood Avenue and built the new house. Looking back now, everything seemed a great waste of time and money. 33 Hatfield Road had been let for twenty-one years, and the wear-and-tear really showed, and the garden was non-existent. The last tenants had left three months ago.

In her own mind, she felt she was coming home, but coming home to what? She turned the key and entered the hall. The wallpaper hung in loose strips on one side, where the roof clearly leaked. It smelt abandoned: the old linoleum was torn and the bare boards in the living room showed a polished surround, which meant that at some time a carpet had filled the centre. Neglect was everywhere. There were five bedrooms, two bathrooms, a large dining room and sitting room, independent servants' quarters and various service rooms, all totally abandoned. In the cold early spring afternoon, it was very forlorn. Beryl walked the length of the wide corridor, opened the back door and went out onto the veranda. There, in the back section, which could not under any circumstances be called a garden, was a double garage, leaning rather curiously to one side, and what had been her father's study, attached to one side, a huge window for light, with many of its panes broken. She sat on an upturned wooden fruit box left by the previous tenants , and stared into complete emptiness. Nothing, just nothing, she thought, after all these years, I have nothing. Then, thinking again, she realised that she had been fooling herself all her married life, she had lived a lie, and now everything had caught up with her. Although not one to run and hide, she felt a wave of total helplessness sweep over her. What was she to do now? She felt no fear or desperation, just a lack of knowing how to move ahead. She sat staring at her father's old studio, pulling her coat tighter round her neck.

Suddenly it came to her. The only way out is to find someone to short-circuit this dilemma. At that moment, the late afternoon sun caught one of the few intact panes in the old studio, and she saw her way out. In her usual direct manner, she took out her mobile phone and dialled Mulberry's number, Mulberry's of all places. "Yes, may I help you?" came Ernest's sharp little voice. "Yes, this is Beryl Kenworth, and I should like to speak to Neville, if I may."One moment", said Ernest in a most uncertain tone. "Mrs Kenworth", said Neville, "what can we do for you?" "I want to speak to you. At what time do you finish this evening?" "In about half-an-hour." "Would you be so good as to come to 33 Hatfield Road? I shall take you to dinner, if that's convenient for you." There was a moment's silence, then Neville said in a slow and calculating manner, "Give me half an hour and I'll be there, and yes, I am free for dinner" and he hung up.

Everyone at Mulberry's shared Beryl's opinion that Raymond had got off very lightly. Neville was intrigued as to what on earth Beryl wanted from him. He knew her only as a customer. What could she possibly need him for? His curiosity knew no bounds, a state he lived through for half-an-hour, having got away ten minutes early from Mulberry's. He now pulled up in front of 33 Hatfield Road. He had noticed the house before, but had always thought it rather sad. As dusk settled in, he opened the gate and knocked on the door. It was duly opened by the matronly figure he knew as Beryl Kenworth.

"Do come in", she said warmly. "The house is in shocking condition!" She had put on the lights in every room. "Let me give you a tour." Neville was fascinated: what could she possibly want? He followed her, listening to her description as they went from room to room. The house was much larger than he had thought it would be and, despite its shabby state, proclaimed that it must once have been quite grand, located as it was on a huge plot, covering almost three normal ones. The tour concluded with the staff quarters and then Beryl opened the back door at the end of the corridor. "Can you see it?" she asked. "It's attached to the side of the double garage. "What is it? All the windows seem to be broken!" "Yes, they are. It was my father's studio." "I didn't know he painted." "Hmm", she murmured, "He couldn't really. His work was terrible. He had the idea that he could paint like the minor Dutch masters: still life, especially flower studies. They were always a step below super-amateur: he had no talent at all. Now that you've seen the place, let's go to dinner!" She turned and went inside and Neville followed. She locked the back door, turned off all the lights, and then, from the shabby hall, they stepped out into a crisp late-spring evening. She locked the front door and said she would meet him at a little restaurant off Main Street.

When they were at last seated, each with a glass of wine, she said boldly, "Well, what do you think of the house?" "It's in terrible condition", he said sharply. "What do you want me to say?" "Only the truth! It's the only way we can go forward." She sipped her wine. Now Neville was really mystified. "I think you'd better come clean", he said. "What do you want from me? You didn't invite me here just to talk about your childhood home!" "Oh, but you're wrong! That's exactly why you are here. I want to share it with you." Neville took a gulp of his wine and stared at her. "What! Share it with me! Are you mad?" "No, not quite! Look here, Nigel! You live in a squalid apartment on Marton Street. You have no studio and, it seems, no opportunities for the future. No, please let me finish! I have this large house and the necessary funds to put it in order, as you know. I don't know you well, but I think that's an advantage. There's the bonus of the studio for your use. What do you say?" "I need another drink!" "Help yourself!" she smiled. His usual razor wit failed him. He had never had an opportunity like this. But Beryl, of all people! And such a big house! He began taking stock, and said, "It's very kind, but don't you think that my private preference for men might pose a problem?" He baited her, but she was ready for it. "I see that as an advantage, a positive advantage. What's your problem? Do you think I shall be embarrassed if you bring a gentleman home for dinner and he stays the night? Forget it, Neville! You'll lead your life and I'll lead mine, not that mine will keep up with yours! We shall definitely be seen as a very odd couple! What do you think?"

At this point, the waitress arrived and they ordered, Beryl then repeated her question. His composure returned and he looked at her. "We can do it on one condition." "What's that?" she asked, narrowing her eyes. "That you change your hairstyle!" She burst into hearty peals of laughter. "We may just make it as real friends!" She laughed again. "Is it really so bad?" she asked. "Truthfully, yes! Your hairstyle and clothes make you look twenty years older." "I suppose you see me as dowdy!" "A bit", he said, "but nothing that can't be remedied, rather like the house!" "What shall we do with the house?" "I suggest we call in Nigel Storey and see what he says about it. We'll speak to Rodney about the garden. It will cost you, you realise." "Of course! That's not a problem! I have sufficient funds and I'll sell the other house on Birdwood Avenue and the beach house, unless you think you will use it. I never go there. It's just an expense!" "Let's start with number 33 and sell the house on Birdwood Avenue. We'll think about the beach house later. Where is it, by the way?" "It's at Portsea, on the side of the cliff. My father must have bought it fifty years ago at least. But do you think Nigel Storey will give a quote for putting number 33 in order? I only ask, because he seems to be working flat out at Brunswick!" "Don't worry! Leave it to me!"

The meal ended with the odd couple making plans about which parts of the house would be their own private domains and which parts they would share. "I want a good kitchen. I like cooking and could do much better than what we've had this evening!" said Beryl in an offhand manner. "You must realise that you can bring your friends to drinks and dinner whenever you want. I like entertaining. For twenty years I've lived with someone who hated guests and only wanted whisky and television." "Sounds like a fun life!" "Yes, a really fun life!" she said sarcastically. "The studio is wholly yours, when it's repaired. I'll give you the key and you can do as you wish!" "Thanks! By the way, we must get the house repainted: it looks shocking. So run-down!" "I know, and I think the roof needs repairing too! We'll see Nigel Storey first and then get going. I have a great deal of the original furniture in storage. I suppose we should go and have a look at it, but let's wait for Nigel and then we can plan better!" They left the restaurant, said goodnight and went their separate ways.

We really will be an odd couple, thought Neville. But what the hell! A studio, a big house, no expenses, and she's not so starchy after all! Beryl's stand in the magistrate's court had redeemed her in the eyes of many. Very few would have had the courage to say what she had said. Some thought her callous to say such things about her own son, but also realised they too could one day be in the same position, with the same responsibility toward the community.

Socially, the most interesting development was between Anne and Lorna, who had known each other since their schooldays. Since Paul and Michael had entered their lives, a relationship developed between them that they had never known before: trust, understanding and sharing, a new experience for both of them. An experience due to this young man with a pivotal role, whom they shared without jealousy or animosity, giving rise to total support for him. Long before the others, Paul realised that these two splendid women gave their support to his and Michael's relationship, and probably loved Michael as much as he did, but without any sort of rivalry, each loving in her own way. Michael was never without one or the other of them, and took it all for granted, as did the others. But the relationship between Anne and Lorna was something much greater: they had common ground; they both loved and supported Michael, without giving a thought to who might be more important. This equal sharing meant that both had a role in Michael's life and were equally committed to it. For Anne, this meant riding with Michael and Patrick, while Lorna was the supportive figure in control of life at home, at Killarney. But what was interesting was the dynamics between Anne and Lorna: for the first time ever, they trusted another woman completely, and without any prejudice, a new development that produced an increasingly calm relationship with Michael. He understood undercurrents very well, the tensions, the sharp words, but now in the haven of Killarney, his whole past was dissolving, and everything was now positive and the only way to go was forward. His love for Paul was total, sometimes to the point of exaggeration, but this was part of his black-and-white scheme of things. Paul was the only person he loved sexually, and while he shared his love with Bernard, Lorna and Anne, it was to Paul that he was totally committed.

Michael was now about nineteen years of age. No one knew exactly how old he was, but that wasn't important in his mind. He had the man he loved, and Cooty, as well as Lorna and Anne, and his world was absolutely secure. In a certain sense, he lived in a super-protected environment that was fostering his development: his ability to paint, his work in the garden and piano lessons, his riding, all this meant that with the support of people who loved him everything was made possible. This was put to the test when Nigel said to him – the work on the Irish room being well advanced – that he needed eight relatively large shell paintings for the end wall. Michael was most taken aback: a shell painting was no problem, but eight of them seemed a great number to him. Even with Mary's help, would he be able to manage it? "As soon as possible!" said Nigel. So Mary and Michael sat down in the studio to tackle Nigel's demand. While Michael was worrying over finishing the paintings, Lorna, Anne and Bernard were working feverishly to organise his birthday party – in fact, his first birthday ever - , which was to fall on St Michael's day, September 29th.

Anne hit on a brilliant solution. "Why not", she said, "go to mass in the morning, then Michael can go riding with Patrick and they can end up at a large marquee by the lake at the bottom of Killarney and Bellevue for an enormous picnic?" "Oh yes!" exclaimed Lorna. "It's the only way to do it! A spring picnic, and I know just the right caterers!" Bernard nodded. He never doubted Lorna's ability to produce the finest of parties at the drop of a hat. "But you see", she said. "It must be a surprise! When Patrick and Michael get to the tent, it must be a surprise! Oh, I'm so looking forward to it!" "Well", said Bernard, "you have only a little over two weeks to get it going! We go halves, or it's not going to happen!" "Oh, Bernard! You're so silly at times! I'll send you half the bill! Who shall we invite? Oh, what fun!"

Both Bernard and Lorna knew very well that the half of the bill for the birthday party would never arrive, but as Anne was so excited, they let matters rest. "We must have Amos, and Stephen and David must come, of course!" Anne said. "Oh! And we must have the Mulberry boys! Oh Bernard", she said slowly, "I heard from Neville that he and Beryl are going to live together, obviously – knowing Neville's background – as friends only, although I must say, I find it rather quaint!" "So do I", said Lorna, "but, on the other hand, why not? Perhaps Neville will enliven Beryl and she will make him a little more settled." "I don't think anyone, either Beryl or anyone else, will manage to tame that rapier-tongue of Neville's, but the relationship may just work. I think we should invite her as well. Let bygones be bygones!" said Anne. "After all, she made a pretty good stand, when you consider it was her only son!" "OK", Bernard replied, "invite whomever you want, but I – and remember this Anne! – shall provide the champagne!" "I accept, Bernard", said Anne airily and smiled. Looking at Lorna, she said, "The cake is yours and Mary's responsibility! There! Everything's arranged!"

But this was not the only surprise concerning Michael's birthday. Lorna wrote out all the invitations and gave them to Mary to post on her way to her weekly shopping. But an idea had occurred to Mary, and instead of going straight to the post office, she turned her car at the main intersection and headed for Rodney's nursery. She went straight to his office, where he greeted her saying, "Can you wait just a minute? I'll be back in ten minutes. Have a look around!" Ten minutes later, he found Mary looking at some well-established white azaleas. "They're quite lovely", she said. "Yes, they're all for the conservatory at Killarney and I've just sent off that large truck you saw at the gate, full of plants and trees for it as well!" "It's on that subject that I want to speak to you, but you must promise me that you'll keep everything I tell you a secret!" Rodney looked rather surprised. He knew Mary quite well now, having dined fairly often at Killarney with Samuel, but not on an intimate level of keeping secrets. "OK, I promise!" he said. "Rodney, will the conservatory be finished for Michael's birthday?" "It should be. Why?" "Will the painting be ready and all the plants and lights in place?" "Yes", replied a somewhat perplexed Rodney, wondering why she was asking him and not Nigel or Bernard. "Well, here is what I want to do! After the birthday picnic, Mrs Lorna has asked me to prepare a light dinner for a few friends, but I thought that with your help we could decorate a large table in the middle of the conservatory as a surprise dinner. What about it? Will you help me?" "Of course I will!" "I'll give you free rein to do what you think is best. I'll only need to know the size of the table for the cloth." "How many guests will there be?" "I think the same group as we had for that lunch some time ago: Mr Bernard, Mrs Lorna, Mrs Rochester, Patrick, Dr Colin, yourself and Samuel, Admiral Watson and Major Keen, and Judge Spender. Have I left anyone out?" "What about the birthday boy and Paul?" "Oh yes", she laughed. "No party without the birthday boy!" "But Mary, it can't really be a surprise! All these people will look at their invitations and talk to one another!" "Oh,

I've thought of that! A little note included with the invitation to this conservatory dinner will threaten them with death if anyone breathes a word about it!" "Very well, Mary. I'll give you a hand. You say I can do what I like?" "Absolutely!" came the reply. "Well, this can be my birthday present for Michael!" "Oh no, Rodney! I insist you send me personally any expenses relating to this venture!" "We'll work it all out later!" smiled Rodney. They shook hands and she walked down the path to her car. Rodney thought to himself, I wonder where that huge wire and metal chandelier is that they used in the local repertory theatre production at Brunswick town hall last year? Neville's sure to know! And he headed for the telephone.

Mary duly posted all the invitations, all sixty-one of them and at the same time handed over eleven cream envelopes bearing the addresses of her chosen guests for the conservatory party. They contained a small card, bidding them to dinner at Killarney at eight o'clock – black tie. With the invitation was a typed note asking each person, including Bernard, Lorna and Paul, not to talk or speak of this event to one another, or they would miserably spoil a special surprise for Michael, and hoping they could contain their curiosity, for which they would be rewarded on the evening. Mary then set out to do her shopping for Killarney and to stock the larder for her gift to Michael of a dinner party in the conservatory.

The reality was a little different. As the day drew nearer and nearer, Anne's ideas evolved greatly: one medium marquee became two enormous red-and-white striped ones, one with a dance floor and the other set up for eating, with the walls and ceiling draped in apricot chiffon and two vast Venetian chandeliers suspended above the tables' white damask. Anne also insisted on lots and lots of good-looking waiters. Anne had a power cable laid underground from Bellevue to the edge of the lake for the lights and orchestra. Everything was organised down to the last tiny detail.

Back at Killarney, the huge birthday cake was well underway: a three-tier dark fruit cake – a little like a wedding cake – with the fruit soaked in brandy. The cake had to be made, according to Mary, as quickly as possible, so that it could rest and then be assembled and decorated, and all in secret. Patrick was called in to help, and his riding lessons took

Michael far from the 'danger zones'. Grateful as everyone was to Patrick, he was even more grateful to them for having Michael to himself. For Patrick, it was like adrenaline just to be with him: it came in a surge, followed by the most sublime calm, a feeling of supreme security. Whatever it was, he felt that it was all he wished for the rest of his life: Michael seemed to produce a balm that made nothing impossible and everything good. Patrick's only problem was that these times together were never as long as he would have wished.

At this time, a very awkward situation occurred that galvanised the Killarney set to a man. One evening, returning from a very late shift, Patrick couldn't find a parking lot near his apartment and so was obliged to leave his car near the corner of the park. He locked his car and started walking the block-and-a-half to his apartment building. He had only taken a few paces, when he heard a girl screaming. He spun around and realised that the sound was coming from the opposite, more heavily wooded side of the park. He rushed over lawns and between the trees and finally came upon two youths attempting a sexual assault on a young girl, who was resisting their efforts. She was now being held by one of the boys, but it was difficult to see clearly, and at three-thirty in the morning, after an eight-hour shift, Patrick was not about to start asking questions. His fist swung swiftly into the face of one of the boys, sending him crashing backwards, and he turned his attention to the other. The boys attempted to defend themselves, but they were no match for a very defiant and aggressive Patrick. Perhaps he should have been less aggressive, but he wasn't: he attacked them viciously. The girl was hysterical. He helped her to her feet and led her away to his car to take her to the hospital, since she was bleeding badly from the mouth. He never gave a thought to the two thugs, one sporting a broken jaw and the other a broken nose, with severe rib injuries. He left them where they were, took the girl to the hospital and alerted the authorities. The girl's parents were telephoned and, at four o'clock in the morning, retrieved their rather battered daughter from the emergency section of Brunswick hospital.

It should all have ended there, but it didn't. One of the louts was, in fact, the son of very important local bigwig, with certain financial backing. The father sued Patrick for excessive violence against his son, whose broken jaw was cited as evidence. Patrick was suspended from duty pending the hearing. The Killarney set serried their ranks: Anne and Bernard went to see Sergeant Reynolds to try and sort out the situation. "It's not the first time", said Sergeant Reynolds, scratching his head. "He has a very quick Irish temper!" "I'd see it as a member of the constabulary doing his duty", said Anne sharply. "Where do we stand?" asked Bernard. "We?" said Sergeant Reynolds. "Well, he's our friend, and if we can help, we will." "Judge Mahoney, that's very kind, but we must see now how this works out with the father, who's prosecuting for excessive violence." "Do you think it will go before a police disciplinary board?" asked Anne. "I don't know, but I certainly hope not! It depends on the father pressing charges." "Who is the father?" asked Bernard slowly. "Andrew Simons" came the reply. "Oh really?" said Bernard and nothing more was said, and after making their goodbyes they left the police station.

"Sergeant Reynolds doesn't seem very supportive", said Anne, as she swept her Mercedes out into the main street. "We shall see about this", said Bernard in a rather secretive manner, making Anne glance in his direction. She dropped Bernard off at Killarney and headed home, but even before the gates of Killarney were behind her, she had got Patrick on her mobile and said, "Come over to Bellevue for dinner *now*!" It was more an order than an invitation, and when he arrived forty minutes later, it was as though a chic evening had been arranged for two dear old friends, despite the undercurrent.

"Listen, Patrick", said Anne, as they sat down for a pre-dinner drink. "Whatever happens with this ridiculous situation, you have a place at Bellevue or Killarney. If the worse comes to the worst and they suspend you indefinitely, you can take the large apartment off the swimming pool for as long as you like. I'll match whatever salary you are making and you can manage the stables here, so that I shan't have to send the horses to Cynthia's stables in winter. It's essential for you to go on giving lessons to Michael, and that's that! Oh, by the way, do you like swordfish? We're having it this evening." Patrick never got used to the way this group rallied around and then carried on business as usual. He wasn't as judgemental as Colin and was much more inclined to accept the inevitable, whereas Dr Colin Campbell thought that they were all a law unto themselves and, albeit a great social opportunist himself, he never approved of their methods or assumptions that whatever they did was right.

Patrick's situation hung only lightly over the forthcoming birthday. Anne was convinced that Bernard, being Bernard, would resolve it all and that, in fact, was what happened. Many years earlier, Bernard had given Andrew Simons's father a very lenient sentence for fraudulent real estate dealings. He now phoned Terry Simons and invited him to Killarney for a drink. The social occasion lasted only long enough for Terry Simons to finish his drink and for Bernard to hint that, if charges were pressed against Patrick Timms, the public prosecutor might be interested in irregularities in a new building estate that Simons was developing on the outskirts of Brunswick. They shook hands and Terry Simons left Killarney with the sure feeling that if he ever saw judgement day, Bernard would be there, making the judicial decision and not necessarily in his favour. The charges against Patrick were dropped to Patrick's great relief, though wondering whether, if Anne were to make the same offer of employment at Bellevue, he should continue working as a policeman or look after the stables and chaperone that beautiful young man called Michael.

After this incident, Patrick increasingly became part of the group. Much to Colin's annoyance, Patrick was often seen in public with Anne or Lorna, but more often with Michael, which Colin viewed as a danger to himself socially. Somehow Patrick had managed to achieve something that Colin couldn't: Michael's affection, and a secure place in the tight Killarney-Bellevue set. He was only a policeman, Colin thought. OK, he was good-looking, but his conversation was limited. How could they all accept Patrick as their social equal? The green-eyed dragon of jealousy gnawed at Colin, and he suffered. When invited to either Killarney or Bellevue, he was very much aware that he was the outsider, not Patrick. Even Rodney and Samuel chatted with Patrick as though they were lifelong friends, and Colin noticed that Samuel was paying more specific attention to Patrick. What really galled Colin, however, was that when Paul and Michael came down to dinner, the party had usually already gathered, and after Bernard, it was Patrick who received a hug and a kiss, never him!

The birthday party arrangements were excellent, and everything was kept a secret from Michael: he never thought for a moment that one enchanted day would be any different from another.

For Mulberry's however, this was not only a top social occasion, but also very good business. Ernest ordered a whole range of fine things in Michael's size, in his favourite colours, so that whenever one of the lucky guests descended on Mulberry's for a gift for Michael's birthday, Ernest and his staff could supply exactly what was required: a chic and perfectly acceptable present, all wrapped in red gloss paper and tied with yards of red ribbon. "Oh, it's almost like Christmas!" chimed Ernest, speaking to the staff. "How exciting! I do believe that our dear Mrs Rochester, as smart as ever, has engaged a chamber orchestra for the luncheon! And chandeliers in the marquees! Oh, what an afternoon it will be! Nothing of this kind has ever occurred in Brunswick before! How exciting!" He babbled on, fussing about the arrangement and stacking of boxes of shirts (all in Michael's size) on the main counter. "I bet you'd like to take him a new bathing costume, wouldn't you Tarzan?" teased Neville. "Ho! Ho!" replied Samuel. "At least he can fill them out much better than you can!" And he walked off to help yet another customer who had received a birthday party invitation.

It was Neville, now much more secure with Beryl's support, who greeted Dr Colin Campbell. "Are we looking for something, Doctor?" Colin smiled weakly. "Yes, I need a gift for Michael." "Oh, you as well!" came the slightly sarcastic comment. "I thought a shirt or a jumper. What do you think?" asked Colin, looking at Neville and then glancing sideways at Samuel. "A bit ordinary: everybody's doing the same, but there are some very nice shoes in his fitting, if you care to come this way, Doctor." Colin glared at Neville. He had never liked him, and his opinion that he was a real bitch was one-hundred-percent accurate, so it was annoying that he had to deal with this supercilious queen. The shoes were indeed beautiful: light tan brogues, American, not English, with the traditional design punched into the fine leather. "They're a little expensive, but they're real quality", murmured Neville. "Very well! Put them on my account and wrap them!" So yet another parcel left Mulberry's in its red wrapping paper and large red satin bow.

To Michael, it was just another house party weekend, with Amos, David, Stephen and a few other friends of both Bernard's and Lorna's, as well as Anne's, who began to fill the two large houses. Much laughter and drink got this birthday weekend off to a good start. No one spoke about the second invitation, and it was kept like a State secret. Michael was pleased to see all his friends from Melbourne, and it never crossed his mind that this weekend was different from any other.

Having risen late on Saturday morning, he and Paul showered together and, as usual, were late for breakfast. Everyone else had gone to take a quick glimpse of the conservatory, now almost finished with most of its plants and trees in place, and the Irish room, now fortunately without the smell of leaking pipes and mould.

Michael left via the gate between to Killarney and Bellevue to join Patrick for his riding lesson. Patrick had been instructed to take them as far as possible from the last-minute preparations by the lake, before returning for the birthday celebrations. For Patrick, the order to disappear with Michael was almost wish fulfilment. They headed their horses in the opposite direction to the lake and the marquees. Patrick smiled inwardly to himself, thinking of the following two wonderful hours of solitude. In Patrick's mind, when he and Michael were alone together, they came close to perfect harmony. Michael always followed Patrick's instructions, and to see them riding together was quite a treat.

At about half-past-twelve, Patrick and Michael headed back to Bellevue, but instead of going straight to the stables, Patrick insisted that they should pass by the lake. Never doubting Patrick's decision, Michael assumed it was normal and off they went. Michael was greatly surprised to see two huge striped marquees by the edge of the lake: no people, no sound, just two big tents. "Patrick, what are these things doing by the lake?" he asked. "If you wait just a minute, you'll find out!" Patrick replied. Near the marquees was an oak tree, to which they tethered their horses. As they approached the marquees, their sides rolled up and sixty people or more, with the aid of the chamber orchestra, started singing 'Happy Birthday'.

Michael was bewildered and looked for Paul, but not seeing him immediately, he seized Patrick's hand and froze slightly. Paul saw this through the crowd and came forward and explained that this party was just for him, and that it was his birthday party. Everyone clapped and cheered. Michael smiled, one hand in Paul's and the other in Patrick's. "Look at that, Tarzan! What wouldn't you do to be in Patrick's place?" teased Neville. "Ho! Ho!" said Samuel and moved toward the bar. "Can I get you some poison or something?" he asked. Michael had never seen so many parcels, all wrapped in glossy red paper with big red satin bows. He was amazed when he realised that he had to open each gift, and thank the donor with a kiss or a hug. Everyone was dressed in smart casual clothes, as requested in the invitation, but it was Michael and Patrick in their riding gear who won the day for being smartest. The orchestra played and people moved from one marquee to the other, chatting and laughing, and taking advantage of the excellent food and wines. At the onset, all eyes focused on Beryl, a very different Beryl, who had lost thirty pounds at the Health Farm, let her bobbed grey hair grow out, and stood at Neville's side, coping very well with his bitchy banter. She looked most acceptable: her hair was now blond, just over the collar of a smart dark-blue Ralph Lauren blazer, white blouse and pale grey slacks and a pair of elegant black flat shoes, rather than her usual 'dykey' footwear, as Neville used to call it. She wore very discreet gold and diamond earrings and a splendid Cartier bracelet that had belonged to her mother. All in all, it was a total make-over, and as everyone said, much for the better. Michael received his gift from her, kissed her on the cheek and said thank-you. A little voice inside Beryl said, "You should have done this a long time ago", and with that, she plunged into the spirit of the party with all the others.

"Samuel", said Rodney, "I have to go. I promised to do something for Judge Mahoney. See you at home, about seven o'clock. Don't be late! Samuel looked very surprised. Why on earth wasn't Rodney staying for the lunch? How odd! Ah, well! There was Michael. . .

Nothing ever changed, and Neville always took advantage of it. When Michael kissed Samuel and thanked him for his gift, Samuel melted. His adrenalin pumped and it was as though his rather large feet no longer touched the ground. Michael also thanked Neville, but shook hands and moved on. "Careful, Tarzan, or you'll fall right out of your tree into a heap, and then we'll have to send for Cheetah!" "Fuck off!"

came the sharp retort, but Samuel was really very happy and didn't refuse a drink from a good-looking young waiter, who made sure his glass was full throughout the entire luncheon.

"Oh, God!" exclaimed Neville in a devilish manner. "Just look! Colin Campbell has got a kiss from Michael! Oh, shock! Horror! Is there a doctor is the house?" This brought shouts of laughter from the Mulberry set and the group around them. "Be quiet, you faded parrots!" said Ernest Mulberry. "You happen to be in smart company, not that some of you would know the difference!" His tone then changed completely, as he saw Anne coming toward them. "Oh Mrs Rochester! What a most delightful luncheon! So very smart and so very you!" "Thank you", she replied. "Would you all like to take a seat at one of the tables? I think we'd better begin, if that's all right!" "Oh, of course, Mrs Rochester!" Anne returned to the noisy hub of the party, giving instructions about the arrangements.

She wasn't stupid or blind. Even Anne could see Samuel's plight, so she sat him where he had a clear view of Michael for the entire meal. The Killarney table sat as they always did. No one, not even Colin would have dared to change their traditional places. The only change that had occurred was to seat Patrick opposite Michael, which annoyed Colin, since before Patrick had arrived on the scene, it had been his coveted place.

Everything went like clockwork. The good-looking waiters were much appreciated by the Mulberry group, but the young waiter who had kept Samuel's glass full couldn't understand why he had become invisible now that Samuel had a view of Michael! Michael himself was overwhelmed by the party, and little by little realised that it was all for him. Maisy O'Brien was there, and all the people he knew and dealt with, from Nigel down to his hairdresser, who was most flattered that she had earned an invitation. Owing to the fine food and wines, the orchestra was almost drowned out by bursts of laughter and the buzz of chatter. At the end of the meal, and after a suitable interval, the cake was brought in. Anne stood up to thank everyone for coming and for their kind gifts. She gave especial thanks to Mary for the cake, but Mary was nowhere to be found. How odd, thought Anne. Rodney's place was also empty. He was doing something for Bernard, Samuel had said, but on Michael's birthday? I must have a word to Bernard, she thought, but in the hustle and bustle of the party, it slipped her mind.

It was now Michael's turn to say thank-you, with which Paul had given him some help. When Michael stood up, Bernard clinked a teaspoon against his glass for silence. As Samuel said later, Michael looked like a god, rising out of a sea of people. He looked around and smiling said, "This is my first birthday party! Thank you, Anne, and thank you all!" He sat down again, everyone applauded, and the cake was cut. The champagne flowed. After this, people rose and moved around talking to each other, gliding in and out of the marquees to take advantage of the sunshine outside. There was a burst of laughter, and Neville's voice was heard saying, "Let's face it, Agnes. You couldn't ride a horse even if there was an armchair strapped onto it!" "Smart arse!" was the only reply and with that, Agnes, a woman in her early fifties, strode over to where the two horses were tethered. Looking at them, she decided that Polly was clearly the more amenable for a woman who had not been on a horse in almost thirty years. "I'll wager ten dollars you can't ride fifty yards!" cried Neville. "I'll make it fifty!" cried someone else. By this time, all the guests were outside, leaving the waiters to tidy up and the orchestra playing for no one. Agnes, having had enough to drink and with just dumb courage, with the help of Patrick got her leg over and sat astride a not altogether happy Polly. Michael she knew and loved, but this hefty matron was another thing altogether. A great cheer went up as Agnes moved Polly away from Patrick's grasp. "You see! Once a rider, always a rider! And I'll be more than happy to take your ten dollars, Neville!" With that, she dug her heels into Polly's flanks. That was enough for Polly, and she bolted toward the lake to screams of laughter from all the guests, including Michael and Bernard. As Polly neared the very edge of the lake, she stopped abruptly and lowered her head, thus sending a fifty-year-old matron hurtling through the air and into the muddy water. The laughter was now unstoppable. Polly returned to where Michael and Patrick stood with Bernard, while Anne sent some waiters to help the much bedraggled Agnes, wet through and covered in mud, into one of the marquees to dry off a little, before going home for a shower. "Would you like the ten dollars now, or later?" teased Neville "Drop dead!" came the retort, bringing hoots of laughter from all.

As Ernest Mulberry said, the luncheon party was the finest, and probably the funniest, that Brunswick has ever seen. Everyone agreed with Ernest as they all headed home that Agnes had provided the best comic relief. Even Anne had to admit that this had been one of her greatest successes.

While all this was taking place, however, preparations were feverishly underway for the evening performance. Mary was working frenetically in the kitchen, and a few "Oh fuck!"s from the conservatory meant that all was not exactly going according to plan.

Both doors to the conservatory – from outside and inside – were locked. When the Killarney party returned from their splendid luncheon, they all took to their beds for a rest before the evening meal. It wasn't till about seven o'clock that Judge Stephen Spender made his appearance in Anne's sitting room in black tie. Ten minutes later, Anne came in herself, in a magnificent strapless burgundy satin evening frock with a train, making this a perfect excuse to open her safe and place around her neck a beautiful ruby necklace set in platinum with matching earrings. "Stephen, do be a darling and fasten the clasp for me!" "Anne, may I ask you something?" "Certainly, darling, so long as it's not my age!" "The invitation for this evening is a total mystery! What is Bernard doing?" "Darling, I haven't a clue!" At that moment, the maid entered. "Mr Timms, Madam!" "Oh what a pleasant surprise!" said Anne, as Patrick rounded the corner in a dinner jacket, looking perfection itself. He said, "I knew you would be going, so I thought I would make myself useful and collect you!" "How thoughtful of you, Patrick, always the gentleman! All right gentlemen, let's see what Bernard has cooked up for us!"

As they reached Killarney, they were followed up the drive by Rodney and Samuel in Samuel's car, and in turn by Colin. They all exchanged greetings and found suitable words of praise for Anne's marvellous gown and jewels. They were shown into the yellow drawing room, where a waiter offered champagne to all. Lorna entered with Bernard, Amos and David, who were staying with them, and five minutes later, Michael with Paul, all dressed as requested by the invitation. A glass of champagne in her hand, Anne was the first to make inquiries. "Well, Bernard, what's the mystery? Do tell! I'm dying to know! I received an exquisite invitation from you." "Not from me, you didn't!" he said. "Oh Lorna, do tell!" "But Anne, I don't know anything about it! I never sent these invitations!" "Well, who did then?" said Anne, looking at the other guests. "I did!" said a voice, and everyone turned to the doorway to see Mary standing there. She moved toward Michael in the centre of the room and put her arm around him. "Happy Birthday, darling! This is my gift and Rodney's!" Anne now looked totally bewildered. "Right! This way!" said Mary, taking Michael by one arm and Rodney by the other. They all traipsed past the ballroom and stopped in front of the door leading to the conservatory. Mary and Rodney stepped back. "Open the door, Michael!" said Mary, "and Happy Birthday!" She kissed him on the cheek and, so as not to miss an opportunity, Rodney did the same.

Michael opened the door and stepped into a wonderland where nothing was real and everything possible. Gasps were heard from all sides, including from Lorna and Bernard. "It's splendid!" cried Anne. "Oh, really, really splendid!" and it was. Rodney had directed the lighting in such a way that the plants and trees looked as though they were floating: you never saw the base, but only the tops of everything. In the centre stood a large table covered with a long white cloth: every accessory that night was white. Over the table hung an enormous wire-and-metal chandelier, painted white, with sixty lighted candles, each provided with a drip tray to catch the melting wax. On the table were the large silver candelabra that had belonged to Bernard's mother, also fitted with white candles, flickering slightly and producing marvellous moving shadow effects.

"Oh Chloe! It's just like our honeymoon!" said Amos, sending everyone into hysterical laughter, even Colin for once seeing the funny side of it. They all found their place-cards and sat down, Lorna at one end and Anne at the other, while Michael, as usual, sat between Bernard and Paul, with Patrick opposite him. "Rodney, this really does you credit!" said Bernard, looking around him. "It's very tasteful and smart." "We aim to please", was Rodney's reply, knowing full well that this evening – the result of many days' work – would definitely pay dividends in every possible way, except one – and that was Michael, beautiful, but infinitely remote. This he knew for a fact, unlike Samuel, who dreamed that one day it was going to happen.

Mary had prepared a splendid meal, with all Michael's favourites. At a certain point early on, Bernard excused himself and went to the kitchen. "Mary", he said, "who is paying for all this?" "Judge Mahoney", she replied quite sharply, "this is my gift and hopefully you will be gracious enough to accept it". Bernard felt a little out of his depth: Mary had never spoken so sharply to him before. "Thank you, Mary, but will you please do me a favour!" "Certainly", said Mary, in a more relaxed manner. "You will find a crate of champagne in the wine cellar. It was brought back from Anne's this afternoon. I'd be most pleased if you would use it!" "Don't worry, Judge!" she laughed. "It's already on ice!"

Bernard returned to a table laughing at Daphne and Chloe jokes. Michael's whole day had been planned and catered for by people who loved him, and he accepted both the events and the people with him as an everyday occurrence. He was happy and the setting, although interesting and pleasant, didn't matter: it was the security that these people provided that really mattered. Colin's opinion – never expressed within earshot of the present company – was that Michael was overindulged and, as a result, just expected more. After all this time, Colin should have come to understand Michael, but he didn't; all he knew was that Michael had an effect on him, as he did on many at the table tonight, and that the real winner was Paul.

The triumph of the dinner was the main course. Mary had discovered in the ballroom, along with the candelabra, a huge silver meat dish and dome. As the waiters brought out the numerous vegetable dishes, they left a large space in front of Bernard for the surprise. Mary brought the huge domed dish and placed it before Bernard, then turned to Michael and said, "Take the top off, Michael!" He duly did so, to reveal an enormous turkey, covered with pineapple slices, halved-cherries in each centre, and topped with a glaze. The two great drumsticks were fitted with frilly end-papers and the turkey itself sat on a bed of roast potatoes. The company applauded and cheered. Mary took the dome and deposited it on a side table, and left Bernard to carve.

It was at this moment that Rodney withdrew from his pocket a remote control, aimed it and pressed a key. In a flash, the whole lighting system changed from white to russet red and gold, the fountain's jets increased and the red lighting made it look like fireworks, Again everyone applauded and cheered, before tucking in to a marvellous turkey dinner in brilliant surroundings. Samuel was not unaware that the same waiter who had looked after him that afternoon was paying him enough attention to make him think that the evening might not necessarily finish here at Killarney, and he was quite correct.

After a marvellous selection of puddings and dessert, the company moved to the yellow drawing room, since the Irish room was still not ready. Coffee, liqueurs and champagne were offered to a very happy and contented crowd.

It was then that Lorna beckoned Michael to join her at the piano. Once seated, he glanced at Lorna for the sign to begin, and off they went: their rendering of 'Chopsticks' was perfect. Michael had started on the right note at the right time, and had finished perfectly. A round of applause was heard. Paul had no idea that Michael had been practicing for months with Lorna and was so proud that he had mastered yet another art. Lorna stood up and went to take some champagne and get Michael's special glass, just as Michael moved to the centre of the stool and, while everyone was talking, suddenly began to play a piece of music that he had heard Lorna play time and time again. It was the theme-song from 'Limelight'. He looked studiedly at the keys and then seemed to relax completely, like a pianist at a piano-bar, looking and then glancing around him, listening to the sound in his head and transmitting it to the keyboard via his fingers. There was absolute silence. Mary had come in with another bottle of champagne, and stood transfixed in the doorway when she saw who was playing. Bernard and Paul were overwhelmed, as were the guests, and Patrick's heart was applauding for all its worth. Emotion got the better of Lorna: she was unable to contain herself and tears rolled down her cheeks. Anne went over to her and put her arm around her for support and handed her a handkerchief. "How could he? How can he?" she wondered. "He can't read music, and besides he has no music in front of him. Whatever it is, he's marvellous!" Michael finished his piece and stood up to cheers and yells: all present felt they had shared something very special with Michael. Michael merely bowed his head in a highly professional manner and said, "Thank you, Lorna!" At that, Lorna again burst into tears, which shocked Michael and made him think something was wrong. He dashed over to Lorna, upsetting a glass on his way. "Lorna, do you feel bad?" he asked. "No darling! I think this is the happiest day of my life", and she held him in her arms. Anne immediately took over, insisting that champagne glasses should be filled again, giving Lorna time to disappear and return without streaks of mascara running down her cheeks. Michael could never play on demand, but only when he felt calm and wanted to did he take to the piano, making Paul's heart swell with pride.

It was late when they all finally headed for their respective rooms: David and Amos's were down the hall past Michael and Paul's. On reaching his, Bernard realised he had forgotten to tell Mary about the arrangements for the following day, so in his pyjamas and dressing gown, he returned downstairs and spoke to Mary and thanked her again for her splendid dinner. Going back upstairs, he noticed that a light had been left on outside David's bedroom, and he tiptoed over so as not to disturb anyone and turned it off. Returning, he passed Michael and Paul's room, as usual with the door ajar, and heard two very sleepy voices, "Paul, goodnight!" "Goodnight, Michael", a short pause and then the two of them together, "Goodnight Toby!" Bernard walked slowly back to his room, took off his dressing gown and slipped into bed, but remained sitting upright. "Bernard, what's wrong?" asked Lorna. "I walked past the boys' room and I overheard them saying goodnight to each other, and then they both said goodnight to the bear." "Oh, Bernard! It's the same every night. You see, it's not just a teddy bear. Toby means everything to Michael: he's a concrete symbol that he can touch. When you gave him the bear, it was like starting all over again. And Toby has become a part of Paul's life as well, but for Paul, Toby signifies his love for Michael." Bernard slid down under the covers. He reached out and held Lorna's hand and said very softly, "Isn't it great having a family?" "Yes, Bernard, it really is great!"

Progress was well underway in the Irish room: the old chimney breast had been opened up and the dark-green marble fireplace installed. The ceiling was finished, the leaves of the hundreds of shamrocks on it picked out in the softest green on a cream background. Neville had had countless arguments about painting them, which was a very time-consuming work. Michael had the last word on the choice of wallpaper: a large dark green damask pattern. The green Bohemian chandelier was hung from the ceiling, rugs and furniture from the ballroom, plus the gilt consoles with the shamrocks and matching mirrors, which were placed between the three tall windows, the latter draped in matching plain dark-green silk and kept in place by huge tassels.

The enormous painting of Polly took pride of place at one end of the room, but on the opposite wall there was still a blank space. With great difficulty and much patient help from Mary, Michael had finished the eight large shell paintings and they had been duly sent off to the framers, but had so far not returned, since Nigel was unhappy about the colour of the mounts. Finally, on a Tuesday morning, they arrived and were ceremoniously hung four above four. Because of their large mounts and gold frames, they filled the entire space extremely well. Michael was very excited, but it meant he would have to wait until Thursday when Bernard and Paul returned from Melbourne to show them his work.

Patrick and Anne were invited to dinner on Wednesday evening and, for the first time, the Irish room was used for drinks. It was unusual for Michael to show any feeling in public, but his paintings had taken on great importance for him, and he was very proud of them, showing them off to lavish praise from Anne and Patrick. But Lorna and Anne knew this would not be enough. What he wanted was Paul and Bernard's approval and waiting until they returned seemed like eternity to him

He was in his chair in the yellow room, watching the drive as he did every Thursday evening, but this evening was different: "wouldn't they ever come?", "why were they late?" - these were the thoughts milling round in his head. Finally he saw the car's lights coming up the drive: he sprang like a cat out of his chair, bounded across the hall and was out on the steps in a flash, just as the car came to a halt.

As they alighted, Bernard and Paul were assaulted by an agitated Michael, speaking very quickly, not something he did very often, and kissing and hugging them both. "Come and see! Come and see! It's a surprise! Really, it's a surprise!" Lorna appeared at the top of the steps.

"It's all right. He's very excited because he has a surprise for you both!" With that, they followed Michael into the Irish room, where they were genuinely surprised to find that in just three days all the furnishings were in place, most of them having come from the ballroom.

"Cooty! Look, look!" Bernard swung around to look: there at the far end, above a green velvet settee, hung the eight shell paintings. He and Paul walked down to inspect them. "They're beautiful, Michael", said Bernard, "really beautiful!" "You're a clever boy!" said Paul, "and I love you!" This was all Michael wanted: the seal of approval from the two most dominant forces in his life. After introducing them to his new paintings, he returned to his usual chatty conversation about what had been happening at Killarney during the last three days they were in Melbourne.

On Saturday, a dinner party saw the usual small group gathered in the Irish room for drinks. Although suitable praise was offered once more for the shell paintings, Michael seemed indifferent, and was much happier talking about the painting of Polly.

CHAPTER EIGHT

A Honeymoon

CHAPTER 8

A Honeymoon

"Bernard, we simply must do something about all that stuff in the ballroom. Most of it's very second rate, pieces we have exchanged from upstairs. I've spoken to Nigel. There are probably four or five good pieces, but the rest is basically junk. Let's make a decision and get rid of it all!" Bernard put his newspaper down, knowing he would have no peace until a decision was reached. "Are you sure it's all junk?" "Go and have a look for yourself! It's the last part of the house to be finished, so let's get it done!" "Oh, very well!" said Bernard, picking up his paper again, "Do whatever you want! The problem's too big for me. You and Nigel decide: sell it all and give the money to a local charity if you like!" "I don't know any local charity, but I'm sure Anne must", she said, rising and heading for the phone.

"Oh, darling! What a good idea!" said Anne. "Actually I don't know of any charity, but I'll ask around." "If you'd like any of the furniture, Anne, please come and take it. You'll be doing us a big favour!" Anne put the receiver down and walked into a space that had once been two rooms.

Nigel, his work more or less finished at Killarney, had been seized by Anne to upgrade all of Bellevue, "top to bottom, darling!" Nigel had never worked so hard: first Killarney, then Bellevue, and now many other homes in the area were all crying out for his expertise. From near bankruptcy, Killarney had led him to engage six new staff members. Financially, he had never had it so good, but it meant constant attention to detail and being strong enough to stand up to Bernard and Anne and win. He had won most of the decorating fights, but in Michael's case, he had floated along with him and they had arrived at a successful conclusion. Even he had to admit that the very dark-green wallpaper in the Irish room look exceedingly good, even if Michael rather than he had closen it.

Nigel looked at the furniture again and said that he would buy the good pieces for his shop. For the rest, he suggested holding an auction to raise money for the repainting and reroofing of their local church, St Mary's, sadly in need of repair. So it was all agreed. With good advertising about town and whippersnippers to cut down all the grass and weeds near the church, the auction was held. Two trucks moved to and fro, ferrying all the pieces of varying quality to St Mary's. The local ladies provided afternoon tea after the auction, which took place at ten o'clock. The turn-out was amazing, and Father O'Brien couldn't believe it: everyone wanted a bit of Killarney! He said a few words to the crowd and then the auctioneers – offering their services free – started the auction. Items worth ten dollars brought eighty: prices were absurd. Lorna said she was very embarrassed that these intelligent local people were paying such prices for junk, not all of which came from Killarney, some being left-over pieces from St Georges Road.

A great sum was raised, covering not only the new roof, but painting both inside and out. Neville chose the colours: the blue interior became a soft apricot, and the grey exterior, cream with white trim. The general opinion was that it was a good face-lift. There was even enough for a new runner down the aisle and a carpet for the sancutuary, quite a luxury for the tiny country village of Morton.

At Killarney, the empty ballroom was a vast and desolate space. The old wooden venetian blinds hung at odd angles, since their cords had rotted, and, as for the curtains! Well, only one window had any left! But the joy of this vast space was the enormous chandelier that Bernard's grandmother had purchased at auction in the 'thirties: a gigantic expanse of crystal suspended from the ceiling, now in the afternoon sunlight sending refracted shafts of pink and blue and yellow onto the pealing wallpaper in the panels around the room. This was the vision that the 'family' saw for the very first time: a completely empty space. Paul disappeared for a moment and returned with a DVD player and two speakers. He brought a long extension from the kitchen and put on some romantic waltzes. All of a sudden, with the sound of the music, the room changed from something purposeless to what it had been designed for: a perfect use. Bernard took Lorna by the arm and they slowly moved around the floor. Paul asked Michael, "Shall we dance?" and made a sweeping bow. Michael was unsure of what he should do, but the moment he was in Paul's arms he managed very well, in fact, too well! Paul said, "Michael, we're dancing! Watch what you do with your hands!" "Don't you like it?" teased Michael. "Michael, behave yourself, or we'll have to stop!" With that, Michael bent toward him and kissed him. "Paul, I like dancing with you!" "Oh, darling, you're impossible! Just impossible!" Michael knew from Paul's tone that he was also having a good time.

"We must use the ballroom again", said Bernard. "I'll have Nigel give it a coat of paint and it will be ready!" "I think there's a great deal more to be done than just a coat of paint!" said Lorna. "Come on, Bernard. We promised Father O'Brien we would have a cup of tea with him at St Mary's. We'll leave you to the dancing, boys!" They left, closing the double doors behind them.

Paul went over and changed the CD for something slower and much more romantic and, in the late afternoon, with the orange sunlight streaming in from the side windows making large irregular shapes on the floor, they moved around the ballroom, completely lost in each other's arms, kissing and swaying to the music. Paul felt a soft mane of black hair on his neck and inclined his head closer to Michael's. He felt complete: no other adjective came close to explaining his feelings. It had been a long time since they had last been alone like this: there was always someone else about. Not that that was a problem, thought Paul, since it made moments like these so much more tangible and real. After a while, the music stopped, and it was Michael who spoke first. "Paul, let's go to bed now!" So the two young men went up to their suite to make love together, completely absorbed by each other, trusting each other and absolutely in love.

Next day, Nigel came over from Bellevue, where he was putting in a new kitchen. "The same as Killarney!" was Anne's demand. The new kitchen at Killarney had been a great success: no frills, everything working and tons of benchtop space. Nigel had fulfilled Mary's order to a tee, with stainless steel and white. It was rather austere, but Mary was very excited. "Everything works at last!" she said. "I can't believe it!" Bernard's slightly ironic comment on receiving the bill for this very expensive kitchen make-over was "Strange! The food tastes exactly the same!"

Lorna took Nigel to the ballroom and he looked about. "Well, the wall panels need repapering, the rest of the walls need painting and the old blinds have to be cleaned and repaired. You want new curtains and the benches round the sides have to be reupholstered. The same sort of thing goes for the supper room, which is rather gloomy, with only one window. I wonder why?" "Nigel, it was only ever used at night!" "I suppose so", he replied in his deep, matter-of-fact voice. "Do you want to keep the same cream and gilt look, or do you want a change?" "Let's keep it the same. The only important thing in the room really is the chandelier. Oh, by the way, can you get somebody to clean it?" "I suppose so, but only after we've finished the work. I'll get some samples of wallpaper and fabrics over before the end of the week." "Nigel, you are a dear! Thank you so much!"

Even with the confusion reigning at Bellevue, Anne lost no time after the birthday party in inviting Colin to dinner. He was much more formal that he had been. "Do help yourself to a drink, darling! I'll be back in a minute!" He over-filled a champagne glass and looked about for a cloth to wipe up the overflow, found a napkin and cleaned up. He looked around the large room: its most impressive feature was the white marble fireplace. The rest he considered a trifle 'old-hat'. He had always thought of it as a very elegant room, filled with charming and interesting pieces. It was true that he was out of sorts and had had a tense day at the clinic, with most of the staff staying well out of his path.

Anne reappeared. "Well, where's my drink?" "Coming", he replied, this time not overfilling the glass and handing it to her with a certain nonchalance. She immediately divined the problem. "Sit down, Colin. We need to talk, I think. What's the problem?" "I have no problem!" he said sharply. "Oh yes you do, darling! You've always been rather transparent!" Anne smiled and sipped her glass. She looked like a cat, he thought and wondered whether he was the mouse. "Well, let's sort everything out before dinner, Colin. The problem's Patrick, isn't it? Or, rather your problem's Patrick – not mine! You should relax a little and give up trying to put everyone into pigeonholes. You can't do it, darling! You've been my dear friend for years and will always be! But it stands to reason that neither of us has just one friend. Patrick is sweet, and is very professionally taking care of my horses and Michael." "And Michael. . ." was Colin's dry response. "Oh, so that's the way it is! You're jealous of the relationship between Patrick and Michael. Really, Colin! You're smarter than that! I spoke to you about Michael some time ago. Michael and Paul are lovers, and always will be. Michael has a string of men who'd kill for just one night. It's never going to happen: he's not like that. Look at Samuel! He's so sweet A perfect body, body-building at the gym three nights a week. He's besotted with Michael. Colin, are you putting yourself in the same category as Samuel?" Anne's voice had now changed; it had become much more businesslike and harder. "No, darling! Let me finish! Patrick is different. His love for Michael. . ." Colin interrupted, "So it's OK for Patrick!" Anne spun round. "Listen very carefully, Colin! If you don't contain this feeling of competitiveness for Michael and your jealousy of Patrick, you'll finish completely with me as your friend! Do you understand? You *are* my friend, but you're poisoning yourself! If you think I see you as a better friend than Patrick, or Patrick as a better friend than you, you've really lost the game. Do you understand me?" The last part of this sentence was said in an icy tone. "Yes, I understand you!" "Fine! Then let's say no more on the subject. Oh, darling! I do hope you like fish done in the microwave. I've personally never tried it, but since Nigel has just torn out the kitchen, we're reduced to a bare minimum! What colour do you think I should do this room? I just can't decide!" She continued as if the first part of the evening had never existed, just like old times, and with the wine and the very tasty fish, he mellowed quickly and the rest of the evening passed very smoothly.

Driving home afterwards, however, the first part of the evening's conversation returned to him and he was very aware of the ultimatum that had been made. Taking a wrong step now would cost him dearly: not only would he be banished from Anne's company and the Killarney set, but Michael. . . .. the thought that he might never see him again sent a cold shiver up his spine. No Michael! It was just too impossibly cruel even to consider, so he must toe the line, even to the extent of being a little more friendly to Patrick. Hmm, he thought, as he drove his car into his garage. Well, at least Patrick is goodlooking. . .

Anne left everything to Nigel and headed for Melbourne for a while, since the dust and noise were driving her mad. She called Lorna a couple of days later to persuade her to come to town and keep her company and, as Michael had a dental appointment, she would take him on the eighth. So it was decided that when Paul and Bernard returned to Melbourne, Lorna, Michael and Toby would go with them. Having notified the staff at St Georges Road, all was ready for them. Michael was not a good traveller and on arrival he said he felt 'a bit bad', and went to lie down. Anne had arranged dinner at her apartment and, when Paul and Bernard came back from work, with Michael feeling much better, they set off for Anne's.

Although in Melbourne they were all having a good time, the same could not be said of Patrick, who felt totally abandoned and, without Michael, his twice-weekly rides alone were a real effort.

Lorna had not entertained for ages at St Georges Road, mainly because she was now more or less permanently at Killarney and Paul and Bernard only used the breakfast room for their meals, so the big formal dining room was virtually never opened. Lorna decided that, since they would be here for a while, she would arrange a large dinner party. So it was the usual group that assembled at seven-thirty for drinks. Amos was late, arriving about eight o'clock, his apology being that he had been held up. In his arms was a large red-wrapped box with a big red satin ribbon. Michael knew instantly it was for him. "Well, Michael! Here's just a little something for you. Now do be careful: they're very fragile!"

He handed the box to Michael and went on to greet the rest of the group. Michael moved across to a circular table and undid the package. He withdrew the first irregular shape, wrapped in white tissue paper and opened it up. It was a magnificent pink and orange shell from – as Amos told them later – the Philippines. He unwrapped the others: the colours were bright and clear, burgundy and pink anemones, long green-and-blue trumpet shells, each more colourful than the next. Michael was very impressed. "I shall be able, I think, to paint one or two", he said as he gently handled the anemones. "It's very spikey, isn't it?" he commented, looking at Amos. "Yes", said Amos. "Be careful you don't drop it!" They all crowded round the table to inspect this splendid shell collection. Michael carefully rewrapped each and returned them all to the box. He then went over to Amos and, on tip-toe, kissed him on the mouth, as a natural gesture of thanks and love. Like Bernard, Amos was by now used to this act of affection, but apart from Paul, they were the only men Michael ever kissed. With others, except for Patrick, whom he always hugged, he shyly shook hands, to their disappointment. Amos once mentioned this to Bernard, saying that he was very proud that Michael was so openly affectionate with him, a stern thin man of six feet two, who only ever shook hands if he was really pushed to do so. They now moved into the dining room, Michael arm-in-arm with Amos, who turned to the following group and whispered loudly in Michael's ear, "I hope Daphne's not going to be jealous!" There were peals of laughter from all, especially from David, who said he was feeling miffed again, laughter too from Judge Stephen Spender, who had known all these men – except for Michael and Paul – all his life and had never seen them so relaxed and 'sent-up', albeit ever so nicely, and who divined instantly that the catalyst was Michael.

Anne noticed Bernard whispering something to Lorna. "Come, come!" she said. "What's the secret?" "Come along; let's sit down!" said Lorna, changing the subject. They all took their regular places. The table may have seen the occasional addition of different men, but never another woman. As usual, the meal was punctuated with gales of laughter and merriment. At a certain point, David came in on a serious note and asked Amos whether his new boat were ready. "What new boat?" asked a curious Anne. "What have you done with the yacht?" "Nothing", replied Amos. "The yacht is in excellent condition. It's the old boat

I bought from Bull's shipyard at Metung. . ." "Why on earth do you want another one?" asked Bernard. "Well, it's like this. You know I have a place at Metung and my yacht's moored there. I went last year to check on some tackle I needed and saw at the shipyard this old boat. It's enormous! It was converted as a cruiser for the Gippsland Lakes in about the nineteen-twenties for the State Governor and family, and was used for a few years by various members of the family for holidays. After that, it was used for cruises and then it was painted in bright colours for children's cruises on the lakes. They planned to scrap it, but as I remembered it as a fine craft when I was young, I decided to buy it, and little by little it's been restored. "How big is it?" asked Paul. "Well, if you're not into boats, it has two decks and two levels, four bedrooms and bathrooms downstairs and a large galley upstairs." "Oh, it *is* big", said Lorna. "Much larger than the yacht!" "Oh, yes! Much larger! I suppose it going to cost me a fortune in mooring fees. You're all most welcome to use it! By the way, Anne: what about your house at Metung?" "Don't speak to me about it! I haven't a clue what to do with it." "Have you got a house at Metung as well?" asked Stephen. "Yes, I do. It was left to me by an aunt, many years ago. I never used it. I'd go down with Amos and his family, but I must confess, it's eight or nine years since I last saw it. In fact, the only thing I see now is the maintenance bill!" "It's quite a house", said Amos, addressing a very curious table. "It's a large Victorian house with a tower that overlooks the lake, the only house with a tower, if I remember right, and a big veranda all around it, plus a large garden." "A jungle, I should think!" interrupted Anne. "It's a most forlorn old house, with lots of sad memories. After her husband died, my Aunt locked herself away, Miss Haversham style, and was quite eccentric. I don't remember the inside very well, but she had a number of windows boarded up – something to do with spiritism: only a certain number of windows for the number of people who lived there. Since she was the only one, she had them all boarded up except for three. I think there's a caretaker's house as well. It's all in a very shabby state, I fear." "How odd" said Paul, "to shut out the sunlight! She must have lived in the twilight for the rest of her life!" "She did! She would receive no visitors and the caretaker did everything. There was, as I recall, a hatch in the outside wall, level with the bench in the kitchen, and all her food passed through the hatch without anyone every seeing her, until the day she died." "What a story!" said David. "Have you ever used the house?" "No. When I used to go to Metung, I always stayed with Amos."

"Now", said Lorna, "Bernard and I have a little story to tell!" "Oh, do tell!" cried Anne. "Well, Bernard!" said Lorna, looking at him. "Hmm!" He looked slowly round the table, and put his arm on Michael's shoulder. "Michael, what do you think of this? Lorna and I are finally going to get married!" Michael looked at Bernard and then turned to Paul. For him, the term marriage meant nothing. He slept with Paul in their bedroom and Bernard slept with Lorna in theirs. He seemed a little confused, but assuming it was affirmative, he replied, "Cooty, that seems very nice!" There were cheers and kisses, congratulations and the clinking of glasses. "Oh darlings! How splendid, how splendid!" chortled Anne."Darlings! you must let me organise the reception. I have some wonderful ideas!" Bernard turned to Anne, "Anne, please don't be offended, but the wedding and reception will be done this way and this way only: a late afternoon wedding at St Mary's Morton and an identical dinner to the one we had for Michael's birthday in the conservatory. I'll have to see if I can convince Rodney to set up the lighting again. That's that! No gifts, just good cheer: that's all we want!"

"Daphne, what shall we wear?" boomed Amos. "Surely you're not going to put on that old lace number with all your medals pinned to your ample bosom!" There were screams of laughter as they all imagined short, plump Major David Keen in layers of lace and medals. It was just too much. Paul had tears of laughter streaming down his face.

Not to be socially out-foxed, Anne now turned and addressed Bernard. "Darling, where are you planning to go for your honeymoon?" Bernard, however, was not about to be forced into something he didn't want. "Oh", he said. "We shall all have to sit down and decide where we would like to go." "All?" Anne asked quizically. "Yes", said Bernard. "Lorna and I have no intention of going anywhere without Michael and Paul!" There was what can only be described as a 'soft' silence, and it was Anne who first broke it. "Bernard, I think yours and Lorna's choice of intimate companions for this special time is superlative!" Applause followed this short, but complete statement, in which Anne had as usual shown herself mistress of any social situation. "Thank you so much, Anne!" said Lorna, suddenly wishing to change the subject, as she could see that Paul was very emotionally moved by Bernard's announcement. Michael smiled: he wasn't even sure what a marriage was, much less what a honeymoon might be.

"Well, if you're looking for a quiet time, with no one around, only one shop and a hotel, lots of boats and nothing else except me to take you through the lake system or to cross and go through Lakes Entrance to the Ocean, where it's very crowded, I place myself at your disposal." Anne was dead silent. Amos had to a certain extent stolen her thunder, since she had all sorts of ideas for the honeymoon. Of all people, it was Michael who turned the whole thing around. "Anne, if we go to this place, and Amos has a house and you have a house, we can all of us", he said, looking round the table, "be together, and that would be very nice!" He looked at Bernard, who leaned over and gave him a kiss, saying "Yes, Michael, that will be very nice!"

Anne immediately sprang back into the conversation. She would go and have a look at the house at Metung this week and see what could be done. "Oh, I'll take a board off here and a board off there, and we'll see what happens!"

The rest of the evening was filled with laughter and anticipation. As the guests were leaving, Bernard said to Amos, "Your idea seems great! If there are not so many people, it's much better for Michael, and that means it's better for us!" "Don't worry, Bernard! We can be completely private on this craft sailing through the lakes system. There won't be any problems. By the way, can Michael swim?" "Of course, he spent all last summer in Anne's pool with Paul!" "Oh, that's great!" "I want everyone who comes to the wedding reception at Killarney and wants to do so, to come on this ten-day holiday at my expense." Anne overheard this and her mind was working sixteen to the dozen. She bade them all good night and gave Michael a big hug. "I love you very much!" she said. As she turned, Lorna said to her, "Well, how do you think you and I are going to look in church?" "You and I?" Anne repeated. "Darling, without you as my matron of honour, I couldn't possibly get married!" "Oh, Lorna! You are divine!" Anne cooed and made for the taxi she had summoned, which disappeared down the drive, followed by the cars of the other guests.

"Well!" said Bernard. "What a fun night! I'm off to bed!" He stopped and looked at Paul and said, "I'm desperately hoping you'll do me the honour of being my best man". "Bernard, that's something I'd be very proud to do!" "Oh!" said Lorna. "And you, my beautiful young man, are going to take me to the altar!" Michael looked at Paul and then hugged Lorna. "Lorna, that will be very nice!"

In their bedroom, Paul took off his coat and hung it up; he then removed his shirt and, turning, saw that Michael hadn't begun to undress and was sitting on the edge of the bed, looking worried. "What's wrong?" asked Paul. "Paul, what's a honeymoon?" Paul sat down next to him, and Michael automatically ran his hand over Paul's well-developed and furry chest. "Darling, it's when two people get married. Then they go on a honeymoon, which is like a holiday together." "Paul, but we are all going on a honeymoon, aren't we?" "Yes, darling, we are. Isn't that great?" Michael stood up in front of Paul and took off all his clothes and put them on a nearby chair. "Paul", he said, turning his head to one side, "if we are going on a honeymoon, does that mean we are married?" "More or less." Paul paused as Michael came toward him. "Yes, darling, you could say that we're married". Michael, totally naked, pushed Paul back on the bed and lay on top of him. "Paul, I like being married to you. I love you!" Paul held him in his strong arms and fought back the tears. After a moment, he said, "Let me undress, and then let's get into bed, you beautiful thing!"

While Paul and Michael were preparing for bed, Anne's mind was working like a threshing machine. Two months! Just two months to get her house at Metung ready for Lorna, Bernard, herself, Paul and Michael, and perhaps even Patrick. Amos would have to take care of the others. Oh, what must she do!

At twelve-thirty, the telephone rang in Nigel's bedroom. Drowsily, he picked it up to hear a most excited Anne on the other end. "What are you talking about?" he asked. "Where? Metung! Are you sure you know what you're talking about? Yes, you're right! I do think you're crazy! What! Tomorrow morning in Melbourne? At what time? Why? How? Oh, very well, Anne, tomorrow at your apartment at nine o'clock!" and he hung up. "It's just not possible! It just isn't possible!" he repeated, as he turned over after setting the alarm clock and went back to sleep.

At nine the following morning, Nigel arrived as bidden, having got up at six to organise his day and race off to Melbourne. "Darling, have you brought your measuring tapes and notebooks?" "Certainly!" he replied, very drily. "Oh, come along, Nigel! The taxi's here!" "Where are we going?" "To Metung, of course!" "What, in a taxi?" "No, silly! I've hired a plane. We don't want to waste time, do we?" Oh God! He thought. This is going to be a nightmare. "Nigel, do you know an architect near Metung?" "Well, sort of. . . He lives at Bairnsdale, about an hour away, I think."

They bundled themselves into the taxi and sped away to Essendon airport, where a small plane was waiting for them. They would fly to the nearest landing strip to Metung, which was at Lakes Entrance, where the caretaker of Anne's property would be waiting, having also been woken at twelve-thirty the night before. Anne asked Nigel to carry a little suitcase, which she opened once they were settled and the little aircraft had taken off. It contained smoked salmon, bread, butter, lemons and a jar of caviar, two glasses and two bottles of champagne. Nigel looked astounded. "Well, darling, we're going to do a day's work, so we must have a decent breakfast, don't you think?" "Of course", he replied weakly. "Now, darling, this is what has to be done. This house has got to be ready in two months, for Bernard and Lorna's honeymoon!" "Really!" he said, lifting his bushy eyebrows. "What condition is it in?" "Well, that's where you come in!" "Oh, is it!" he said. "You did telephone your architect friend to meet us at Metung, didn't you, before we took off?" "Yes, Anne!" he said, a little sharply. "Don't worry, darling! Everything will be fine!" She smiled, "Be a dear and open the bottle! I'm so thirsty!"

The plane touched down – or as Anne described it later, 'bounced down' – on an empty paddock with a tin shed at one end. It taxied over to where a lone Range Rover was waiting, with a very overweight woman at the steering wheel. She cried out, "Jump in!" and off they sped to Metung.

Nigel was expecting a surprise, but not this! His architect friend was dutifully waiting at the front gate, through which a German shepherd dog was barking and baring his teeth. What a wonderful introduction, thought Nigel. "How do you do?" purred Anne, "and how charming of you to rush to my aid!" Nigel thought she was laying it on a bit thick, but said nothing. Jan, the overweight wife of the caretaker, took the rather aggressive Alsatian and chained him up. "Well, let's have a look inside, shall we?" smiled Anne. It was a large Victorian weatherboard house, built on a steeply sloping plot, so that in front, on the lower side, the house had two storeys, while at the back it was level with the upper part of the land. Paint was peeling everywhere. There were verandas on all sides, but its interesting architectural feature was its tower on the far side, which looked out across the lake. The garden was in reasonable condition, since this was what the caretaker was paid to do, although Anne had her own ideas about something a little smarter.

The front door opened to a musty smell that was quite overwhelming. "Is the electricity on?" Anne asked Jan. "Oh, yes! Just try the switches." This proved that there was indeed some form of electricity. "Why are the windows boarded up?" asked the architect. "Don't ask!" said Anne, and she turned to Jan. "Jan, bring your husband and elder son here at once and carefully remove all the boards that have been nailed over the windows!" "What, now?" asked Jan. "Of course now!" snapped Anne. The architect was called Ted, and it was to him Anne turned, "Ted, dear, just keep an eye on those two taking the boards off the windows. I don't want any damage". Ted was nonplussed: here he was, being used like a foreman on a building site, but when he heard Anne snap at Jan once more, something told him it was better to acquiesce. Anne and Nigel went upstairs to what was the main living room, whose windows were the first to be unboarded. Suddenly, the late morning sunlight streamed into a very shabby, but decent-sized sitting room. The rest of the house was the same: in fair condition, with no water infiltrations owing to the caretaker's diligence, although everything was shabby and out of date. Anne called Ted to join them and asked him to check the bathrooms. "There should be three or four, I don't remember. Then come back and see me." Ted was not used to being spoken to in this manner, let alone a short, elegantly dressed woman, but he did what he was asked. "Well, Nigel, start measuring!" she said. "I think this room" – and she meant the sitting room – "should be white and pale blue. Yes, that's it! Do you think any of this furniture is worth saving?" He had a look around. "Not a single piece! Get rid of it all." "Well, we can still use some of the furniture from Lancell Road, with some new settees and so on, and beds, of course. I leave it all up to you!" She smiled at Nigel. "Jan", she called. "When the boys have taken all the planks off all the windows, I want you to open them to get rid of this stale smell!"

Anne then turned to Ted, "I want the house repainted inside and out - Nigel will give you the colours – and the kitchen and bathrooms completely modernised. You can check with Nigel: he knows my taste. And it must be finished in less than two months." "It's impossible!" gasped Ted. "I pay cash!" smiled Anne. Ted looked at this woman and felt that it didn't matter what he wanted or did, she would have the last say, and this was a very good summing up of his new customer, Mrs. Anne Rochester.

Anne now called in Jan's husband and said to him, "Sell all the furniture: everything. If you want some bits and pieces, keep them, and give me an itemised list of the pieces sold. The only thing that is not to be sold is the light fixture in the living room: that stays!" "Really!" said Nigel. "I thought we were doing a sleek holiday hide-away!" "We are, darling, complete with a twenty-light Venetian chandelier! It will look divine. Take some of the curtains back with you, and you can copy them if you like. Jan will get them down for you." A somewhat dismayed Jan disappeared and returned with a ladder to take down the curtains and valences that Nigel wanted. As Nigel said later, Jan looked a little like a circus elephant standing on a small drum, taking down the curtains. "Jan, dear", purred Anne. "I want this place scrubbed from top to bottom. If you need extra help, get it, but get it organised at once. Remember, if this place is not in perfect condition in two months' time, I may be tempted to sell everything, house and all, and that would mean having to pension off you and your husband! But I'm sure I shan't have to" – and here there was a long pause – "shall I dear?"

It was a worried Jan who sped about, making sure that all was as Mrs Rochester required. To Jan's husband, Anne said, "I hire you to look after the garden and lawns: that means weeding the garden and mowing the lawn. They look very scruffy now, but I'm sure all will be well. Oh, by the way, I see that some of the picket fence is missing. Have it seen to and have the whole front fence cleaned and repainted white. Thank you!" She smiled and went inside to see what Ted and Nigel were doing. "All under control?" "Well", said Ted, "it may take a plumber more than two months to fix all this". "Oh no it won't, Ted dear!" she said, narrowing her eyes, "because you are going to use three or four plumbers together to finish on time. Do you understand?" Ted glared at her and then motioned that he did indeed understand the urgency. "Nigel will be here a lot during these two months, so between the two of you, everything will be shipshape. I believe that is the expression." Although Nigel was used to this behaviour, Ted most certainly was not, and as he pulled his car out from in front of the house, he had an awful feeling that Mrs Rochester was going to make his life hell for the next two months. He was dead right.

"Nigel, darling! Everything done?" "well, sort of! Yes, OK! I'll come back next week for things like painting the rooms, but for today, we've finished!" "Good, Jan dear, do drive us back to the landing strip. Our plane is waiting." "Certainly, Mrs Rochester. They left through the front gate, where the Alsation was straining on his chain. "It looks so much better with all the windows unboarded", said Anne. "Yes indeed!" was Nigel's dull reply.

Ted drove back to his Bairnsdale office feeling numb. He wished he could have told Anne to go to hell, but he was in hot water financially, owing to an extremely bad investment and to the fact that his storage shed was full of items his clients had at the last moment refused to accept and for which he had got caught with the bill. In one sense, Anne was a blessing and, financially, might just save his scrawny neck, but on the other hand, ending up as a slave to Mrs Rochester's whims was not pleasant. A thought then crossed his mind: the kitchen. "Oh God!" he said aloud, "If only it fits! If only!" He had been left at the very last minute with a super deluxe stainless steel kitchen that had cost a fortune, and he had to get rid of it, since the retailer refused to take it back. In his office files, he found the glossy brochure with all the measurements. He went straight back to his car and returned to the house at Metung, where Jan and family were most surprised to see him. He rushed to the kitchen and with his tape began to compare the measurements with the brochure. "It fits! It fits!" He jumped for joy. "That's a great load off my shoulders, and the window doesn't even have to be changed!" He phoned Nigel next day to say that everything was under control and that the new kitchen was perfect, with no problems at all. For the first time in months, Ted felt he was on top of things: his client had money, and he was out to get as much as he could. But although things had started well, it was not to continue that way for Ted. Three days after he had called Nigel boasting that he had everything under control, Anne happened to be in Nigel's workroom, selecting fabric for the big sitting room at Metung. She was not happy with any of the samples, and the fabric she wanted would not be available in time for everything to be made up. She was looking about the workroom, when an assistant interrupted and said Nigel was wanted on the phone. So Nigel went into the showroom in front and took the call in his office, sandwiched between the two rooms. Everyone could hear the conversation, owing to Nigel's considerable voice projection. "What!" he screamed. "How?" The weak little voice on the other end belonged to Ted. One of the workmen who was repairing a sheet of iron on the roof at Metung had stepped sideways, missed his footing and vanished through the ceiling inside. Of all the ceilings, it was the one in the living room. Since it was an old lath and plaster ceiling, a quarter of it had collapsed under the weight of the worker, who fell to the floor. "I don't believe it! So everything is shipshape, is it? The chandelier?" No, apparently that had not been damaged, but what was Ted to do now? "I'll tell you exactly what to do!" screamed Nigel. It was unlike him to lose his temper, but things were getting on top of him workwise. You'll find a plasterer to put an entire new ceiling in, and in the centre you'll fit the largest prefabricated dome you can find. Send me copies of cornices and get going, or else you know we may decide to delay payment for a year or so! By the way, have the chandelier fixed properly in the centre of the dome, because if anything happens to it, we'll sue!" Nigel slammed the phone down.

He held his head in his hands a moment, before returning to the workroom and Anne. "A problem, Nigel?" she asked. "Oh, just another job. Workmen are so sloppy these days!" He hadn't got the courage or strength to tell Anne that the disaster was hers. "Nigel, while you were on the phone, I noticed these two rolls of pale blue silk damask. I think these will do perfectly." "Sorry, Anne! They're not mine." "Not yours!" she said. "But the wrapping paper says 'Rolands' and they went out of business ten or twelve years ago!" "Yes, I know. They were brought here by a Mrs Weymouth seven years ago or so, and they've been here ever since." "Well, perhaps I could have a word with this Mrs Weymouth and make an offer. Open up one of the bolts and let me have a look!" "You can have a look, Anne, but as for Mrs Weymouth, she's now dead, and this belongs to her daughter, Silvia." "Nigel, I must have it! How many yards?" "About twenty yards in each bolt, so there's quite a lot of it." "Enough for the sitting room at Metung?" "Yes, and plenty over for the accessories." "How much do you think it's worth on today's market?" "This is French silk damask from Lyons, as the label indicates, and would probably fetch between six hundred and one thousand dollars a yard." "Good heavens, Nigel! Do you think this Sylvia knows this?" "I doubt it. She runs the lost dogs' home here at Brunswick. A rough diamond, I'm told." "Really! Do you have the telephone number of this dogs' home?" "Just a moment, I'll find it for you." He duly handed Anne the phone number and sat back to watch the world's greatest actress begin to spin a web. "May I speak to Miss Syvia Weymouth, please?" "Speak'n!" came the reply. "Oh Miss Weymouth, how charming that I've finally found you!" purred Anne. "Call me Silv; everyone else does!" "Oh Silv", said Anne. "I'm Anne Rochester and I wonder whether you would be free to join me for lunch at Bellevue tomorrow?" "Oh shit, yeah! Sounds great!" "How kind of you to accept my invitation! Do you know where Bellevue is?" "Sure do! You've got horses. We lot that luv animals should always stick together!" "How well put, Silv! Shall we say noon tomorrow? Wonderful! Till tomorrow!" Nigel smiled and thought, she really wants this silk and she's going to put on quite a show to get it at her price.

"Oh Nigel, what have I done?" she said. "I haven't got a kitchen at Bellevue!" "Well, have the food sent in from a local restaurant or hotel. I don't see the problem." "No, I suppose not", she said, making her goodbyes and then heading for the best local hotel. They were most accomodating to Mrs Rochester and said yes, yes to everything. Beef, yes, definitely, she thought. A dog person would probably prefer beef. Beef tornados: perfect! Sweets, yes! All organised, she left and drove back to Bellevue, thinking, "So it seems she a very rough diamond!"

On arrival, she explained to her staff what she wanted for the following day, and then called one of the workmen to bring a ladder and take down in the small dining room the Arthur Streeton landscape from the chimney breast and replace it with a ghastly print in a white frame, portraying two collies. Hmm, she thought: that should bait the trap!

Next day, dressed very smartly, but casually – no jewelry, which was something unheard of for Anne – she waited patiently for Sylvia Weymouth to arrive. Precisely at noon, a small jeep-like car screamed up the drive. She heard the brakes slammed on just outside the front door, scattering gravel everywhere. Anne herself opened the door. "Silv, how nice to meet you!" Sylvia Weymouth was not so tall, but extremely overweight, dressed in a pair of stretch jeans and a rainbow-striped jumper and matching beret, beneath which poked out a lot of long unruly hennaed hair. She had a perky face and dark brown eyes. Being a consumate actress, Anne carried it off very well: the mouse was being lured into the trap.

They went to the small sitting room for a drink, Anne apologising for the state of the house, explaining that renovations are necessary. "Aw, don't give it a thought! I've lived in joints worse than this!" "Really?" said Anne with a weak smile. "What would you like to drink?" "Well, seein' we're goin' all posh, I'll have a red: I usually drink beer. Good stuff, beer! Can't stand that champagne stuff: it's bats' piss!" Anne suddenly realised that somewhere along the way, Sylv had missed something in her social education. She offered Silv a glass of red and poured herself half a glass of the same, not daring to offend Silv's sensitivities by opening a bottle of champagne.

"Cheers!" said Sylv, gulping the glassful down in one go, "I really like pleasantries, but, God, I'm starving!" "Oh, do come through to the dining room. We'll eat at once. I suppose you have so much to do?" "Oh yeah! It never stops for us charity guys, we're always helping someone. Personally, I'm in charge of the lost dogs: poor bastards, pitched out! You know, if I ever catch anyone who abandons a pup, he'll get a fair kick up the arse from me!" Anne had the sinking feeling that lunch was going to last forever.

Anne ate practically nothing. Silv managed to spill the gravy as well as the red wine all over the cloth, causing Anne to say, "Oh Silv, who cares, as long as we're together!" "I see you like dogs. Lovely painting over the fire! You got real taste! I like it very much. I suppose it's done by that Rembrandt guy!" "Do you really like it?" asked Anne. "Yeah! Lots! It would look great in my lounge room. I've just had the walls painted saffron. I'm going through an ethnic experience." "I'm sure you are", said Anne, looking at the mess on the table. "Hey, I say Mrs R., you haven't got any more of that yummy meat, have you?" "I'll just check with the kitchen. Do help youself to some more wine. Don't worry! There's another bottle open!" as she noticed Sylv draining the 'red', as she called it. Anne made for the kitchen. "Have we got any more of that beef?" "Certainly, Mrs Rochester, tons of it!" "What do you mean, 'tons of it'?" "Well, someone at the hotel made a mistake and put a '1' in front of the '2', so the meat is for twelve, not for two." "Oh, I don't care! Just put some more meat on a plate marked 'Fido' and bring it in!" "'Fido', Mrs Rochester?" "I was just thinking aloud!" She returned to the dining room. "Silv, how are the finances going at the dogs' home?" "Piss poor, Mrs R!" Anne found the abbreviating of her name most annoying, but she bore it. "Well, I think we should come to an arrangement!" "Oh, yeah! Well, a donation would be most welcome." "I had thought more of a business arrangement", said Anne, beginning to move in for the kill. "You see, Sylv, I was at Mr Nigel Storey's place the other day, and I saw you have a couple of bolts of blue fabric there." "Aw, shit, yeah! It's real precious! Me mum got it years ago." "I wonder whether you might consider selling it to me. I'd be happy to give you the picture of the dogs above the fireplace, to show you my goodwill." "Wow! Mrs R. You're a goodie!" "How much do you want for the fabric, Sylv?" "Now, listen, Mrs R. I didn't come down in the last shower like. I'd want a good price for the stuff!" "Like what, Sylv?" "I'd want a hunderd and fifty dollars for each roll. It's real precious stuff y'know!" "I'm sure it is, Sylv!" purred Anne and fetched her bag from the other side of the room. After a search, she pulled out three one-hundred dollar notes. "Shall we say we have a deal, Sylv?" "Shit, yeah! Mrs. R. It's a deal! Oh fuck, is that the time? I've got to pick up a dog from the vet." "I'll get a man to take your picture down", said Anne, standing. "No sweat, Mrs R.!" And with that, upsetting half a glass of claret onto the cloth, Sylv swung her antique dining chair round, climbed onto it and unhooked the painting. Before heading for the door, she pulled a plastic bag out of her pocket and scraped the food left on the table into it, including the rolls and pudding. "It's OK, Mrs R. I always carry a doggy bag. Some of them will be eating real good tonight!"

As Anne opened the front door to let Sylvia out, she saw Patrick's car coming up the drive. He pulled up, said hello to Sylvia, genuinely surprised that they made jeans in such extraordinarily large sizes. "Bye!" screamed Sylvia, heading off at great speed to collect her dog from the vet.

"Who on earth was that?" asked Patrick. "A long story. . . Do come in and have some lunch! I'm exhausted!" Anne took him into the small sitting room. "Open a bottle of champagne, please!" Whilst he was doing it, she dialled Nigel on her cell phone. He replied, "I've already started cutting it". "Thank you, darling!" and she hung up. "Please pour me a glass, Patrick! I'll be back in a moment!" She sped to what was now her temporary kitchen. "Clean up the whole dining room at once! Put a fresh cloth on the table, hang the picture up again and prepare lunch for Constable Timms and myself. Have we got any smoked salmon for an appetizer?" "Yes, Mrs Rochester!" "Well, get on with it please!" Anne returned via her bedroom with diamond earrings and a splendid matching bracelet.

"Had a fun morning?" said Patrick. "I can't begin to tell you! I hadn't realised 'rough diamonds' could be quite so rough!" Patrick looked at Anne and frowned. "Don't worry! It's not important! Oh, by the way, Patrick, when do you take your annual holiday?" "Funny you should ask that! Sergeant Reynolds and I worked them out this morning. I've got the afternoon off since I've worked three night shifts. At the end of this month, I have a break." "Oh no, Patrick! That won't do at all!" "What do you mean 'it won't do'?" "Well, Bernard and Lorna are to be married in two months' time." "Oh!" he said, "but what has that to do with me? Anyway, I thought they were married." "Patrick, you will contact Sergeant Reynolds, or I will, and change your vacation to coincide with the wedding and honeymoon." Patrick looked totally lost; he couldn't make head or tail of what Bernard and Lorna's wedding had to do with him. "Patrick dear, you're invited to the wedding and are going on the honeymoon!" "Excuse me, Mrs Rochester", said the maid. "The dining room is now in order, if you're ready." "Thank you", Anne replied. "Come along, Patrick. Bring the bottle with you!"

"Anne, please! I don't understand why on earth the Mahoneys would want me on their honeymoon!" "Oh, darling! We're all going, and you must come because Michael will need company when he goes riding!" "What!" was the reply. At this point, Anne explained everything to him. "You must come! I shan't take 'no' for an answer!" A holiday with Michael, thought Patrick. I don't believe it! "I knew you'd say yes", purred Anne. "And, of course, you'll be staying with me, Bernard and Lorna, Paul and Michael. Oh, what a big happy family! Hmm, you know, Patrick, I've become quite peckish after this morning's work! Do help yourself to some more salmon. Oh, yes, I will have another glass! Thank you so much!"

And that was that. Again, Patrick's lifestyle was turned upside down by Anne. He drove straight back to the office after lunch. "But it's your afternoon off!" said Sergeant Reynolds from behind the desk. "Nothing wrong, is there?" "Well, wrong, no! Just a little adjusting to be done!" and five minuted later a smiling Patrick left the police station, mentally planning a holiday in about two months, with Michael and his extended family. Wow! A holiday at Metung, at the top! Patrick knew Metung well. As a boy he had spent some of his school vacations there with his aunt and uncle, who grazed cattle about one-and-a-half miles from the Metung bridge. "I can't believe it!" he said over and over again to himself. "Wow!"

About one week later, everyone returned to Killarney, but just before the 'transfer', Paul had to fulfil an obligation to take Michael to dinner at his sister and brother-in-law's house at Camberwell. Michael was very silent in the car. He had always been a bad traveller, and the stopping and starting at traffic lights tended to upset his stomach. Paul pulled into the drive and Janet was immediately on the veranda. "Hi boys!" she said. "It's a quiet night with no children! How about that?" Michael got out of his side of the car, while Janet greeted Paul, and Michael stood there like a statue. "Oh, Paul!" said Janet, in a very quiet voice. "He really is beautiful! Peter said he'd changed, but he's beautiful!" "Well, at least shake hands!" said Paul. "Are we invited inside?" "Oh, yes! Yes! Oh do come in! I seem to have forgotten my manners!"

They entered the hall to see Peter coming towards them. "How are you Paul, Michael? You look great!" Michael smiled weakly and took

Paul's hand. He felt very unsure in this situation. He didn't remember Peter very well, but he knew he belonged to the past, and not a very pleasant past. "Let's go into the sitting room", said Peter, "and I'll get us all a drink!" Janet had been primed about this evening and everything was perfect: the special champagne glass for Michael; the fish meal; no one walked too close behind him. Janet was fascinated: he was the most beautiful creature she had ever seen. As they entered the sitting room, two great cobalt eyes slowly and systematically surveyed everything. "Paul, do come and have a look at the dining room! I've had it redone." It was the room least used in the house, but it was Janet's pride and joy. The last time he had seen it, it was pale green, but now it boasted a strong gold-and-white Victorian baroque wallpaper, with plain matching silk curtains over the big bay window. "Quite a change!" said Paul. "Oh, do tell me you love it!" begged Janet. "I love it to bits!" laughed Paul. "Oh, Paul! Michael's just splendid. From Peter's description, it was impossible to get any picture together. He, he. . . well, he's just so perfect, so. . .aesthetic! Yes, that's the word I want, 'aesthetic'! Are you both just as happy now as you were to start with?" "A million times more!" came Paul's reply. "She put her arms round his neck and kissed him. "I wish you both all the happiness in the world. You both honestly deserve it!" "Thanks", he said quietly, and went on to admire her silver collection.

In the meantime, Peter had been talking to Michael in the sittingroom, but Michael was only answering 'yes' or 'no'. The phone rang in the hall. "Just a minute! I'll be back!" said Peter. Michael moved over to the upright piano in the corner and took off the stool the sheet music that one of Janet's daughters had been practicing. He ran his fingers lazily over the keys and then began to play exactly as he had on the night of his birthday. He was totally unaware of the effect this had on Janet, but more particularly on Peter, who had immediately hung up on his call, claiming an emergency, and was now standing in the doorway, a picture of total disbelief. It wasn't possible! How could he possibly play like that, with extreme dyslexia? Yet there he is, beautiful and talented! I just can't believe it! Janet was far more emotional, and blinked back her tears as she held Paul's arm. She whispered, "He's an angel! A real angel!" Michael finished the piece and Paul walked over and kissed him.

"You're a very clever young man!" he said. "Let's have a drink!" Peter got the drinks in a semi-trance.

The evening passed pleasantly enough, but Michael was very quiet, not making any conversation at all. Straight after their dessert, Paul explained that tomorrow they were off to Killarney, and therefore needed an early night. If the conversation had been pleasant but lacking in animation, it certainly made up for it after the guests had left. "You told me his head was shaved! You didn't say he had big blue eyes. His hair is wonderful! He's like a filmstar, only better!" "It's almost two years since I last saw him and he's changed a lot: he's beautiful!" "*I* said that!" cried Janet. "Give me another glass of champagne! Let's finish it! By the way, there's another bottle in the fridge!" "Good heavens, we'll be drunk!" "Oh, I don't care!" said Janet. "You told me he hadn't got a chance, that he couldn't do anything complicated! Did you hear him?" she went on excitedly, "he played very well!" "What was the name of the piece?" asked Peter. "It's the theme from 'Limelight', the Charlie Chaplin film. It's so romantic! I think the first lines go, 'I'll be seeing you eternally'. Oh, he's brilliant! I should have asked him to play something after dinner." But what Janet did not understand was that Michael could only play like that when he felt like it, even at Killarney. If pressed to play, he'd play Chopsticks with Lorna, and nothing else. So what Janet and Peter had heard was a unique performance, although Janet was convinced he would be a concert pianist. "And he played without music! Peter, you don't think that perhaps you had the wrong file, and got them mixed up. I mean, this can't be the person you got Paul to take two years ago! Patients with severe dyslexia don't change radically, do they?" "As for mixing up the files", he said sarcastically, "that just didn't happen! But radical change like that, I honestly would have said the chances were one million to one, and he's the one in a million, that's the secret!" Peter looked at Janet, "If you breathe a word of this, I'll divorce you!" "Oh, that sounds serious!" "It goes against the books, but I think it's love that's turned Michael around. Yes, Janet. I'm certain of it. It's Paul's love and the group he lives with that supports him. It can't be proved, but I'll lay a bet with any man or woman" he said smiling, "that Paul is the key that opened that chance for Michael, and when he opened it up, Michael flowered!" "You must drink champagne more often", said Janet. "Your diagnosis is very romantic!"

Michael resumed his riding lessons with an overjoyed Patrick, and his painting lessons with Mary. His new box of coloured shells kept him and Mary very busy. Lorna suggested to Michael that it would be nice to give a painting to Amos. "Lorna, that is a nice idea", he said. "I'll do one for Amos and two for Anne. Mr Nigel asked to do them as a surprise for Anne's new house near the water. " "Oh darling, what a wonderful idea! She'll be so happy!" "Yes, I think so", said Michael in a quite matter-of-fact way, as he disappeared toward the kitchen to talk the project over with Mary while tasting a fresh batch of macaroons that he knew were due to come out of the oven.

During the following weeks, Lorna noticed a lot of whispering between Mary and Michael, and so guessed that another surprise of some sort was on the way.

Nigel was often now at Bellevue. Nigel kept her posted on all events at Metung, but was anything but pleased when she insisted that one of the larger guest bedrooms must have a double shower. "But that bathroom is more than half-finished!" he moaned. "I don't care! The boys must have what they're used to!" was Anne's sharp response. "Get Ted to start moving on that at once! Oh Nigel, the curtains! I know they must look splendid! What colour have you decided on for the walls?" "Well", he sighed. "I tried white, but it's too stark with the pale blue, so I added a few cups of blue to the large drums of white paint, and it's so much better and softer!" "And the furniture?" asked Anne. "Everything's fine!" replied Nigel, and stood up to leave. "Oh darling! It just slipped my mind! I must have the grand piano from Lansell Road set up. Do get a decent piano tuner in, since it hasn't been used for years." It was on the tip of his tongue to say something, but he stopped himself. "Oh, I forgot", she said. "Do you remember Sylvia Weymouth, from whom I purchased the blue silk? Well, I have a problem, Nigel!" Oh, God! he thought, yet another. "Well, our Sylv happens to be a very hefty rough diamond, as you put it, and when she stepped on my dining room chair to take a print down, she left a large dent in the upholstery, in the form of a desert boot." "What was she doing on the chair?" "Taking down a print from the wall?" "But if I remember clearly, you haven't got any prints in the small dining room." "Ah, well. . ." there came a silence, then, "It was a little game really, to clinch a business deal!" Nigel just looked at her and, in a resigned manner, said he would have a look at the chair on his way out. "Thank you, darling! You're so good to me!" And how! he thought.

It was an irate Ted who was informed that one of the bathrooms had to have a double shower fitted. "But it's half-done", he wailed. "Then half-undo it, and finish it with a double shower!" The expletives were sharp and to the point. As the deadline for finishing the house drew ever nearer, Ted and Nigel's relationship became brittle, to say the least. Whenever Ted's telephone rang, he shuddered, terrified that a certain Mrs Rochester had changed her mind, yet again. Nigel went up to Metung with Amos one weekend, which was entirely spent trying to calm down the caretaker, his wife and son, into whom Anne had put the fear of being dismissed if the house wasn't ready on time. Ted, who had a short temper and no patience left at all, had never had such a high-pressure project and wasn't coping as well as he ought. He was also not happy about having an interior decorator ordering him about, but tolerated it since the alternative of direct contact with Anne was something he knew he was unable to cope with. At times there was an army of workers on the project, each getting in the other's way, lots of bad language, yelling and laughter.

Nigel took the nervous caretaker into the dining room and told him to look out of the window. There was no view as such across the lake, since the window looked directly onto a thicket of hedge and trees, with the remains of an old hen house, plastic drums of various sizes and colours and the wreck of an old car, with its doors missing. "Well", said Nigel, "what do you think Mrs Rochester is going to think about this view?" "I'll have it all moved at once", the caretaker said, white-faced, and hurriedly disappeared. Nigel could hear him yelling at his son, "Get all that stuff cleared away at once, or we'll all be out on the street on our arses!" Nigel smile. Another project underway! He walked back into the sitting room. The two narrow windows had been taken out and now a pair of french windows opened on to the veranda with a spectacular view over the lake. The new ceiling was in place, and the dome, he thought, looked very well, since it meant that the Venetian chandelier was now two feet higher, making it just a little less intrusive. It was currently wrapped up to protect it from dust and paint. "Ted!"

called Nigel. Ted came into the room, very red-faced. "The cretins have put the wrong taps in the wrong bathrooms, and it all has to be done again!" "Don't worry", said Nigel. "That's only half a day wasted!" "Oh God!" said Ted. "I can't wait for this project to be over! I'm going crazy! I have nightmares about Mrs Rochester coming after me with tigers and lions! I think I'm going mad!" "Or you simply have a vivid imagination!" replied Nigel. "Remember that the floor-sanders are in on Monday, after which, make sure there's no mark on the floors! The dust should have settled by Wednesday, so we can begin sealing them. What about the tiling in the bathroom with the double shower?" "Don't speak to me about it! One of the workmen dropped a box of tiles off the back of his truck and smashed every single one of them!" "What!" exclaimed a horrified Nigel. "What have you done about it?" "Well, we can't get the same tiles in such a short time, so I decided to do the whole bathroom in marble tiles." "In marble tiles! What is that going to cost?" "I remembered I had them from another job, two years ago, and there were just enough." "What colour are they?" "A sort of terracotta." "You're a very lucky man, Ted! That's the same colour as the boys' bathroom at Killarney. Mrs Rochester will be delighted!" Ted had no idea what Nigel was talking about, but the words 'Mrs Rochester' associated with 'delighted' made him feel that perhaps he was going to win through this project after all.

Since Nigel way staying with Amos as his guest for the weekend, Amos took advantage of the fact to ask for a few hints about making his house a little more presentable for the coming honeymoon. Three hours later, with measuring tape and sketching block, Nigel was ready to join Amos, and they headed off to the hotel for dinner, talking about colours and fabrics.

At Killarney, the wedding plans were well advanced, and clothing and such had been worked out to a tee. Mary had arranged the menu and, with Samuel's help, Rodney had once more managed to set up the lighting in the conservatory. If Rodney was overwhelmed by being asked to join the wedding party and then, if he could, manage the honeymoon, Samuel was walking a foot above the ground and was for once crowing over Neville. Ernest had given Samuel permission to take ten days off, and the thought of being close to Michael was beyond his dreams, as well as the all-expenses-paid holiday.

It was at Mulberry's that an incident occurred on Monday morning. The night before, Ernest had imbibed just a little too much and, as a result, had a terrible hangover. He arrived at work, looking rather wrung-out, hoisted himself into his little pulpit and buried his aching head in his cupped hands. The usual banter was going on among the staff. "Be quiet, you faded parrots!" he shrieked, and silence reigned. Before long, however, the bitchiness started up again. "What are we going to give the Mahoneys as a gift?" Neville asked, baiting Ernest. "Oh, I don't know! I just can't think at all today!" "What! Only today?" quipped Neville. Ernest lifted his head and glared at him. "I'd be very careful if I were you!" he hissed, or you may be asking your dear Beryl for a job asa permanent gardener!" The dart hit the mark. Neville narrowed his eyes as only he could do, and crossed the floor to unpack a box full of shirts, in silence. Not to lose an opportunity, Samuel struck in with, "Oh, now I know what to get for you for Christmas! A pair of gardening gloves! What colour do you prefer?" Neville spun round. "Don't push too hard, Tarzan, or you might just find you've fallen out of your tree!" He returned to unpacking the new collection of summer shirts.

At that moment, Anne swept through the door. "Good morning all!" Ernest struggled to his feet. "Oh, and to what do we owe the pleasure of this visit, Mrs Rochester?" "Oh, Ernest! I should like a word in private, if I may!" "Oh, but of course, Mrs Rochester! My office is through the door on the right." The staff were more than curious. As a rule, Anne spoke her mind in front of anybody, but this time she wanted something special, thought Samuel and the others.

"Do sit down, Mrs Rochester!" "Ernest, this is a very delicate matter, and I must insist on complete confidentiality." "Oh, but of course, Mrs Rochester! As our most esteemed customer, anything you wish will be done with complete discretion!" "Oh, Ernest, I knew I could count on you one hundred percent!" she said smiling. "How kind!" was Ernest's reply. "Well, it has to do with the Mahoney honeymoon. . ." "Oh, yes! Such excitement! I wonder whether a gift from the store would be appropriate?" "No, I don't think so, but a letter or a card would be." "Oh thank you so much!" oozed Ernest. "I have been in such a quandry as to what to do, what was appropriate to the situation. Now you have solved the problem for me. So what may I do for you?" "Would you shut the door properly! This information is very private!" "Of course, how silly of me not to have closed it properly when we came in!" For a man with a hangover, Ernest was giving a very good performance.

"Well", Anne began. "The honeymoon or holiday at Metung will be in less than a month, and since Samuel is attending with Rodney, it is a delicate matter of funding." "Yes", said Ernest, with no idea of what she was talking about, while his headache was terrible. "I'm going to speak to you about another guest, who will be attending." "Oh yes, and who could that be?" Ernest asked, now more curious than ever. "Constable Timms", came the reply. "Constable Timms, Mrs Rochester? I'm sorry, I don't understand!" "Well, for ten days at Metung, Constable Timms will need a considerable wardrobe. Summer things, you know: nice shirts, trousers, shorts, shoes, swimsuits. You know the sort of things he will need." "But Mrs Rochester, there's no problem! We have a large range of superior clothing in his fitting. I don't see where the problem lies!" "I don't want Constable Timms to be out-of-pocket over this, you understand." "I'm not sure that I do, Mrs Rochester." "When I bring him in this week, I want you to insist on opening an account for him, but you will debit mine." "You want me to send you the account for Constable Timms's wardrobe, so as to speak?" "Exactly!" "Without either him or the staff here knowing about it?" "That's exactly what I want, Ernest, and when I come in with him later on in the week, we'll pick out a shirt here and one of this and one of that. I want you to ensure there will be enough for the ten days we shall be at Metung." "Oh, Mrs Rochester, you can reply on my keeping your secret! When all the clothing is packaged, shall we send it to his address or yours?" and he smiled weakly. "His, of course! I'll explain it all to him later, after the deed is done, so as to speak. He's a very proud young man, so we must be very diplomatic", said Anne, rising. "It shall be done exactly as you wish. Not one member of the staff will know what is happening. I'll choose all the pieces myself." "Do remember", said Anne, "the look should be young, but smart!" "Well, you've come to the right place for that. Thank you so much for your confidence, Mrs Rochester." "A great pleasure, and I shall look forward to seeing you later this week with Constable Timms!" With that, Anne left the office, saying good morning to the staff, and walked out happily to a sunny morning thinking, hmm! another situation solved!

Anne knew very well however that this was going to take a lot of very careful handling, if Patrick were not to be offended, or his pride hurt. But, Anne reasoned, he only had a constable's wages and it wasn't fair that all of a sudden he should have to spend a considerable amount of money to keep up with the rest of them. But what if he refused to take the clothes, she thought. Of course, Michael! She could use Michael as a wedge to convince Patrick to accept the package from Mulberry's. Of course, how silly, she thought, not to have reasoned that out before. With that, she headed up the street to Nigel's store, to speak to him about a dinner service she wanted.

Anne entered the store, where, to her surprise, there were three other women looking at fabric samples and decorator items generally. Usually there was never anyone in the shop. Business must be looking up! How nice for Nigel, she thought, without realising that Killarney and Bellevue, not to mention Metung, were Nigel's main income earners, and as a result of this work he had received a great deal more in the way of orders than ever before. "Is Mr Storey in?" Anne asked the assistant, all dressed in black. "I'll go and see at once, Mrs Rochester!" One of the other women in the shop turned sharply around and said good morning to Anne. "Come on through, Mrs Rochester! Mr Storey is in the workroom." As Anne entered the workroom, she stopped dead in her tracks: hanging on one wall were two blue silk damask curtains and pelmets. The effect was quite overwhelming.

"Nigel, darling, they're brilliant! They're a masterpiece!" "Well", said Nigel, "when you consider that there are five windows in that big room, you can multiply the effect by five!" "Oh, I'm so pleased!" she purred. "Oh yes! Just as I imagined!" Nigel raised his eyebrows a little. "Everything else under control? I thought I might go down to Metung and have a look at the progress." "I wouldn't, just yet", he said. "Let's get it all cleaned up a bit first. I know you'd like to see the curtains up, so let's give it ten days or so and I'll come down with you and we can check it out together!" "Excellent! Well, in ten days then. Oh, by the way, Nigel, the kitchen at Bellevue is so inconvenient and the staff are complaining all the time!" "The new kitchen at Bellevue will be ready by the end of the week, we hope!" "We certainly do! I can't do any large-scale entertaining at all. It's very trying!" "I'm sure it is", said Nigel very dryly. "What about all the things in the house at Metung: sheets, towels, tablecloths, plates, kitchen equipment and so on?" "Almost finished! Most of the stuff has been sent and is being stored in the caretaker's spare bedroom. Now, just be patient. Remember, ten days' time!" "Very well, Nigel! I'll catch you soon! The kitchen at Bellevue in a week! Excellent!" "I said, 'I hope'!" Exactly darling, in a week!" and with that she left and went back to Bellevue.

One last task to go, organising a touchy Colin for the honeymoon, and that would be done this evening: a quiet little dinner, with just Colin and herself. Oh! I hope it won't be difficult! She thought.

Colin arrived at Bellevue, and Anne met him at the door, elegantly groomed and with beautiful emeralds set classically by Van Cleef & Arpels, with diamonds surrounding each considerably sized emerald. Colin was duly impressed and they went to the small sitting room, since the large one was still being altered.

Anne began on a carefree note, but saw at once that Colin was extremely tense. "Darling, do relax! What's wrong?" she asked casually. Colin was not about to tell her that his so-called invisible wife was making life very difficult for him: a ten-day holiday with Anne Rochester was the last straw! It didn't matter what he explained about the honeymoon, she wasn't buying any of it. Heaven knows what she would have thought if she had realised that the aim of this holiday for him was to be as close as possible to a beautiful young man with thick black bushy hair and cobalt-blue eyes and the body of a god. So he simply told Anne there were a few problems at the clinic. "Colin, ten days away from all this will make a new man of you!" Of that he was in no doubt, but being able to get away was the problem. "Darling, you can please yourself. You can either stay with me at Metung, or with Amos." For some reason, Colin over-reacted. "Would you prefer me to stay with Amos?" he said sarcastically. Anne was genuinely surprised. "Colin, what do you mean?" "Exactly what I said. Paul, Michael and, I suppose, Patrick all tucked up in your newly-renovated mansion!" Anne realised at once that this was not going to be a quiet little evening with Colin. "Darling, what exactly is wrong?" She stood up and walked to the sideboard and topped up her glass. She then refilled Colin's glass, and put the bottle back in the silver wine cooler. "It seems", said Colin, still in an aggressive state of mind, "that as usual I've been left to last. I'm surprised it worries me since it happens so often!" Anne now realised that this was not going to be solved with a couple of bottles of champagne. "Colin", she said very sternly. "The problems you have in your private life are not to be brought into my house. I won't have it! I'm here as a friend of many years. I, together with Amos, am offering you a ten-day holiday with all our friends. Really, darling", she said, narrowing her eyes so that her feline aspect was quite visible, "I thought that with a bit of planning and common sense, you could end up not sleeping alone for ten long nights. . ." "What do you mean?" he snapped. "Let's talk about your options over dinner, shall we, Colin dear?" They moved to the small dining room in silence.

"Colin, we're not going to play cat-and-mouse, are we?" "No!" came the angry retort. "Very well, then. I do hear on the grapevine that, well, what should I say?" Colin's face relaxed and became the old Colin again. Anne could bait him with just a few inuendos. "Well", he said, smiling. "What have you heard on the grapevine?" "Well, darling", she purred. "It's only casual information, but I do have it on quite good authority." "Oh, Anne! You're such a tease!" "Darling, refresh the glasses!" Conversation lulled while the maid brought in the first course and left. "All done in the microwave, I fear. I haven't got a kitchen till Friday. What a nuisance! I expect you'll have to rough it this evening!" "Anne!" he said firmly. "Oh, of course! Well, it seems that Samuel is most delighted that you'll be with us at Metung." She looked down at the Oysters Kilpatrick and then slowly raised her eyes to meet Colin's. "Won't that be nice for everyone?" Colin said nothing for a moment and then, "Where is he staying?" "Oh, with Amos! Amos has quite a large house. I believe Nigel is freshening it up a bit. Hopefully that means getting rid of those hideous printed cretonne curtains in the living room, with all those nautical themes." Anne laughed, as did Colin. "Are they really awful?" "Awful? They're abominable, chosen by his wife, I believe. No taste, I fear. Obviously, none at all!" They both laughed again. "Oh darling, it's so good to see you relaxed! Metung will be really good for you." "What clothes shall I need? Look, I can come for a few days and then return for the weekend." "Darling, what a good idea! Without you the whole honeymoon would be a real flop. Do, oh do! Get yourself organised. It will be fun!"

After that, the evening paced along very well, but Anne was not unaware of the undercurrent of his jealousy of Patrick – not Paul, as one might think. It was the good-looking Patrick who somehow or other turned Colin into a green dragon of all-consuming jealousy. It wasn't just that Michael was extremely attached to Patrick and made no secret of it. Anne, too, was very fond of him, so Colin saw Patrick as getting the best of both worlds and leaving him only as an onlooker. At Killarney, everyone liked Patrick. Bernard and Lorna were very close to him, and in a very short time, he had managed to be part of Killarney. There was never a dinner party that Patrick was not invited to, and if he had a night shift, the whole party was changed just so he could attend. This never happened for Colin. At Killarney, he was an outsider and knew that his invitation always came via Anne, and this annoyed him. He was a doctor in charge of a major clinic; he had had a good public school education, whereas who was Patrick? A good-looking Irish Australian, a policeman of the lowest rank! Yet he always came first, not Colin. With Michael too! Yes, with Michael! The riding lessons twice a week, with the policeforce changing rosters so that Patrick could ride with Michael; the way Michael hugged him in public. It was galling! This evening the green dragon bit very deep.

Anne had baited the trap for Colin with Samuel. She was sure that if Colin and Patrick were staying in different houses, a happy honeymoon was much more likely. The last thing she wanted was a public scene: that would ruin everything for Lorna and Bernard. This is going to be much more difficult than I thought, she mused: much more difficult!

Anne, it seemed, had the energy of twenty: she never stopped a moment, and her brain was working overtime. Two days after her evening with Colin, she persuaded Patrick to go with her to Mulberry's. This time, Ernest was in much better condition and he had remembered everything Anne had told him about Patrick. He started talking about a pair of casual linen trousers for the waterside, as he described it, and took all Patrick's measurements, shoe size, etc. Patrick was a little confused. He had never shopped at Mulberry's, which was frankly too expensive for him, but there was Anne chatting to all the boys and Samuel, taking more than a casual interest in Patrick's being measured up by Ernest. Patrick felt a little uncomfortable in this environment, and wasn't even sure what he was doing there. "Exactly!" said Ernest. "Yes, perfect! I have everything now!" "We must have a shirt!" said Anne, in order to cover tracks, and a shirt was duly selected, a very fine plain white voile. "A very good choice, Constable. You'll be well-equipped now for drinks on the veranda, if I may say so." The pair of linen trousers was selected and everything left at that. "No, no, no!" beseeched Ernest. "No money! You now have an open account with us, and we are most pleased to have you on our books. I'll have the goods delivered to your address the minute the trousers have been altered! Good afternoon, Mrs Rochester! So nice to see you again!" "Oh, Ernest! I must bring Michael in!" "Down, Jane!" smiled Neville to Samuel. "I think we need some shorts, it's now so hot!" "Whenever you're ready, Mrs Rochester, the store is at your disposal!"

"Well, perhaps he'll need a new swimsuit", teased Neville. "Just think, you could swing down from the light fixtures and carry Michael up to the top of the shirt display! Go for it, Tarzan!" "Well, you never know!" smiled Samuel. "I'll let you know what happens after my ten-day, all-expenses-paid honeymoon is over. Do take care not to tear your frock when you're trimming the roses in Beryl's garden!" "Arsehole!" was Neville's bitchy rejoinder.

One week later, and three weeks to go before the wedding, a delivery van arrived at the police station, saying they had some parcels for Constable Timms. They had been brought here, because there was no answer at his apartment. Patrick didn't look up. "Just leave it here!" he said. "All of them?" asked the man. Patrick spun round on his chair and was amazed to see eight large Mulberry bags placed on the counter. "There must be some mistake", he said. "There should only be one shirt and one pair of trousers!" "No, Constable! These are all yours. Mr Mulberry packed them himself. I had to wait for him. Will you sign here please?" Patrick picked up the pen and signed the delivery docket. "'Bye, Constable! Have a good holiday!" The whole town knew about the honeymoon through Samuel and Neville's chatty gossip grapevine.

Patrick looked at the parcels, feeling wholly unsure as to what he should do. I'll ring Mulberry's: there must be some mistake. He was put through to Ernest. "Oh no, Constable Timms! It's all for you! We at Mulberry's want you to be our smartest representative on the honeymoon. Do have the most wonderful time! Goodbye, Constable!" and Ernest hung up.

Patrick was now absolutely nonplussed. The packages had to be paid for! Where would he get the money? He phoned Anne in a great state. "Patrick, when you've finished your shift, take your new clothes home and then come and see me at Bellevue." When he arrived, Anne greeted him at the door and took him to the small sitting room. "I just don't understand", he said, becoming agitated. "I can't pay for all that stuff! I saw the shop's prices the other day: they're astronomical!" Judging that this could get out of hand, Anne immediately reversed her strategy. "Open a bottle", she said, in a matter-of-fact sort of way. She sat down, opened her handbag and withdrew her chequebook. "Thank you, darling!" she said, accepting a glass of champagne. Patrick had now become so used to drinking champagne, it seemed quite natural to open a bottle and pour it out. "Now, Patrick. How long have you been teaching Michael to ride? Well over a year, wouldn't you say?" He looked rather startled: suddenly fear struck him. Was Anne going to stop the riding lessons? "I. . . I don't remember exactly", he said, his face beginning to whiten. "Sit down, Patrick", Anne said in a very businesslike way. "If you have been giving these lessons for all this time, plus extras, how much do you think I owe you?" With that, she took a pen and opened her chequebook. "But Anne, you don't understand. For me, being with Michael and teaching him is the most wonderful thing that has ever happened", he blurted, and then became bright red with embarrasment. "I wouldn't accept one cent from anyone for this. You've all been so kind to me in every way. I don't know why you're putting me in this awkward and embarrassing situation. " "Patrick, darling! Michael loves you very much." At this, Patrick calmed down. "I confess I ordered the parcels from Mulberry's, but they're not just from me for everything you do for me, but they're from Michael as well. You mean such a lot to him. Without his riding twice a week, heaven knows, I couldn't always be with him. Bernard and Lorna trust you compeletly, as does Paul. These packages from Mulberry's are only a way for us all to say thank-you, especially Michael. Oh, by the way, darling, you'll be staying with me at Metung; the others will be at Amos's. Now is everything settled?"

As always, Patrick had the feeling that with these people he was not in control. It was like living in a wonderful cottonwool world, where even if you fell over, you could never get hurt. "Yes, thank-you, Anne, but I find all this very embarassing!" "Don't, darling! Just enjoy life, and remember that we need and love you very much. Besides, I'm dead curious to see what kind of bathing costume Ernest has chosen for you!" She laughed. "Oh Patrick! The only people in the world who know about the packages from Mulberry's are myself, Ernest Mulberry and you, and I think we should leave it just like that, don't you?" "Yes, Anne, that's fine! Thank you!" he said quietly. "You must stay for dinner! Do say you will! I need someone to laugh with this evening. It's been a long day! Oh, did I tell you that Sylv has left a permanent impression on her dining room chair? When she stood on it, she left the inprint of a giant desert boot!" Patrick laughed. "I was very surprised they made jeans so large!" They smiled at each other. "Another glass before dinner?" he said. "Absolutely, perhaps even two!"

It was now summer, and the boys spent a lot of their spare time in Anne's pool, much to her delight, as well as Patrick's. If he thought Michael was elegance personified on horseback, in his bathing costume he was absolutely overwhelming. Ah! He thought. Ten beautiful long days of this at Metung! Wow!

The wedding plans were going apace and the only person who was edgy was Anne. Nigel had been to the Metung house three times and not told her about the visits until afterwards. "Everything, every last detail is under control! Don't worry, Anne! When you arrive with the others, your summer villa will be waiting for you!" This was still far from true, however. When a very nervous and agitated Ted found that yet another mistake had been made in the downstairs bedroom, he came out onto the upstairs veranda and in a fit of rage stamped his foot. The whole wooden flooring beneath him gave way, and Ted disappeared to waist level in the space below the flooring. One of the workmen pulled him out, laughing. "You'll be all right, mate!" Ted's trousers were ripped on both sides and he had bad grazes on both legs. "You're really lucky you didn't get your balls ripped off", said the perky workman. "Oh fuck off!" was Ted's gentlemanly response, as he limped toward his car. At this moment, the large Alsatian, who had just broken his chain, saw Ted as easy meat and raced toward him. Ted sped through the new front gate and slammed it behind him. He leaned against the picket fence as the Alsatian was called back to the caretaker's house, and he looked down at his grazed legs. As he got to his car, he heard a workman yell out, "You bloody idiot. I've just painted that bloody fence, and you've leant all over it! You fool! Now I'll have to touch it all up!" Ted removed his coat to see white stripes like a zebra imprinted on it. He threw it in the back of the car. Mrs Rochester or no Mrs Rochester, I'm going to build igloos at the pole, he thought, rubbing his bruised and battered legs.

"Of course you'll have to refloor all the veranda! Get going!" shouted Nigel down the phone. "This job gets worse every day", moaned Ted. "I'm cut to pieces!" "Believe me, if this house is not up to scratch in just three weeks, Mrs Rochester will cut you up all by herself! I'm not joking! Get another firm in to do it at once!" An exhausted and very frazzled Ted hung up and looked through his directory to find a company that could lay a new veranda floor in less than two weeks.

Anne had also taken it upon herself to send Rodney down to 'smarten it up, darling', as she said, 'the garden is so dreary'. Rodney had had a little over a month and a half and, with two assistants, had worked very hard to upgrade the garden, with the caretaker complaining about the maintenance he'd be obliged to do.

After Nigel had spoken to a distrait and damaged Ted, his shop assistant said that Mr Michael Mahoney and Miss Mary Ryan were here to see him. He stood up and asked her to show them into his office. "How are we?" he said in his deep voice, brushing his schoolboy haircut to one side. "Mr Nigel, we've finished all the shells." "Very good, you've been working!" Mary opened a cardboard folder, which contained six shell paintings. "My God!" said Nigel. "These are very good indeed!" He spread them out. "Oh, this pair is great! Those strong pinks and oranges are very effective!" "Mr Nigel, those two are for Cooty and Lorna and those two are for Anne's new house." "She'll be thrilled!" he replied. "And the other two?" "The big curly shell that is all yellow is for Amos, and the dramatic one is for Patrick." "Why do you think it's dramatic?" Nigel asked. "Well, we've made the shadow very dark. I did this a long time ago, but it turned out bad. Then Mary helped me with a dramatic shadow and now it's good!" Mary had indeed helped Michael with this last painting. Like everything in Michael's life, if it started off as a difficult project, he blocked, so this picture had remained for six months in the planpress until Mary coaxed him to finish it, using terms like 'dramatic shading', which helped. "Well, we'll frame the pair for Bernard and Lorna like this", and Nigel placed a sample of mounting board against the side of the painting. "What do you think?" "Oh yes, that is very nice!" "And I think for Mrs Rochester, we shall use a very pale blue, as I've just the place for them in her new house. But you must keep it a secret!" "Oh, yes!" answered Michael. "Also the one for Amos. I've made some changes to his living room at Metung and this will do very well to put over the fireplace. I'll give it a specially large mount. What colour mount would you like for your dramatic picture of the nautilus shell for Constable Timms?" "I don't know", said Michael, and looked at Mary. "What do you think?" "I think, darling, we'll have to leave it to Mr Nigel to decide." "Yes, I think we will."

Nigel now addressed Mary, "I'll have the frames ready in four or five days. I'll keep the paintings for Amos and Anne and will make up two parcels, one for Bernard and Lorna and the other for Constable Timms, or would you like to give them one each for the wedding?" Michael thought about it. "One each would be nice, then they each have a present!" "Good idea, plus a separate parcel for Constable Timms. Now let me write all this information on the outer border. Ok, right! That's done!" He smiled at Mary, "I'll use Paul's account, I assume?" She smiled back, "I think so!" "Fine! I'll call you, Mary, when the three paintings for the Mahoneys and for Patrick are framed and ready. We don't want to spoil the surprise, do we Michael?" "No, we want it to be a big surprise!" Bernard had stated emphatically that there were to be no gifts, but Mary thought the paintings would be something they would treasure as a memento of the day, and since Michael had produced them, she was sure Bernard would accept them at once.

Another little drama was also being acted out at Brunswick. This time, it was Father O'Brien, who had promised Bernard a Latin mass for the wedding. He was speaking to the headmaster of the local Senior Catholic School. "I'm really most concerned", he said. "It's been so long since I've said a Latin mass, and especially facing the altar. I've decided to have a rehearsal, meaning I'll say a mass in Latin on the Friday just before the wedding." "At what time?" asked the headmaster. "I'll do it instead of the usual ten-thirty Friday mass. Hardly anyone comes, so there should be no problem." Now, can you run the Latin Mass sheets off for me, since my printer's not working again?" "Yes, that's fine! The new one here is wonderful. This new technology is splendid!" "Yes, indeed!" "Father, I'll get the girls in the office to do it. How many copies do you want?" "Oh, about twenty-five. Judge Mahoney told me it will be a very intimate ceremony; strictly family!" "Well, you were lucky that his furniture auction paid for the complete renovation of St Mary's! The least you can do is to give him a decent Latin mass!" "Yes", said Father O'Brien. He left the school complex and headed back to the main church in Brunswick to see if he could find a white chasuble set with all the pieces and have it dry-cleaned for Saturday.

Friday arrived and Father O'Brien had no altar boy, so having placed the chalice and paten covered with veil and burse on the credence table, he carried in the thurible. The temporary modern altar had been removed. Earlier he had lighted the six tall candles on the old high altar in their very dirty brass candlesticks. He heard some noise in the church, but assumed it was some of his old parishioners talking, but on entering from the sacristy, he stopped dead. The church was packed: the entire upper forms of the Catholic School were there to hear, probably for the first time in their lives, a mass in Latin. The headmaster had taken it upon himself to give his senior students the opportunity to see what a traditional mass was like, deeming it a genuine and important part of their education. He had even insisted on the school choir attending, and Mrs Cunningham had been requested to play the organ.

Father O'Brien censed the altar and the mass began. The choir was good, but the Latin responses poor, although everyone tried their best. Father O'Brien realised that at the wedding next day the responses would be no better. The only piece in the school choir's repertoire was Mozart's *Ave Verum*. At the end of the mass, most of the students were very positive about it, since they had probably missed a dreary lesson.

The choirmaster later said he had spoken to the headmaster, and that the choir members were more than happy to repeat their performance at the wedding. As the choirmaster put it, "As Judge Mahoney paid for the restoration of the church, I think it's the least we can do!" "Oh dear!" thought Father O'Brien, "this is not going to be a quiet little family wedding at all!"

Just three days earlier, Lorna and Anne were having a drink in the yellow room, and Anne said, "Settled?" "Well, with me, yes, absolutely. But it's up to Mary." "Not a problem", smiled Anne. Lorna topped up Anne's ever-empty glass and rang for Mary. Mary duly arrived with a "Yes, may I help?" It was Anne who replied, "Do come and sit down!" By now, Mary knew Anne very well. She had a way of saying things and a tone she used when she wanted something. "Yes, Mrs Rochester!" "Mary dear!" Mary now knew that Anne wanted something 'important'. "As you know, at the end of the week, we are all off to Metung for ten days." "Yes, Mrs Rochester!" "Well, I have a proposal for you. You know that Mrs Robbins has had to leave my service because of ill health. So I want you to come with us and take over the running of my whole house at Metung. You will have your salary here as usual and I shall be more than happy to pay you a generous fee on top. What do you say?" "Well, Mrs Rochester, at present we're all going flat out for the wedding breakfast here!" "Don't worry, Mrs Barnes can clean up afterwards, and, really Mary, I don't know what would happen if Michael were left to the mercy of some local cook!" The trap was baited. "Yes, Mrs Rochester, I'll come. What's your budget for the ten days?" "Whatever you want, so long as the food is as good as it is here at Killarney! That's more than satisfactory for me. I'll leave you the caretaker's number. Her name's Jan and she will stock up whatever you ask her for. She can charge to my account, so there's no problem. I'll get Jan to hire a girl to help you full time for the ten days. Oh Mary! You are a dream! Thank you so much!" "Thank you for thinking of me, Mrs Rochester!" said Mary and left the room to the sound of champagne glasses clinking together.

For Mary, this involved major planning for three menus per day. They might eat out once or twice, but if it was like Killarney everyone preferred to return and eat at home. Mary knew that Anne had used Michael as bait, because the idea of ten days without Michael was too much. She hastened back to the kitchen to make the final arrangements for the wedding breakfast in the conservatory and to make orders via Jan for Metung.

Michael was bursting with his effort to keep a secret: more than one day was difficult, but five days? The parcels arrived via Mary and she hid them at her studio: two larged framed shell paintings in separate parcels, wrapped in white with big bows and a little bunch of silk flowers entwined in the bow. The other package was more masculine, in burgundy with gold and burgundy ribbons. "Michael", said Paul, "why are you giving Patrick a present on Bernard and Lorna's wedding day?" "Paul, I think it's right, because when everyone gets a present and you don't, it's not very nice, and no one gives Patrick a present." If only he knew how much the Mulberry bags had added up to, he would have realised that this time Patrick had not been without his share of presents, but since neither Paul nor Michael was aware of this secret, Paul thought his reasoning quite valid, although just a little odd. But after all, this was Michael. "Well, where's *my* present?" teased Paul. "But you have me all the time! That's *your* present!" and Michael laughed his soft deep laugh. Paul put his arms around him and smiled. "Yes, Michael, that's the nicest present in the world! Now, hurry up! We're expected at Anne's for a swim! Michael! Behave yourself! Or we'll never get to Anne's!"

Waiting till the morning of the wedding was eternity for Michael, but it finally arrived, and at six a.m. he was down at Mary's for the gifts for Bernard and Lorna, wearing only a dressing gown. "But aren't you going to give them the presents at dinner this evening?" "Oh, Mary! Can't I give them now?" he wailed. "I can't wait all day. I'm sure I'll feel bad!" "Oh, very well! Go and get dressed and I'll bring the presents to the kitchen. Excitedly, Michael cleared the stairs two at a time and entered his and Paul's bedroom. Paul was still half-asleep. "We're going to give them their presents now!" cried Michael. "Oh Michael, what time is it?" "I don't know! Come on, Paul!" and he pulled back the bed covers. "Paul!" he said threateningly. "OK Michael, get dressed and get the presents. I'm coming!" As he hauled himself out of bed and pulled on some loose clothes, Michael was already dressed and was in the kitchen, just as Mary came through the back door. "When do you want to give Patrick his picture?" "Tonight will be good for Patrick!" "Very well! I'll put it back!" He carried the two large parcels upstairs and called out to Paul. "Paul, hurry!" Paul duly arrived and knocked on Bernard and Lorna's bedroom door. "May we come in?" No sooner had Bernard's drowsy voice given the affirmative than Michael was sitting on the edge of the bed. "Cooty, this is for you, and this is for Lorna!" "It's Michael's idea", said Paul quickly, seeing Bernard's frown. Lorna opened hers first. "Oh Michael, it's beautiful! Oh, darling!" and she leaned across and kissed him, although he was fidgetting like a cat on hot bricks. "Cooty, open it quickly!" he said. Bernard opened the wrapping paper to find the pair to Lorna's painting. He didn't say anything, but pulled Michael into his arms, with a great lump in his throat. "It's beautiful, Michael!" was all he could say. "Come on, Michael! Let Lorna and Bernard get ready! Remember, today is their big day!" "Yeah!" yelled Michael. "Today we wear funny clothes!" meaning mourning suits, which were hanging ready to be put on in their respective rooms.

The morning passed quickly, with the telephone ringing continually. Amos and David were staying at Killarney and Stephen, as usual, was at Bellevue. Amos heard the yelling and laughter and realised that Michael was up and about. Much praise was given to Michael's paintings, and Amos was most pleased that his gift of the box of shells had been put to just the right use. He was not to know that a surprise lay in store for him at Metung.

At this point, we must returnto the Wednesday before the wedding. At six-thirty in the morning, two enormous removal trucks, carefully packed the evening before, left Brunswick for Metung, following a car, also filled with boxes large and small, driven by a slightly nervous Nigel, two girls from his workroom, plus Rodney, who was to give the garden a last look-over and see that everything was all right.

After three-and-a-half long hours, they pulled up in front of the Metung house, to find a little van outside, carrying a lot of advertising and announcing that it belonged to the piano tuner.

"Take this stuff off carefully, or you'll answer to Mrs Rochester!" said Nigel. The removal men – four to each truck – were extremely careful. None of them knew this woman, but the way Nigel spoke was enough to convince them! The first thing Nigel rushed to see was the veranda flooring: all done! All totally redone! Bravo, Ted! Under Nigel's direction, the girls hung the curtains, unpacked crockery, cutlery, stacked towels. As soon as the new beds were in place, they were made up, all the spare linen stacked in the right places. The precision was amazing. When Ted limped into the house half-an-hour later, first making sure that the Alsatian was safely chained up, he couldn't believe it. The grand piano was in place and the tuner was working on it, accompanying Nigel's directions – "No, not there! Yes, that's fine!" – with the clink-clink of the piano keys. Nigel had thought of everything, down to coordinated soaps for each bathroom. Nothing was left to chance. "Very well!" he said to one of his girls, "Up you go and get the plastic off the chandelier!" In less than two-and-a-half hours, it was finished, down to the cushions on the settees. Michael's pictures were hung in a prominent position, with lamps, rugs, decorative objects, occasional chairs, all upholstered to blend softly with each room. The show-stopper, however, was the main living room: this vast space had previously been two rooms, which Ted had knocked into one, right across the upper part of the house. It was very elegant, with two french windows at one end, opening onto the wide veranda, and three other symmetrically-spaced tall narrow windows, down the opposite side, all draped in the famous pale-blue silk damask. The polished floors had large white rugs with pale blue borders, and pieces of antique furniture shone, as did the vast Venetian chandelier in the centre of the new dome fitted into the ceiling.

"All done, I think!" said Nigel, and called Jan. "On Sunday, everyone will be here. Now, listen! On Saturday you will get the white lilies from the florist's. All you have to do is fill these three vases." He pointed at three crystal cylinders. "I've already phoned the florist. Don't forget!" "Oh, I shan't!" said a nervous Jan, and methodically jotted it down on her note pad, filled with writing on page after page. Rodney, too, was satisfied with the clean, gleaming exterior. The garden looked neater and a standard box tree stood sentinel on either side of the glossy black front door, with shining brass fittings.

"Good job on the veranda, Ted!" "Thanks!" replied a rather worn-out and nervous Ted. "Do you think she'll like the kitchen?" "Oh, I don't think she'll care! I imagine she won't ever go into it!" "Oh really!" said Ted, somewhat dejectedly, "it happens to be a good one!" "So I see from the account", said Nigel. "Well, we've finished here! Off to the hotel for something to eat and then the last things for Amos's house and we're done!" He fluffed up a cushion for the third time. "Mrs Rochester will pay you herself when she arrives, either Sunday or Monday." "She could post it to me if she likes", said Ted nervously. "It's all the same to me!" They departed, leaving a fully furnished holiday home with every imaginable luxury, all completed in two months. "Never, never again!" thought Nigel. "I'm just too old for all the stress!"

As expected, the wedding was over-the-top: it was anything but a quiet country wedding. When Bernard and Paul reached the church, they were surprised to see a school bus outside. On entering, faced with the school choir beaming at him, Bernard felt that, as usual, the arrangements had been taken out of his hands. He and Paul were welcomed by Father O'Brien wearing a beautiful nineteenth century white French chasuble. "The choir wasn't exactly my idea, Bernard, but there it is!" and he smiled weakly. The church filled quickly, not only with locals, but with people who had driven down from Brunswick to see the show. Rodney and Samuel, together with Colin, entered and took their place, then came Anne on Patrick's arm. One of the women in the congregation was heard to say, "Oh, look, Mrs Rochester, with the policeman. I hope she hasn't done anything wrong! Is she wearing handcuffs?" Anne was dressed in a soft rusty pink with cream accessories, including an enormous picture hat and her usual amount of jewelry. Patrick led her to her seat, just opposite Paul, the prie-dieu just in front of them with the chairs being for Bernard and Lorna.As the car drew up with Lorna and Michael, the choir began. Lorna entered, wearing a beautiful cream silk frock, very simple, with matching short jacket that according to Neville was bleached to death. Around her neck was a double string of beautiful graded Broome pearls: even Anne raised her eyebrows at them. But Lorna and Michael slowly moving up the aisle together drew all eyes: he so perfect in every way, his hair groomed perfectly. He looked wonderful. As Neville said later, being the fount of all social chitchat around Brunswick, the bride was so elegant, but her escort was divine. He even noted that Michael was wearing the famous ruby cufflinks.

Michael led Lorna to Bernard's side, and then stepped back to join Paul, with Anne just opposite on her chair.

Just before the mass began, Paul leant over and whispered to Michael, "I love you!" Michael smiled and said nothing. The mass went off without a hitch, except that during the collect, the choir started the *Ave Verum*.

Michael had never heard anything like it, and he thought it wonderful the way the music rose and dropped. When mass was over the bride and groom walked out arm-in-arm. Patrick moved in and took Anne's arm and the boys followed together, to a large crowd outside, clapping and wishing them all the best for the future.

Then it was back to Killarney for drinks and dinner in the conservatory. Rodney had indeed done his bit and the lighting was fabulous: the glittering of the fountain had an extraordinary effect, while the palm trees all had special lighting from the front. Rodney had spent hours up the ladder getting it right. They all sat down to another of Mary's extravaganzas: marvellous food, excellent wines, and everyone had a wonderful time. Anne positively refused to take off her hat. "I can't, darling", she said to Samuel. "My hair is probably ruined!" Everybody laughed. Mary came up to Michael's side and whispered to him. He stood up and followed her into the kitchen. "Here it is, darling", she said, and he took the burgundy-wrapped parcel and returned to the conservatory. When he entered with the parcel there was a silence. They all thought quite naturally that it was a gift for the bride and groom (earlier, Paul had spoken to Bernard and Lorna about this, and Lorna was very touched that Michael should think that Patrick never received a gift). Michael went round the end of the table, where Bernard and Lorna were sitting, to Patrick, who sat opposite him. "It's for you!" he said. The silence was electric, since no one except Bernard, Lorna and Paul knew what the gift was. Patrick first looked surprised, then embarrassed. "But Michael, it's not my birthday!" "Patrick, today you have another birthday!" replied Michael and leant down to hug him. Two seats up, Colin winced. "Patrick, open it!" begged Michael. Everyone was still watching the outcome as Patrick opened the large flat parcel: to his astonishment, it was the painting of the nautilus shell, with a soft coffee-coloured mount, almost the same as the lightest colour on the shell. Patrick stood up and embraced Michael, and in a small, weak voice said, "Thank you very much!" They could all see that it was a very emotional moment for Patrick. Anne immediately started conversation at her end of the table, just as Lorna did at hers. Michael went back to his seat and the festivities sparked up again with a few Chloe and Daphne jokes.

At half-past-one, Bernard brought the evening to a close, telling everyone that they must be back at Killarney at nine the next morning for the trip to Metung. As they all rose, talking and laughing, Patrick gently took Paul's arm. "I don't think I deserve this beautiful painting", he said, to which Paul answered, "You do deserve it", and squeezed his arm. "Michael is very fond of you, and so am I."

Patrick heard Anne calling for him, since he was taking her and Stephen back to Bellevue. He left with his picture under his arm and, after dropping the others at Bellevue and reaching his own small apartment, he propped it up on the chest-of-drawers and sat on his bed staring at it, as though it brought with it another facet of his life, which to a certain extent it had. The fact that Michael had chosen such a public way of presenting the picture was for Patrick a symbol of being accepted. Nothing like this had ever happened to him before. He shook his head, undressed and got into bed. "Tomorrow, Metung!" he thought, ten beautiful days with a twenty-year-old, who had completely captivated him, giving him for the first time a direction for his life. Smiling to himself, he murmured, "Tomorrow, Metung!"

Organisation the following day was precise. Mary left a six a.m. and Mrs Barnes prepared a late breakfast for everyone. All the equipment and riding gear were loaded onto a small van, which left at nine o'clock for Metung. The others departed about an hour later. Colin, Samuel and Rodney left in one car, Bernard and Lorna in another, Amos, Stephen and David travelled together, as did a rather over-anxious Anne and Patrick. Paul and Michael went on their own and Colin had given Michael some car-sickness tablets an hour before they started. Paul said, however, that if Michael felt sick, he'd stop, so he wasn't sure when they would arrive at Metung, but not to worry, since they could keep in touch by cell phone. Paul's was the last car to pull out of the drive. Anne and Patrick had been the first. "Oh, I hope everything is all right!" she said plaintively. "Of course it is!" said Patrick. "Nigel's a wizard!"

Just as Paul started his engine, he heard a scream from the house, and saw Mrs Barnes crying, "Mr Paul, wait!" She was carrying a medium-sized wicker hamper with a large piece of canvas on top, and under her arm was Toby. "Oh, Mr Paul, I almost forgot! Mary would kill me if I hadn't remembered!" "What's in the hamper?" Paul asked, getting out of the car. "That's right, Mr Paul, put it flat on the back seat and the rug can go on the floor. Here we are Michael! I'm sure Toby is going to have a nice holiday, just like you!" "Yes, I think so", he smiled. "But what is in the hamper?" "Oh, Mr Paul, it's your lunch!" "Our lunch!" "Yes, Mr Paul! Mary thought that since Michael is not such a good traveller, you could stop along the way and have a picnic to break the long journey." "God bless Mary!" said Paul. He said goodbye to Mrs Barnes, hopped back into the car and started off down the drive. "Michael!" said Paul sharply. "Not while I'm driving!" Michael smiled, "But you like it!" "But not when I'm driving! You're impossible, Michael!"

The first car with Patrick and Anne sped off and Rodney, who was driving behind, soon lost sight of them. "I'm glad it's a policeman driving at that speed!" chipped in Samuel. "It's probably to do with Anne's worries about the house, which she hasn't seen since the first day she went down there with Nigel a couple of months ago. Perhaps we'll all end up sleeping at Amos's together, which could prove interesting, particularly the tight sleeping arrangements!" "Don't count your chickens before they're hatched, Samuel!" countered Rodney.

But Samuel was right. Anne was generally as cool as a cucumber, but today in the bright sun and heat, she was extremely agitated. What if the damned house isn't finished? she thought, then realising she hadn't got Mary's mobile number for an update on the state of the house, which had been Patrick's idea. "Oh, darling! Of course!" and she rang Lorna, who gave her Mary's number. "Come on, come on!" sighed Anne as the number rang. "Yes, may I help you?" came the reply. "Oh, thank God, Mary! It's Anne. What's the house like?" "Don't worry, Mrs Rochester. It's all finished and looks great. You'll be very happy with it, I'm sure." "Thank you, Mary" replied a much calmer Anne. "Is the champagne on ice?" "Absolutely! Look forward to seeing you in a few hours! Goodbye!" "I knew everything would be fine!" she said, looking at Patrick. "You didn't! That's why you phoned Mary!" and he started laughing. "Patrick, you're impossible!" she said, repeating what Paul said to Michael when he wouldn't do as Paul wanted.

With the tablets Colin had given him, and Toby sitting on his lap, Michael travelled quite well for some time, but after a couple of hours he told Paul that he didn't feel too well. Paul looked for the nearest side road and turned off. He drove five hundred yards down a sandy track and pulled into what seemed to be a forgotten gateway. He turned off the engine and got out. Michael also alighted and walked about for a few minutes. When he returned, Paul had spread out the canvas cloth beneath the gumstrees in a little clearing back from the track. On the other side the canvas was lined with fluffy tartan blanket. The hamper stood at the edge. "Would you like to open it, Michael?" Paul asked. Michael unlatched the two clasps and lifted the lid. Inside was a masterpiece of Mary's: chicken drumsticks with paper 'frills', a container of smoked salmon on a bed of ice in a plastic bag to keep it cool, all kinds of delicious food that Michael adored, and to one side was a bottle of champagne in a cooler bag and two old-fashioned champagne glasses. Once he began to eat, Michael felt so much better, especially with a glass of champagne. Paul noticed there was also a champagne stopper: a clever idea, since consuming the lot and driving on a very hot day was not the best thing he could do. Michael lay on his back in the shade, having eaten a hearty meal. This time it was Paul was snuggled up to him and ran his hand over Michael's chest and kissed him. Some time later, they departed in high spirits on the last leg of their journey.

The closer they got to Metung, the more excited Anne became. "Oh, I do hope all is well!" "Oh, do settle down, Anne! Everything is going to be fine. Look", Patrick said, "we've crossed the bridge and I can see the tower!" "Oh darling, it looks so different with a new coat of paint! Oh, darling Nigel!" The car pulled up in front of the house and Patrick got out and openedthe new picket gates, and then drove up to the front door. Anne was out in a flash and gave a quick glance over the front garden, the pair of bay laurels in square terracotta pots. Perfect, perfect, she thought. The front door opened and Mary welcomed Mrs Rochester to her new home. "I must see everything immediately, Mary!" She opened the two downstair bedrooms, complete with their bathrooms. Yes, colour excellent. Then she mounted the broad stair to the living room. "Good heavens!" she exclaimed, with Patrick just behind her. "The man's a genius!" A magnificent designer-type living room opened up in front of her: all perfect, the blue silk drapes, the carpets, and on the blank internal wall hung two large shell pictures. Anne went closer to get a better look. "Oh, these are Michael's work!" she said with genuine surprise. "Yes, Mrs Rochester, he wanted to give you a special present for your new home!" The squiggly writing at the bottom of each picture said 'To Anne, with all my love – Michael'. Anne stood transfixed and realised that tears were forming in her eyes. It wasn't that last night she thought that Michael had forgotten her when he was giving his pictures to the others, but that he had kept this gift as a surprise for her was overwhelming. She dabbed her eyes with a handkerchief, only to see the mascara marks. "I'll strangle that cretin at the beauty bar! She said that this stuff was waterproof!" She proceeded to inspect the whole house, and was delighted when she found that a double shower had been fitted in one bedroom, exactly the same colour as the boys' bathroom at Killarney. She went back to the sitting room and then realised that what had once been two ordinary windows at the far end of the room were now two french windows leading out onto the veranda. "Oh, yes! Yes!" she cried. "Patrick! Open a bottle! We must celebrate!" She walked out onto the veranda, which had been completed with small tables for four and comfortable chairs with loose covers in pale blue linen. I couldn't have done it better myself, she thought. While waiting for Patrick to come with the drinks, she telephoned Nigel. "Nigel, darling! I can't begin to tell you what a brilliant – yes, darling, 'brilliant' – job you've done. The living room! The french windows! Oh, Nigel! And the chandelier in the dome! How original!" If only she knew, thought Nigel. "Dear Anne, if you're pleased, so am I!" "Darling, when all the band's not here and you want to get away" – there came a pause – "the property's yours!" "Anne, thank you very much!" "Darling, even the flowers! How thoughtful! Oh, but Michael's paintings! What can I say?" "Perfect for the room!" came his reply. "Yes, darling, perfect for the room! He hasn't arrived yet, but I'll give him a hug for you!" "Yes please!" and a gale of very hearty laughter followed.

Amos and company arrived at the same time as Rodney and co. They first went to Anne's, where they were welcomed with hugs and the usual bottles were opened. Ten minutes later, Bernard and Lorna arrived. Everyone, to Anne's satisfaction, thought the house divine. Tours through each room were obligatory, but it was Amos who in the sitting room spied the two paintings of shells he had recently given Michael. He didn't feel envious, or did he? He justified his feelings by thinking that he, and he alone, had given Michael the subjects through which his creativity could evolve. Yes, that was it: the master behind the master!

Anne played the hostess to perfection: no one could have asked for more, finger food on the veranda, with expectations of Mary's banquet that evening. What more could anyone want?

But Anne felt a sensation, light as a feather. She checked her guests carefully and realised that the feather she had been brushed with was Colin. What was different, because different he was? She knew him so well, and knew that something was up. Now, she thought, which number at this afternoon luncheon was it? Patrick? No, so who was it?

Finally, Paul and Michael arrived, one hour and a half after the others, both smiling, Michael with Toby under his arm. Bernard couldn't help it: whenever he saw Michael with the bear, he felt a pride that had no rational basis, but just that the bear, Michael Mahoney and Bernard Mahony were one!

"Come along, Daphne!" chimed Amos. "To the love-nest!" This provoked screams of laughter, especially from Samuel, who felt he was finally part of this group. He had always been a little uncomfortable in the so-called Killarney set, but for the first time he felt a social equal and laughed heartily with the rest.

Anne's sixth sense was electric. Why wasn't she having problems with Colin? Why had he so willingly accepted staying at Amos's and hadn't put on his usual prima donna performance because he was not staying with her? So Samuel was weaving his web around Dr Campbell, was he? Hmm! she thought, it's taken them some time to clear the corners!

"Come along, Daphne, over the threshold!" "Oh, not again, I just can't bear it!" From the street, through a high paling fence ,with much laughter, the boys entered a beautiful property built in the nineteen-sixties Cape Cod style, shipped all the way to Australia. A very large house: with the trees, from the street you saw nothing but a bit of roof, but most houses at Metung were like that, discreet, quiet. No one could – or should we say 'ought to' –know what lay behind those tall weathered fences. Anne's house was the only exception in the old part of Metung: it screamed high chic, and even after sixty years of abandon, its look was totally acceptable.

Once inside the gate, while the rest of the guests were surprised – especially Stephen and David, who had stayed there on many occasions - Amos was flabbergasted. Nigel and come and had taken measurements and that was that. What they now saw was a complete make-over, no structural alterations except for the chimney breast, but the cosy-folksy look was gone. Inside, all the drab bits of furniture from other houses that inevitably ended up in holiday homes were gone – the awful clashing carpets, the odd lounge chairs – and the look was smart. With the exception of David and Stephen, none of them having been here before, they assumed that Amos, Anne, Lorna and Bernard all had the same taste. They all complimented a very surprised Amos, while Stephen took over and showed all the first-time guests to their rooms.

David noticed how quiet Amos had become, standing in front of what had once been a nasty rock- faced fireplace, but was now chic with travertine, the chimney breast plastered. Amos was transfixed. David broke the spell. "It's beautiful, Amos, It's a very lovely rendering of the shell!" Amos moved closer to Michael's painting on the chimney breast, beautifully mounted in its gilt frame and read at the bottom in Michael's squiggly hand 'To Amos, with all my love – Michael'. Amos wanted to say something smart to David, but the words didn't come. "I know", said David, softly. "He's a very special boy!" Amos tried to pull himself together, but as only David was present, he let his emotion show, and his tears of joy genuinely moved David, who took it as a mark of great friendship.

Everyone found the sleeping arrangements to their liking. Amos's house had six bedrooms, though the bathrooms were a problem. The house and garden went directly to the lake, and were completely private. Samuel was in seventh heaven, and said to Rodney, "This is the only way to fly!" Rodney, knowing a little more about the ten days to come, said "You haven't seen anything yet!"

At seven-thirty, they were all back at Anne's for dinner. Anne was at her best. Everyone toasted the bride and groom again, and then they moved into the dining room. The seating was as always and never altered: everyone knew his place from wherever the old-fashioned champagne glass was set. Before the company took their seats, however, Rodney asked for a moment's attention as he had something to say. This seemed strange, since he was always quiet, getting things done, but never putting himself forward. While they all stood behind their chairs, he asked Anne to use a remote control device, to which she replied, "Anything, darling, so long as it sings!" Everyone laughed as she pressed the button. Through the open bay window, where once there had been a derelict henhouse, an enormous urn lit up, surrounded by bushes and trees in a soft white light. "Wow" was the consensus. "Rodney, darling! It's wonderful!" cooed Anne. "You're such a marvel! It's simply the top!" "Thank you, Anne", he said and everyone applauded.

Anne, however, was carefully keeping her ear to the ground to catch any undercurrents that evening, which finished very well, with drinks on the veranda until quite late. Michael and Paul made an early exit, after Amos had thanked Michael in private for his beautiful painting. Paul got up first from his chair on the veranda and said, "Thanks for everything! We'll catch up with you in the morning!" Michael did his round giving a kiss or a hug as expected, or a handshake. Everyone noted that he kissed Amos, since as a rule Michael never kissed any man apart from Paul and Bernard. When he got to Patrick, he gave him his usual hug and Patrick asked, "Do you want to go riding in the morning?" "Oh yes!" said Michael. "Will it be early?" "It will have to be", said Amos. "We're going out on the boat for lunch!" "We can manage that", said Patrick. "We'll be back by twelve-thirty, OK?" "Yes, perfect!" "Can you be ready at seven-thirty tomorrow morning?" Patrick asked Michael. "Yes!" smiled Michael. "I think so!" and they headed off to bed, but not before making a visit to the kitchen. Paul embraced Mary "Thank you so much for the picnic. We couldn't have got here without it!" "Mary, the chicken was very nice! I ate both pieces with the paper on the ends." "I hope you both enjoyed it", she said. "Goodnight, Mary!" they both repeated and off they went to the bedroom Nigel had designed for them. "Very nice!" as Michael put it, "but it's not really tortoise, is it?"

Patrick was up early. His bedroom was downstairs and so he had to ascend the staircase for a hearty breakfast prepared by Mary and served on the veranda. He was wearing shorts and a shirt open to the third or fourth button. Michael duly arrived, having been pushed out of bed by Paul, who thought that, having woken him at six for his riding appointment, he could now go back to bed and catch up on his sleep. Michael came for breakfast on the veranda wearing only a pair of shorts. He hugged Patrick as usual, but because he was still a little sleepy, he held on to him longer. Patrick felt the electricity and gently pulled himself away, worried that a certain part of his anatomy defied gravity when in contact with Michael's body. Thank goodness for Mulberry's rather ample shorts. They finished breakfast and drove to a riding school just over a mile from Metung. Michael was assigned a mare that he was sure was Polly's sister. For the first time, Patrick took Michael over a set of jumps, calling to him to lean forward, and then sit up straight. The manager of the riding school-cum-farm was totally indifferent to her clients: they paid and she happily took their cash, and that was that! She was dressed in a very large pair of jodhpurs and a man's loose red cotton shirt and riding boots. Michael wore his hat, since Patrick refused to let him ride without it, but because it was so hot and only eight-fifteen in the morning, his attire consisted of jodhpurs, boots and a white shirt, with the sleeves rolled up and the front open wide. The first jumps were low and Michael took them easily, the horse feeling Michael and Michael the horse. Patrick kept a strict eye on his equestrian ward, but when he reined in and went to speak to the owner in her red shirt, Michael decided he would take the much higher jumps, set up one after another. He turned his mare and touched and spoke to her as though she were Polly. "Go, Polly!" he said. When Patrick turned to see Michael taking two high jumps, with no real experience, he panicked, knowing that any yelling or calling would only confuse the boy. So he called out, "Lean back!" then "Now forward!" and Michael and his 'new' Polly cleared the jumps without a hitch. Patrick was very concerned as he took Michael into his arms and hugged him. "We did very well!" smiled Michael. "Yes!" said Patrick, relieved, "and thank the saints you're in one piece!" They collected their tackle and headed back to Metung, while the red-shirted manageress opened a bottle of beer and, drinking straight from the bottle, thought aloud, "Why are gay men so good looking! It doesn't seem fucking fair!" and then lumbered into her office to answer an insistent telephone.

When they arrived at Anne's, Michael was quite elated. "We took two jumps, one after the other, and there were four bars! It was very good!" he told Paul. Not understanding anything about the equestrian world,

Paul accepted that with Patrick, it must be fine. It was a very nervous Patrick who explained to Anne and Lorna Michael's somewhat reckless adventure that morning. Anne looked at Patrick, "Did he hold his seat?" "Yes, perfectly!" "And he moved with the horse?" "Yes", said Patrick, very weakly. "Well", said Anne, "all I have to say is that Michael is very lucky to have such a good instructor, wouldn't you, Lorna?" "Yes!" said a somewhat nervous Lorna, "but there wasn't any risk, was there?" "Oh, a little!" said Patrick, breathlessly, "a little!" "Well, you must both be more careful, please!" pleaded Lorna. "Promise!" said Patrick, and helped himself to a sizable glass of champagne, still shaking a little on thinking of the potential consequences of a fall.

Everyone was ready for the lunch, prepared – or organised – by David and Amos. David was a regular patron of a restaurant close to his home in East Melbourne and when the chef retired he had come to live at Lakes Entrance. David contacted him and, for ten days' top pay, he took over the cooking at Amos's, and on the boat. Today they were all ready for the boat trip. Paul and Lorna were concerned that Michael might be sea-sick, but it didn't happen. Everyone wore bathing suits, and Samuel looked like a labrador waiting for Michael to take him for a walk. The afternoon was splendid. It was the first time Michael had tasted barbecued fish with a hot sauce, and he loved it, so David felt doubly content that his friend the chef had pleased them all, especially Michael. When the boat moored at a quiet spot along the banks of the Tambo river, everyone was in and out of the water. Well, not quite everyone! Anne, wearing the chic-est swimsuit, never entered the water. "Come on!" pleaded Samuel, as Colin dived in. "Thanks, but no, darling!" It's far too wet!" It was of course Michael, in the very swimsuit that Samuel had sold to him at Mulberry's, who was the star. Paul knew that everybody thought Michael was beautiful but, as time went by, he never felt jealous of the fact. Samuel wore his heart on his sleeve: he only had to touch Michael and his feet wouldn't feel the ground for a week! Everyone knew this except Michael, who just accepted that Samuel was Rodney's friend. Rodney himself was not blind to Michael's sexual attraction, since it was so overwhelming that it intensified thoughts that might otherwise have been merely speculation. It was Patrick who had the most trouble while swimming: all it took was for Michael to hold him or play with him in the water and he immediately realised he had much less control over his anatomy than he thought.

On the evening of the second day of the holiday, Bernard, who had insisted on paying for everything but found it all organised by the others, insisted on giving Mary a break by taking the group to dinner at the only local hotel. He booked for nine o'clock. They all had drinks at Anne's and then walked the one hundred yards to the hotel. Before leaving, Anne went into the dining room and, since the door to the kitchen was ajar, she saw Mary giving Patrick what seemed to be dancing lessons on doing the 'hokey-pokey'. How odd, she thought. What on earth is going on? She then proceeded to forget about it entirely.

Since the hotel dining room was rather full, they had to squeeze their chairs together, but even so, owing to the noise, it was very difficult to make youself heard unless you were very close. Anne had a funny feeling. What on earth was Patrick doing, continually staring at Michael, she wondered. Orders were taken. What with the noise and tight space, Patrick was the first to see it. Bernard was speaking to Stephen on one side of Michael and on the other Paul had leaned over to speak to Rodney, when someone walked behind Michael and, having to squeeze by, touched him on the shoulders. Patrick saw his hand go up and his head go down. He sprang up, upsetting his wine, and moved with incredible dexteritybetween chairs and tables. He lifted Michael up, even before Bernard and Paul had realised what was happening, although when he saw Patrick moving so quickly, Paul understood that something was wrong. With Lorna, Patrick and Paul made their way through the crowded hotel and onto the terrace in front. Michael was shaking: the ghost of the past had returned to haunt him. Lorna took control. "Paul, take him back to Anne's. Wait a moment, Patrick!" she said, and rushed back to the table. "All of you finish your meal here and have a drink at Amos's afterwards. If you all come back now, Michael will feel even more distressed!" She left and joined Patrick outside. "Will you come with us, or would you prefer to stay with the others?" For Patrick, it was like being invited to the very inner circle. "No", he said, "I should like to be with you. I don't want to go back inside!" "Good!" said Lorna, and immediately dialled Mary. "Mary, we've had a problem. Could you possibly manage dinner for four on the veranda now?" "Is it

340

Michael?" asked Mary. "Yes, it is, I'm afraid!" "Ready in five minutes!" said Mary and hung up. Michael settled down a little with Patrick talking to him about his riding, but he held Paul's hand tighly for the one hundred yards to Anne's house.

Having the girl there to help her, Mary was shouting instructions. The poor girl had no idea about the drama, or why a meal for four had to be produced in five minutes. Mary rushed about between the kitchen and overseeing the table. "Never", she shouted, "ever put Michael's glass in a place where he hasn't got his back to the wall! Never!" The girl's impression was of being in a horror movie, where at any moment Dracula would sweep down and plunge his teeth into her neck, just because she had placed a glass in the wrong position.

When the four arrived, everything was calm and in order, and it was a very different Mary from the one who had attacked her assistant a minute before. Calm and sensible, she welcomed them, saying she had heard that the hotel food was bad and was glad to have them back for a good meal. Michael accepted it all and became much more tranquil, but an underlying tension was still there. Drinks were poured and they all talked about the fun lunch on the boat. Michael stood up, and everyone expected him to go to the bathroom, but he went into the sitting room, walked past the piano and returned to it, then he lifted the lid and sat down. Mary, coming through with the first course, froze when she saw him lean forward, then backward. Then he began playing exactly what he remembered from the wedding four days before: Mozart's *Ave Verum*. The effect was electric. The three on the veranda stood and watched through the french windows. Michael played as though it were the last thing he was going to do in his whole life: it was like an outlet for all his fears from the past. Lorna felt every note strike her heart. He was wonderful, but more than that, he was special. When he finished, he stood up, turned round and saw Mary. "Mary, I'm so hungry!" he said. "Just as well, darling!" she said, sniffing back the tears. "I've prepared something very special for you!" "Mary, you're always making special things for me! You're very nice!" Michael returned to the table, ready for his dinner, but Mary had to put the tray down on a small table to wipe her eyes before serving the meal.

Meanwhile, at the hotel, everyone settled back to a more sober evening, though since four of them had left, they had a little more space. Samuel made no secret of the fact that the young Italian waiter was very much his cup of tea, and had to bear being the brunt of everyone's jokes. "But of course!" said Anne, "I'm such a fool! Mary was instructing Patrick, before he left the house this evening, about Michael in crowds. Why are we all so stupid!" There was complete silence. Despite the evening's upset, Anne had detected something else. When they had all moved their cramped chairs apart, Colin and Rodney didn't and Rodney went on talking to Colin with his arm along the back of Colin's chair. Anne, being Anne, dropped her napkin and in the act of retrieving it glanced quickly under the table: two knees were touching. "Hooray!" she thought. "So it's Colin and Rodney, not Colin and Samuel! Well, well! What a holiday!"

When dinner was over, Samuel made excuses to stay and see his waiter, and Colin and Rodney said they would have another drink. Bernard, Stephen, Amos, David and Anne walked to Amos's house, seventy yards in the other direction from Anne's, through the warm summer evening. When they got there, it was Anne's turn to be surprised. Nigel had totally revamped the living room and bedrooms. "But Amos, it looks so splendid!" "Don't you mean less cosy?" Amos replied. "Oh, Amos! How could you say such a thing! But you're right!" She laughed and spied Michael's painting over the new travertine fireplace. "Well, it looks like we both made it!" she said. "It looks wonderful here!" "You know", said Amos, settling into a comfortable chair, "I confess I've always been very envious of you, Stephen!" "Of me!" said a surprised Stephen. "Yes, you. When Michael gave you the little painting of the clam shell – years ago now it seems – I confess I was envious." "Now that won't be necessary", said David, "because you have a bigger one!" This brought peals of laughter. After half an hour, Anne said she was ready to retire, since tomorrow they were to have dinner on board on the lake. "Sounds great!" said Bernard. "We're looking forward to it!"

In the balmy night air, Anne and Bernard walked arm-in-arm back to Anne's place. "Oh, Bernard! Are you a betting man?" "Well, it depends on the odds!" "I'll lay you a bet that one person in this group is going to return to Brunswick a much happier person." "Samuel will always find fun", he said. "Oh, but Bernard, I'm not talking of Samuel!" "Who are you talking about then?" "It's only a guess." "Oh Anne! I hate these charades! Hurry up and tell me, or I shall lose interest at once!" "Bernard! Don't you dare! It's Colin!" "Colin, what do you mean 'Colin'?" "Colin and Rodney!" "You mean. . .?" "Yes", she interrupted. "Isn't it wonderful! Now I can manage Patrick without any jealousy!" "Anne!" he stopped. "Are you planning an affair with Patrick? Not that I have anything against it! He's a splendid man, honest, reliable, and very handsome!" "Oh Bernard! For a judge, you can be so stupid! I gave up sex for champagne at twenty, and see no reason to return to the past! No, I want to employ Patrick as an overseer. Don't you see how good it would be? He could take Michael riding every morning." "Anne, just a minute! He has a career! You can't expect him to drop everything just for you – Ok for us too!" "He must, Bernard, he must! I shall see how I can arrange it!" "Don't interfere with his career, Anne!" "Is that a judicial ruling, Bernard?" she asked, a little sarcastically.

They reached home, found that everyone had called it a night, and in turn they also retired.

Next morning, Anne rose early and went to the kitchen. "Mary, I want to thank you for last night. You're just divine! You saved everything, especially with your warning to Patrick. Thank you so very, very much!" "Mrs Rochester, Michael is the most important thing in my life", Mary said very soberly, "and, like you, I also go out of my way to protect him". "Yes, Mary, but you go much further than we do!" She smiled at Anne and asked where she would like her breakfast. "On the veranda. Is anyone else up?" "Oh, yes, Mrs Rochester! Paul and Michael have gone for a walk along the lake. They said they'd be back in a hour or so for lunch." Anne walked onto the veranda, complete with dark glasses, to cope with the bright, sunny morning. "May I join you?" said a voice. "Oh Lorna, please do!" "Mary", called Anne. "Could we make it breakfast for two?" "Bernard's asleep. He was very concerned about Michael. Did anyone tell you about the piano performance last night?" "No, I haven't seen anyone! What happened?" asked a surprised Anne. But before Lorna could reply, a large breakfast tray was placed on the table. "He played like an angel!" said Mary. "I couldn't help crying!" "It was splendid!" said Lorna, and she explained Michael's performance at the piano. "He's really amazing!" said Anne. When they were alone, she said to Lorna, "Did Bernard tell you about. . ." "Yes!" interrupted Lorna. "Colin and Rodney! Well, who would have thought it?" Someone else arrived for breakfast. It was Patrick. As he picked up the morning newspaper, he overheard Anne's voice on the veranda, slightly agitated, saying "But it's perfect! With Colin occupied with Rodney, I don't have to cope with Colin's jealousy of Patrick. I must get Patrick to leave the policeforce and come and live at Bellevue. He can have the big apartment near the swimming pool, or one of the suites in the big house, if Nigel ever finishes them. Nigel told me he's having great difficulty converting the small dining room into a Chinese-style kiosk." "Whatever gave you that idea?" asked Lorna. "Oh, Michael, of course!" "Oh, of course!" echoed Lorna weakly. "Do you think, darling, if I went to Sergeant Reynolds and told him Patrick was a horse rustler, he would fire him?" "I don't think he'd believe you!" said Patrick, coming out to join them for breakfast. Although shocked that she had been overheard, in a split second Anne managed to turn the situation around. "Well, darling! What about car-theft, so as to bring it all up to date?" "Anne, please!" said Patrick, sitting down. Lorna noticed that today Patrick was much handsomer and more relaxed than she remembered: his black, wavy hair, black-brown eyes, broad chest, and muscled legs revealed by his shorts. "Oh Patrick, darling", said Anne slowly. "You can have and do what you wish. I'll pay you whatever salary you want!" "Anne, I've got a career!" "Don't be silly, Patrick! We all need you much more than Sergeant Reynolds does! And just think, darling", she said even more slowly, "what if they transferred you somewhere else, a long way from Morton! Whatever would you do?" "I've thought of that!" he said, looking down at the floor. "I don't know what I would do!" Anne had now baited her trap. Lorna watched in silence as Anne's voice rose and dropped, making the most of every word she used. "Darling Patrick, if that occurred, Bernard, Amos, Stephen – all of us – would obviously do our best to help, but could we guarantee it? I hope so!" Here, she finished her coffee and returned her cup to the saucer, looking as forlorn as possible as she reached over and grasped his left arm. She then played her trump card. "Patrick, darling", she began. "I suppose Bernard's right when he says we must respect your career." "But, Patrick", she said, removing her dark glasses, "what about Michael? Without you he'd be completely lost! You saw what happened last night. You were the one who came to the rescue first, you held him and took him out of danger!" Now came the thrust: "Patrick, he loves you very much. You know that life without you, for him and for us, would be impossible!"

There was a silence that no one had the courage to break. Finally, it was Lorna who, smiling, came to Anne's rescue with "We couldn't possibly do without you. Besides, Patrick, seeing that you're now also Michael's croquet partner, any idea of your not remaining is just unthinkable!" Patrick stood up and walked over to the cast-iron balustrade. He turned and faced the women, leaning back. "You're asking me a lot, Anne!" "I know, darling, but it's not just for me! It's for all of us, but more espcially for Michael. He sees us as family, but you and Mary have a super-special role in his life, and without either of you two, he could only regress. His progress is linked to the certainty that you're always there: he's sure of you and loves you both." At that point, Mary, who had come to collect the breakfast things, overheard the last part of Anne's discourse and burst into tears. Anne and Lorna didn't move a finger: it was Patrick who went over to comfort Mary. She apologised and thanked Anne for her generous comments and left, sniffing. "Well, darling, what do you say?" "I'll give you my decision on the last day of the holiday, but you'll . have to respect my decision!" "Certainly!" said Anne, with eyes cast down. Patrick replied, "I'm going to have a shower and then I promised to help Amos arrange a thing or two for dinner on the boat tonight. I'll see you later for lunch!"

Anne put her finger to her lips, warning Lorna not to say anything. She stood up, went inside and returned with a bottle of champagne and two glasses. She opened the bottle in dead silence, poured it out, looked at Lorna and said, "I think we have a minder for Michael for life! What do you think, darling?" They clinked glasses. "I hadn't realised you'd been to drama school, Anne!" "I haven't! It's just natural talent!" They both laughed. "He's divine, isn't he?" "Yes", said Lorna. "Let's hope his decision is in our favour!" "Oh, it's certain to be!" answered Anne, very sure-of-herself. "What! Drinking so early in the morning?" said Bernard, as he came onto the veranda. "Just celebrating a little secret", said Anne. "We can't tell you until the end of the holiday!" "Oh, really!" said Bernard, disinterestedly.

The two groups separated for lunch, but joined up in the evening for the trip on the lake with dinner aboard. The boat was lit up and looked magic. "Patrick", said Lorna, when he handed her a drink. "You're really one of the best dressed men in our group!" Anne overheard this and, when Lorna moved away, winked at Patrick, who did the same. The evening was a great success and Amos was very proud that this large craft was being used exactly as he had hoped. The group now fitted together very well, after two or three days of adjustment. There was no stress, and everyone – especially Michael – was having a wonderful time. For Michael it was all new, since he had never seen a big lake and never been on a boat before. He probably thought that all boats had this level of luxury. The chef once again lived up to David's expectations, and supper on board was something that even Anne had to admit was a pleasant experience.

So the days went by, each one pleasanter than the next. Only one little adventure occurred, causing a change of plans. Nearly every morning, Michael and Patrick went to the riding school, and one morning the red-shirted owner was in her office and a very brisk argument was going on. The man with her screamed, "I'll sue!" Patrick popped his head round the door. "Help youself!" said the red-shirted manageress, so they went to collect their horses as usual. The one Michael usually rode was, however, in a separate little paddock, unsaddled. Michael called, "Polly! Polly" and the horse came over. Patrick took a saddle from the rack and saddled her up for Michael, and out they went toward the jumps. "Let me take the four-bar one", begged Michael. "No! You'll take the two-bar, then the three-bar! Sit up straight, Michael!" demanded Patrick. They started and, although Michael was unaware of what was going on, Patrick noticed that the owner and the agitated man with her kept pointing at Michael. "What's wrong?" thought Patrick, but since no one called them, they stayed at the jumps. As usual, Michael got his way, and took the high jump very professionally. "Good, Michael! You did that very well!" Michael felt a swell of pride as Polly n° Two and he cantered to the far side of the meadow and took the small jumps all over again.

When their morning ride was over, they returned to the enclosure when the owner was waiting. They dismounted. "I gotta thank you guys", she said. "That arsehole you saw earlier was going to sue me. You see, that horse", she said, looking at Patrick, "the one your boyfriend was riding, threw that arsehole's son and broke his arm. Pity it wasn't his flaming neck! Wanna drink?" she asked, while downing a half-bottle of beer. Patrick felt a little awkward at being labelled Michael's boyfriend, but also surprised that he was so little embarrassed by it. "When he took all the jumps I guess even that arsehole realised it didn't have anything to do with the horse and everything to do with his stupid son's inability to ride. So thanks a lot for the demo, boys! By the way, all future riding here on you holiday is on the house! Have a great day!" She disappeared into her office to answer yet another insistent caller.

Next day, everyone was on the boat again and they started off at eleven. Later they moored at the most isolated part of the lake and swam and the boys lay on the deck sunbathing. Of all of them, Michael tanned most quickly, owing to his olive skin. Anne sat with Lorna in a silk wrap over her matching swimsuit that never touched the water, decked in gold jewelry. She lifted her dark glasses and glanced at the younger members of the group: Michael, the youngest, Samuel, Rodney, Paul, Patrick and Colin, all lying in the sun. She topped Lorna's glass up and said, looking at the boys, "You know, Lorna, there's a very old Australian expression 'You wouldn't be dead for quids'!" Lorna roared with laughter. "Oh, Anne!" she said, unable to stop laughing, "You're so right!"

Feeling sleepy, Michael moved close to Paul and rested his head on Paul's chest, as he did every night. Paul ran his fingers through Michael's thick black mane of hair and felt absolutely content.

Later in the day, before they returned to Metung, the boys went swimming again. As Patrick pulled himself back onto the boat, Samuel grasped his hand and helped him aboard. Samuel ran his hand down Patrick's wet side. Patrick smiled and looked at him. "Thanks for the help, but no, thanks!" Samuel's reply was quick and sharp, "You know where to find me!"

The holiday-cum-honeymoon was reaching an end. Amos insisted that their last meal should be on the boat on the lake, and everyone enthusiastically agreed. After lunch, Michael went to Bernard and said, "Cooty, is everyone going to be on the boat this evening?" "Yes, Michael, everyone!" "Even Mary?" Bernard looked at him, "How stupid of me, Michael! I shall go and ask her at once!" He stood up and disappeared into the kitchen. "Oh, but Judge Mahoney! I couldn't!" said Mary. "I'm afraid you must!" he smiled. "Michael's orders!" He left and explained to Anne, who immediately phoned Amos to make sure another setting was laid for Mary.

It was a breathtaking evening, warm, with a slight breeze, and everybody in good shape after their holiday. So many things had happened, and so many had been consolidated: all but one, and Anne waited patiently, but nervously, for Patrick's reply to her offer.

After a wonderful meal, Amos stood up and thanked everybody for coming to Metung, claiming that he'd never enjoyed himself so much. Anne then took the floor and asked Michael whether he had enjoyed his stay. "Yes!" was his answer. Anne used Michael's affirmative to make a proposal to Bernard and Amos. "Well, now we've had a splendid holiday, what do you say to making it an annual event?" "I'm all for that!" cried Amos. "So am I!" said Bernard. "Good!" said Anne. "So it's settled! Once a year, at least, every year! Hooray!"

"I suppose", said a much mellowed Colin, with his arm round the back of Rodney's chair, to Patrick, "it's back to work, like all of us?" Anne pricked up her ears at once, as did Lorna. "Yes", said Patrick, "work, work!" and he smiled. "But I'm changing addresses this year." "Oh!" said Colin. "Are you taking a new apartment?" "I really don't know in which part of Bellevue I'll be living, but it'll work out somehow!" Colin was dumbfounded. He looked first at Patrick, then at Anne, who suddenly looked like a cat that had got at the cream. "Isn't that lovely, Michael?" she smiled. "You can now go riding every day!"

CHAPTER NINE

Home At Killarney

CHAPTER 9

Home At Killarney

The moment Michael got back to Killarney, he handed Toby to Paul and raced off to see whether his bronze geese were still in their place in the Red Garden. Then he dashed to the bottom of the garden, through the gate that divided Killarney from Bellevue and straight to the stable yard. "Polly, Polly!" he called, but she wasn't in the stables, so he turned and headed for the paddock, where a slightly fatter Polly – having had no exercise for two weeks – cantered up and nuzzled Michael's neck. Patrick, who had arrived back two hours before Paul and Michael, came out to see what the noise was about. Michael called to Patrick, "Polly's happy we're home! Look, I think she's getting fat!" He laughed: a very suntanned Michael in a white shirt and dark blue shorts, providing a vision that convinced Patrick that he had been right to accept Anne's offer.

Originally, Patrick had thought that the apartment near the swimming pool was the best idea, but Anne wouldn't have it. "Darling, it's far too much like staff quarters. Stay there for the time being, since Nigel hasn't finished your suite yet. In two weeks, he said, it will all be done!" Yet again, he was allowing his life to be organised for him, and he realised that being a passive employee worked very well. Paul was looking after his pension plan, all contributions being paid by Bernard, who had made it quite clear that since he looked after Michael when they weren't there, he would pay, and that was that. Anne paid his wages, exactly as she had said, double what he had been getting in the police force, plus extras such as accomodation, meals, etc. Who would have thought that picking a beautiful boy up out of the mud two-and-a-half years ago would have led to a total revolution in his lifestyle!

When he went to Melbourne with Anne and everyone from Killarney, he stayed at Anne's large apartment. It gave Michael the greatest pleasure to say to Henry O'Connor at Brown's, "Mr Patrick is my guest!" Henry always smiled and said, "Of course, Michael! How nice of you to bring a friend!"

Colin eventually got over his initial shock and inevitable jealousy, since he had quite a lot to rearrange in his own life: his wife left him and returned to her parents, but her father was wise enough to realise that a handsome doctor in a large and growing country town was basically a good investment. Colin demanded a contract and a share of the clinic's profits, which was agreed to after many weeks of haggling. Once the legal documents were signed, he and Rodney looked round for a country property near Morton and eventually found a small and very run-down farm with an even more run-down large Edwardian weatherboard house. It was well set back from the road and the pair of them decided that with a bit of time they could sort things out, meaning, of course, that Nigel was again called upon to save the day, and Rodney indulged his fantasies in laying out a special garden around the house.

One afternoon, Anne received a call from Samuel, asking if he could see her. "Certainly, darling! Come to dinner!" "I'd like to see you alone", he said. "Fine! Make it tomorrow evening! Patrick is going to Killarney to play croquet and is staying for dinner. I've copped out of sports: not really my thing!"

Bernard, Michael and Patrick were playing croquet, while Lorna and Paul sat watching them from the pavilion, now fully restored. Michael was always so animated when playing this game, which he and Patrick did very often. They particularly liked playing after sunset, lighting the candles on top of the hoops. When the ball went through a hoop, the little bell would ring. Essential to this was Rodney's clever garden lighting, which gave a diffused effect over the croquet court.

Samuel arrived and three minutes after being given a drink, spilled the beans. He wanted Anne to ask the owner of the best hotel in Brunswick – the Royal –, whom she knew very well, to take on his Italian waiter friend, the one he had met on holiday at Metung. "Well darling", said Anne, "I can certainly try. What sort of position is he looking for?" "Oh, a waiter's job!" said Samuel. "Oh dear! That won't do at all! What about trainee chef for the big dining room? I think that would be much more suitable. Leave it to me. I'm sure we can organise something!" "Oh, Anne! Thanks!" In private, he addressed her as Anne, but in public always as Mrs Rochester, an arrangement she liked very much. "Anne, could I possibly see your Chinese room?" "But, darling! It's not finished! In fact, it's not really started!" "Well, everyone in Brunswick is talking about it!" "Are they?" said Anne, smiling. "I wonder how they found out about it!" She winked at Samuel, both knowing quite well that 'Neville the mouth', as Samuel called him, had been broadcasting it for weeks, although no one had actually seen it.

That room had been a nightmare for Nigel, and he had come very close to abandoning the project. Anne was at her most difficult. The first wallpaper that went up, she had Nigel take down. "Nigel!" she said, sharply. I said 'Chinese as in "eighteenth century chinoiserie", not as in "Chinese take-away"!" This made Nigel angry. "It's not easy, Anne", he said in a sarcastic tone, "to pull eighteenth century Chinese scenic wallpaper out of a hat!" "I want the one Michael showed me, with figures walking about at the bottom." "Well!" said Nigel, "in that case, we shall have to ask Michael to give up painting shells and start painting eighteenth century Chinese wallpaper!" Realising Nigel was angry, Anne backed off a little. "I know it's very difficult, Nigel, and I'm sorry, but that's what I want!" "Do you!" he snapped. So the Chinese room was the only one not completed in a fully renovated Bellevue. Nigel had decorator friends in Melbourne, but not one of them could help him.

Then, a month or so later, with all work suspended on the small dining room à la chinoise, Nigel received a call from – of all people – his old working colleague from Bairnsdale, Ted the architect. "Nigel", Ted began, "I suppose I couldn't interest you in about thirty painted panels, could I? I've been renovating a house at Lindenow, and there are two trunks of this painted stuff up in the attic." "What sort of panels are they? I mean what's the subject?" "I only saw one, and some of them are badly torn, but it's oriental stuff!" "Ted, have you got the trunks with you?" "Yes, they're in the hallway of my office. Do you think they're worth anything?" "I'll tell you in the morning. I'll leave here at six, so I'll see you around ten-thirty-eleven o'clock!" "Ok! I'll be in my office!"

At precisely eleven o'clock, Nigel's tall frame stalked into Ted's office. "Well!" he said, "are these the trunks?" "Yes! By the way, Nigel: good morning!" "Oh, good morning!" mumbled Nigel, as he opened the first trunk. The panels were damaged, but were nineteenth century, Nigel thought. The reason they were in poor condition was that they had been taken off the walls of another room at some time. With Ted's help, he unrolled the first roll completely. Joy of joys! There were two large Chinese figures, each holding a lamp on a long bamboo pole. "Have you got a customer for this stuff?" asked Ted. "Yes! A certain Mrs Rochester!" Ted paled. "Oh, her!" "Yes, her!" "How much do you want for the lot, remembering that they're not in good condition, or would you prefer to negotiate directly with Mrs Rochester herself?" "No, no!" cried Ted. "That blasted house at Metung was enough for me! The woman selling the stuff wants five hundred dollars, and my commission is one hundred. What do you think?" "I'll pay the five hundred and send you the one hundred dollars only if I can salvage what I need from the trunks!" "Ok!" said Ted, seeing his trick to get a quick hundred dollars wasn't going to work. The thought of negotiating with Anne was out of the question.

Before returning to Brunswick, Nigel phoned Anne, who was with Patrick, looking at the work to be done on a very rundown stable block. "Darling! I knew you could do it!" she cried. "How marvellous! Oh!" – a short silence – "Oh, I see! Well, I'll ask Lorna. You'd better go straight to Killarney when you arrive, if we need that sort of space. Oh! That may be a little more difficult, but I'm sure I can manage something!" Her voice was now much more sober. "Yes, yes! Very well, six o'clock at Killarney!" and she hung up. She at once telephoned Lorna. "Darling! How are you?" cooed Anne. Lorna knew instantly that Anne wanted something. "I'm fine, darling!" she replied. "I thought we might just walk over to see you!" "Why don't you and Patrick come for lunch?" "Good idea! Thank you, Lorna! We'll be over about midday!" and Anne hung up. Patrick leaned back against the stable door and looked at Anne. "A problem?" he smiled. "A technical hitch, but I'm sure I can manage something!"

At exactly twelve noon, Patrick and Anne entered Killarney by the back gate, and were met by Michael. "Darling, you look fabulous!" He kissed Anne's cheek as usual and gave Patrick his ever-expected hug. Michael was in great form, chatting on to them, when Anne suddenly stopped in her tracks. "Good heavens!" she exclaimed. "It's enormous!" This was the first time she had seen the conservatory from outside: a vast glistening palace of cream cast-iron and glass, with a green tropical jungle trapped inside. "We're having lunch there today", said Michael. "I like it very much. Rodney has shown me how to open the windows in the roof to let the hot air out, but you must close them at night!" An inspection of the Red Garden was obligatory, before going on to the house. Patrick claimed jokingly that he was the better croquet player, to which Michael laughingly said, "No, Patrick! You are not!" and took him by the hand to the conservatory to explain the computer system for opening and closing the glass roof panels.

"Would you like a drink, Anne?" smiled Lorna as she welcomed her. Then they followed the boys towards the conservatory. Lorna had laid a table for four, right in the centre, and the sunny day's light, filtered through the palms and other exotics, was indeed pleasant. "Well, Anne", said Lorna, when they were all seated, "what do you want?" "Lorna, dear, what do you mean?" "Come on, Anne! I know it when you're up to something!" "Well, it's like this. Apparently, Nigel has found - at Lindenow of all places! – two trunks full of Chinese wallpaper. But, and this is the problem, the paper seems to be very damaged, and since we need a large space to lay it all out, I'm afraid, Lorna, that I took the liberty of telling him to bring it here to Killarney at six o'clock, so that we can lay it out on the ballroom floor! That's quite a liberty, I know, but I knew you'd forgive me!" "Oh, is that all, Anne? Good heavens, it's no problem at all!" Patrick refilled Anne's glass. "Lorna, this is such a divine place, a perfect setting for lunch!" She wants something else,

Patrick thought, having very quickly learned Anne's power games. "Oh, Lorna!" "Yes?" replied the unsuspecting Lorna. "There is another little thing. . .." "Really Anne? And what can that be?" "Well, I think I shall have to have Mary's help in repainting the pieces that are missing. Nigel seems to think that she's the only talented artist in the area. Taking all this stuff to Melbourne and back would take months, and we'll never be able to get the room finished!" "Hmm!" sighed Lorna. "This puts a different light on things" It will depend how much time is needed, and first of all you'll have to ask Mary!" "Who has to ask me something?" smiled Mary, bringing in a large silver tray with the first course, which she set on a side table, from which she served each of the guests. "Dearest Mary", began Anne and recounted her plight to her. "Well!" said Mary. "It's really not up to me!" Lorna interrupted, "I suppose with Mrs Barnes in the kitchen, we could all muddle through?" "Oh, it's not that! I'd have to seek my assistant's permission!" She smiled and went back to the kitchen with an empty tray. Anne looked puzzled and then, in her quick feline manner, turned slowly toward Michael, who suddenly became aware that everyone was staring at him. "Anne", he said, "are you all right?" "Oh, yes, darling! I have a little job for you. I knowyou'd like to help Patrick and me!" "Leave me out of this!" smiled Patrick. "Darling", said Anne, looking sharply at Patrick, "we're living in restricted conditions: no small dining room, and, to make things worse", she now turned to Lorna, "we're being slowly poisoned!" "Poisoned!" "Yes, darling, you heard me: poisoned! That Jennifer Walkley is really too much! Making mistake after mistake in the kitchen. Only the other evening, I had to ask Patrick exactly what it was we were eating. I think it was some kind of meat à la miaow. . . Dear me! There's no difference in taste between one thing and another. I shall probably have to get Sylv up from the dogs' home to see whether she can tell me if we're eating pet food. Thank goodness she can't foul up smoked salmon. Oh, I'm wrong! Yes she can! Remember, Patrick? She chopped all the delicious slices up into tiny pieces and put them on some dry old crackers, finishing off her pièce de resistance with a blob of tomato paste and a sage leaf on top. Really, it just won't do!" Everyone knew Anne was quite serious. Lorna knew from Mary that Anne's new cook was terrified of her, which made her make mistake after mistake. Lorna also knew that Anne was not the easiest woman to work for, especially if you were another woman. "I've been thinking", Anne said, returning to the subject of cooks, "of offering Mary a huge salary and spiriting her away to Bellevue! – Don't worry, Lorna! I wouldn't dare! I know Bernard would put me in the women's prison within five minutes for stealing staff!" She laughed. "Now, darling, do you think you could help me?" she said softly to Michael, who replied, "I don't know what to do!" "Don't worry, sweetie! Mary will take charge, so I take it that it's in the affirmative! Oh goody! Another glass, Patrick darling!"

In high spirits, she went back to her problems with her cook, which had Lorna and Patrick in stiches. Michael didn't quite grasp the finer points, and didn't understand why Anne had taken to eating cat food. On returning with the main course, Mary was greeted by a smiling Anne. "Of course, Mary, all the time you and your assistant spend on this project will be recompensed handsomely!" "Let's see the work, then my assistant and I", she said, looking at Michael, "will decide!" "Well, it will all be laid out on the ballroom floor at six o'clock, and we can all have a peep", replied Anne.

At exactly six o'clock, Nigel's small van pulled up under the porte cochère, and he got out and rang the bell. "Well, good afternoon, Nigel!" said Lorna. "We're all agog to see the Chinese wallpaper!" "Can someone give me a hand with the trunks?" "I'll send the boys", said Lorna and disappeared, to be replaced by Patrick and Michael. The two wooden trunks were carried in and placed on the ballroom floor. "I'll need something to hold the papers flat: a weight at either end." "Michael!" said Lorna. "Rodney brought two bundles of stakes yesterday for the roses. I saw them standing by the side of the shed. Bring them in and we'll use them to hold the papers down." Michael rushed out to collect the bundles of stakes. He was so curious: two trunks of Chinese men! He was quite unable to imagine what form they would take, even though he had seen the photograph in the book on interior decoration. There were no wooden trunks involved.

Nigel opened the first trunk, took out a roll and held one end while Patrick unrolled it and held the other and Michael placed the stakes at either end to stop it from rolling up again. This they did again, and again, and again. This operation produced a shower of white powder, which Nigel explained was the old wallpaper paste that had crystallised with time. "They're beautiful!" said Lorna. "They're rather damaged!" retorted Anne, moving around to see them all. In looking at a still unrolled one, Mary noticed a number pencilled on the back. She checked the others and found that they, too, all bore a number. Mary thought it possible that the numbers might provide the original order and, when arranged side-by-side on the ballroom floor, an enormous scene unfolded, with two figures on each roll, holding lamps, chasing butterflies and other genteel behaviour of the Chinese court. Michael was most impressed by the birds. "They look very real", he said, "But they all look frightened!" "They do, a bit", said Nigel. On all the rolls, the top part was badly damaged and in some places the paper was missing. Mary had a good look at it. "It's because they used another kind of glue at the top, which didn't come away as easily as the other." Nigel measured the length. "Hmm, the length's fine for the room, but the problem is that so much of the top is missing, as much as eighteen to twenty-four inches on some of the rolls." "Mr Nigel, why don't you put a fence at the bottom, then?" They all turned and looked at Michael. "A fence, darling?" said Anne. "If we put a fence, we couldn't see the figures!" "Anne, just a minute!" and he disappeared, leaving a not-too-convinced Anne and Mary, looking at the torn sides of the sheets.

"Mr Nigel, look! Look, we can put a fence at the bottom and make the pictures short!" Nigel took the book Michael had returned with, and exclaimed, "A genius, Anne! This boy's a genius! He's saved the day!" "Darling, how wonderful of you!" said Anne, who then turned in a mystified manner and said to Nigel, "How?" "This book shows wainscotting up to about three feet. If I fit wainscotting around the whole room, we can cut off the badly damaged top part of the rolls completely before putting them on the walls, which will save a great deal of repainting on the top sections!" "And if", added Mary, "my assistant and I glue Japanese rice peper behind all the tears on the sides and repaint the missing pieces, when the sheets are put on the walls, we can touch up any little bits left over. But it would be much easier for us to do it first, here on a long tressle table, and we can probably get rid of the old crystallised paste with a soft brush." "Done!" cried Nigel. "Wainscotting it is!" Anne was a little unsure about the final effect, and it must be remembered that her small dining room was fifteen by fifteen feet, making for a very dramatic effect. Since Nigel had all the measurements with him, he did a quick calculation. "Well", he said, "we're two feet short for finishing the room. Mary, do you think you could mock up a strip to finish it off, plus two others, just blue with a bird, for over the window and over the door?" "My assistant and I could probably manage something!" Well, that was that. Patrick and Lorna were most impressed with it all, Anne less so, owing to the poor condition of the rolls.

At that moment, Anne's mobile phone rang. "Rather short notice, wouldn't you say, Kevin? After all, you're the mayor and you have got a secretary, and I'm called at the last moment! Someone important cancelled!" There was a silence. "Hmm! Which hotel? Oh, the Royal! What time? No, I have my own transport, thank you! I'll see you at seven-thirty! Goodbye!" She switched off her phone. "Lorna darling, will you look after Patrick this evening? I have a mission to accomplish! Yes, a mission!" she said slowly. "Patrick's always welcome here!" said Lorna, linking one arm through his and one through Michael's. "Well, darling", said Anne to Patrick. "I can see you're literally in good hands, so I'll leave you to some twilight croquet!" "Oh, yes!" cried Michael. "I'm going to win again!" He had taken to the game like a duck to water. As Lorna said, he was so animated and so happy playing with either Bernard or Patrick, although he preferred Bernard, because Patrick wouldn't let him win, whilst Bernard always did. This resulted in a healthy competitive spirit between Patrick and Michael.

Anne walked backthrough the gate linking the two properties, and immediately made for the kitchen and a slightly distressed Jennifer. She gave a series of sharp orders, "Don't cut the salmon" being the first, and left directions for a supper to be served for three or four persons in the sitting room. No, Jennifer would not be required for the evening. All she had to do was have everything prepared, and that was that.

She went up and showered and put a great deal of thought into her frock and jewelry for the evening. A local event, she thought: a dreary Rotarian evening, with someone speaking on the environment and local rights. That calls for the sapphires encrusted with diamonds, she mused. Yes, that's what I need! But she was going not because she was interested in listening to someone on the environment and the meal, she was after something far more important.

She was slightly late arriving at the Royal, and made just the right entrance, perfectly groomed and beautifully bejewelled: most of the men present paid her genuine compliments, the women's were quite so genuine. The speech was in the large reception room, with about a hundred persons craning to see Mrs Rochester, who sat beside the Mayor. As Anne said later, the discourse was thankfully short and, to her surprise, the menu was quite ordinary. She scanned the room and noted to her great joy that Ernest Mulberry and staff sat at one table. Just as I thought, she said to herself. She waved her hand at their table, on the other side of the room, and moved her bejewelled fingers in sign of greeting. Ernest half-stood and bowed. The others remained seated, but bowed in acknowledgement of the great honour she was bestowing on them. Between the courses, a great number of people left the room to smoke outside on the terrace, smoking being forbidden in the dining area.

It was during the first of these so-called breaks that Anne managed, without much trouble, to attract the attentionof the Royal's owner, a great friend of hers. "Albert, you look wonderful!" "You're lying", he said, "but I like it!" "Darling, how's the kitchen going?" "Very well! We've had a little problem with that Italian boy you sent us, but now that's all settled!" "Oh!" said Anne. "What was the problem? I do feel so completely responsible!" The only other people left at the table were two senior women Rotary members, who stopped talking and pointed their ears in the direction of what they thought might be interesting gossip to relay at the Golf Club's Wednesday Ladies' Day. They were disappointed, as they couldn't understand the meaning of Anne's comments.

"Do tell me what the problem was", she cooed. "Well, he's a nice boy, but he doesn't like cooking for large numbers, only small groups, and I'm afraid the locals are not yet ready for his menus. But with a little more self-discipline, he may just do here." "Oh how sad for you! I suppose you've got many young men waiting in the wings, so as to speak. . ." "There are always some young people who want to learn!" He smiled and she returned the smile, after which he returned to oversee the kitchens. The next course was served, after which the smokers returned to the terrace. As soon as the exodus began, Anne signalled to a waitress.

"Yes, Mrs Rochester?" "At the Mulberry table, do you see Samuel, the boy with the blond hair?" "Oh yes, Mrs Rochester! Everyone knows Samuel!" "Good!" she said. "Go and ask him to come here at once!" In a flash, the message was passed and Samuel seated himself in a vacant chair next to Anne. "How are you this evening?" he began, very formally. "Oh, fine!" said Anne, in an off-hand manner. She leaned closer to him and dropped her voice, so as to disguise their conversation under all the noise in the room. "Samuel, are you still seeing your Italian friend?" she asked, dropping her eyes. "Off and on", he replied with nonchalance. "Is it off or on this evening?" she asked. He blushed a little. "Actually, I'm seeing him after this do!" "Listen, Samuel!" she said in a particularly demanding tone. "Collect him after this boring event and bring him directly to Bellevue for supper! Do you understand?" "Yes", he replied, having no idea what Anne had in mind. She had not wanted to see his Italian friend before, so what was up, he wondered.

Anne feigned weariness, to cover her actual boredom, and left early. She had to wait almost two hours before the car came up the drive with Samuel and his Italian friend. She opened the front door, and the performance began. "Darlings, do come in!" The large sitting room was gently lit, and there was soft background music. They sat down and she asked in the most charming manner if Mario would be so kind as to open the bottle (if truth be known, it was the second!). He did so with professional skill, presented Anne, then Samuel with a glass of champagne, and took one himself. Samuel felt uncomfortable. He had the feeling that the cat was going to pounce, and he was dead right. "Mario" Anne began, "do you like working at the Royal?" "It's OK!" he said in a whisper. "I'm told you'd prefer to work for small groups, rather than the kind of evening we had tonight. How would you rate the food this evening, Mario dear?" "I thought it was pretty ordinary", he said, gaining a little confidence at being asked a professional question. "Oh, dearest Mario, I couldn't agree more! We have so much in common!" The mouse was almost within the cat's grasp! If Samuel felt uncomfortable before, a certain fear was now settling in this huge, expensively decorated room: a young man and a dynamic, bejewelled woman in front of him. He felt he was entirely out of his depth. He watched and listened as Anne drew Mario further and further, closer and closer to a beautiful jewelled paw with extremely sharp claws.

"Darling, are you getting apprenticeship wages at the Royal?" "Yes, it's not much really, but I suppose it's the experience that counts." Now the paw struck, and Samuel felt completely stupid at not having grasped what Anne was leading up to. "Mario, let's say I double your wages, with a flat by the swimmng pool thrown in of course, and you start work for me tomorrow!" There was dead silence. "But what about the Hotel?" "Don't worry, darling. I know the owner very well. We're old friends! Samuel will help you move in, won't you darling?" Samuel realised he'd been used, but the side benefits from Anne's generosity and the holiday at Metung made the scales balance. "Well, boys! I'll let you go! You obviously have a pleasant night planned!" she said, smiling. Mario went bright red. "Oh, Mario dear! I almost forgot to tell you", she said slowly, "you'll get a bonus on your ever-increasing salary if you keep your cuisine to the highest level of your imagination. Till tomorrow then! Goodnight boys!" She closed the door and went back to the sitting room, only to hear the front door reopen as Patrick entered. "Sorry I'm so late! Hey! I almost hit a car coming out of the drive!" "Oh, I'm glad you didn't do that, Patrick! You might have startled our new chef!"

Mario was everything Anne desired: his personal habits were discreet, his cooking delicious, and his fish dishes were heaven. "What more could one ask for?" she said to Patrick. "At least we shan't live in fear of a nondescript casserole à la Kiticat!" It was with great pleasure that Anne took the good-looking Mario to meet all the suppliers for Bellevue. First, Mr Mathews the butcher. "Only the best cuts, of course!" she purred. "Mario is only into quality!" Then off to Maisie O'Brien, who thought he was a nice lad. At Maisie's, Anne – Mario noted – changed tack. "Mario, you must always listen to Mrs O'Brien, she always has the best fruit and vegetables in town." "Thank you!" responded Maisie. "And here is a sack for our boy! He's growing into a beautiful young man!" and she handed Mario a red string sack of carrots and apples for Michael to give to Polly. Mario, too, appreciated Michael's beauty. He thought him very exotic, but was not quite so besotted as Samuel. Having made her round of introductions and made clear who signed for what, she instructed that all accounts should be sent once a month to Bellevue as usual.

Whilst Mary and Michael were working at restoring the Chinese panels, Nigel had the wainscotting installed by a local carpenter. At the moment, as Nigel was wont to say, the saints were at last lending a helping hand in that Anne developed an abcess under a wisdom tooth. So off to Melbourne she went for ten days, freeing everyone from her criticism with regard to the Chinese room. To start with, Mary had problems with Michael on the work. He held the tears in the long sheets together and she, using a special glue, stuck the rice paper over the tears, except that Michael tended to misjudge the tension needed, which created difficulties. Then Mary hit on the idea of reversing roles, which worked very well indeed, and they managed to finish all the work in one full day. When dry, the rolls were reversed and Mary began to touch up the scratches and tears, using a long tressle table in the ballroom. The small sheets that needed to go over the window and door were copied from the existing design, which left only the two-foot strip that would be fitted between the door jamb and the corner of the room where the light switch was. For this, she traced only one figure, since the old sheets were twenty-six inches wide, with two figures each. She painted nearly all the strip, except for the figure, which she took to her studio to do and was strangely secretive about. Nigel had the wainscotting painted a creamy sage, ripped out the fireplace and replaced it with a simple travertine frame on three sides. Four tiny spots were fitted into the ceiling on either side of the room to softly illuminate the walls. Then the hanging began. It took three days, with all kinds of problems cropping up, but finally it was all in place, but not, alas, in its original position. Half the sheets had a figure facing right and half a figure facing left: on the far side of the room they joined well, but at the centre of the chimney breast they didn't fit well at all, with mountains at a strange height and bamboo poles that didn't match. Mary was called in to repaint and had to create a joining pattern, changing the height of the mountains, introducing new birds and, in the foreground, altered the height of the grass and bushes.

Except for Nigel, the wallpaper hanger and Mary, entry was forbidden to all until the work was completed. Nigel had found what he thought must have come from a picture theatre, a central brass light fixture with three large dragons, each with moustaches and wings. It had sixteen little red glass panels through which the light shone. It wasn't the first time he has used it in an interior: the first was in the living room he had decorated for a married woman. When she turned on the switch and saw red patches of light dotted all over her very conservative living room – "basic beige", as Nigel called it – she made him remove it, saying it made the room look like a brothel: "foreign art and red lights", she complained! Nigel had the well-worn light fixture cleaned and replaced the sixteen little red panes with ordinary frosted glass: success! It fitted perfectly! Finally, all the panels were in position, the silk taffeta curtains were the same colour as the wainscotting, their zigzag pelmets hung with little bells that Nigel had acquired at the local hardware store in Brunswick. He fitted a brass cylinder tightly to the narrow end of a long bamboo cane, which could be used to touch the bells and make them ring. He had fitted this up for someone he knew would be a regular guest, his great blue eyes always watching to see whether the bells really worked.

It was the last day before Anne's return: the furniture was put back into the room, comprising a round table, six chairs, plus two on either side of a very simple mahogony sideboard, opposite the fireplace. "Ready at last!" and "Never again!" Nigel said to himself. As he left the room, the maid in the corridor heard him say "Goodnight Michael!" He shut the door to the Chinese room and, a very weary decorator, wended his way back to Brunswick. "Poor old thing!" the maid said to Mario in the kitchen. "He's losing his marbles! 'Course, I know why: she's a very difficult person! She had him change that room three times. No wonder he's going off the rails, talking to himself. It's the first sign, you know! Mark my words, it'll be her fault if they have to put him away. Mark my words!" she repeated, leaving a confused cook without any clear idea of what she was talking about.

Although she was bursting with social plans, it was a very anxious Mrs Rochester who, with Patrick, opened the door and flicked on the light switch. The room took a little time to light up completely, so the effect was much more dramatic. "Just as I imagined!" she said. "Perfect! Just perfect! Oh, Nigel is an angel!" She looked closely at the panels. "Mary and Michael have done a wonderful job! Oh, a black tie dinner, tomorrow evening! Oh, Patrick, by the way, there's a Mulberry package I picked up for you! It's absolutley divine! Would you get it

364

from the car, please?" As he returned, he heard her exclaim, "Fabulous!" "Ingenious!" "I love it to bits!" "How divine!" Then, as he came into the room, "Patrick, Patrick! Have you seen that figure? So clever! Oh, Mary is a genius!" Patrick smiled, "It's clever, isn't it?" "Clever, darling! Has he seen it?" "No, Mary and Nigel have kept it as a surprise!" There it was: the figure on the strip of paper, just on the left as one entered the door. It was identical to all the others, with the same colours and textures, but the face! The face was a portrait of Michael! "I love it!" said Anne "Oh, open the bag!" "Anne, I told you. . .!" "Darling, don't tell me anything!" She laughed. "Since you're now working for me, that's your evening uniform!" He withdrew a beautiful dinner jacket from the package, plus a fly-collar shirt and tie. "So smart, don't you think, darling? Oh, let's have a drink to celebrate! By the way, you'll have to ask Lorna to tie the bow for you: I'm hopeless! She does it for all the boys at Killarney!"

The following evening, Mario was in fine form. The guests arrived in black tie, but this evening Anne had insisted that Mary should join them and, rather than risk a tongue-lashing from Anne, she acquiesced. To begin with, she felt very awkward sitting down and not being in charge of the culinary delights.

After pleasantries and drinks, during which Patrick asked Lorna to give him lessons at tying a bow-tie, they moved into the new Chinese dining room. Together with the others, Michael was fascinated by the last figure near the door. Mary was given a round of applause before they all took their traditional places. On Michael's plate there was a little package, as there was also on Mary's , although she had an envelope too. Both of them looked enquiringly at Anne. "Well, darlings, open them up!" Mary was the first to open hers, since Michael found it difficult to get the tiny bow undone. "Oh, goodness!" exclaimed Mary. "I can't possibly accept this!" "My dear", said Anne, raising her glass. "You can't possibly refuse the token!" Mary pulled out of the slightly faded velvet interior a pair of diamond earrings set in gold. "They'll suit you perfectly, Mary. Go into the hall and use the mirror there, and then let's all see the effect!" Mary dutifully did as she was asked, removed her little gold sleepers and inserted the diamond earrings. She returned to the room. "Perfect, just perfect!" said Lorna. "When I was in Melbourne with that beastly dental problem, I went to the bank and looked through the things in my safe deposit. I've no idea where these came from, but they screamed 'Mary' at me, so that was that!" "You look like a film star!" said Bernard. "A toast to the artist from Killarney!" "Hear, hear!" everyone replied. "Put the envelope in your purse, Mary, and we'll say no more about it! Michael, you're a bit slow opening your package!" "Anne, the string is very tight!" he said. Paul took the package and cut the ribbon. Michael opened the lid of the little box and there they were! Paul was shocked and started to say something, but Anne beat him to it. "No, Paul! It's my gift and that's that! I'm sure Mary would agree that this room could never have been completed without Michael's aid!" "Anne's quite right!" said Mary. "I couldn't have done the work without my assistant!" In Michael's hand were two diamond cufflinks, with four large diamonds set side-by-side in each link, making a square, and surrounded with diamonds half their size, forming a border. "Once upon a time, they were earrings, but they didn't suit me. I had them made into cufflinks to give to my father years ago, but he passed on before they were ready. So now, they go to the right man, but on one condition!" Everyone looked at Anne. "Well, since you now have two sets," – Michael was wearing his ruby set – "when Paul needs a pair, you can share them!" "Anne, they're very nice! I like them very much!" Michael stood up and went round the table to give her a kiss.

The evening passed splendidly. It wasn't until the dessert was finished, just before they moved to the sitting room, that Patrick introduced Michael to the polished bamboo rod, which Anne had not so far noticed, hidden in the copious folds of the silk curtains. "You use the rod to ring the bells!" said Patrick. Using the rod, Michael gently touched one of the bells hanging from the pelmet. "You'll have to strike it a little harder", said Patrick, and with another stroke, the bell rang. "Oh, how positively perfect!" smiled a contented Anne. Just as they were leaving, Anne whispered to Mary, "If I have any problems catering-wise with Mario, may I ask your advice?" Mary smiled, "Of course you can! He's a nice lad. I like him".

It wasn't until Mary had gone home, changed, taken off her diamond earrings and put her sleepers back in that she remembered the envelope in her handbag. She opened it up: inside were six one-hundred-dollar notes, and Anne's card, which said simply, 'Thank you, Anne'.

The following Sunday was like most Sundays: mass at eleven and back to Killarney for lunch. They were six, as usual. Colin and Rodney were occasionally invited, but were mostly busy with their new house, or else Colin was on duty at the clinic, now that he was a senior director. After lunch, Michael pestered them all to play croquet and so they all went along to the croquet lawn, where Anne, Lorna and Paul sat in the shade of the little pavilion and chatted, while Patrick, Michael and Bernard played. Bernard always let Michael win, but not Patrick. He liked to challenge Michael and push him to his furthest limits, as he did when riding. The game over, Bernard said he felt tired and went indoors, while Michael pulled Paul onto the lawn to try and teach him how to play. He stood right behind Paul and put his own hands on top of Paul's , showing him how to use the mallet. "Michael, what are you doing?" asked Paul, as Michael's hand slid up his arm. "Michael, behave yourself! You're impossible!" He kissed him and they returned to the other three, hand-in-hand.

Paul went to get another bottle of champagne, but the little refrigerator was empty. "Darling", he said to Michael, "would you please bring us another from the kitchen? Take the empty one with you!" Michael bounded across the front lawn, past the big fountain with the men having a shower and in through the front door. At that moment, everything changed: as he went in, he saw Bernard lying on the hall floor. He rushed back to the front door, screaming "Cooty! It's Cooty! He's asleep on the floor!" and rushed back in. In the kitchen, Mary heard Michael scream and sped into the hall, where she found Bernard lying unconscious. She grabbed a cushion off one of the hall chairs and put it under his head. "Stay there! Don't move!" she said to Michael, and fled to the phone. She had Colin's mobile number and called him. "Doctor! Please come with an ambulance! Bernard has collapsed. He's breathing slowly, but he's unconscious!" Colin literally dropped everything: the tray of instruments he was carrying crashed to the floor. "Emergency!" he yelled. In a moment, the clinic's ambulance pulled out down Main Street, its siren blaring, followed by Colin's car, in hot pursuit.

Michael's scream had brought everyone from the croquet lawn, running to the house. Paul was first and rushed to Bernard's side. "Don't touch him!" warned Mary. Lorna burst into tears. "It's all right, Lorna!" said Mary. "His breathing's regular!" She took his pulse. "I don't know what's wrong!" "Call an ambulance!" said Lorna. "It's on its way!" replied Mary. They all just stood there, feeling helpless. Michael was terrified. He couldn't understand why Bernard wouldn't get up. Seeing his white face, Mary said to Paul, "Look after Michael: he doesn't seem very well!" Paul put his arms round Michael as he began to sob. "Where's that damned doctor?" came Anne's determined voice. "Open the gates!" said Lorna. Mary went to press the button and the huge gates swung open, awaiting the ambulance and Colin. At this point, Bernard regained consciousness. "Don't move!" said Mary and Michael knelt by him, tears dripping down his cheeks. "Cooty! Cooty! Don't go to sleep!" "I'm all right!" said Bernard. "I've just had a fall!" he reached out and took Michael's hand and smiled, "Everything's all right! Don't worry, Michael!"

Five minutes went by, then ten: it seemed an eternity. Suddenly, they all turned to the doorway, whence they could hear the distant siren of the ambulance. "Come on! Come on!" said Patrick. In a few moments, followed by Colin's car, the ambulance sped up the drive.

"Hi!" said a very worried Colin. "What's happened?" "We have no idea! Michael found him here. He just said he felt tired and went indoors!" said Lorna. The men put him on a stretcher and wheeled him to the ambulance, and with Colin again in hot pursuit, Bernard was rushed off to the clinic. They all followed, leaving only Mary at home and promising to let her know of any change. Paul asked Colin, "Is it a heart attack?" "I don't think so", he replied. "We shall be running tests. Do you know if Bernard is diabetic?" "No", said Paul. "You'll have to ask Lorna." Colin went to speak to Lorna. "I've no idea", she said. "Bernard has always enjoyed such good health. I don't even know whether he has ever had a test for diabetes."

Colin left, and returned thirty minutes later. "He seems better now, but I want to keep him here overnight and run a fuller set of tests on him tomorrow. You can see him, but only for a minute. He's very tired!" They all filed in. The first thing Bernard saw was Michael's eyes, red from crying. He went up to Bernard. "Cooty, don't go away! Cooty, you have to be with me!" "I won't go away, darling. I'll always be here!" The moment was electric, and Anne left the room in tears. It had never crossed anyone's mind that Bernard would not be there: he was the patriarch of the group. It was unthinkable that he wouldn't be there always: he was only sixty-seven; he wasn't old! Lorna held his hand. "We have to go. They only gave us a few minutes. Try to rest, Bernard! We'll be back first thing in the morning!" She kissed him, as did Michael, and they all left, Michael holding Paul's hand very tightly. In the carpark, they said their goodbyes quietly.

When the three of them got back to Killarney, they were met by an anxious Mary, who cried, "How is he?" "He's still conscious, but very tired." "Thank the blessed saints for that!" she said and disappeared into the kitchen. Five minutes later, she came back to the yellow room, bearing a teatray. A hot cup of tea was just what they needed, but they drank it in a strange silence, Michael sitting very close to Paul. "I'm sure everything will be fine, Lorna! It's probably some imbalance in Bernard's system!" Paul was searching for words that wouldn't upset Lorna any more than necessary.

No one slept very well at Killarney that night. Paul found himself trying to comfort both Lorna and Michael, but at times Michael was inconsolable, and this helped Lorna, since in comforting Michael she had to present everything from a positive point of view. It was the first time Paul had seen Michael take Toby off his shelf and take him to bed. The two of them lay there holding one another, with Toby somewhere in the middle, and in the end they dropped off to sleep, exhausted from worry.

Bernard didn't come home next day, since Colin insisted that he musn't leave the clinic until he knew exactly what was wrong with him. The second day, Bernard was as well as ever, and as difficult as could be. "I won't be told what to do!" he ranted. "I'm going home, and that's that!" Colin finally gave in, and Paul and Lorna collected a very aggressive Bernard and took him back to Killarney. Michael was waiting in his usual place in the yellow room for the car to come up the drive. It seemed hours since Lorna and Paul had left, but at last the car drew up under the porte cochère. As Bernard climbed out, Michael cleared the steps in a single jump and was in Bernard's arms. "It's all right now, Michael. It's all right!" "Cooty, I was very frightened you would go away!" He began to cry. "I'm here now, Michael! You don't have to cry now! Perhaps we'll have a game of croquet tomorrow: what do you think?" "Cooty, that would be very nice!" he said, drying his eyes with a handkerchief Paul gave him.

It was a sombre group that entered the house, but things settled down. Bernard seemed as he always was. They dined at Anne's the following evening, but there was an edge to the occasion, because no one knew what was wrong with Bernard and why he had passed out like that.

At the end of the week, Colin called and they all gathered in the Irish room, including Mary. "Bernard", said Colin. "You have nothing wrong with your heart at all. We've run all the tests, and what you're suffering from is, as I suspected, diabetes!" "What!" said Bernard. "Is that all?" "Bernard, you'll have to be careful. I'm going to give Mary a diet sheet, because there are certain things you can and can't eat. If you don't stick to this diet properly, you may pass out again. Your pancreas doesn't produce enough insulin for your body, so if you don't stick to the diet, you'll have to have regular insulin injections. So that's it! You must make up your mind!" he said sternly. "Yours is not an advanced case of diabetes, but you must watch yourself and monitor the results of the diet. You'll have to come to see me at least once a month for a check-up. Do you understand, Bernard?" Colin spoke like a schoolmaster correcting a naughty pupil. "Of course I understand!" Bernard said sarcastically. "I'm not stupid!" "Well, let's see how things work out then!" said Colin. "I've got to go! Rodney is having some twenty-foot trees delivered this afternoon, and I'm supposed to be there. A token appearance, I think. You must come and see the progress. In fact, if you're not doing anything next Saturday, we're having some people over for lunch. No black tie!" Lorna and Paul laughed. "OK, we'll give you a call during the week to confirm. Thank you, Colin, so much for coming so promptly with the ambulance the other day! We really appreciate everything you've done!" "Yes", said Bernard. "Thanks, Colin!" "I'll see you out", said Paul.

In front of Colin's car, Paul said, "I think Bernard's going to be a difficult patient, but I promise we'll do our very best!" "You know", said

Colin, getting into his car, "the best medicine for Bernard just now is a young man with blue eyes and a mane of black hair! Goodbye, Paul! I hope to see you all next Saturday for lunch!" and he drove out onto the main road as the big iron gates closed behind him.

As Colin predicted, Michael was exactly what Bernard needed. Bernard realised that, of all the people he loved in the world, Michael was the most fragile, and leaving him alone was just not going to happen, not if he had anything to do with it. Well, he thought to himself, that will probably mean eating raw carrots and dried seaweed.

The following Tuesday, Bernard, Paul, Michael and Anne left for Melbourne together, since Michael's dental work had to be finished. Lorna didn't feel well, and stayed at Killarney. On Wednesday morning, she received news that the nineteen-year-old son of a family that had worked at Killarney in the past had been killed in a terrible car accident, a Saturday-night victim , as the person driving had had too much alcohol. The boy had been killed outright, as the driver missed a bend and drove straight into a sturdy telegraph post. Lorna phoned Patrick and asked whether he would accompany her to the funeral at St Mary's. Patrick promptly collected her at ten forty-five and in ten minutes they were there. Lorna dressed in black and carried a mantilla, which she always wore at mass nowadays. They sat in the third row, since the Killarney pew was filled with mourners. As everyone filed out of church after mass, Patrick stood up, but Lorna took his arm and motioned to him to sit down again. She whispered to him, "I need to ask you something!" "Anything, Lorna!" "Since Bernard's collapse, I've been very worried. I have to ask you to make a difficult promise!" Patrick said nothing but turned to face her. "I want you to promise here, in front of the Blessed Sacrament, that if anything happens to Bernard and me, you will look after Paul and Michael!" She tightened her grip on his arm. "Paul can't always be with Michael, and Michael needs you, Patrick. He loves you and trusts you, and so does Paul. I shall only feel comfortable if you can make me this promise!" "Lorna, of course I'll look after them, but I shan't have to think about it for some years yet!" "Let's hope so, Patrick!" She smiled. "Thank you! Shall we go now?" Slightly happier, Lorna and Patrick left the church. As they got into the car, she said, "Patrick, this is between you and me!" "Certainly! Oh, by the way, I'm taking you back to Bellevue for lunch. I telephoned Mary earlier, because Mario said he would prepare us a splendid lunch alla italiana!" "Patrick, you are a dear!"

Lunch was a great success. This was one of the rare times that Lorna had spoken to Patrick at any length, and she began to understand why Anne – always very careful about trusting anyone – had handed over to him the running of Bellevue, including supervising the repair and rebuilding of the stable block. She listened with great care as he described Michael's achievements. "He's wonderful! He listens to instructions and never takes offence at any correction. I'm very proud of his riding!" As he continued in this vein, Lorna felt herself relax. If anything should happen, she knew that Patrick would look after Michael. She was also keenly aware that Michael loved Patrick, and after this lunch, she was absolutely certain it was reciprocated.

The others got back from Melbourne as usual on Thursday evening, to be greeted on the doorstep of Killarney by Lorna and Patrick, Anne having been told earlier that she was staying to dinner. Anne and Lorna linked arms and went in. "Your cook is a dream!" Lorna said. "I had a delicious lunch on Wednesday, after the funeral!" "Oh, how was it? I hate funerals! Let's talk of happier things!" pleaded Anne. Michael was very pleased that Patrick was there, and chatted to him, which he never did as a rule. "Patrick, we went to the club. It was very nice, and I saw Amos and David and Stephen there!" He stopped to call to Paul, "Paul, please open the boot of the car! I have a surprise!" Paul threw him the keys. "Michael, shut it properly when you're through!" In the boot was a long parcel, wrapped in paper from a sporting store. "Patrick, take the paper off! Patrick, there are two of them! Quick!" Patrick removed the paper and found two new croquet mallets. "Patrick, they're very nice! Look at them! I preferthe one with the red handle. You can have the other one with the black handle. Oh, I shall be able to win much more easily!" He smiled. "Oh!" said Patrick, "but if I have one that's new, and you have one that's new, then I shall probably win!" Not being too sure about this, Michael said, "We shall have to play then and see. Perhaps after dinner you could light the candles on the hoops. I'm sure I shall win!" he said confidently. Michael closed the car boot and they went inside, leaving the new mallets on the veranda together with the torn wrapping paper. He returned the car keys to Paul. "Paul, Patrick and I are going to play after dinner!" "Michael, Patrick's probably tired. He's been working on the new stables at Bellevue!" "Well", said Michael, with his deep laugh. "That's a good thing: then I can win!" This time, Patrick laughed, "You're becoming sneaky, Michael!" and everyone joined in the laughter.

As dinner began, the main topic of conversation was the lunch on Saturday. "I wonder how many are invited", said Bernard. "I hope not a crowd: I couldn't bear it!" "Oh, come on, Bernard", said Anne. "It's their first social event since they bought the house!" "Where is it, exactly?" asked Patrick. "It's about three miles before Morton, on the old bridge road." "Is it finished yet?" asked Paul. "I'm not sure", said Anne. "The last time I spoke to Rodney about it, he said they were well under way! Oh, Bernard, before I forget! Rodney said there's been a mix-up. Some of the roses he sent here belong to Bellevue, and vice-versa. He said he would sort it out next week, after the luncheon weekend!" Rodney had done well out of Anne and Bernard: their big gardens had been totally overhauled and the changes had made a great difference to both. He had been well-paid for the work but, as Anne said, it was worth every penny. This was one subject on which Bernard agreed totally. At Killarney, the red garden was changed by Rodney three times a year, and he had done all the landscaping for the croquet lawn, and had planted eighty rhododendrons, filling in where some had died and continuing the line right down the drive. Mr Barnes was not so happy with Rodney, and was always saying to his wife, "It might look pretty, but it's me who has to do all the work!"

Saturday arrived and they were bidden for between twelve-thirty and one o'clock. Michael and Paul were late getting up – strange, since they had not had a late night! – since Michael awoke in a devilish mood. By the time they got down to breakfast, Bernard had already finished and was looking at the plans of the property, to see what land was left between him and Anne, after taking that large slice for the croquet lawn. Rodney had made various suggestions, but neither Anne nor Bernard felt any further extension to their large gardens necessary, so the rest was being used for grazing by the three horses.

They got to Rodney's and Colin's new home about one o'clock. "Goodness! There are quite a lot of cars!" said Lorna. "Oh, look! Park near Anne's car, and we'll walk down the drive a bit. It will be easier to get away if we want to leave early!" They moved toward the house, and the first people they saw were Patrick and Anne, who said, "Darlings, we've just arrived, all three of us!" Mario, as Samuel's friend, was also invited, as were Neville and Beryl. There were about thirty people, plus caterers. They walked through the garden gate, with a large fish pond on the left, surrounded by exotic shrubs. "Rodney's done so much! It's wonderful!" said Anne. The garden had an oriental flavour, though not strictly oriental in design. They moved down to a paved area, just outside the back of the house: a great tressel table had been laid with a white cloth and plates of hors d'oeuvres. Waiters moved around with trays of wine for the guests. This gave rise to a small problem, since Samuel and Neville started their usual sparring competition, but what with the hot weather and plentiful supply of wine, their repartee became electric, much to the entertainment of the other guests.

Someone overheard two matrons, both of whom had seen Anne arrive with Patrick. "Well!" said the shorter of the two. "I see Mrs Rochester is with Constable Timms! Hmm!" "Oh no, dear!" said the other. "He's not a constable now!" "Really? What is he then?" "Oh, he's a concubine!" came the sarcastic reply. "Really?" said the first. "What rank in the constabulary is that?"

Neville entered the house through a sliding glass door, part of a wall of glass looking onto a large area of decking, with black bamboo at one end and a huge group of hydrangeas at the other. The banter between Neville and Samuel became incandescent and Neville left in a huff, slamming shut the glass door. One of the waitresses hurrying along with two trays of hors d'oeuvres walked straight into it. There was a terrible bang, as her head hit the door, together with the trays, squashing their content against the glass, where it stuck for a minute or two, before sliding down to join the mess on the floor. The waitress was not hurt, but somewhat confused as the other catering staff rushed to her aid. Colin was furious, but not really sure whether it had been an accident or whether Samuel and Neville were having a lot of fun at his expense. "Look!" teased Neville. "Tarzan, you could screech through the bamboo, looking for Cheetah! Ho ho!" Colin overheard this, and said sharply to Neville, overheard by many other guests, "If you don't quieten down, I'll do a lobotomy on you!" "Oh, Doctor! With your own fair hands! Let's get going!" quipped Neville.

Colin was now getting very angry. He had always disliked Neville, but to be made a fool of in his own home was absolutely not on. After this Neville and Samuel settled down a little, until a high-pitched shriek was heard. Neville was doubled up with laughter at Samuel extracting himself from the large group of hydrangeas at the end of the decking. By now, everyone was in high spirits, and even Bernard thought it funny, but not Colin. "I fell! I'm sorry!" said Samuel, who had now had a lot to drink, but wasn't absolutely sure that Neville hadn't pushed him.

Lunch continued, voices rose, and the noise became louder. Neville took a piece of chicken from the table, but in doing so, managed to get his ankle caught in one end of the long white table cloth. He fell forward, straight into Colin's back, making him start forward and splash red wine all over the person he was talking to. Anne was in fits of laughter, but Colin was black with rage. "I caught my foot!" said Neville, weakly. "Really?" screamed Colin, and roughly pushed him backwards. Neville lost his balance and collapsed onto the end of the tressel, which came down under his weight, with a whole load of plates, glasses, wine, food, almost completely covering him. As Neville attempted to get to his feet, Samuel screamed out, "Rodney! Have you still got those old peacock feathers? We could stick them up Neville's arse and use him for a centre-piece!" Everyone had been affected by the spirit of mayhem, and there were gales of laughter. Colin had had it! He said to Neville, "I think you had better leave!" to which he replied, as quick as a flash, "Oh doctor! I thought you'd never ask!" He got up and limped toward the front gate, with food falling off his new jacket and pâté and dips dripping off his shoes. A last shot from Samuel made him turn round suddenly: he slipped and slid into the fish pond. "Darling!" screamed Samuel. "Make up your mind! Do you want to be a fruit salad or a mermaid?" Again gales of laughter from all the guests. Neville was so angry at Samuel that he picked up a small pot containing some rare plant and launched it in Samuel's direction. The latter saw it coming and ducked behind Colin, who caught it full on the back of his new Harris tweed (Mulberry's, of course!)

The rest of the party was tame, except for one incident. Samuel passed Anne and, with a straight face, asked her whether she was in training for the black-and-white minstrel show, before walking on. Anne looked at Lorna, who had to point out that, as a result of all the tears of laughter, her mascara had run. "The bitch!" Anne snapped, and disappeared into the bathroom for repairs.

Everyone was exhausted after a power-packed afternoon. Next day, all the guests phoned Colin and said that it had been the funniest luncheon they had ever attended, and that they had had a splendid time. Colin accepted the thanks, but thought the compliments were a little backhanded.

Although Neville and Samuel had had their moments of hilarity at the party, a very rude awakening awaited them on Monday morning at work. Ernest had been told all about the shenanigans at the party by a friend, and when they reached the shop he was as black as thunder. He stepped down from his little pulpit and screamed at them, "How could you be such cretins! Your behaviour was intolerable! If you wish to play the fool in public, do so, but not with my customers, do you understand? Now listen", he said, wagging his finger at them, "if a certain Doctor Colin Campbell closes his account here, I promise you both, you're fired!" Looking at Neville, he added sarcastically, "Perhaps you should ask Mrs Beryl for a pair of gardening gloves, because I have a feeling you're going to need them! I'll give you one hour, and in that time the pair of you will separately telephone Dr Campbell and apologise! Do you understand?" This he said in an icy tone and stalked across to his office, slamming the door behind him.

Samuel and Neville looked at each other: they had never contemplated an attack from this quarter. "You first, Neville! You did the most damage!" "Me!" screamed Neville. "If you hadn't started it!" The office door opened. "Neville, use the office phone. Dr Campbell is waiting. I have decided to hasten the process!" Ernest was not letting anyone make his business look unprofessional. So one after the other, they apologised, Ernest standing beside them and making sure that everything was sorted out and Dr Campbell placated. The rest of the day went very quietly for the staff at Mulberry's.

The following Saturday saw another luncheon, but a much more sedate one, at Bellevue, to which Anne had invited Lorna, Bernard, Michael and Patrick, Paul, Colin and Rodney. She thought she'd make Samuel wait awhile for his black-and-white minstrel quip, which she'd not forgotten. Lorna had found the line brilliant, but hadn't dared laugh, knowing that Anne's sense of humour was excellent providing the joke was not on her. Michael and Patrick were to join them direct from their ride – "Come on as you are, boys! Don't bother to change if you're late! Lunch is at one-thirty precisely!"

Patrick had sought and obtained permission from the next-door landowner, who also had a boundary with the State forest, so that they could cross his land to reach the forest, where the Country Fire Authority had cleared an old overgrown track for some miles in case it was needed as an access road for firefighters. Sergeant Reynolds had also kindly interceded and got permission for them to go riding along the re-opened trail. Michael was very excited on Friday evening and took Patrick's advice to breakfast early with him at Bellevue and set out directly afterwards. He woke at six, and a sleepy Paul said, "Have a shower, darling, and off to breakfast! No, Michael! I said *you* have a shower, not me! I'm going back to sleep!"

Michael showered and dressed in his riding outfit, kissed Paul and said he would see him at lunch, after which he slid a cold hand between the sheets. "Michael! Michael! Your hand's freezing!" "Paul, you like it!" "Get out and have a nice ride, beautiful! See you at one o'clock!" Michael bounded downstairs and out through the kitchen to face a beautiful sunny morning. He raced to the bottom of the garden, through the gate, and up to Bellevue for breakfast with Patrick. He entered the back door near the kitchen and met Patrick coming down the corridor. "Well, young man! You are punctual! Are you hungry?" "A little", he smiled. "Come on, Mario has got breakfast ready!"

Mario was overwhelmed on seeing Michael dressed other than in formal clothes, his white shirt open in front, jodhpurs and shiny brown riding boots, carrying his black riding cap. He gasped audibly "Wow!"

and then blushed as Patrick looked at him and asked, "Is breakfast ready?" They ate a hearty breakfast and Michael had three slices of toast and marmalade as well, which he loved, hence the boxes of oranges that Maisie O'Brien sent to Mary, who had now become an expert marmalade maker.

Then off to the stables and away to discover a new trail. Michael couldn't believe his eyes as they entered the forest, its tall trees on both sides of the track. The silence was broken only by birdsong and the cawing of the crows. The scent of the eucalypts in the morning sun was heady and he loved it. After a while, with very little conversation, he pulled Polly over very close to Patrick's horse. "Patrick", he said, "are you married?" "Why do you ask?" "Well, I sometimes don't understand why people get married. Cooty and Lorna got married, but they are the same as before. Why do people marry?" "What a question!" replied Patrick. "Generally, people marry because they love the other person." "Oh!" said Michael thoughtfully, "I suppose you're right, because Cooty and Lorna love one another, but I love them too, though I'm not married to them. It's very strange! But I love Paul, so I must be married to Paul, musn't I?" "In a certain sense, yes", said Patrick slowly, not looking at Michael. For some reason, he was starting to feel angry, and didn't really know why. "Patrick, if we're married to everyone we love, then I'm married to you and you're married to me! Hmm, that's very nice!" and he reached over and squeezed Patrick's arm. "Patrick, that's very nice", he repeated.

Patrick suddenly felt excitement speed through his body, leaving no part untouched. He blinked: there was still something he was unable to control. He reined in his horse, as did Michael, and said, "Michael, you're the most wonderful person in the world!" He daren't use the word 'love' in case Michael misconstrued his intentions, although his intention was very clear. What Michael felt for Patrick, Patrick felt for Michael one hundred times over.

"Come on! If we don't start back now, we'll be late and Anne won't be pleased!" "I'll race you to the bend at the bottom!" and Michael turned Polly around and set off at a gallop, with Patrick in hot pursuit. It wasn't that Michael was mentally limited; he was dyslexic, yes, but the fact that he didn't grasp certain situations was simply because he had no concept of things that everyone else takes for granted, owing to a whole life spent in an institution, remaining as quiet as possible so as not to attract violent attention: his world could not exapnd. He had seen very little other than his day-to-day experience: he had no challenges, except to survive, so concepts like marriage were a mystery to him. He understood love, because that was manifestted in Paul, both physically and mentally, and this gave him confidence to open his eyes and look around him unafraid.

For some reason, he never enjoyed watching television: it made no mark on him, so his only teacher was life. In the hands of Bernard, Lorna, Paul and Anne, he just accepted what they did, how they lived. He was able to cancel out his past and set his feet to the future, not a planned future, to be sure, but he accepted what they arranged for him, which in his mind was obviously right. He never queried their decisions, nor considered that he was being protected from the rough world he had known until then. Thus beginning again in a new environment where the common denominator was love, he flourished, and the change resulting from the protection and love offered him by this small group was evident in his rapid development.

If Mario had been overwhelmed by Michael at breakfast time, when he led them into the sitting room he was, like Samuel, besotted with him, Michael's hair was all over the place, his shirt opened even one button lower, and his jodhpurs filled out where they should be. "A god!" he thought, "they really do exist!" then realising that he was staring at Michael, he made a quick exit, to be ready to serve lunch, since it was now already one-fifteen. Michael and Patrick entered the sitting room in their socks, and were greeted by all. "How was the ride?" asked Bernard. "Cooty, it was very nice! No noise! It was very strange. I like it very much. Patrick, can we go again?" "Certainly!" said Patrick with a smile, floating above the ground. Both Rodney and Colin noticed not only a radiant Michael, but a very handsome, dark riding instructor, who today seemed to have a special secret, making him blissfully content.

Conversation in the dining room clearly dwelt on the previous Saturday's lunch. "What a disaster!" said Rodney. "Not at all!" said Lorna. "Look at Bellevue and Killarney. We have lunch and dinner parties all the time, but in a couple of days, everyone has forgotten them. You and Colin have had your first social luncheon and people around here will be talking about it for years to come! The only problem is that whenever you have a party, your guests will want the same entertainment!" "They can forget that!" snapped Colin. "You have no idea the mess those two delinquents caused!" "Be that as it may", said Anne. "It was still a pretty funny afternoon. I do hope your fish have not changed their diet and are demanding pâté served on a leather shoe!" Even Colin laughed. "I have a very big hole in my hydrangea patch", said Rodney. "It will stay that way now till next season. It's a pity Samuel goes in for body-building, since it means that he can flatten hydrangeas very successfully!" "I found your garden very interesting", said Bernard. "I had a look around while the comic relief was taking place. You've both done so much in such a short time!" "Not me!" said Colin. "Rodney's the genius! I don't know one plant from another." "By the way, Rodney", Bernard continued, "have you sorted out the mix-up between the Bellevue and Killarney roses? Lorna told me about it." "Yes. All the labels with a 'B' obviously belong here, and the ones with a 'K' are for Killarney. When the boy delivered them, he mixed them up. I've spoken to Mr Barnes and he's returning the ones marked 'B' and Anne's gardener is doing the same for those marked 'K'." "Good!" said Bernard, and then changed the subject. "Anne, are you coming to town next week for Amos's birthday? The party's on Wednesday evening at Brown's. Lorna and Michael are coming down with us on Tuesday morning." "We'll be down sometime Tuesday, I think. We have an appointment with a plumber: something to do with drains on the stable block, but I'll give you a call, Lorna, when we get away!" 'We', it was this word that grated slightly on Colin, the 'we' obviously meant an elated, darkly handsome Patrick, who was in his usual place, smiling, opposite Michael. This cat must have got at the cream, he thought uncharitably, and in a way he was right. In such a short time in Anne's employ, Patrick had taken over the running and expenditure at Bellevue, plus organising the staff, both casual and permanent. As Anne said to Lorna later when they were alone, "Darling, I have absolutely no idea how I managed before Patrick. He's divine: riding with Michael in the mornings. I rarely go out now, perhaps just once a week to keep in form, but the boys live for it!" "Yes, they do!" smiled a knowing Lorna.

After Anne's delicious lunch, Rodney and Colin both said, "So much better than KitKat blando!" ending the afternoon at Anne's on a funny note. Once home, Colin slumped down onto a settee. "Would you like another glass of happiness?" asked Rodney. "Oh God! I have to work in the morning, but it's only two hours! Why not!" "A very pleasant lunch, don't you think?" said Rodney. "Oh yes, fine!" said Colin, in an off-hand manner. "Oh Dr. Campbell, what's disturbing you?" said a slightly sarcastic Rodney, sitting down beside him and giving him a kiss. "What's wrong, doctor?" "Nothing!" "Not true! Let's start again!" A pause ensued, then Colin, with the glass of wine in his hand, looked at Rodney. "You know what annoys me most about that lot: it's the way they handle Michael!" "Really?" "Yes, really! The pampering! Come on, he'll be twenty-one this year, and he always has to sit between Bernard and Paul, with Patrick opposite, and a special champagne glass in front of him! It's just ridiculous! It's not normal!" "Oh Colin, what's your definition of 'normal'? Because I personally know many men in this situation: married, kids, and the boyfriend on the side. Don't raise your eyebrows! You're a classic case, and just look at Samuel! All – and I mean all,except for Mario – the trade he picks up in this large country town are married men! So you're quite right, Colin: Michael isn't normal!" "You know what I mean!" "No, Colin, honestly I don't! At the best you seem a hypochrite. You seem to be writing the rules according to Dr Colin Campbell. You can't grasp the reality between what should be seen as correct – or, as you put it, 'normal' – and what actually happens. For me, Michael is the most normal young man in the world. He loves someone with all his heart, but he shares that love with the people around him." "Oh, that's ridiculous! He lives in a fools' paradise! Without them, where is he?" "Come on, Colin! He'll never be without one or the other, emotionally or financially, for the rest of his life!" Colin reached over and said, "Pour me another drink!" "Please!" responded Rodney. "It's the mollycoddling I think is detrimental to Michael's development." "You know, Colin, you haven't once in this conversation criticised Michael: everyone else, but not him. Colin, you're completely transparent!" "What's that supposed to mean?" "Come on, Colin! You're as much in love, or infatuated, with Michael as everyone else. You think that if he were under your wing – or bedcover – it would be better for him, but it wouldn't! Come on, we all love him, and we'd all like a slice of the cake, but we can't have it! Look at Samuel: body beautiful, a real tart, sleeps with anybody once or twice, but when he sees Michael, part of his system goes crazy! He's not just infatuated, in love, or whatever. He changes physically and it's only Michael who produces that effect on him!" "Oh, it's only because he can't get him!" "That's not true! I know Samuel well, how shall I say?" "Intimately!" came the sharp response. "Yes, well! Come on, Colin! You were married to a woman and I don't go round passing bitchy comments!" said Rodney briskly. "Michael has some magic – oh, I know he's very beautiful! – but it's that quiet elusive Irish magic, as Patrick calls it. I think that's it, it's magic!" "And, of course, *he* would know, wouldn't he?" – here the teeth began to show – "Who is this Patrick, who now commands sea and shore?" spat Colin, now quite drunk, but determined to have his say, free from any inhibition. "Riding lessons in the morning; now into the State forest for a gallop here and there!"

Rodney refilled Colin's glass, thinking a hangover in the morning might not be a bad thing for our Dr Campbell. "Oh, yes!" Colin continued, removing his shoes and making grandiose movements with his arms. "And we are so grateful to dear Constable Patrick Timms for his generous offer to step down from the constabulary and take dearest Michael riding!" "You're jealous!" "I'm not!" "Oh, yes you are, Colin! You think somehow along the way you've missed out! Michael remains with Paul and now he shares part of his life with Patrick, and not with you!" "Not with you either!" Colin spat back. "Come on, Colin, get over it! The more you relax with Michael, the more he'll get to like you, but this chip-on-the-shoulder routine will ruin your every opportunity. You risk Michael's keeping you at arm's length for ever!" Colin finished his glass and stared straight ahead, through the glass wall and into the well'lit garden. He said absolutely nothing, as though he had no power to respond. It was all there: Rodney was right! He had misjudged some things, but, drunk as he was, he was sure he hadn't misjudged everything. With Rodney's arm round his shoulder, he slowly mulled over the term 'normal'. As if he were mind-reading, Rodney softly said to Colin, You know, sweetie, the only normal person I can say I honestly know is Michael!" Colin started to interrupt. "Let me finish! He has a lover, and not a bad one at all!" Feeling rather playful now, Rodney said, "Have you seen Paul at Anne's swimming pool? Not bad, really! So, he has a faithful and handsome lover, plus a family, not to mention Mary, who adores him! Listen, I tell you, if you make one wrong move with

Michael, and Mary were there, arsenic on your smoked salmon would be guaranteed!" Colin laughed. "I guess you're right!" "Colin, look! We have a good relationship, you and I, but please don't destroy it through jealousy!" "What jealousy?" Colin responded sharply. "Patrick" came the reply. "I couldn't care less about him!" "Oh yes you could! He's the one Michael's with, not you, or for that matter, not me, but that's it! I'm sure Patrick is completely in love with Michael!" "Oh, without a doubt!" said Colin sarcastically. "Colin, Patrick's another back-up system for this beautiful guy! You know what he deals in, Michael: he deals in the most precious commodity that exists!" Colin pulled himself up from his slumped position on the settee, and Rodney said, "He deals in unconditional love!" and poured Colin another drink from the bottle. "You may as well finish the last bit", he said, pouring it into his glass. "That's a very neat expression!" said Colin. "Oh, it is! It's the neatest and most honest expression in the world. Michael is totally pure. He's not like us, being very cautious and gauging what we can get from this person or that. It's not part of his vocabulary. When he loves, the consequences don't matter. He loves because he feels it right. Look, if Anne had given him a pair of cuff-links made out of bottletops, he would have loved them just the same. He loves them because she gave them to him, and that's that. He accepts without judging: it's what he feels inside that matters!" "He's just lucky he landed on his feet", said a drunk and slightly spiteful Colin. "Darling, we've all had a good education and a good background. We've nothing to complain about, except that when we were twenty-one we weren't given five million dollars!" said Rodney, and laughed. "But Michael had nothing, Colin, nothing: until three days after his eighteenth birthday; the kids at the institution constantly tormented him and hit him!" "Yes, yes! I know all that!" "Well, where's your charity, Colin? It doesn't cost a cent." Silence followed, broken by Colin, who said slowly, owing to his large intake of alcohol, "I'm not really jealous, you know. It's just that, well, I always feel an outsider. They stick together very tightly, the Killarney lot, and Anne and Patrick make no allowance for anyone who's not part of the inner circle." At your age, Colin, you have to make your own circle – or our circle – and stop feeling inferior. They're a special group, financially, idea-wise, religiously, they're all as one and if there's a problem for one of them, the others automatically rush to protect. Michael is the most vulnerable, so it's only natural to assume that they are going to protect him more vehemently. Remember, he has the wherewithall to repay them tenfold. As I said, they're a group of very sophisticated and very nice people, but their currency is unconditional love, and Michael is the richest of them all!"

Again there was silence, then Colin said, "Rodney, I think I'm drunk!" "Good! I think you need to be drunk more often! It's an Irish essential. Do you need a hand?" "Do you hate me, Rodney?" "No, Colin, I love you! All you have to do is realise it, and our relationship can grow. It's all up to you! Come on, Doctor! I'm going to get you to bed and see if I can change your shift first thing in the morning, because I have this funny feeling you're not going to be 'a well belle'!"

On Monday after lunch, Bernard and Lorna were watching Michael and Paul play croquet, when Anne's car drew up, and she and Patrick alighted. "Over here!" cried Bernard. "Oh, goodness! All that energy wasted on sport! Darlings, how are we?" "Patrick, come and save me!" called Paul, and Patrick took his place. "Patrick doesn't play so well", smiled Michael. After the first round, they were even, so Michael insisted they play another round to decide the winner. Michael was wearing a pale-blue shirt with rolled up sleeves, open in front to show a very tanned chest, and a pair of cream trousers, which fitted – thought Patrick – extremely well.

While they were playing and laughing, the other four relaxed with a drink in the pavilion. "I must say, Bernard", said Anne, "this is a sweet little pavilion! I forget where you got it." "From the Wallace estate. Gosh, that's a sad place! I went past with Paul the other day. It's all gone, not only the old house, but the fools have completely demolished the garden: not a tree left!" "And the rhododendrons?" "Gone, too, I'm afraid. There should be a law to stop people demolishing history, otherwise Australia will eventually end up with a bland mixture of mediocre suburban architecture!" "I couldn't agree more!" said Anne. "We're taxed higher than anyone else, to keep this country's heritage in one piece! It's positively ridiculous! Oh, Bernard! Amos said absolutely no gifts for his birthday on Wednesday!" "Very sensible indeed!" replied Bernard.

Back on the croquet lawn, Michael was now losing the second round to Patrick. "Patrick, don't be so good!" he exclaimed, but Patrick went ahead and won. Michael swung his mallet to and fro in his hand and turned to the others, sitting in the shade and applauding the victor. Then he turned back to Patrick, put his arms around him and, for the very first time, kissed him. "Patrick!" he said severely, with his head to one side. "You're impossible!" bringing shouts of laughter from the pavilion. "Come and have a drink! You're both champions!" cried Lorna. As they crossed the lawn, Patrick's feet never touched the ground.

Early Tuesday morning, they set out all four for Melbourne, Michael with a parcel on his knee. He still couldn't cope with long car journeys and, even with the tablets that Colin had prescribed, the trip was not pleasant for him. He fingered the string on the parcel he was holding, which contained, not one, but three shell paintings: one large one of a big white shell with a bright yellow interior and spikes all over it, while the other two were ones he had started a long time ago and had now completed. There had been no time to frame them, so Mary had cut the mounts, glued the pictures in, and covered each separately with a large sheet of cellophane, before wrapping them all together in a brown-paper parcel.

Mary was pleased that they would be away for a few days, as she was working on a secret project. She had found a frame in the old staff quarters above the supper-room, where the chandeliers had been stored, and had asked Bernard whether she might have it. It lacked one whole corner, but was a beautiful double swept french frame, not so large, about ten inches by eighteen. She took it to Nigel and asked whether he knew anyone who could restore it. He said he did, so she left it with him and, on a canvas stretched to fit the frame, started her little masterpiece. With her new camera, she had taken forty or fifty photographs of Michael, and had used some for his portrait on the Chinese wallpaper at Bellevue. Now she was working on a proper portrait, but knew it would be useless asking Michael to sit for it, as he never stayed still for a moment.

The evening of Amos's birthday arrived, and they all went to Brown's for dinner, where Amos had booked a small private dining room. At the door, Henry O'Connor greeted Michael with, "Michael, how many guests do you have tonight?" "I think a lot", he said, looking behind him at the rest of the party getting out of taxis. "Well, that's fine! It means that the Admiral will be surrounded by a wonderful group of people!" He held the big glass door open and ushered them all into the sitting room area, where Amos, David and Stephen were waiting for them. "Happy birthday, darling!" said Anne. "Twenty-one again! Oh, how sensible!" Michael kissed Amos and wished him a happy birthday, then went over to a side table where the newspapers were kept and opened his brown-paper parcel. Inside were one large and two smaller stiff, flat parcels wrapped in gold with white ribbons. Mary had done a fine job. "This is for you, Amos! You can use it at Metung. I think it would look very nice!" Amos's six foot-two frame rose and he embraced Michael. "You're very kind, Michael!" he said, and opened his gift. "It's beautiful, Michael, really beautiful!" At that point, Michael realised he had two other presents and, as Henry came personally to take their drink order, Michael swung round and handed him one of the packages. "This is for you, Henry", he said shyly. Henry was quite overcome, "But Michael, it's not my birthday!" "Oh!" replied Michael, I think it should be! I think you will like the present." "I don't know what to say", said Henry. "This is a genuine honour", and he held out his hand. Michael took no notice of it, and hugged him. Henry opened his parcel and was overwhelmed that Michael should have made him a gift at the same time as Admiral Watson. "You're very kind", he said softly. "I'll just go and get some refreshments for you all", and he disappeared.

This left Michael with one other parecl: he now made straight for David, saying, "This is for you. It's not right you don't have one too. I hope you like it. It is a nice shell, all pink and red inside!" Major Keen said nothing at all, but the tears in his eyes were quite sufficient. Lorna moved across and put her arm through his. "It's fine, David! You don't have to say anything! Oh, here's Henry! A little champagne for all!" David put the package down unopened on the arm of his chair and took a handkerchief from his pocket. In a quavering voice, he said, "Michael, thank you so very much. You are very, very kind!" and set about opening it. It was, as Michael had said, a fine painting of a shell in reds and pinks. "It will go very well in our living room, Daphne!" said Amos, to break the emotion. David laughed. "I had thought, Chloe, that it might look better in our boudoir!" "Did you dear?" Everyone laughed. As Henry handed round the glasses, Bernard rose and said, "Happy birthday, Amos!"

"Well, young man", said Amos, "it's your birthday soon! Goodness! You'll be twenty-one: that mean's you'll be a man!" "Really?" said Michael. "Amos, why do you become a man at twenty-one?" "It's a tradition. It means that at that moment, you become legally responsible for everything you do!" "But do you change when you become a man?" David interjected, "Michael, we use the term 'man', when we think of someone who is responsible, kind, and thinks of others rather than himself. I think most of us here tonight would agree with that definition, and if we all agree on it, then you, Michael, have been a man since the first time we met you, almost three years ago, and I, for one, am very proud to be your friend!" "Hear! Hear!" said Stephen. "A toast to Michael!" Michael wasn't quite sure about the finer points, but he knew that what David had said was definitely in the affirmative.

"What would you like to do for your birthday, Michael?" asked Amos. Michael stood up and went across to where Amos sat in his armchair, and sat on the arm; he slid one arm around his neck. "Oh Amos, I thought", he said slowly, that we could all go to Metung and you could let us sleep on your boat on the lake. . ." and he smiled. "A brilliant idea! Yes, it's a great idea, but I'll let you boys sleep on board!" said Anne. "Your table is ready, Admiral!" "Thank you, Henry! Come along all of you! This occasion happens only once a year!" "Thank goodness for that!" quipped Anne. Michael was very excited. "Amos, can we really sleep on the water all night? Oh, that will be very nice! I shall like it very much!" He squeezed Paul's hand. "Paul, just think, Amos will make us sailors! Won't that be fun?" "It will be great fun, darling!" said Paul, just wondering how on earth all the arrangements could be made. But he relaxed, knowing that, between Anne and Lorna, everything would work out satisfactorily as usual.

The evening passed very pleasantly. Patrick had originally felt a little ill at ease with Stephen, Amos and David, but because he was one of the party, he was accepted as an equal, exchanging points of view, enjoying the humour, and he found that, with time, it was as if he had always known them. Michael made them all laugh when he said to David – who, although stout, was an excellent croquet player – that Patrick had become too good a player now. It was interesting that, at Killarney, it was Michael who marshalled them all into playing croquet. "It's funny!" said Amos. "I always thought croquet was a game for senior citizens and was basically a thing of the past. But it's not true at all. It's a rather skilfull game! It's good that you two", looking at Anne and Bernard, "have come to an arrangement: swimming at Anne's and croquet at Bernard's, since otherwise you would probably have to field separate teams!" "We came to a sophisticated arrangement, Bernard and I, and it works out very well", said Anne. "Riding, swimming, croquet: we have it all, wouldn't you say?" and she looked around the table with a contented smile.

Michael's birthday was two months away, but Anne began the hunt for the perfect gift. What could she get him? In desperation, she called on Nigel. "Darling, what am I to do? I can buy some more clothing, but I want something deliciously special! Please help me!" she sighed. "Well", said Nigel, with a poker-straight face, "There really is only one gift to get Michael." "Oh, do tell! What is it?" "A display case for his shells." "Oh, Nigel! You're a genius, a genius! Not a word to anyone! But, Nigel, where am I going to find one, and what type?" wailed Anne. "Come with me to the storage shed behind the workrooms." The assistants all half-stood and said, "Good morning, Mrs Rochester!" "Good morning, all!" came the reply. "Nigel, don't tell me you have a display case stored in the shed out here!" He didn't answer, but opened the padlock, then the lock on the door, and they stepped into the gloom. "Just a minute, I'll turn on the light!" he said in a matter-of-fact way. A flash of crude neon lit up the storeroom. "Nigel, what a mess! How do you know where anything is?" "Do you want a display case, or not?" was the dry reply. "Sorry, darling! Of course I want the display case!" He threaded his way through a forest of furniture and accessories in various states of repair. "Here we are!" he said, and stopped. "Well!" said Anne, looking all around. "I can't see a display case at all!" "Here, look!" and he pointed to a square cupboard, with a Boulle front door and two big decorative handles, the kind you find on antique pianos, either side . The top was in shocking condition, split and very badly marked. "Nigel!" said Anne sharply, "If you've brought me here to waste time, I shall be very angry! This isn't a display case!" "Yet!" came the reply. "But, Nigel, how could you possibly use this as a display case when it has a solid door! You can't see inside at all!" "Oh, ye of little faith!" "Faith or not, I just can't see what you're talking about!" "Listen: the base is in good condition. We have the surface renovated, and on top I'll have the cabinet-maker create a sort of large glass obelisk with black wooden supports to match the base, with a decorative gold urn on top. Inside, the shelves will be of clear glass, and I'll fit into the base, which is now the top of the little cabinet, a light to illuminate all the shells on the clear glass shelves." "Nigel, that's perfect!" said Anne. "It will fit precisely on the other side of the fireplace in the boys' bedroom, matching all the other Boulle furniture! A tortoise display case, yes! Nigel, yes! You are a genius, but can we have it all ready in two months?" she queried. "If Metung was finished in two months, a display case is a push-over!" "Oh, Nigel! You must promise: not a word to a living soul! A tortoise display case! He'll love it, and he'll be able to see it every day! Perfect, perfect! I leave it all to you, darling, but remember it's a secret!" And a very buoyant Mrs Rochester sailed through the workrooms and out through the shop, sure that she had found the perfect gift for Michael's twenty-first birthday.

As always, Anne was to the fore of all the organisation for the coming event, and had lunch alone with Lorna at Bellevue, with Mario moving silently about, one dish more exotic than the next. Anne began to go over the arrangements. "Sleeping, the same as before, darling, except that the other bedroom next to Patrick's can be used by Mario. They'll have to share a bathroom, but you know, darling, boys love it! Mary will have the spare room and bathroom at Jan the caretaker's. Now that's accomodation organised!" "Just a minute", said Lorna. Why on earth do we need two cooks?" "Darling, of course we need them. You don't expect Mary to don a swimsuit and waterwings and splash all the way to the boat each morning to make the boys' breakfast and do backstroke to get back here to do something for us! Oh, that wouldn't do at all! We must be absolutely realistic!" "Yes, I suppose so", replied a slightly defeated Lorna. "Two cooks, of course!" "Well, they will stay on the boat two nights at the most, Anne. We're only going for four days! I'm sure Hannibal crossing the Alps never needed so much planning!" "Oh, darling! Don't exaggerate!" "Now, Amos's boat sleeps six, with two double and two single cabins, or whatever you call them. That means one single for Amos, one single for Bernard – although why he is doing this, I'm not sure! – a double for the boys, and who shall we put in with Mario, I wonder? she said mischievously. "Who would you suggest, Lorna? Patrick or Samuel, which one? Hmm, I shall have to study this little problem, but based on past experience, I suppose Samuel would be best. We don't want to break new ground now, do we?" She gave a wicked grin. "Anne, you are terrible! Poor Mario!" "Oh darling! Remember we took him home from Metung last time as a – what could one say? – souvenir? Anyway, it worked out very well! But darling, I've been talking to Colin, and it appears that people who suffer from car-sickness don't necessarily suffer from sea- or air-sickness. So I'll take Mario and Michael, and Paul, if he wishes, and we'll fly down. Isn't that a great idea?" "I'm not at all sure!" said Lorna. "Even though for the ten days we spent at Metung, Michael was fine on the boat, a plane – and a small one at that – is quite another thing!" "Don't worry, I have it all in hand! I'll have a word with Paul. Mario or Mary can make a brunch that we can tuck into to break the journey and Michael will arrive in tip-top condition! Oh, I must write all this down! Jan can collect us from Lakes Entrance, or field or paddock, or what you will!" "Don't make any arrangements before speaking to Paul. Promise me that!" "Very well! He's home the night after next!" "Oh no, darling! I'll call him tonight. He'll be at St Georges Road, won't he?" "Yes, he goes to the gym, and he and Bernard are home after eight-thirty, so you'll catch him there!"

"Anne, darling, what have you decided to get Michael for a present? We're completely stumped. Bernard says a good watch, but I really don't know, since he already has one. What did you say you were getting?" "I didn't" said Anne, looking at her plate. "Anne, aren't you going to tell me, for heaven's sake! Imagine if we bought the same thing!" "Highly improbable, Lorna! It's a super-secret!" "Really, Anne, do tell!" "I can't! You'll have to wait and see what it is with the others! Oh, how I do love surprises!" "I'm sure you do!" said Lorna in a slightly sarcastic manner.

"She won't tell me anything, Bernard! She's like a cat that's caught one mouse and is ready for the next!" "Typical!" was Bernard's reply over the phone. "I think a watch, or another Toby. I just can't think of anything! He's already got everything!" "What is Paul getting him?" "Well, he doesn't know either. He suggested a watch. Oh Lorna, why is it so difficult to buy a present?" "I don't know, Bernard, but difficult it is, since we need two gifts – one from you and me, and one from Paul. A watch is one, but what about the other?" "I haven't a clue. I wish I could do shell paintings! That would solve the problem!" "Oh Bernard, please be sensible! Time's running out and you and Paul had better put your thinking caps on!"

Bernard did just that. He had seen a television programme that gave him an idea. Next day he telephoned Rodney. "Yes, Bernard, it's here, but in what condition, I'm not sure!" Rodney replied. "Yes, I suppose so. By when? You're pushing it, Bernard! In secret! Have it finished and in place in secret? I'll try, Bernard, but no promises! And the contents? OK, I'll see what I can arrange!" "Bernard's crazy", thought Rodney. "Doing all this as a birthday present for Michael, and in secret!"

Bernard told Lorna he had worked out the gift problem, but that it was to remain a secret till the day. At the next opportunity, Lorna took Paul aside. "Listen, Paul: Bernard, Anne and Mary have all decided to get or buy a present for Michael, but are keeping it a secret! Paul, what are we two going to do?" "Another watch is useless", said Paul. "You and Bernard got that beautiful Cartier watch for him for his last birthday. I say, Lorna, let's do the same as the others. We'll buy a gift together, but we'll keep it secret as well!" "Good idea, darling! But what?" He leant over and whispered in her ear. "Paul, Bernard will have a fit. You know how he is!" "Think about it, and let me know what you think by the end of the evening, and I'll see whether I can make arrangement for it. Otherwise, you'd better come up with another idea quickly!"

Although Michael's birthday fell on a Wednesday, the party was shifted to Thursday evening, when they would all be together, since the following day was their departure for Metung. But it was on Tuesday that everything happened. Although Paul thought Anne's offer to fly them to Metung was very generous, he was very concerned about the consequencesif Michael felt sick on the plane. It wasn't as though he could get out and have a walk and breathe some fresh air. Up in the clouds, it could be a nasty experience, and up to the last moment he was undecided.

Bernard arranged for Lorna to be away from Killarney on the Tuesday morning, and Michael was out riding with Patrick, so the coast was clear. Mary had to be brought into the secret, as she had also with Anne's gift, arranging the furniture in the boys' bedroom and having the collection of shells ready to fit into Nigel's newly created Boulle display case. No one knew about Mary's gift, except Nigel, and again it was Mary who had to assist Paul and Lorna with theirs. Patrick said to Anne that he thought it was the givers who were having more fun than the recipient. Having made sure the coast was clear, Mary phoned Rodney and soon two big trucks came up the drive, each bearing half a large white metal structure. The workmen disappeared into the conservatory, where they had to move huge pots of trees around before starting work. When Lorna got home after running Bernard's errand - popping into Mulberry's for yet another gift just in case everything went wrong with hers and Paul's gift – she was most startled to be told by Mary that the conservatory was to remain locked and no one was to enter it before Thursday evening. "Judge Mahoney's orders!" she said sternly. "Something to do with a birthday gift. Rodney is sorting it all out!" "Really, how pleasant for them all!" came Lorna's sharp reply.

Nigel phoned a very nervous Mary on Wednesday morning. "You'd better bring the canvas here, since the frame arrived late last night and it's very delicate. I've got a small bench, clamps and some thick felt. Can you bring it this morning?" he said in his calm, matter-of-fact manner. "I'll come at once", said Mary. She told Lorna she had to dash to Brunswick for something to do with a birthday present. A moment later, her little car went beetling down the drive with a flat rectangular package on the back seat, covered with a sheet.

"This gets madder and madder", thought Lorna, and immediately phoned Paul at work. "Paul, it's Lorna. Well, how did we go? Really? What colour? Oh, white! Sounds divine! Great! See you on Thursday! Everything here is completely out-of-hand: secret after secret! It's crazy! Yes, everything's organised for Metung. Yes, I'm very concerned about the flight, too! I might give Colin a call and double check what he told Anne. Looking forward to seeing you! Goodbye, darling!"

Mary walked into Nigel's showroom with the covered painting under her arm. "I have an appointment with Mr Storey", she said. "Come through!" cried Nigel, hearing her voice. She went through to the workroom and there it was, fully restored and regilded. "Oh, Nigel! It's beautiful! It's so, well, grand!" "Yes, I have to confess that when it came back last night even I was a bit surprised. But let's see the canvas!" Nigel was not one to over-enthuse. He was a calculator: he knew exactly what in the decorating world went with what and he had many years' experience in the trade, but when Mary removed the sheet from the painting, he was so startled he said nothing for a moment. He just sat down and stared at the canvas. "Do you think it's the best thing you've ever done?" he asked. Mary's quiet answer was, "Yes, I honestly think it is!" The two of them seemed transfixed. The image was a half-torso of Michael, painted in the style and colours of an eighteenth-century portrait, perhaps by Reynolds, with a red silk and velvet drape across one shoulder and his naked chest, his mane of black hair and electric blue eyes that seemed to follow you, no matter where you were. "Mary, this is a very, very fine painting of a young classical god. It's splendid! Now let's see how he will look in his new frame. The effect was stunning. "We've done it! It's perfect! The big green velvet ribbon and bow are ready!" "What green ribbon?" asked Mary. "Well, it has to hang in the Irish room, and since there's no space left on the walls, I've decided to hang it over the mirror above the fireplace. You know, that huge, dreary thing, Bernard insisted on keeping! You know, the one that leant against the window in the ballroom!" "Yes, yes", said Mary, "but Nigel, hanging a painting on top of that big mirror. . .!" "It's very French! I've done it before. I've always disliked the frame of that mirror. I think Bernard's grandmother must have found it in a railway waiting room! This will be the finishing touch to the room!" "But what about the weight of the picture and frame?" "Don't worry!" he said. A strong copper wire runs through the centre of the ribbon and will be attached to the top of the mirror on the wall. Leave the painting with me and I'll bring it when I bring Anne's gift on Thursday morning. Don't forget the shells!" "How many do you need?" "About twelve showy ones: that should do it, I think! I'll see you Thursday morning after Michael's gone riding."

It was a busy time for Mary, preparing a dinner party for eleven, phoning Jan at Metung to ensure all the provisions had been purchased. Amos and David were house guests, while Stephen, as always, stayed with Anne. They couldn't all stay at Metung for the same length of time, some were coming only for the weekend, including Colin, Rodney and Samuel owing to work, while Stephen and Bernard had to be back on Tuesday, but if everything else worked out, the others might stay on all week. The only person not caught up in the frenzied organisation was Michael, who took every day as it came. In Michael's mind, everything was possible: it was a mere step from asking Patrick, Paul, Lorna, Bernard or Anne to its happening instantly. The only thing different now was that he was barred from the conservatory for three days, just like Lorna. "Lorna, perhaps Cooty will never let us in again!" he said with a certain conviction. "I don't think that would be very nice, do you? We won't be able to have lunch there any more", he said in a dejected tone. "Darling, of course we will! We have to wait and see what Bernard is keeping as a surprise!" "Hmm!" came the response, as Mary insisted he have another slice of the Atlantic salmon she had cooked in foil, with just a hint of oil and a few herbs. "Do you like it, Michael?" Mary asked. "Mary, it's very nice. I like it very much!" "I'm glad!" she smiled and left the vast dining room where the two of them were lunching alone.

After lunch, Lorna insisted on playing their duet together. It was always the same: if he started a split second behind her, all was well, but if he missed the beginning, he lost the thread, which was what happened now. "Lorna, I'm very bad today, I'm sorry!" "Darling, it doesn't matter! Everyone has good days and bad days!" She was interrupted by Mary coming into the room, saying there was a call for her. Michael sat alone, as if in a trance, moving his fingers over the keys, but just half-an-inch above them, as though he were playing in his mind. Then down they came, in a crescendo of sound and he began playing. It was again the theme from 'Limelight' and every note struck with an intensity that rendered it electric. Lorna and Mary stood transfixed in the doorway, not daring to disturb him. He finished and spun round on the piano stool. Looking out through the big bay window, he heaved a great sigh and turned once more to see Mary and Lorna. "They won't be home until tomorrow!" he said very softly. Lorna swept up to him and held him. "Tomorrow's not so far away, darling!"

On Wednesday, Anne held a dinner party for Michael's official birthday. Lorna and Michael were the chief guests, plus Patrick, Rodney and

Samuel. "Black ties everyone!" was the demand issued from Bellevue. When they arrived, Patrick came up to Lorna and said, "Would you tie this bloody thing for me, please? Anne refuses to have a ready-made one in her house! A bit boring, don't you think? It looks just the same!" "Come here, handsome! I'll see what I can do!" and in a flash the tie was knotted perfectly. "Thanks!" said Patrick. Anne had to make different seating arrangements, since Paul and Bernard were missing: Patrick sat in Paul's place, with Samuel opposite, and Lorna sat on Michael's other side. Samuel was in seventh heaven. Later, Anne said to Lorna that he looked just like a big labrador with a lead in his mouth, waiting for his master to take him for a run!

Mario produced a masterpiece of fusion cooking, with lots of the freshest vegetables. He had become an intimate friend of Maisie O'Brien, so Bellevue now shared the best of the goods with Killarney.

Thursday opened as a warm early-summer day. Michael went riding, or – to be a little more accurate – jumping, with Patrick, so the morning was free for Nigel to come with an assistant. Lorna was most surprised to see him heading up the staircase with a cupboard base, followed by his assistant carrying a large glass obelisk with a big gilded urn on top. "Nigel, may I ask what you are doing?" called Lorna from the bottom of the stairs, as Mary rushed up with a big box of shells. "No, Lorna! I can't tell! It's a secret!" he replied, in his matter-of-fact voice. They were fifteen minutes in the bedroom before coming down. They headed for the Irish room. "Get the tall ladder!" called Nigel to the assistant. Lorna left them to it: all this rushing about was impossible, and it was supposed to be a secret!

She took the chance of going upstairs when she heard a drill boring into the wall of the Irish room. "No point in worrying!" she thought. "I haven't been able to enter my own conservatory for three days!" She entered the boys' bedroom and there it stood, the most beautiful display case: a glass obelisk on top of a Boulle base, lighted from the bottom. In the top section under the urn, four glass shelves held the most beautiful shells that Amos had given Michael over the past two years. It was a small masterpiece! So that's Anne's secret, she thought, seeing a card tied to the little gilt nob on the obelisk that read 'With all my love, Anne'. As she went downstairs, she saw Nigel leaving with

his assistant, saying to Mary, Sorry about the dust, but drills are drills!"
"It's no problem", Mary replied. "Oh, Nigel, how much do I owe you
for the frame?" "Mary dear, it's on the house! Give Michael my love
for his birthday!" and he left via the front door, only to return to say,
"Goodbye, Lorna!"

"Bedroom, Irish room, conservatory! This place is turning into a lunatic
asylum!" she thought. "What's happening here?" She walked into the
Irish room, just as Mary was starting to clean up the plaster dust from
the drill holes. "Mary!" was all she said, and sat down quite heavily on
the arm of the settee. She just stared at the portrait. After a moment or
two, Mary felt embarrassed, since she still said nothing and the silence
grew. Finally, it was Mary who broke it. "Do you like it?" she asked
quietly, with the dustpan still in her hand. "Mary, it's Michael! It's so
beautiful! Oh Mary, it's beautiful!" Mary left Lorna just staring at the
portrait. Lorna went to the door and turned the chandelier full on, so
as to see the portrait's quality better. "It's love! She couldn't have done
it without all that she felt for him! It's just splendid!"

At this point, Michael arrived back from riding and, realising that the
lights were on in the Irish room, he entered, to find Lorna still gazing
above the fireplace. "Lorna!" he started on a sentence only to stop
abruptly on seeing his own image in the gilt frame. He said nothing,
but moved very close to Lorna. After a prolonged silence, he said, "Mary
did this, didn't she?" "Yes, darling! She did it for you, for your birthday!
It's beautiful, don't you think?" "Lorna, it's very nice, but you don't need
a painting of me. I'm always here!" he said softly. She held him very
tightly. "Darling, go and tell Mary that you like it very much, and then
you can go up to your bedroom to see Anne's surprise!"

As bidden, leaving Lorna still mesmerised by the portrait, he went to the
kitchen, where Mary was working. He came and put his arms around
her. "Mary, it's very beautiful! You're very clever indeed! I like it very
much, thank you!" and he kissed her. "I'm glad you like it!" she said
shyly. "I think you had better have a look in your bedroom!"

Michael climbed the stairs and walked down the corridor to his
bedroom. He entered, and there it was on the other side of the fireplace
with the light on and his collection of shells, seemingly suspended in

mid-air. He rushed down the corridor. "Lorna, Lorna! All my shells are here in a piece of tortoise furniture! Look at all the shells Amos gave me!" Lorna came up and pretended she hadn't seen it before. "Wow! Isn't that splendid?" "Oh, yes! It's very, very nice!" "Why don't we call Anne, and you can tell her how much you like it?" This was duly done, with Anne cooing and saying she would see him later that evening.

As the afternoon wore on, Michael went to his chair in the yellow room, beside the piano, and looked out of the window, waiting for the car that would bring Cooty and Paul home. This evening, however, there were two cars: first Bernard arrived in his, and then thirty minutes later came Paul. When Bernard arrived, Michael was ecstatic. "Cooty, Cooty! I'm in a picture in the Irish room! Come and see! I look like I've come out of the swimming pool!" "Really?" said Bernard, perplexed, and having no knowledge of Mary's gift. They entered the Irish room to find Lorna having a drink by herself, since no one else had yet arrived. "Hello, darling", she said to Bernard. "What do you think?" The portrait affected Bernard in a strange way: he wanted to say something, but choked. He looked at Lorna. "I know", she said. "It's Michael, frozen in time. It's quite beautiful, isn't it?" "The portrait seems to know a great deal more than we do!" he said seriously. "But so he does, Bernard, and we both know that's the truth!" "Yes", replied Bernard, "that's the truth!" "Cooty, come to my bedroom! Look, look!" Michael led Bernard to see the Boulle display case. "It's beautiful, Michael! Look at all the shells!" "Cooty, do you like it?" "Very much!" "So do I!" "Now, young man, come with me! I have something for you!" He linked arms with Michael and headed for the conservatory. Bernard called Mary as they passed the kitchen and she gave him the key. He unlocked the door and they went in. On the blank wall of the house now stood an enormous aviary, all cream, to match the conservatory, with six big Rosella parrots in it. "Cooty!" said Michael in amazement. "Look! They're all red and blue! What are they?" "They're parrots!" Michael only knew the word from Mulberry's, where Ernest used it for his staff when he got angry with them, but these were wonderful! One of them spread his wings and flew to a higher branch. The flash of colour as he moved through the air, only to fold his wings when he alighted on the branch was magic for Michael! Their colours were splendid. "Cooty! They're so nice! I like them so much!" he said. "Well", said Bernard, "they're all yours! Now you'll have to learn to look after them!" "Oh yes!" said Michael, and he looked at Bernard very concernedly. "Cooty, how do you look after a parrot?" Bernard laughed, "As long as you like them, that's fine!"

While they were in the conservatory watching the parrots, Paul arrived. Lorna greeted him, "Can you believe it? Bernard is in the conservatory. He's bought Michael six parrots! Oh Paul! They're beautiful, really beautiful! Mary!" she called, and when Mary answered, "Tell Michael and Bernard to come to the yellow room!" When they came in, they found Lorna and Paul holding a little animal by turns. "Good heavens!" said Bernard. "It's a lamb!" "No", said Paul, "actually it's a dog. He's a Bedlingham. He just looks like a lamb!" Michael went over and kissed Paul. He seemed very shy of the dog. "Here, hold him, darling! He's your birthday present from Lorna and me!" "Oh Paul", said Michael, "he's very tiny. Where does he sleep?" "For now, in Mary's apartment, then we'll see what happens later!" The dog yawned and struggled to get down. Michael put him down and he walked around the room. Then Mary entered and saw him. "Not here!" she said, and whisked him away to the garden, where he relieved himself and then returned with Mary. He trotted after Michael as they moved to the Irish room.

At that moment, cars were heard in the drive and Mary opened the door to Amos and David with cases in their hands. "They greeted her with "Don't worry, Mary! We know the way!" and were followed by Colin, Rodney and Samuel. Ten minutes later, Anne, Patrick and Stephen arrived. In turn, they moved from one extravagant and imaginative gift to the other, with a tiny Bedlingham puppy (later to bear the name 'Sebastian') under everyone's feet. "He's very nice, isn't he?" Michael said to Patrick. "I don't really think he's a dog, he's a funny lamb!" Patrick gave Michael a hug and wished him happy birthday, then said, "We shall have to introduce him to Polly very soon!" "Patrick, do you think Polly will like him?" "If we introduce them slowly, they'll get to like each other. Here, this is for you! It's not quite as exciting as your other gifts, but 'happy birthday' all the same!" They all watched as Michael unwrapped the black paper from what turned out to be a box, and carefully opened the lid. "Patrick, it's a shell!" said Michael, but as he withdrew the large nautilus shell, he realised it was attached to a base. The base was an Atlas on a square plinth, but instead of holding the world, he held this shell. The mouth of the shell had been fitted with an engraved silver lid that opened on a hinge. Michael was fascinated. "Patrick", he said, "this is a very rich shell. It comes with lots of decorations!" Everyone laughed. He then hugged and kissed Patrick, as was now his habit. Patrick had purchased the shell many years ago, and although he had a certain affection for it, he was certain that tonight was the night to hand it on to Michael.

As they all moved to the red dining room for the birthday dinner, Paul lingered a moment, gazing at the portrait. His three years with Michael all flooded back: here Michael was immortalised, while the reality was a young man constantly changing and developing. He glanced at the painting once more before joining the others, wondering that the speechless, frightened little eighteen-year-old of three years ago, with his bloody face and shirt and shaven head, could have become such a perfect swan: the ugly duckling was now gone for ever. The wonderful warm feeling he felt inside was the knowledge that this beautiful creature was his, and that the love they shared was something no one could take away. "Paul, are you coming?" called Lorna. Paul looked at the portrait and winked, then headed for the dining room and a Mary extravaganza, concerned only about the flight the next morning.

They were all up early. Paul and Michael left Killarney and picked up Anne and Mario and the essential wicker hamper, and drove straight to Essenden airport, where the plane was waiting for them. "Darling", said Anne, "it's going to be a fabulous adventure! You'll love it!" Paul was not so sure. They climbed into the four-seater passenger plane, with Anne and Mario in front and Paul and Michael behind. Michael had taken his tablets exactly one hour before, and seemed in high spirits. The plane taxied to the runway and then took off. Michael got quite a shock at the lift-off sensation. Part of his chest seemed stuck to the back of his seat. Then he looked out of the window, his hand still firmly in Paul's. The earth beneath them was as he had never imagined it, all divided into strange squares, rectangles and every irregular shape you could imagine. He was fascinated. "Paul, we're like birds!" he said. "Do birds see this when they fly?" "Yes, I suppose they do. What do you think of it?" "The ground seems a long way away", he said nervously, watching a little red speck that was obviously a car moving along a road.

"Everything is very small, very, very small!" After half-an-hour, Anne instructed Mario, who was not at all convinced that a light aircraft was an ideal form of transport, to open up the hamper and serve the food and drink. He had excelled himself in making wonderful tasty morsels: easy-to eat finger-food. "Another drink, anyone?" Anne turned to see how Michael was. "Fine, darling! Next trip, Paris! Oh what fun!"

They arrived at Lakes Entrance and taxied over to where Jan was waiting with the Range Rover. Michael felt a little odd, but not at all unwell: it was a totally white-faced Mario who climbed very shakily out of the plane and leant up against the car. "Oh dear!" said Anne. "Well, you can't win them all!" They all piled into the car and set off for Metung, with the window open so that Mario could feel the fresh breeze on his bleached-out face.

Being somewhere he remembered, Michael felt at home at once and walked around the veranda, leaning over the cast-iron balustrade to look at the lake. The others arrived three hours later, by which time Mario, feeling a fraction more human, had prepared a light lunch for them all on the veranda. "Cooty! Cooty! I've been in a plane! It's so high off the ground!" This was the cry that greeted Bernard and Lorna. "How do you feel?" asked Lorna. "Oh, good! I was a little frightened when we started, but it was very nice!" Anne reported that Mario had not found the flight very nice, so it was arranged that he should return by car with Patrick and Mary. By four-thirty, they were all there: the same group as before stayed with Anne and the others with Amos. Only Stephen was not present: he would be arriving tomorrow.

On Mary's arrival, she took charge in the kitchen at once, much to Mario's relief, meaning that he could finally go and lie down. Their evening meal was at Anne's. "Patrick, what has happened to the little dog?" asked Michael. "Well, Mr and Mrs Barnes are looking after Sebastian", as he had been named by Bernard, "and when we go home he will live with Mary and you will have to look after him!" "Hmm!" he sighed. "I have to look after six parrots and Sebastian. I think it's going to be a lot of work!" Patrick laughed. "Everyone will give you a hand!" "Patrick, are you sure that Sebastian isn't a lamb? We saw those lambs the other day when we went riding. He seems very much the same!" "He does look the same, but he's a dog!" Conversation was animated over dinner, with a very excited Michael anticipating sleeping on Amos's boat the following evening. "I do hope Mario has no problems on board", said Lorna. "Well, he didn't last year when we were here, so here's hoping, or else we'll have to make our own breakfast. Not really a difficult task at all!" said Amos. "Paul and I can rustle up a smart breakfast and you, Chloe, can serve it in your new uniform with matching apron and cap!" This provoked screams of laughter. "I'm sorry, Amos! My days of serving are well and truly over, I'm afraid!" David said, with a nose-in-the-air attitude. "Besides, I don't think that, on a boat, with a tray and high heels, I could possibly manage at my age!"

Next morning, Michael went riding with Patrick at the nearby riding school, where the girl with the red shirt remembered them. "Hi!" she greeted them. "How have you been?" "Great!" said Patrick. "They're both saddled over there. Same horses you had last time, and remember, it's on the house! Your boyfriend pulled me out of a tight corner last year! You see", she said, scratching her head, "I never forget a favour! Have a good ride. The hurdles are up, you can use them if you want!" "My boyfriend!" thought Patrick and smiled, "my boyfriend!"

Lunch was on board, with dinner at Amos's, then it was all aboard again for a night on the lake. Michael was very excited. Amos and the others walked down to the pier where the boat was moored. Mario and Mary had prepared everything for breakfast next day. Amos stepped on deck, followed by Bernard, Michael, Paul, Samuel and Mario. There were four cabins below deck and two tiny bathrooms separating the cabins, with a corridor right down the middle, so it was possible to exit both in front and at the rear, with the large saloon and galley kitchen above. Michael and Paul took one large cabin and Amos the other, since Bernard wouldn't hear of Amos giving up his cabin for him. Of the two smaller ones with bunks, one was taken by Bernard and the other by Samuel and Mario.

As they pulled away from the jetty and made for the open lake, Michael went up with Amos and was delighted to steer the boat – under Amos's direction – to the far side, where they were to moor for the night. The others went to the saloon, where Mario offered drinks while they chugged across the lake.

When they reached the far end of the lake, Amos downed anchor and he and Michael joined the others. Another thing Michael liked immensely were the lights on board, a floating house with lights and all! "How nice!" he thought.

The evening wore on, with jokes and discussions. It was Paul who said to Mario, "Please sit down with us and have a drink. We are all here to have a good time and don't stand on ceremony!" "Thanks!" said Mario, and he helped himself to a whisky and joined the others. At about twelve-thirty, they decided to call it a day, and they all went to their respective cabins. Samuel looked longingly as Michael followed Paul down the steps. "Hand me the glasses, Samuel, and put your eyes back in their sockets!" said Mario.

Michael decided he wanted to sleep near the porthole, so that he could see the morning first, but in order to do this, he had to climb naked over Paul, to get to the other side. "Michael, be careful!" said Paul, which for some reason Michael found funny, and started laughing in his deep voice. "Shh! The others are trying to. . ." He never finished. Michael kissed him and pressed his lips for a long time on Paul's. When he moved to the other side, he turned round to Paul and put his head on his chest and held him tightly.

Next morning, Michael awoke to a loud splash and, through the porthole, saw Samuel swimming alongside. He scrambled over Paul, who was still half-asleep, pulled on his swimsuit and rushed up the narrow stairway. He jumped into the water, yelling and having a great time. By this stage, everyone had been awakened by the noise, and Samuel was in seventh heaven swimming and playing with his idol. After about twenty minutes, Michael felt tired and started to swim back to the boat, when he realised he was in trouble. So did Samuel, who immediately swam over and guided him back to the boat, making funny jokes so that he would not feel afraid. "OK, you water-babies, come and have breakfast!" said Paul, as he helped Michael on board. "I'll be there in a moment!" said Samuel, who suddenly realised that with his tiny swimsuit, it took little imagination to see the effect Michael had on him.

Breakfast was served in grand style, everyone dressed in shorts and shirt, except for Mario, with black trousers, white shirt, black tie amd white jacket with gold epaulettes. He and Mary had arranged a bumper breakfast. "Goodness! You couldn't have a breakfast like this at any of the good hotels", said Bernard. The table was set with white damask and flowers in low silver vases, with large jugs of orange juice and champagne, which was Anne's suggestion, of course. There was fruit, cereal, bacon, eggs, sausages, liver, toast: enough food for double the number of people, and all served piping hot. "I'm starving!" said Samuel and tucked into enough for three. "A growing boy!" laughed Amos.

After breakfast, they cruised along the far side of the lake and returned to the jetty, tied up and jumped off. "Amos! Can we do this tomorrow night, please?" "I don't see why not! That's what I bought the craft for! Certainly! Why not?" "Oh, let's leave everything here then, shall we?" said Paul. "I'll give someone else a turn", said Bernard and took his bag, which Michael slung over his shoulder. They headed to their respective residences.

The only difference that evening was that Patrick took Bernard's place. While swimming next morning, Patrick discovered that Michael couldn't swim at all well, and at times panicked. It was fine in the swimming pool, where the sides were close and where you can mostly touch the bottom. But in the lake it was different. He asked Paul whether he would mind his teaching Michael to swim properly. "Not at all!" said Paul. "I'd be grateful! He'll listen to you, but with me he just wants to play around!" So it was decided, but – like Samuel – Patrick realised that Michael's sexual magnetism might cause a few touchy moments, but it would be worth the effort. Back on deck, Michael was calm this time, since Patrick had not left his side. This fact brought a slight tinge of green envy to Samuel: Patrick could hold him, but if *he* tried, he was sure the result would not be the same!

Over another luxurious breakfast, with all in shorts and Michael in an open shirt with his wet mane of black hair, were four young menwho thought he was the most beautiful thing in the world, but only Paul had the right to reach over and kiss him.

So the weekend passed without a cloud in the sky. Colin and Rodney stayed only one night, Stephen, Samuel and Bernard three, leaving the rest with Mary and Mario. The week ended with Michael plaguing

Amos for another night on board, which Amos was only too happy to do. It seemed to Amos that fate had dealt him a lucky card with this boat, because he couldn't remember being happier and more content, with Michael scurrying around on board, wearing Amos's captain's cap.

Finally, it was time to go home. David and Amos stayed on for another week, but the others departed, except that this time Mario returned with Patrick and Lorna and Anne, Michael and Paul headed across the field to board the little plane, with Paul carrying the little wicker hamper for the return journey.

Back at Killarney, everything returned to normal, except for the addition of Sebastian, who developed a great attachment to Michael and Mary, and wasn't at all keen on Mr Barnes. So they settled down, waiting for the next social event.

There came one evening, however, that was to change forever the lives of Michael, Paul and Patrick. It seemed just like any other Friday evening, but it was to turn out anything but ordinary.

They were sitting in the Irish room for drinks before dinner, when Bernard said, "We have something to say to you!" The three boys looked at one another, realising that Bernard was also speaking for Lorna and Anne. "Keeping secrets is fine, but the girls and I see no point to keeping a secret that affects your futures. It concerns our wills." "Bernard", started Paul. "Please, Paul, let me finish! Anne, Lorna and I have left everything to you and Michael, lock, stock and barrel. The difference in Anne's case", at which point Anne interrupted. "In my case, I leave everything to Paul and Michael, but Bellevue and the funds for its upkeep is left to Patrick for his lifetime. You boys have Killarney, so Bellevue will be no use to you, although the deed to the property will be yours, Paul, as I said, but it's for Patrick's use for the rest of his life!" Patrick said nothing, looking totally overwhelmed: he just didn't know what to say. Michael, although he hadn't grasped the ramifications of what Bernard had told them, went over and put his arm around Patrick and said, "Now you're real family forever", and he kissed him, making the tears run down his cheeks. Paul handed him a handkerchief and smiled, "Michael's right! The six of us will always be together!"

Bernard said to Paul, "We can look over the fine points next week in town!" "Well, now that's all settled, what about a drink?" said Anne, with a wave of her hand.

Anne smiled a knowing smile at Patrick. About two weeks earlier, Anne had awoken at about five o'clock and realised she had left her tablets in the kitchen the night before. She got up and went along the carpeted corridor to fetch them and, on passing Patricks suite – the door slightly ajar – heard a soft conversation, which implied that the second person must have been in his room all night. "Well, well!" she smiled to herself. "Everything has worked out perfectly! Fancy Mario and Patrick! Well, that should secure the staff!" She returned to her room with her bottle of pills. "Well, fancy that! Good for Patrick!"

"Well, now that's all settled", said Anne, have you heard about the drama in Highfield Road last night?" "What drama?" asled Lorna curiously, and Anne recounted what she had heard from Samuel that afternoon.

It had not been a good day for Eric Kenworth. He was now divorced, living on a small pension, and drinking heavily with what acquaintances he had left, when he heard that his own masterpiece, his very own house that he had designed, was up for sale. He couldn't believe it. Although the house did belong to Beryl, he just couldn't believe she would put it on the market. He rose and made for his canary yellow jeep and sped off in the direction of the house on Birdwood Drive. To his horror, there was indeed a large 'For Sale' sign, and diagonally across it was a large black strip with florescent green letters saying "SOLD". He was furious. He turned his jeep quickly, scraping a parked car and drove to Highfield Road, to have it out with Beryl, since up to then he had been sure that in time he could have persuaded her to let him live there, even if not with her.

It was the time of evening Beryl most enjoyed. Dinner was organised, thanks to Neville's culinary skills, and they sat having a drink, discussing the day's events and laughing generally at someone else's expense.

It was at this point that Beryl and Neville heard a screech of tyres and, a moment later, a forceful battering of the front door knocker. Beryl rose and crossed the room into the hall. She swung open the front door to be confronted by a slightly drunk and very agitated Eric. "What do you want?" she demanded. "How could you sell the house?" he yelled at her. Neville was immediately at Beryl's side. "Beryl should consider herself lucky to have found a buyer for that architectural monstrosity", he said sarcastically. Eric pushed past Beryl and made for Neville. Last time he had felt like flattening him at Mulberyy's, Samuel had intervened, but this time there was no Samuel. He took a swing at Neville, who was too nimble for him and headed into the nearest room, which was the dining room, where he used the large table as a barrier. Eric's use of expletives was extraordinary. In all their married life together, Beryl had never heard him use such language. Quick as could be, Beryl grabbed her mobile phone from the hall table and rang Sergeant Reynolds to say she had an emergency on her hands.Eric was yelling and swinging punches at Neville, who replied with stinging comments, making Beryl highly distressed. She rushed to the living room to seek a weapon and found it in the form of a poker. She dashed back to the scene of the fray, just as Eric hurled a plate a Neville and caught him on the shoulder. "You fag!" yelled Eric. "I'll kill you!" That was enough for Beryl, who was now behind Eric. She took a swing and hit him on his side with the poker, just as she did with her favourite driving iron. Down he went, bringing the tablecloth and everything on it with a ghastly crash to the floor. "Make one move, Eric, and I promise I'll render you senseless!" He lay on the floor, groaning in pain. "Just a moment, I'll be back!" cried Neville and disappeared only to return just as Sergeant Reynolds' car, siren screaming, pulled up outside. He rushed in with his assistant, only to witness the oddest scene: Beryl, standing over a groaning Eric, threatening him with the poker, and Neville, who had brought them both a drink from the other room. "OK, on your feet!" said Sergeant Reynolds, and he and his assistant dragged Eric into a vertical position. Whether he was confused, or in pain, or drunk was unclear, but what was clear was the punch he threw, which caught Sergeant Reynolds just under his eye. "You lot are all the fucking same!" Eric shouted. "Handcuff him!" ordered Sergeant Reynolds, in a determined cold voice. "I'm so sorry!" cried Beryl. "Are you all right!" "I'll get some ice!" said Neville, and returned with several cubes of ice wrapped up in a kitchen cloth. "Thanks!" said Sergeant Reynolds sharply. "A night in the cells after we have breathalised you and charges will be laid tomorrow!" He looked around at the dining room floor, covered in broken crockery and glass. "May we clean it up?" asked Neville. "Yes!" said Sergeant Reynolds, holding the icepack against his throbbing cheekbone. "I hope you won't have a black eye!" said Beryl in a worried voice. "But thanks for coming so quickly to the rescue!" "It's fine!" said Sergeant Reynolds with an icy voice. I'll contact you about charges tomorrow. Take him to the car!" he said to his assistant. "You're all poofs!" was Eric's parting comment. "Why not a month in the cells on bread and water?" chirped Neville. "A good idea!" said Sergeant Reynolds as he left.

"Oh, what a mess!" cried Beryl. "Oh, by the way", she said sharply to Neville, narrowing her eyes, "where did you disappear to after I struck Eric?" "Oh, I went to turn the oven down. We don't want an over-cooked chicken, do we?" He handed her a glass of wine and the two of them dissolved in helpless laughter, standing in a sea of broken crockery and glass.

Even after Anne's disclosure of the high jinks in Highfield Road, dinner was a quiet affair, with both Patrick and Paul realising the consequences of the two wills, although Michael seemed oblivious to it all and chatted on with Bernard, Lorna and Anne. Before Anne and Patrick left, Michael told Patrick he would be up early in the morning, since Anne was taking him to the hairdresser.

At Killarney, they had all retired, when Bernard realised he had left his keys in the conservatory and decided to go down and retrieve them. "Leave it till the morning", said Lorna. "They won't go anywhere!" "I prefer to get them now!" he said and disappeared. On his return, he went toward the boys' room to turn off the lamp on the hall table and heard, "Paul, goodnight!", "Goodnight, Michael!" and then they chorused in sleepy voices, "Goodnight, Toby!". "It's good to be back home at Killarney", thought Bernard, wending his way back to his bedroom, with tears in his eyes.